By
Ariel Brouillette

Copyright © 2025 Ariel Brouillette.

All rights reserved. No part of this publication may be reproduced, distributed, or transmitted in any form or by any means, including photocopying, recording, or other electronic or mechanical methods, without the prior written permission of the publisher, except in the case of brief quotations embodied in critical reviews and certain other noncommercial uses permitted by copyright law. For permission requests, write to the publisher, addressed "Attention: Permissions Coordinator," at the address below.

ISBN: 9798274134927 (Paperback)

Library of Congress Control Number: 00000000000

Any references to historical events, real people, religions, or real places are used fictitiously. Names, characters, and places are products of the author's imagination.

Front cover image by Artist Ariel Brouillette.

Book design by Designer Ariel Brouillette.

Printed by Amazon, Inc., in the United States of America.

First printing edition 2025.

www.Arielbrouillette.com

Content Warning

This novel contains themes and situations that may be distressing or triggering for some readers. Please proceed with care and prioritize your well-being.
Dear Death includes the following content warnings:

- Death and mortality, including the death of a main character (HEA)

- Torture and violence, including ritualistic harm

- Power imbalances in romantic and supernatural relationships

- Toxic relationships and manipulation

- Death, murder, and references to ritual sacrifice

- Explicit sexual content (18+)

- Supernatural horror, including demonic transformation and body horror

- Religious themes, reinterpretations of Heaven, Hell, God, and the Devil

- Psychological tension, fear, and panic

This is a dark paranormal romance intended for mature audiences (18+). Reader discretion is advised.

This book is for everyone who's ever felt like an outcast.

It's for every person who's ever tried to bend themselves to fit society's idea of who they should be, and for everyone who said f*ck that and stayed feral.

Be you.

Chapter 1

Opal

I've spent my entire life trying to figure out what happened after death. Turns out, I should've paid more attention to what happened *before* I met him.

Unloading the van wasn't hard. We didn't bring much gear this time: a spirit box, two EMF detectors, and a DSLR held together with duct tape and spite. After three years in the Paranormal Investigation Club of Atlanta, I'd gotten used to the rhythm of these ghost hunts.

Though, tonight? My stomach knew better. Something wrong was in the air. Not ghost-wrong. Not even demon-wrong.

Something-lurking-beneath-your-skin-wrong. I knew because I was pretty sure I'd encountered a demon once in a cave out in the mountains. The footage had put us on the charts and kicked off the success of our channel.

Still, I needed new footage. *Spooky Ghouls*, my channel, was bleeding sub-scribers like it had offended the algorithm gods personally. After three weeks of zero evidence, my analytics graph had taken a cliff dive into obscurity.

My friends and fellow film crew lounged near the cemetery gate, laughing at something Lucian had said—probably another inside joke I'd somehow aged out of.

Nyxie was livestreaming already, perfectly posed in her red leather miniskirt and platform boots. Her phone was at the right angle to let the setting sun gild her silver hair like she was in a shampoo commercial. Lyric, her not-sister-but-forever-twin, leaned against her, tossing back her head with a laugh that rang a little too crisp.

Thane adjusted his oversized sunglasses like it wasn't overcast and tapped at his phone with purpose. Probably updating our socials with something dramatic.

Not one of them moved to help me unload. I yanked the tripod out from beneath a blanket of cables and barely caught the camera bag before it hit the dirt.

They were here for the vibes, not the work. They always were. Sometimes I told myself I didn't care. That it didn't matter if they treated me like the unpaid intern on my own shoot. *They came for the aesthetic. I came for answers.*

I needed death to mean something. All the ghosts in the world couldn't tell me why some people died screaming and others went quiet. Why death took some and not others. Why only silence answered when I begged the other side for a reply.

Was something on the other side? Did we vanish? Or was someone or something waiting? I didn't want jump scares or EMF blips. I wanted proof that life didn't just end.

"Do I look too washed out?" Nyxie asked without looking at me, angling her phone slightly and adjusting the exposure.

"You look dead," Lyric said brightly. "In the best way."

"Perfect." Nyxie smirked. "I want the followers thinking I crawled out of a crypt, not a Sephora."

Lyric giggled and leaned closer to the camera.

"Spooky Ghouls, welcome to our death day shoot," she purred. "We're summoning more than spirits tonight!"

Thane glanced at me over his phone. "Are you still hauling gear? Sweaty isn't spooky."

"So help me," I snapped, nearly dropping the rest of the tripods as I yanked them free from the cords.

"She's fine," Nyxie said, tossing her hair. "It's her thing. Gritty ghost girl. It's off brand if she starts acting like a princess."

I forced a smile. This was the job. The role. The way it always went.

"Thanks for the support."

Lyric slid off the wall and twirled toward me, her skirt flaring out like smoke. "What are best friends for, boo?" she said.

I turned to Lucian. "Did you bring it?" I asked, slamming the trunk shut harder than necessary.

Lucian, my boyfriend since junior year, all golden-retriever charm, flashed that smile that made girls hand over their hearts like currency. Me included.

"Of course," he said, tugging a worn, leather-bound book from his backpack. "Still don't know why my dad had this, but hey . . . cool points for antique witchy vibes, right?"

He handed it over. The moment it touched my palms, I knew something was wrong. It was cold. Not temperature-cold. *Grave-cold.* Like it hadn't been touched by sunlight in decades.

I ran my fingers along the cracked spine. Symbols I didn't recognize shimmered in the corners faintly. Maybe ink. Maybe something else.

"This looks . . . old," I murmured.

Lucian bit into an apple as sunlight caught in his hair, making his curls look like strands of actual gold. "Dad said it's been in the family for generations. Probably some ancient heirloom nonsense. You know how politicians love pretending their roots are more meaningful than they actually are."

Ancient nonsense was exactly what I was hoping for.

Lucian slung an arm around my shoulders and grabbed one of the duffels with his free hand, easygoing as ever. His warmth didn't quite reach me, but I leaned in anyway.

"Come on, babe. Let's get set up."

He tossed the apple over the cemetery gate. It hit a headstone with a dull thunk. I winced and he grinned. His blue eyes caught mine, boyish, blameless, and stupidly beautiful. I gave him a flat look and followed behind him.

Everyone sprang into motion the moment the cameras came out. Figures. Now they had energy: dragging gear, striking poses, debating angles like this was a magazine shoot, not a ghost hunt. Not a summoning.

The air had that crisp, early autumn bite—cool enough for sweaters, warm enough to deny that winter was coming. Leaves skittered across the gravel, dry and restless. The scent of damp moss and decaying leaves hung just beneath the perfume of pumpkin-spice body spray wafting from *someone's* oversized hoodie. Okay, I'll admit it. It was mine.

"If this turns out decent," Thane said, hauling the spirit box to a cracked stone bench, "we could use it for the Halloween special in a few weeks. Imagine the thumbnail: blood, crypts, and cleavage."

The sun bled into the horizon, casting the cemetery in that perfect golden hue influencers worshipped. All soft light and filtered decomposition. It felt curated. It felt cursed, wrong . . . Everything seemed to feel wrong these days.

I knelt near the center plot and started lighting the black candles I'd brought—soy-based, hand-poured. The lighter clicked in my fingers, wind teasing the flame.

Nyxie crouched beside me and pulled something from her velvet tote.

A dagger.

Ornate. Curved. Beautiful in that *this-should-not-be-here* kind of way. The hilt was wrapped in something that looked like leather. The blade glinted, etched with symbols that curled like roots or veins, nothing overwrought. Nothing fake.

"Use this," she said casually, turning it over. "It'll look insane on camera."

"Where did you even get that?" I asked, backing up half a step.

"Antique shop," Nyxie said smoothly. "Or maybe a haunted house. Does it matter?"

Lyric leaned in, her grin too wide.

"You should totally cut your palm. Just a little. Shock factor, babe."

"That's what the people want," Nyxie cooed, already prepping her phone. "Pain, drama, and a girl bleeding in the candlelight."

"Is that even safe?" I asked, brows lifting.

I glanced at Lucian.

He shrugged.

"Might boost the algorithm," he said with a crooked smile that didn't quite reach his eyes.

The sun dipped lower behind the trees, casting long shadows that draped over the headstones like shrouds. The candles flickered, uneasy, uncertain. The spirit box sputtered to life, chattering in static tongues between frequencies. Even Nyxie put her phone away, and for a breath, it felt real. Like maybe, for once, it wasn't just about clicks or clout or subscriber spikes.

Like maybe we were all here to find something. Like maybe I wasn't the only one who believed.

Lucian adjusted one of the mics clipped to his shirt and turned toward me with a small, private smile.

"Hey."

"Hey," I echoed, brushing windblown hair from my face. "Did we really get everyone to shut up at once? That's got to be a record."

"Don't jinx it," he said, smirking. "You know Thane's literally waiting for the chance to start monologing about lens flares and dust again."

"We'll lose the light by then," I said, glancing at the sky. "This spot's perfect, though."

"Did you plan that?" he asked, stepping closer. "Please tell me you didn't scout this place just for the vibes."

"What if I did?" I teased. "You'd still film it."

"Yeah," he admitted, softer now. "I would."

The air between us grew quiet, thick, almost tender. The rest of the world seemed to pull back like a tide.

"I'm gonna miss this," he said. "Us. The hunts. Editing until three in the morning and pretending I know what I'm doing."

"You mostly pick spooky fonts and argue with Thane about transitions."

"Guilty." He laughed, and for a second, it felt easy again. "But still . . . It's our thing."

"You sure you have to go?" I asked, quieter.

He nodded. "Family trip. Can't say no without it turning into a lecture."

"Right. Legacy. Optics. All that fun stuff."

"Hey." He nudged me lightly with his shoulder. "You'll be fine without me. You always are."

I smiled, but it didn't reach my eyes.

"Yeah," I said. "I'm getting really good at that. How long will you be gone?"

"Just the week. Dad's dragging us to that lake house in North Carolina. Zero signal, so I won't be much help from there."

"Thane and I can handle it," I said, trying to sound chill. "We've survived worse. Remember Savannah?"

"Barely," he teased. "You almost set that inn on fire."

"It was one candle," I muttered. "And a very flammable curtain. We're definitely not welcome back." I laughed.

"I'm serious, though. I'll miss you." His voice dipped, quiet and sincere.

"I'll miss you too," I said, too quickly.

Lucian stepped forward and, with exaggerated care, hoisted me onto a moss-draped headstone. "You okay?" he asked softly.

"I will be," I said. "After we get something real tonight."

"You really think something's gonna show?"

"I think something already has."

He didn't ask what I meant. Didn't look at the dagger still tucked in Nyxie's bag. Didn't look at the book in mine.

He kissed me. Soft. Slow. Familiar enough to hurt.

"Alright, lovebirds!" Thane's voice cut through the moment like a slap of glitter. "You can make out later—some of us have content to create."

"Seriously, Lucian," he added, waving his phone like a wand, "if you ruin my lighting with another forehead nuzzle, I *will* hex you. On camera. With filters."

Lucian groaned, still leaning into me, his breath ghosting across my cheek.

"Mood killer," he murmured.

"Fashion killer," Thane shot back. "Pick one. I don't have time to fix both."

"That's Thane," I whispered back. "Romance assassin."

Lucian and I pulled apart and moved to our places. Lucian clicked the camera into place, his usual smirk slipping into something quieter, focused. Intent.

Thane fussed with the lighting one last time, muttering to himself. Nyxie counted down from three like she was cueing a runway model. Even Lyric paused, brushing invisible lint from her jacket, before glancing toward me with something like expectation. Nyxie said, "Ready?"

I lied and said, "Yeah."

I took a breath that felt too deep and stepped into frame.

"Welcome back, ghouls and grave walkers," I said, flashing my practiced grin at the lens. "We're live from the oldest cemetery in Atlanta, where tonight, *Spooky Ghouls* is digging into some uncharted haunted history."

I tossed a glance over my shoulder, the kind of look that made for good cuts in post.

"But that's not all. Tonight we're trying something . . . older. A little ritual we found in a book that probably shouldn't exist. So, grab your sage, cross your fingers, and maybe don't watch this one alone."

Lucian gave me a thumbs-up from behind the camera. Thane adjusted mic levels with unusual silence. The sun was nearly gone now, just bruised streaks of lavender and rust bleeding across the sky. Shadows crawled across the cracked tombstones. I turned back toward the altar we'd arranged, a slab of stone dressed in wax, salt, and intention. The leather-bound book sat in the center like it belonged there.

Like it had been waiting for me.

"You're really gonna read it?" Nyxie asked, crouching low beside a headstone. Her voice pitched half-thrilled, half-daring.

"She has to," Lyric added, stepping closer. "You already teased it. Come on, Opal. Commit. You know how this works. Shock factor."

I hesitated. The pages fluttered in the windless air.

"We don't actually know what it says," I murmured.

"That's the point," Thane chimed in, eyes glinting through his too-dark sunglasses. "We're not here for accuracy. We're here for reaction."

"What if it's real?" I asked, quieter.

That earned a laugh from Lyric.

"Then we'll make sure to tag you in the viral clip."

"Seriously, Opal." Lucian's voice took on a gentler tone. "You don't have to do anything you don't want to. But . . . this is kind of perfect. Creepy book. Historic cemetery. Right before Halloween? It's the whole vibe."

"Right," I said, heart thudding. "The vibe . . ." I glanced at the book. The words didn't look like English. Didn't even look like they belonged to this world. My fingers reached out anyway, tracing the edge of the page like it might bite.

"Okay," I breathed.

Nyxie held out the dagger again, the blade catching what little light remained. "You don't have to cut deep. Just enough for, you know . . . effect."

I hesitated, book in one hand, dagger in the other. The handle felt wrong. "Fine," I murmured. "But just a nick."

I inhaled and glanced down at the Latin scrawl inked on the page. I couldn't pronounce half of it, but that had never stopped a spooky segment before. I had no idea what the words meant, but they sounded ancient, and powerful.

"Voco pastorem spirituum..." The chant felt thick in my mouth, syllables dragging like wet cloth.

". . . finis omnium rerum et initium aeternitatis . . ."

The wind stirred, brushing my hair back. I pressed on, voice tightening.

". . . voco in tenebris circumfusa civium spiritus veteris . . ."

"*Louder*," Lyric whispered, camera locked on my face.

". . . et novi qui occurrit finis ipsum vitae extremum . . ."

Something shifted.

The sky darkened too fast, like someone had turned down the dimmer on the world. The cemetery felt wrong now, like the graves were listening.

My voice shook as I reached the final line:

"Cain . . . hoc mihi ligare, alligare . . ."

I blinked. The letters blurred.

"Cain . . ." The air cracked.

Then . . . I did it.

Before I could change my mind, I pressed the dagger into my palm and drew a sharp, shallow line. Pain bloomed hot and immediate, and my blood hit the open page like ink in water.

For a heartbeat, nothing happened. No thunder. No ghostly moan. No twitching candle flames.

Just silence stretching tight, then—

Every candle blew out at once.

The darkness swallowed us whole, and the ground beneath our feet shuddered—not a tremor, a warning. A long, low wail rose from somewhere beneath the earth, too deep to be wind, too wet and human to be anything natural. It wasn't sound. It was *pressure*. It crawled through the soles of my shoes, up my spine, into the roots of my teeth. My ears rang. My skin burned cold.

I couldn't breathe. My lungs forgot how, and then . . . the shadows moved. Not around us. Toward us, toward me. They slithered between the graves, pooling in the center of the circle, crawling over each other like something starved. They rose, dragging a shape from the dark. Humanoid but wrong. Too tall. Shoulders too sharp. Limbs that twitched with frame-skipping stutters like bad film spliced together.

He glitched into existence.

There. Not there. There again, smearing at the edges like blood on glass. A black hood obscured most of his face, but I could *feel* him looking, and he was furious.

The kind of rage that hummed against your bones and made your blood try to run in the other direction. The kind of rage that existed before time.

"What the hell is that?" Lucian backed up fast, tripping over a headstone.

Thane's hands shook as he fumbled at the tripod. "Is this part of it?" he yelled, his voice cracking.

"Nope. Nope. Nope!" Lyric spun and bolted, Nyxie right behind her, clutching her phone, no longer filming. Just running. The tripod toppled over and clunked against a headstone.

"Guys—wait!" I turned, voice raw. "Don't just—"

They didn't even hesitate. Even Lucian. He abandoned his sound gear in a puddle and ran toward me, muttering under his breath, "Oh my god, oh my god," as he scooped up the book. Then, he bolted.

I Ie didn't look back. *They didn't even hesitate.* That was what stung the most. None of them did. And then I was alone. Well . . . me and him.

The figure took a step forward. The shadows peeled off him in slow, writhing strands, like they didn't want to let go. His form jittered. One moment, he was hooded and humanoid. The next, skeletal.

". . . Who the fuck summoned me?"

The voice didn't only land in my ears. It skinned something inside me. Not loud. Wrong. Smoke hissed from beneath his hood, thick, oily, and slow. It coiled out in lazy tendrils, the shape of breath from something that didn't need to breathe. Something pretending.

One hand flexed at his side, the fingers too long. The air around him pulsed and warped, like the world itself couldn't bear to look at him.

Then he smiled. If you could call it that. The grin split wide beneath the hood. Too wide. Wrong.

"You."

It wasn't a name. It was a sentence. A verdict. A death knell. I couldn't move. The shadows shifted. His head tilted slightly, studying me like a bored god dissecting an insect.

"I was in the middle of a conversation," he said, voice sharp. "That was very rude."

His tone stayed casual, conversational and deadly. He stepped closer. The air went thin. My lungs locked. Smoke drifted toward me again, and this time I could smell it . . . Cigarettes.

My legs wouldn't move. My brain clawed for logic, escape, anything, but only static answered. Under it all pulsed one clear certainty: Something ancient and furious had just marked me for borrowed time.

"I didn't know what I was doing," I whispered. My voice cracked around the edges.

"No shit." He clicked his tongue. "Tell you what . . ." he drawled. "Since you interrupted me . . ."

Another step. The ground didn't creak. It *curled.*

" . . . I'll give you a five-second head start. Five."

My mouth fell open. The rest of me didn't follow. Not yet. He rolled his neck. Bone popped. The hood shifted like he was watching me, waiting for me to scream.

"Four."

My heart slammed against my ribs hard enough I thought they might crack. *MOVE.* My body didn't respond. I couldn't move. Not until—

"Three."

I ran.

Gravestones blurred past as I slipped on damp grass, caught on snarled roots, clipped rusted iron fences I didn't remember seeing before. The cold bit into my lungs as I gasped, heart ricocheting wildly in my ribs.

Behind me . . . footsteps, walking slowly. Measured. Mocking. And yet, every second, they sounded closer.

"Two," he called, light and lilting now. Almost cheerful. Almost merciful.

The trees swallowed me whole.

Branches clawed at my arms, tore at my jacket, left lines of fire across my skin. My breath sawed in and out, shallow and desperate. I didn't dare look back. I knew what I'd see.

Stillness, silence, a flash of him there then gone again, and then—

"Boo."

I screamed and swerved hard to the left, barely missing a cracked headstone. My shoulder slammed into stone. Pain sparked, but I stayed upright, barely.

His laughter rolled through the cemetery, low and delighted, like he'd waited lifetimes to enjoy this. "You humans," he said, voice echoing from nowhere and everywhere. "Always running, as if that ever works."

"I told you," he murmured.

Suddenly, he was in front of me. Just . . . there. One blink, and he'd crossed the world.

"Five seconds."

I froze. Too late. My foot caught on something half-buried. Bone? Branch? It didn't matter. I fell hard, my palms skidding on mud, my knees cracking, the air punched from my lungs in a wheeze.

I hardly had time to scream before he was on me. His shadow fell over mine as he straddled me in the mud, slow, deliberate, inevitable. One hand braced beside my hip. The other reached forward.

For my throat.

"You shouldn't have called me, little thing," he whispered.

His fingers curled around my neck with ease. The kind of touch someone only has when they've done this a thousand times. A million.

I clawed at his wrist. Kicked. Thrashed. Screamed. He didn't even flinch.

His hood fell back, and I saw him. For a second, I thought he was a ghost. Something conjured by blood and ancient words I didn't understand. But ghosts didn't breathe. They didn't drip rainwater from their lashes. They didn't look this solid or this furious.

His skin was pale as bone. Not sickly. Perfect. Too flawless. Cold and smooth like marble left out in the dark. Water clung to him in silver rivulets, trailing down the angles of his throat.

Black hair fell in damp waves across his forehead, tangled and tousled, veiling one eye, and his hoodie, soaked and slashed open down the front, revealed a body that looked carved from shadow and sin.

Sculpted muscle inked in black: Twisting vines, grinning skulls, and flowers curled across tattooed ribs. His eyes were black voids, emotionless and bottomless. He stared at me like I was the most irritating thing he'd seen all century. Then, his grip tightened.

I braced for pain, for death, but . . . Nothing happened.

His hand was still at my throat, but the pressure wavered. Not from mercy. From something else. He blinked once. Then again. His breath hitched, one short, shocked inhale, and his grip faltered. Confusion flickered beneath the clinical detachment.

No snap. No choke. No blissful drop into oblivion. His expression changed, but not to rage. To something worse: Fear.

Without warning, he shoved off me. Hard. His boots kicked up mud as he turned and bolted for the tree line. He vanished for half a heartbeat and then slammed back into the clearing like a rubber band stretched too far.

Something yanked him out of thin air and hurled him into the dirt. His hoodie tore wider, the fabric soaked, clinging to him.

Mud smeared across his chest, his arms, his jaw. He looked like a fallen god that had been dragged through a battlefield and dropped at my feet.

He tried again and again.

Every time, the world yanked him back like a tether. Not to this place but to me. By the fourth attempt, he was panting, shoulders heaving, knees sinking into wet grass, head bowed.

My body buzzed with leftover terror. Scraped palms burned. My throat ached from screaming. Still . . . I crawled forward. Whatever he was—ghost, monster, god—felt more real than anything else in this cemetery.

" . . . Are you okay?"

He looked up slowly.

Those ink-black eyes met mine.

He glared at me with the kind of hatred that felt earned.

"What the fuck did you do to me?"

Chapter 2

Cain

One second, I was in the middle of a conversation, the next I was being ripped through realms. Wherever I was, it was night. *Perfect. Where the fuck am I?*

I blinked, scanning the scene. A dime-store séance. Candles flickering. Idiots playing ghost hunter like it was a fucking game.

There were no witches with true lineage. No cloaked cult leaders dripping in ancient blood. No clever warlocks trading souls for secrets. Just a gaggle of clout-chasing narcissists wearing curated leather and rhinestone pentagrams, staging a séance for a photo op.

And yet, it had worked. Against all reason, against every natural law written in ash and blood and smoke, they'd managed to call me forth. *That* was enough to yank me out of Hell? Why? Why here? Why her? Seriously? *Ah well, fuck it, they're all dead anyway.* The moment I breached the veil, half-shadow, half-corpse, they fled.

One of them snatched the leather-bound book from the crumbled altar like he understood even a fragment of what it contained. Another crushed their camera underfoot in the scramble, the lens shattering with a sound like a bone snapping clean.

Cowards, all of them.

Whether it was choice or paralysis, one girl remained. She didn't run . . . She didn't even flinch. She stared at me, standing motionless in the center of the broken circle. Rain clung to her in uneven patterns, catching on her pink hair.

Her skin was pale. Not in the romantic way but in the way that pointed to too many nights inside, lit only by the ghostly glow of a cheap lamp.

Blood ran freely from her open palm, down her wrist, dripping onto the fractured stone below. Her wide green eyes locked on me with a gaze that teetered between reverence and ruin. It wasn't fear that rooted her in place, no . . . It was fascination.

I loathed it—loathed that expression on her face, the desperate curiosity that mortals wore when they thought that they'd summoned a god, not a consequence. She was clearly a girl with a death wish, or maybe she just had no sense of self-preservation.

I liked her already.

"You've got five seconds," I said almost gently—like a parent offering up a game, like a god offering mercy. Just to be nice. Just to play.

"Run."

She ran.

And fuck, she looked good doing it.

Boots skidding through damp, uneven grass. Her legs catching in the long drag of her sweater. Pink hair snapping behind her like a streak of smoke, like a dying flare swallowed by the dark. Her breath tore from her throat in shallow, frantic bursts, each one sharper than the last, terrified and *delicious*.

She ran fast for a mortal. Her panic gave her speed. I let her think she had a chance. Let her believe distance mattered. Let her flail through the graves as if the dead would pity her. Let her scrape her body open on protruding roots and broken angel wings, her skin catching on rusted gates and ancient thorns. It didn't matter. She belonged to me now.

I could've ended it. I could've crossed the distance between us in the breaths between her screams. Could've wrapped my fingers around that delicate throat, snapped her spine, and added her name to my ledger. But I didn't. Because I liked the hunt.

I liked the taste of panic in the air, the fear in their eyes. I liked the way their footfalls faltered when they realized my shadows were right behind them. She ran like she didn't know she was already mine.

And that?

That was foreplay.

Because I wanted to watch her die.

That was the moment I lived for. The only real thrill left in this all. The only thing that still kicked something alive inside this rotting shell of a body: ancient, half-forgotten, and almost dead.

I walked the same crooked path she tore through, letting my footsteps stretch and breathe, never getting too far away.

I whispered low and wrong, just enough for her to hear.

"Left."

She turned right.

Good girl.

She stumbled over a half-buried headstone and pitched forward with a yelp, knees slamming into the cold, damp soil. Her palms caught her weight, scraping raw, blood mixing with earth and the scent of her fear. She twisted, gasping, eyes darting right and left as she tried to rise, but it was too late.

I smiled.

Game over.

I dropped on her, easy as night. I straddled her and leaned in, grabbing her throat with my hand. Her breath hitched like it was her last—and it should've been. This was the part where her soul left her eyes. Where her body went still. Except . . . it didn't. Heat bloomed under my palms, her thready pulse the stubborn thing that should have stopped by now.

Nothing happened. There was no flicker, no drop, no snap. Just her, blinking up at me. I frowned and squeezed harder, her soft skin reddening under my grip. Still. Fucking. Nothing. My gut twisted. Something was wrong. She wouldn't die. This girl wasn't just another tally mark in my book. No, she refused. I leapt off her like she'd burned me. Which was bullshit. I didn't panic. I didn't feel . . . Not like that. Not anymore. No one survived my touch . . . No one has ever been able to. I bolted while I ripped a hole into reality. Jumped into the rift, slipped into the void like I always do.

Except—

Snap.

I got yanked back. Hard.

Like the world had a grip on my ribs and wasn't letting go.

"What the fuck?"

I tried again and pushed deeper this time. Shifted planes, clawed through space itself with my bare hands.

Snap. I tried again.

Snap. Again.

SNAP.

Every time I got loose, something invisible *slammed* me back into the mud. By the fifth try, I'd torn my hoodie completely. The fabric split, baring my chest to the cold night air, tattoos exposed, wet and gleaming. Black vines, coiled bones, grim faces locked in silent screams.

I was panting, covered in mud, and *furious*.

I glanced back at her. She crawled forward. Knees muddy, scraped up from the fall. Hair clinging to her cheeks. Big green eyes still locked on me like I wasn't the monster here. Like I was something new. I hated the way she looked at me. Like I was beautiful.

I wasn't.

"... Are you okay?" she whispered.

I stared.

Was she *serious*?

I'd tried to strangle the life out of her—*literally*—and here she was, crawling closer like a girl inspecting a wounded animal. Like if she just got near enough, she might coax something soft out of me. That kind of softness? It got people killed.

I glared at her like she'd offered to hug a guillotine. *I'm Death, sweetheart. I don't do okay.* I stood, still glaring down at her like she was the broken piece in a machine that had never once failed me.

"What the fuck do you mean, *okay*?" I snapped.

She gulped.

Good.

At least *something* was right about this nightmare. She was scared. That was the natural order of things. Mortals feared me. The wise ones ran. The really smart ones died fast. But this girl? She just looked up at me like I was some wounded animal.

My lip curled. "What the fuck did you *do* to me?"

She tried to stand. Her leg buckled. Blood smeared down her knee. She stumbled right into me.

Her palms hit my chest.

My hand caught her back automatically—reflex, not compassion. She stared up at me, eyes wide, green as fresh-cut grass after a storm.

And for half a second—

No.

Nope.

I shoved her.

Hard.

She hit the mud with a gasp, hair plastered to her face, dirt streaking her cheeks like war paint. I shook my hand out like I'd touched something infected.

What the actual fuck was this?

I looked at her.

Really looked.

Tried to cut through the visual noise, the blood, the rain-slick sweater, the stupidly fragile expression on her face. Tried to focus. Find the thread I always felt . . . the line that tethered mortals to their exit, to the ledger. The little hum beneath the surface that whispered, *Mine, soon.*

With her?

There was nothing.

No flicker. No tick. No timer counting down her breaths.

Just silence.

A void where death should've been coiled, waiting. It hit me like a punch to the ribs, sharp, off-balance. Like the floor had dropped out beneath me, and I'd forgotten how gravity worked. Every time I moved too far, something pulled. Not physically. Worse. Existentially.

Like the universe had reached past the veil, sunk its claws into the meat of my ribs, and stitched me to her, this pink-haired mortal trainwreck with blood on her hands and leftover glitter on her shoes. A girl who looked like a haunted doll and smelled like drugstore pumpkin, vanilla, and graveyard dirt. Like she was my goddamn center of gravity.

Disgusting.

"Great," I muttered, voice flat with cosmic disdain. "Fucking brilliant." I kicked the nearest tombstone.

The crack echoed into the night, and the stone split clean down the middle, shards sliding to the wet earth with a satisfying *thunk*. She jerked back fast, slipping in the mud, her hands scraping raw as she caught herself.

"Who took the book?"

She blinked, still dazed. "Book?"

She hesitated. Of course she did. Her eyes flicked to the ruined headstone like it might save her. "Lucian," she said finally. "Uh—my boyfriend did."

I turned away before I said something worse. Before I reminded her that her boyfriend wasn't coming back. That she was stuck with me. That the two worst things she had ever said were *yes* to a dare and a Latin phrase she didn't understand.

And now? Now she was bound to the thing that made gods flinch. Somehow, I was stuck babysitting the human equivalent of a glitter bomb.

Fan-fucking-tastic.

Rain was coming down harder now, soaking us both. She looked like a disaster: muddy, scraped up, sweater clinging to her, hair stuck to her face like she was a half-drowned ghost. We were still tethered. Two ends of a chain neither of us could see, forged by a spell she and her friends had probably found in an antique store it had no business being in.

I felt along the link again. It wasn't just stuck. It was *anchored*. I dragged in a breath: pointless but grounding. My hands clenched. My teeth ached from the tension. I wanted to scream, to burn the whole fucking cemetery to ash, to tear through whatever goddamn thread was sewing me to her.

Instead . . .

I glanced up.

The rain hit my face in heavy, ice-cold drops, one after another, sliding down my jaw, soaking into the torn fabric at my shoulders. I let it. Just for a second. Let it fall. Let it touch me.

I hated it.

I blinked once and turned back to her, the moment evaporating like steam off a tombstone.

"This," I said, voice flat and final, "needs to be broken. Now."

She opened her mouth, definitely about to ask what I was or how or why, and I shut it down with a look.

"Don't ask. I'm not giving you a name. I'm not giving you answers. All you need to know is that this"—I pointed between us—"wasn't supposed to happen."

She flinched but didn't argue. Finally, something was sinking in. I reached into the dark and pulled. The shadows curled upward like skeletal smoke, folding inward into a narrow, quivering doorway.

"Where do you live?" I asked.

She hesitated. "Midtown."

Of course.

I sighed, long and dramatic. "Perfect."

The shadows stirred, hating this. Hating *her*.

"Let's go, Final Girl."

She didn't move.

Just stared, wide-eyed and frozen, at the rip in the air behind me. A jagged, seething wound in the fabric of reality, slick with shadows and whispered secrets no human brain was built to comprehend. The kind of sound that slithered into your bones and convinced your spine to pack up and leave.

Smart girl.

Even without knowing *what* it was, she could feel it. Could feel the wrongness of it like cold breath on her neck. She scrambled backward on her palms, heels sliding in the mud like she could somehow outrun what she'd already shackled herself to.

I sighed. Loudly. Dramatically. Like a man forced to chaperone a haunted sleepover.

"Oh, for fuck's sake."

I reached down without ceremony.

She squeaked, something between *wait* and *no*, but I wasn't exactly in the mood for negotiation. I grabbed her by the arm and yanked her upright like a drenched cat I didn't want to deal with. She stumbled and winced but didn't die.

Damn it.

I let go fast, half-expecting her to crumple. Fade. Combust into glitter and bad decisions. But nope, still breathing. Still tethered. Still stubbornly, *annoyingly* alive.

"Fuck, that's weird," I muttered, mostly to myself, shaking out my hand like her skin had left a mark I couldn't see or unfeel. My fingers twitched, the sensation crawling up my spine like bad static.

I leaned in, menace pouring off me like smoke from a fire that never died. She flinched, which made me feel marginally better about the entire mess.

"You're stuck with me," I said, low and flat, like a curse disguised as a fact. "And I'm not interested in playing twenty questions in the fucking rain."

I tilted my head, letting the shadows peel off me just enough to show her what I was. Not the full face, just the suggestion. The shape under the hood. The decay behind the grin.

"So," I said, voice all knives and bored apathy. "Your place . . ."

A beat.

". . . or mine?"

She swallowed hard.

Good.

I grinned, sharp, humorless, the kind of smile that cracked mirrors. "Choose fast, sweetheart. My patience died a few millennia ago."

"M-mine," she squeaked.

I smirked, dragging a hand through my hair as the shadows closed in behind us.

"Atta girl."

I jerked my chin toward the tear in reality, still pulsing, still irritated, still bleeding shadows like the world itself was trying to reject the wound. The edges curled and twitched like they hated being held open this long, like the void was ready to snap shut and swallow us both for the crime of loitering.

"Let's go," I said, voice dry as bone dust.

She hesitated then finally stepped through, spine straight, breath choppy, like she was walking into her own funeral.

Cute.

I followed.

The world stitched itself back around us with all the subtlety of a migraine. We landed on some generic-ass residential street in Midtown. A sad little tree sat hunched in a concrete cutout, probably questioning its life choices. A low brick wall tried and failed to look quaint.

"This—this way," she said quickly, avoiding my eyes.

I trailed after her, my boots hitting the pavement like it had personally offended me. The sidewalk was cracked beneath us, crooked like everything else in this dimension. I glared at it, just in case.

We climbed a narrow staircase to the second floor. She fumbled with her keys, still trembling, still pretending this was normal, and the door creaked open onto a room that made my spine physically recoil.

Pink.

Everywhere.

Walls, rugs, throw pillows, curtains, *carnage by cupcake*. The place looked like someone had murdered a Care Bear and tried to cover it up with good vibes. Pastel chaos bled into every corner, lit by soft gold star string lights and one obnoxiously bright neon sign that read "dead inside" in a loopy, lowercase script and buzzed like a threat and a confession.

I stepped inside like the floor might melt beneath me. She mumbled something about getting towels. I didn't hear her. I was too busy dying inside.

Dripping, furious, and surrounded by marshmallow-core, I stood there like a gargoyle at the gates of hell's gift shop. My eyes scanned the room, noting the pastel skull mug collection, the bone-shaped candle, the taxidermy bat wearing a fucking *flower crown*.

Was this a haunted house?

Or a Hot Topic clearance bin that had developed sentience and then depression?

I turned slowly. Took it all in. "I want to die . . . again," I muttered, and I meant it.

As I drifted deeper, past the cloud-pink rug and the aggressively glittering ghost figurines, something changed. The air shifted. It started subtle. A shadowed corner. A shelf half-concealed from the soft, golden lamplight.

And on it—bones.

Real ones.

An articulated cat skeleton, posed delicately, glass eyes wide like it had something left to say. A snake mid-strike, frozen in time, tension still rippling through its curved spine. A scattered congregation of vertebrae and jawbones, some bleached white, others still carrying the yellowed kiss of age. And nestled at the center, the crown jewel of this necrotic diorama—a human skull.

Not plastic. Not some party-store Halloween prop.

A *real* one.

Hairline crack along the temple. Teeth mostly intact. Still kissed by graveyard dirt she hadn't quite scrubbed clean. The kind of relic that had lived a full, finite life and now lingered as decor in a pastel mausoleum.

I tilted my head, something sharp growing behind my ribs. Not anger. Not disgust.

Interest.

Dark. Dangerous. Utterly delighted.

"Bad girl," I muttered, a grin blooming across my face, wide and utterly unholy.

I crouched to examine it, running a finger along the curve of its cheekbone like I was reacquainting myself with an old friend. The rest of the apartment—the marshmallow madness, the scented candles, the aesthetic death denial—was noise.

This?

This was music.

I rose slowly, scanning the rest of the wall. Graveyard photos, all black and white and reverent. Obituaries clipped and framed like postcards from the other side. Wax-stained votives. A pressed flower nestled between two ribs. An altar. A sick little altar built from curiosity and compulsion. A love letter to Death, and she hadn't even *known*.

Interesting.

Very interesting.

I didn't hear her return until I felt her presence. Behind me. Small. Breathing like she was afraid it would offend the silence.

"Here," she squeaked.

I turned and she stood there, a towel held in both hands like they might bite her if she held them wrong. Her cheeks were pink from the cold, or the nerves, and her eyes were wide, jittery, but underneath the fear, something flickered.

Not defiance.

Not bravery.

Fascination.

Well, well.

I stared a beat too long. Then, finally, I snatched the towel from her fingers like I was doing *her* a favor. "Thanks," I said, smirking. The kind of smirk that wasn't meant to comfort. "Cozy place. You bring all your monsters here, or am I just the lucky one?"

I toweled off slowly, mostly to irritate her. Droplets ran down my neck, carving through the grime, soaking into the waistband of my ruined hoodie. The fabric clung to me, but at least I wasn't dripping on her aggressively pink rug anymore. She watched me like I was a bomb she wasn't sure was finished ticking.

"I don't bring anyone here," she snapped, voice sharper than I expected.

That got my attention. I cocked a brow. "Is that supposed to make me feel special?"

She didn't answer. Just turned away too quickly and started fussing with the mess near the door—wet boots, keys, whatever. Her hands shook a little, and she tried to hide it.

"Well," I said, grin creeping back, "I did give you a choice. You picked me."

She whipped around. "There *was* no choice."

"I dunno." I leaned against her skull shelf, casual as anything. "Sounded like a choice. *Your place or mine.* You chose yours. Which, I gotta say, was smart. My place has screaming walls and a dress code."

She crossed her arms. Defensive. Or maybe cold. Or maybe she was hiding the way her fingers were fidgeting with the hem of her shirt.

She wasn't looking at me. She was looking around me, like if she studied me sideways, she'd see through the layers. Or maybe see something she wasn't supposed to.

The tension changed—not just fear now. Not just shock. Something itchier. Edging toward awe.

She stared at me, jaw clenched. The tension practically vibrated between us now, fear, frustration, something else she didn't want to name.

Then, quietly: "Do ghosts even have a home?"

That was when it got irritating. I dropped the towel on her floor with a wet *smack*. "I'm not a fucking ghost," I said, voice low and final. "And no—I'm not telling you what I am."

I stepped closer, enough to feel her breath hitch. "I didn't ask to be here. You dragged me out of something a lot bigger than your wannabe-YouTuber stunt, and now I'm chained to you until we fix it."

She blinked.

"But sure," I added, gesturing to the mess of bones and blush behind her. "Let's pretend this is a *normal night* in your freakshow Barbie dreamhouse."

"I don't want you here," she said suddenly, voice firmer than before. "Just like you don't want to be here."

I turned slowly, blinking once. "Well, *good*," I replied flatly.

I stepped around her, cracking my neck like I was shaking off the entire idea of this glitter-drenched hellhole. The tension popped along my spine, a release of something feral and barely contained.

My soaked hoodie clung to me like a second skin. I yanked it off with a growl and tossed it onto her ghost-print ottoman, where it landed with a dramatic splat.

Pink couch. Pink rug. Bone collection. Haunted bat with a tiara. *What even is this place?*

I didn't look at her as I said, "Tomorrow we get that book—and I'm gone."

Silence stretched for too long. I paused mid-pace. "What?"

"About that . . ." she said, voice small now.

I turned. Eyes snapped to hers like a trigger had been pulled. I didn't say anything. Just waited. Watched her squirm.

She fiddled with the hem of her sleeve, not meeting my eyes. "Lucian's . . . gone."

"Gone *where*?"

"Family trip. North Carolina. For the week."

Fuck. I laughed once, short and sharp. No humor, all venom. "Of course he is," I muttered. "Because why wouldn't your wet paper towel of a boyfriend take off with the one object tying me to this walking nightmare."

Her chin lifted slightly, like she wanted to defend him, but she didn't. Because even *she* knew it was bullshit. I stepped forward again, slow and dangerous. "So, let me get this straight. You summoned something you didn't understand. Botched the ritual. Bound me here. And now the one thing we need to undo it is on a family vacation in the middle of the fucking woods?"

She nodded.

I stared at her.

Then tilted my head and smiled, all teeth.

"Oh, you are *so* lucky I can't kill you."

I closed the last bit of distance between us. Her back hit the wall with a soft *thud*, and I braced one hand beside her head, the other curling gently—mockingly—around her throat. Not squeezing. Not yet.

Just *reminding* her.

My skin was still damp, the tattoos along my chest and ribs stark against the pale canvas of my body. I felt her breath hitch as she stared, either at my face or at the way death looked shirtless. I leaned in, my mouth close to her ear, voice heated enough to melt steel.

"If I *could*," I whispered, "you'd already be bones in that pretty collection of yours." She trembled, but she didn't look away.

So fucking interesting.

CHAPTER 3

Opal

I was beginning to seriously question whether letting—whatever he was—into my apartment had been a good idea. Scratch that. It had *never* been a good idea. It was the kind of decision you'd scream at horror movie girls for making while clutching a throw pillow and vowing you'd never be that stupid. Final Girl vibes but with worse boundaries and better décor.

He hadn't said a word in ages. Just prowled the perimeter of my apartment like a caged predator, shoulders loose, head low, full of dangerous thoughts he wasn't bothering to leash. Him a panther, and me the morbid idiot who'd cracked open the supernatural zoo gate with a smile.

I didn't know what he was. A ghost? A demon? Some corpse-chic reaper I'd accidentally summoned? All I knew was this: He was terrifying . . . and gorgeous. I was teetering on the edge of a full-blown existential spiral when my phone pinged. I fumbled for it on the counter, grateful for the distraction. Lucian's name lit the screen.

You okay babe?

No. I was not okay. I was furious. *You left me. You and everyone else. You ran like the cast in every supernatural slasher I've ever loved.* I didn't say that.

Instead, I typed:

I'm safe. Back at home.

The reply came fast.

What the fuck was that thing?

My eyes flicked to the corner of the room. He was still there. Curled into the old recliner like it had been carved for him. Like he'd been waiting in it since the beginning of time, and I'd just stumbled, uninvited, into his cathedral of stillness. The lamplight bent around him but never touched, refusing to grace whatever the fuck he was with warmth.

One knee hooked over the armrest, fingers draped lazily, his posture a study in indifferent threat. His eyes were voids. Not metaphoric, not poetic. Real, fathomless, unnatural black. Not the absence of light, but the consumption of it. Pits of black carved out of existence and stitched into a face too beautiful to be trusted.

He hadn't blinked.

Not once.

Creepy fucker.

He looked . . . bored, but beneath that boredom, beneath the cold composure, something cruel watched me. The shadows watched too. I felt them. Icy fingers dragged up my spine, slow and impersonal, like something was counting my vertebrae. It was the kind of pressure that said that tragedy was on deck, and the world knew it. No reason. Pure animal panic lighting up my ribs.

My fingers tapped the keyboard so they wouldn't shake. I answered Lucian.

I don't know.

Because that was the truth. He was the most unsettling creature I'd ever seen. His teeth gleamed like a promise. His tattoos seemed like they'd been carved, not inked, into his skin, black vines and bones and ancient things that didn't translate into mortal languages. The worst part? He'd already tried to kill me and failed, and now he sat there, staring at me like he would figure out how to get it done one way or another.

Lucian left me on read, and I pocketed my phone. My heart thudded harder against my ribs, traitorously loud. I imagined he could hear it. That he was *listening* to it the way hunters listened for wounded animals. Under the fear, beneath the static, something else sparked: curiosity.

I'd spent years chasing ghosts. Digging through grave dirt for proof that something waited on the other side. Filming cemeteries and abandoned hospitals for views and whispers and cold spots that never whispered back. And now . . . there he was. This was real. Angry and shirtless, of all things, glaring at me from my grandmother's recliner like I'd interrupted something important.

Despite the dread, despite the way my bones still remembered how it felt when he'd grabbed my throat, I couldn't look away. Because this was the answer. This was everything I'd ever wanted to believe in, breathing . . . in my room.

He moved, but not fast, oh no. That would've been a mercy.

He unfolded from the recliner like a skin-walker testing the limits of flesh. His joints moved too smooth, too fluid. There was something deeply wrong in the elegance of it. Something *inhuman* in how he took his time, how he let me watch every frame of it.

I froze.

He didn't look at me. He stared at my collection, drifted toward the far wall, *my* wall. The shrine of curated oddities I'd built like a mausoleum disguised in pink: bones bleached and bartered for, funeral cards pressed into glass, black-and-white graveyard photos that felt like love letters to entropy. Trinkets no one else had wanted. Things forgotten, discarded, dead.

I'd rescued them. Named them. Loved them. His fingers ghosted over the shelf like he was reading braille carved into bone. Gentle. Reverent. Like the whole arrangement wasn't an aesthetic, but an altar, and he was a god who'd forgotten he had worshippers.

He moved to the dagger. The curved one with the silver filigree handle, the one I'd found at a dead woman's estate sale after outbidding a man who'd sworn it was cursed. He picked it up like it *recognized* him.

He twirled it with lazy precision, fingers deft, practiced, like it belonged in his hands. The pink glow from my "dead inside" sign buzzed across the blade, painting it like something out of a blood-slick fairytale. He was way too good at twirling that damn knife. He watched the glimmer as it spun with an intensity that screamed *mildly insane.*

"You really have a thing for Death, don't you?" he asked. The way he said "Death" wasn't vague. He said it like a name—a person, not a thing.

I swallowed. "It's just ... something I've always found interesting." It was my fallback line. The one I gave interviewers and nosy commenters who called me "cute-creepy" and asked if I was okay or needed help.

He didn't blink.

"Don't lie to me, Opal."

He appeared in front of me before I'd even registered the distance closing. Breath warm against my cheek. Not human warmth. Old warmth: funeral pyre, last breath, end-of-summer warmth. I backed up, spine brushing the cold wall behind me. I had nowhere to go. He pressed in too close. His presence swallowed the air. The shadows seemed to still for him.

"How do you know my name?" I whispered, but the words cracked and fell apart on my tongue.

He didn't answer right away. Just smiled and dragged his thumb across a faded birthday card on the wall behind me like it was some sacred script only he could read.

"Tell the truth," he murmured. Then he looked at me, really looked, and the world stopped.

Something twisted inside me. My chest fluttered in the worst way. I was prey again. Caught between awe and terror.

"I think it's beautiful," I breathed. It slipped out without my permission.

He stilled. The grin wavered. His eyes narrowed, and whatever thread of amusement he'd been hanging from snapped. Suddenly, he pressed the dagger to my ribs, right beneath my heart. The metal bit hard and I gasped, but there was no pain, no blood. Just pressure.

His brows furrowed. Jaw clenched. Like the laws of nature had spat in his face. He pushed harder. Still nothing. No slice. No scream. Just the sound of my heart racing behind my ribs, *thudding* like it was trying to escape somehow.

He stared at the dagger, then at me.

My breath came ragged now. Too fast. Chest rising, throat tight. He made my knees weak in the worst way. Like gravity didn't work properly around him. Like I might fold under the sheer weight of being seen, of being so close to something that wasn't supposed to let me live, and yet . . .

"Damn it," he muttered, voice rough, teeth clenched. He yanked the dagger away and flung it onto the bed like it had offended him and started pacing, breathing heavy, angry.

I pressed a hand to my ribs where the blade had kissed me, half-expecting to find a gash, blood, anything, but there was nothing. No tear in the skin. No sting. Just a phantom ache and the echo of pressure. I straightened slowly. Not out of defiance, exactly. More like instinct. Like a plant leaning toward a storm because it hadn't learned self-preservation.

He couldn't hurt me.

And that . . . that gave me a little confidence. I straightened, rubbing my side where the blade had pressed against my ribs. The skin there still tingled with phantom pressure, but I was intact.

"Did you just try to kill me?" I asked, voice a little too steady. "Again?"

His head snapped toward me, fast and sharp, like a predator scenting a challenge. His eyes locked with mine, and suddenly the air got heavy, thick, and electric, like the moment before a lightning strike. He didn't deny it, but he didn't apologize either. Of course he didn't.

Every part of my brain still running on survival instinct was waving red flags and shouting, *What the fuck are you doing*. Still, there was something that pulled at me like gravity with teeth. Not attraction, exactly. Obsession, maybe? I needed to understand. Because if I didn't? Then what was the point of all of this? The graveyards, the bones, the ghost videos, the need I couldn't name.

So I opened my stupid, shaking mouth. "What *are* you?" I asked, before reason could stop me.

He turned fully now, arms folding across his bare chest, tattoos shifting subtly in the lamplight. The light still refused to touch him properly. He looked like a statue sculpted from bad decisions, red flags, and grave dirt—so, my type. God help me. Then, with casual cruelty, he reached back and plucked a cigarette from the pocket of his ruined hoodie, crumpled on the ottoman behind him, and slid it between his teeth. No hurry. No drama. Just practiced boredom. The ember flared red as his eyes pinned me in place.

"Wouldn't you like to know," he said, voice curling like the smoke that drifted from his mouth, slow, deliberate, and smug.

"I would, actually."

I wanted to know if something like him *could* exist. If everything I'd believed about the veil between this world and the next was real. If I was right. If I wasn't crazy.

He took a step toward me, and it was enough to chill the air between us. The shadows stirred like loyal dogs at his heels, silent and sentient.

"You're terrifying," I breathed, and I meant it. Truly.

"I'm aware," he said, laughing as smoke slinked from his lips like a secret.

"So. . . are you not going to tell me?" I asked, because apparently I'd decided to poke the bear with a stick and hope it didn't eat me for dessert.

He was already back in the recliner, shirtless, cigarette dangling from his lips like punctuation. One leg slung over the armrest, posture a study in disrespect. His body gleamed faintly with leftover rainwater, shadows licking over his inked ribs like they missed him. His eyes, half-lidded and dangerous, followed me from the dark like a lion debating if I was worth the effort to pounce.

"You're a freak, you know that?" he said, voice slow and lazy.

I blinked. "You're just now figuring that out?"

He grinned.

Wide. Pleased. A little feral.

"Most people cry when I show up," he said. "They beg. Bargain. Shit themselves, if they're particularly honest." He tilted his head slightly, eyes never leaving mine. "But you? You've got a bone collection next to a Hello Kitty incense holder and a neon death shrine in millennial pink."

I flushed, but not with shame. Not really.

Because he wasn't mocking me.

He was *amused*.

"I kinda like that," he said, voice softer now but no less dangerous.

Something fluttered low in my stomach. God, what was *wrong* with me?

I sat on my bed, trying to keep my voice steady. "Not a ghost," I said, ticking it off. "You confirmed that. Not a demon?"

He didn't deny it. Didn't confirm it either. Just smiled again, wider this time. Sharp. Wrong.

"Keep trying, Little Ghoul."

I narrowed my eyes. "I'm not a little—"

"I'm whatever makes your heart beat like that."

The room went still.

I opened my mouth. Closed it again.

Because . . . yeah.

It *was* beating like that.

Hard. Loud. A drumline in my ribs. He made me feel like I was one breath away from either screaming or laughing or spontaneously combusting.

He watched me for a moment longer, then stretched out like a cat, arms behind his head, tattoos flexing across his bare chest like inked armor.

It was late.

The kind of late where everything feels unreal, where silence weighs heavier and shadows press in like they're listening.

But we were still at it.

Back and forth.

Me, half-curled on the edge of my bed, blanket draped over my legs like a half-hearted shield.

Him, sprawled across the recliner like a pagan god at rest. Bare-chested, comfortable, and immovable.

"You're exhausting," I muttered, rubbing my forehead.

He smirked. "You're the one who summoned me, sweetheart. You could've just lit some candles and saged the place like a normal spiritual disaster."

"God, shut *up*," I snapped before I could think better of it.

A laugh slipped out of him.

It rumbled from his chest like distant thunder, like something that lived under your bed and only came out when the lights were off.

The sound made my skin prickle. Not just fear, *anticipation*. Maybe he wasn't all menace and death threats.

He leaned his head back, letting the shadows eat half his face. "There it is. Finally growing a spine."

"I'm not scared of you."

That was a lie. Kind of.

Because, yes, I was scared, but I was also something else. Intrigued. Pulled in. I didn't want to run anymore. I wanted to understand him. I wanted to make sense of the thing sitting across the room like darkness personified, smoking in front of a neon death shrine like it was just another Tuesday.

He arched a brow. "Could've fooled me an hour ago. You were trembling like a little rabbit."

I stared at him.

"Yeah? Well, you tried to kill me."

"And *failed*," he said. "Still hurts my ego." The words sounded bored and wistful.

I didn't know whether to laugh or scream or throw a pillow at his stupid, beautiful face, and I couldn't help the grin tugging at my mouth. "Good."

He narrowed his eyes, but there was amusement under the sharp edges.

"You're lucky I can't rip you apart."

"You've said that already."

"I meant it."

"You always this dramatic, or is it just when you're wet and shirtless in a stranger's room?"

That made him sit up straighter. The grin returned, wider this time, almost impressed. "Careful, Little Ghoul. Keep flirting, and I might think you're into this."

My face flushed so fast it felt like whiplash. "You wish," I muttered, trying to bury the heat crawling up my neck.

He tilted his head, all sharp angles and shit-eating confidence, watching me like I was some bizarre new species he couldn't wait to dissect.

"Oh, I *know*," he said, voice curling with smug darkness. "The heartbeat never lies."

Goddamnit.

"I hate you."

"Sure, you do." He stretched like a lazy beast, every muscle moving with sinful ease. "Keep saying it. Maybe someday you'll believe it."

"I have a boyfriend." It came out brittle. Defensive. Stupid.

His grin didn't falter. "That's unfortunate."

"Not a chance, asshole."

That finally made him laugh, low and amused, the kind of laugh that made your spine tense without knowing why. "Good," he said, settling deeper into the chair like this was his living room. "I just like watching you squirm and be all uncomfortable anyway."

I rolled my eyes so hard it hurt. "You're impossible."

"I'm *inevitable*."

The silence stretched again, full of tension and unspoken things I didn't dare name. I turned off the lamp and slid under the blanket, still facing him even in the dark.

"Goodnight, asshole," I muttered.

"Sweet dreams, freak."

I woke up cold. Not the kind of cold that brushed my skin and left. The cold that *settled*. Sank deep into my bones. The room was too dark and deathly silent. Not the good kind of silence either. No, this silence felt wrong. It pressed in from all sides, dense and watchful. Like the world was holding its breath.

I turned over slowly, praying with every rational part of me that it had all been a dream.

The graveyard. The blood . . . *Him*.

Just stress. Just static from one of my more cursed videos.

But then, I glanced at the recliner, and he was still there.

Only . . . he wasn't the same.

Not the version I'd argued with. Not the shirtless, smug nightmare curled in my grandmother's furniture like he owned the place. No. What sat in that chair looked like something that shouldn't move. A corpse. He looked mummified. Like he'd died long before I was born, and someone had forgotten to bury him properly.

Skin slack and gray, parchment-thin, stretched over bone that jutted too sharp and too still. Parts of him were missing. A cheek sagged like wet paper. One eye was sunken so deep it looked hollow, a pit of nothing. His limbs were locked at awkward angles, stiff with the kind of stillness that had *nothing* to do with sleep.

His tattoos remained, but they were broken now. Faded across rotting flesh. Black lines that once moved like shadow now fractured by decay. My breath caught mid-throat. He looked like Death.

Finally, I screamed.

My body reacted before my brain caught up. I scrambled back in bed, limbs flailing, blanket caught around my legs. I kicked it off and slammed into the headboard, hands shaking, lungs collapsing in on themselves. My heart punched the inside of my ribs like it was trying to make a break for it.

The corpse twitched and jerked sharply. Then it *gasped*. A sharp, desperate inhale, like someone surfacing from deep water, air tearing back into lungs that hadn't needed it in centuries.

Color bled back into him like pigment touching water and pooled beneath his skin. Bones shifted. Aligned. Flesh snapped taut. His jaw clicked. His fingers flexed. The eye, the sunken one, refilled behind its lid like someone was pouring life back into it with trembling hands. I couldn't look away. I wanted to, but I couldn't.

He was reassembling. Alive again.

Beautiful again.

Wrong again.

He collapsed out of the chair, hitting the floor like a puppet with cut strings. Then, he was at my side. One blink, and he was kneeling by the bed, sudden and silent and too close. Shadows clung to him like they didn't want to let go, coiling around his bare shoulders, reluctant to release their claim. He moved carefully, deliberately, like one wrong twitch might spook me or break *him*.

His hand lifted, palm out, no threat in the gesture. Just stillness. But his *face*, god, his face. That was what froze me. His skin was back to that impossible smoothness, pale as snowfall, flawless as porcelain glinting in the dark, but something about it didn't feel right anymore. Now that I'd seen what was underneath, the perfection felt . . . like a lie wearing makeup. His lips still carried that faint, dead blue, like the blood hadn't figured out how to run warm again. Like death had kissed him once and never quite let go . . . and his eyes—

They weren't black now. They weren't void. They were just *tired*. Tired in a way that no mortal could understand. Tired in a way that made the word eternity feel too small.

"Opal," he said again, softer this time. His voice barely scraped the air.

"It's okay." I wasn't sure if he was trying to calm me or convince himself. I couldn't breathe. My back hit the headboard. "What—what the *fuck* was that?!"

He winced. "I'm sorry. I should have warned you. Or just . . . not fallen asleep."

I stared at him, wide-eyed, still shaking.

"You looked *dead*."

"I was," he said simply. "Kinda."

"That's not *normal*!"

"No shit."

He reached out like he was going to touch my arm but stopped short, fingers hovering. "Most people don't see me like that," he said, and for the first time he sounded . . . apologetic. Maybe even *embarrassed*. "I don't usually sleep. I don't like it."

My heart was still racing, my skin clammy. I could still *see* it. The bone. The withered skin. The *truth*. And now he appeared whole again. Human, almost. But I couldn't shake the memory of him breaking apart like wet paper.

"Why?" I whispered, voice hoarse. "Why do you . . . turn into that?"

He didn't move. Didn't blink.

"Because that's what happens when I sleep," he said. "The body you see? It's not real. It's . . . glamour, tattoos and all. As long as I'm awake, it holds, but when I rest—when I stop *trying*—I go back to what I really am."

"And what's that?"

He smiled, but it didn't reach his eyes.

"Something that's been dead a very, very long time."

I didn't know what to say to that.

He looked down at the floor like it had insulted him, then slowly pushed himself to his feet. The movement was smooth again, his usual unnatural grace returning like a mask sliding back into place.

I followed him with my eyes, still curled against the headboard, blanket clutched to my chest.

He ran a hand through his hair and muttered, "I should've warned you. I just . . . forgot."

"You *forgot* that you turn into a corpse when you sleep?"

He shot me a look. "Sorry, princess, didn't realize I needed a disclaimer."

My nerves flared again, terror mingling with exhaustion and something almost like pity.

"I'm not a princess."

"No," he said, more to himself than me. "You're worse. You're *curious*."

He turned to face me fully, eyes dark, shoulders tense.

"I don't sleep for a reason, Opal. It's not for comfort. It's not for peace. When I sleep, I'm not hiding. You saw the part most people are smart enough to fear."

"I *am* scared," I whispered.

He nodded once. "Good." But he didn't say it like he meant it. He said it like it disappointed him.

"What the fuck are you?" I asked, the question falling out of me before I could stop it.

He froze for a beat, then turned away with a sound that wasn't quite a sigh. It was deeper—a growl. Like the question scraped something raw inside him. "Opal," he said, voice strained and low, "you really don't want the truth."

I flinched.

He looked . . . disappointed. Not in me, but in himself. "Just trust me when I say you don't want to know what you trapped. It's probably best if you stopped asking questions." His eyes cut away from mine, jaw tight. Something in his expression shifted, like he'd pulled a curtain shut behind his gaze. "Got it?"

I didn't answer.

He didn't wait.

"Go back to sleep, Opal."

"I'm not sure I can," I whispered.

He didn't reply. Just threw an arm over his eyes, slouching back in the chair like he was done. Conversation over.

"You'll get used to it," he said flatly.

I stared at him. At the way the shadows coiled around the recliner like they missed him. Like they *belonged* to him. Like they were shaped by his presence and now didn't quite know what to do without him moving.

The silence pressed harder.

"I don't think I want to get used to it."

He let out a breath—slow, worn, ancient.

"Too late."

CHAPTER 4

Cain

I didn't fall back asleep. Should've known better than to try. Sleep never worked right for me anyway. I never really rested—I blacked out like a corpse until the world clawed me back. But that little flicker of quiet after we got here? Stupid and weak . . . a moment of silence I let happen.

I cursed myself for it.

Now I was awake, stretched out in the corner of her room like some stray she'd let in out of the storm. Hoodie still damp, boots still muddy, shadows curling around my fingers like bored snakes.

I watched her.

Pink hair splayed across a pillow that looked like it cost eight bucks and three hours of indecision at Target. She was breathing slow, even . . . sleeping.

Fucking sleeping.

With me five feet away.

That was either the dumbest thing she'd ever done or the most metal.

She seemed small in the dark. Fragile in a way that wasn't weakness, just mortal. Tucked in like she didn't know the world had sharp teeth. Like she hadn't summoned a literal death god and botched the landing. Like I wasn't still sitting here, trying to puzzle out why she wasn't dead yet, and how to make it happen.

I could've killed her half a dozen times by now. Should've. I wanted to, at least in theory, but every time I tried, something cracked in the machinery, something jammed, like the universe was holding its breath. Like she was . . . wrong. In the way I was wrong.

I flexed my fingers, watching the shadows coil tighter. Restless. Hungry. I really wanted to kill something. Her, preferably. Just to prove I still could. Just to make the crack in the system go quiet. But I hadn't, and that fact was a bullet rattling around my skull.

She was different. Different in a way I didn't like. I dragged a hand over my face and exhaled slowly through my nose.

"What the fuck is wrong with you?" I muttered.

She didn't flinch. Didn't stir.

Still sleeping.

Which, again—*what?*

I stood and paced, slow and quiet. Studio apartment. One room, scarcely furnished. Cheap desk with a cracked monitor. Weird collection of jars on the shelves: bones, feathers, teeth. Pink curtains. Fairy lights. A murder aesthetic dipped in glitter. *My* personal hell.

I'd touched thousands, millions. Gods, kings, monsters. Every one of them bent to the rules. Every one of them *ended*.

But her?

She had *no time*.

That clock I'd always felt, the one ticking under every soul like a countdown, was silent. Nothing. Like Death had skipped her. Like she wasn't part of the system. Wasn't mine to write in the ledger.

That was dangerous.

Not just to me. To the whole fucking world. The balance, the thing I was made to protect. Because there's only one thing worse than dying: not being able to. I knew that hell firsthand.

The itch started again. That crawl under my skin that said to move. Chaos clawing at me for release.

I needed to ruin something soft. Something that thought it was safe. That was when I saw it. Spray paint. Black. Nestled on a shelf beside a candle and a cursed-looking scrapbook of headstones.

Of course it was black.

It was stupid . . . and *perfect*.

I shook the can. The rattle sounded like a heartbeat. The intake of air before a scream. These walls were too clean. Too pink. Pretending death was cute. It made my hands itch. Time to fix that. I picked the spot between the closet and her haunted-ass altar and went to work. My tag. A skull, grinning, jagged, hollow-eyed. I'd left this mark everywhere something died. Every city. Every body. And I'd leave it here too. Because one day, tomorrow, next century . . . I'd kill her.

As soon as the leash snapped, I'd make it beautiful. Not the art—the murder. The art was the signature. I stepped back and looked at it. It was perfect. I turned and scanned the room for something else to bleed. I grabbed a stuffed animal on her nightstand, some pastel bear or rabbit or whatever, and I stabbed it.

Then I saw him. Tucked in the corner of her wall collage. A Polaroid. The boyfriend. Smiling like an idiot. I plucked it off the wall and stared for a while. I hated this guy's face already. I grabbed a Sharpie from her altar shelf. Thick black ink bled across his face: devil horns, x's over the eyes, fangs, a stupid little speech bubble:

"Sorry I ran."

I pinned it back and grinned. Then I dropped into the recliner like I hadn't just defiled her pastel sanctuary with petty vengeance.

I lit a cigarette.

Gods, I needed it. The smoke detector beeped, and I looked at it nasty. It went quiet.

The smoke curled through the air like it belonged here more than I did. It was the only thing that still tasted like anything. Food? Ash. Drink? Ash. But this? This worked.

I pulled hard. Let the burn scald its way into my lungs and held it there. But not because I had to. Because I needed to feel something. The nicotine hit. Sharp. Fast. Blessedly numbing.

For a second, the screaming edges of my mind dulled. The rage, the boredom, the constant itch to destroy, all quieted just enough to make the stillness tolerable.

I exhaled slowly, watching the smoke drift to the ceiling. It wouldn't kill me. Nothing would. But at least it reminded me I still had a body.

Even if it wasn't technically alive. Even if my heart only beat when it remembered to. I flicked the ash into a pink ceramic skull on the nightstand probably meant for incense.

Even better.

The sun started to peek through the blinds. Weak, golden slats of morning light spilled across the room, chasing shadows off the floor. The air smelled like fabric softener and cheap ghosts.

I took another drag off the cigarette, now just a glowing stub between my fingers. The ember hissed in the ashtray as I crushed it, smoke curling up like it was reluctant to die.

Daylight.

Perfect.

Maybe now we can commit a felony before breakfast. Break in somewhere and steal that damn book back. A little B&E to kick off the morning. Stretch the legs. Violate some privacy. You know . . . therapy.

I stood, shadows peeling off my frame like they'd rather stay tangled in the dark. I rolled my shoulders, stiff from sleeping in a recliner designed for people who hadn't committed cosmic crimes.

"Rise and shine, Little Ghoul," I said, voice rough from smoke. "We've got a boyfriend to rob."

She blinked, rubbing her eyes like she was still trying to figure out which part of this was the dream or the nightmare.

". . . What?" she mumbled.

"We're getting that book back," I said, already pulling on my boots like I hadn't just graffitied her perfect little wall. "I'm not sitting around for a week so your boyfriend can come home from the woods, or wherever he's gone to emotionally repress and be aggressively mediocre." I crossed my arms and stared down at her. "We break this bond, and I go back to doing what I like to do, and you go back to whatever the fuck all of this is." I gestured to her room.

She glared at me, baffled. "Right now? It's *barely* morning."

"Exactly. Fewer witnesses. Better parking." I grabbed her jacket and tossed it at her like it was a bomb she could decide to disarm or wear. "Let's go."

She caught it, still blinking. "You—you want me to *break into Lucian's house*?"

"No." I pointed at myself. "*I'm* breaking in. You're just my emotional support cryptid."

Opal sat on the corner of the bed, hoodie crumpled in her lap. "This is insane."

I huffed. "We'll be in and out. You can even wait outside. Pretend you don't know me."

"That's easy," she muttered, pulling her hoodie over her head. "You're impossible."

"Glad we agree."

She muttered something under her breath that sounded suspiciously like *asshole*.

I smiled, sharp and satisfied. "Language, Final Girl."

She glared at me. "I need to eat before we go. I'm starving."

"Fine."

I leaned back against the wall, arms crossed, watching her rummage through the mini fridge like she was preparing for a midnight picnic instead of a felony. She pulled out bread, butter, cheese. Simple. Mortal. My stomach twisted at the smell before I even realized it.

She glanced at me over her shoulder. "You want one?"

"No."

"Come on." She set the skillet on the hot plate, dropping butter in with a hiss. "You can't live on cigarettes and a bad attitude."

I pushed off the wall, stalking closer until the shadows at my feet curled along the linoleum. "I don't eat."

She snorted. "Everyone eats."

"Not me." My voice came out flat.

"You mean . . . you don't *like* to?" she asked carefully.

I stared at the bread browning in the pan. My jaw ached. "I mean I can't." The words hung there, raw. "I remember the taste," I muttered, softer now. "Once. But that was a lifetime ago."

Her eyes widened. She didn't say anything, which almost made it worse.

"Now?" I forced a smirk that felt like glass in my mouth. "Everything turns to ash. Wine, blood, your precious grilled cheese. It's nothing."

Her lips parted. "So, you're—"

"Starving," I snapped, sharper than I meant. Then quieter, because the truth always cut deepest when whispered: "Always."

The butter popped in the pan. She looked down at it. "That sounds like hell," she whispered.

I leaned in close, let my grin sharpen until she shivered. "That's the idea, Little Ghoul. Now eat your sandwich," I said, snatching my jacket from the chair. "We've got a house to rob." I watched as she bit into it then glanced away. "So . . ." I said, dragging out the word, voice sharp enough to cut. "No search party?"

Her hands stilled.

"What?"

"Your little ghost-hunting posse." I raised a brow. "Not even a text?"

"They probably . . ." she started, then stopped. Swallowed. Tried again. "They didn't know what happened. Not really."

"Pretty sure they saw me crawl out of the ground like a pissed-off curse," I muttered. "Hard to miss."

She didn't answer.

Didn't look at me, either.

"Right," I said, lips curling. "Guess they were just busy."

I saw the twitch in her jaw. The truth she didn't want to name. And the ache hiding behind it.

"Whatever," she said, brushing past me. "Let's just get the book."

That's when she saw it. Her eyes widened, scanning the wall behind me like she was seeing it for the first time, and really, she was.

"Oh my *god*."

"Yes?" I replied, leaning against the doorframe, voice soaked in half-sarcasm.

Her eyes narrowed. Her jaw clenched. The flicker of rage was immediate and beautiful. "What did you do to my wall?!"

I shrugged, completely unbothered. "Improved it. You're welcome."

She gawked from me to the black-dripping skull grinning out from the drywall like it wanted to devour her throw pillows. Then something in her shifted. Her breath caught. "That tag . . ." She stepped closer, slower this time. Like the paint might let her in on a secret.

"That's been on the news," she said, voice quieter. "People think it's a gang symbol. Or a warning, or—" She looked back at me. Really *looked*.

"They said it shows up where there've been mass murders."

I sighed, offended. "A gang?" I scoffed, voice going guttural, like a growl that had learned manners. "That's *insulting*."

Then, lower. Flat. Honest. "I claim my work."

Her mouth opened. No words. She just stared, and I stared right back. Because watching her put it together? Watching her realize what exactly it was that was sleeping in her recliner? That was better than the art.

Her pulse picked up. I didn't even have to hear it. I could feel it. Like static in the air. Like the room had shifted to a different frequency. Her eyes stayed locked on the skull dripping down her wall, but I saw the tremble in her hands. There it was. The fear finally settling in. And gods, it looked good on her. I pushed off the doorframe and took a slow step toward her.

"I love this part," I murmured.

She blinked, backing up one step. "What part?" she asked, voice tight.

I grinned. "The part where you realize you didn't just summon something weird and annoying. You summoned something ancient. Something wrong."

She pressed her back to the wall, as if that would do anything to stop me. I kept my voice soft, almost gentle. That made it worse. "You see it now, don't you?" I crooked my head. "You didn't pull some cursed little ghostie out of a graveyard. You dragged *me* out."

Her breath hitched. I heard it.

"You want to know how many places that skull has shown up?" I asked, stepping in close enough to make her nerves jump.

"I don't."

I leaned in next to her ear and whispered, "You sure?"

She flinched. "You're sick."

I smirked. "Takes one to summon one, sweetheart."

She clenched her jaw. "I didn't know what I was doing."

"Oh, I know. That's what makes it delicious." I tapped a finger against my temple. "You weren't trying to call me. You just wanted a ghost. A little fun. Something spooky to spike your views."

She didn't answer. I saw it in her eyes, the regret. The realization. I stepped even closer, lowering my voice. "Congratulations, Opal. You didn't open the door," I said. "You left it unlocked and invited a monster in." I grabbed her arm. "Now let's go."

It was still weird, being able to touch someone. The contact hummed deep under my skin—something I wasn't supposed to feel. Something I shouldn't be bound to.

"Wait," she said, yanking back with more force than I expected. "How do I know you won't kill me once the spell is broken?"

Smart girl.

I smiled, slow and sharp. "You don't."

She crossed her arms. Brave again. "Promise."

I raised an eyebrow. "Excuse me?"

"You have to promise you won't kill me if I help you."

Fuck. That was annoying.

I felt the wall tighten around me. Felt something shift in the tether. I didn't like it. Not one goddamn bit.

She shouldn't be able to do that. Shouldn't be able to push. Shouldn't be able to ask things from me and have the bond respond like it mattered. She didn't know my name. She didn't know the rules. She had no power. Or at least, she shouldn't. I clenched my jaw, eyes narrowing.

"Fine," I growled. That didn't mean I meant it. Didn't mean she was safe. The bond might keep her alive now, but the second it was gone? The second I was free? I could snap her like a twig. I would, eventually, and I'd enjoy it. Might as well have had my fingers crossed. Because I wanted to see her bleed.

"Good. Okay," she said, nodding like we'd just sealed a business deal instead of dancing around murder.

She turned, casual as anything. "Before we go, I want to test something."

I narrowed my eyes. "What?"

"Just . . . stay here."

I blinked. She slipped out the door and closed it behind her with a soft click. I stood there. Waiting. Counting.

What the hell was she doing?

The tug hit me hard. One moment, I was in her apartment, perfectly stationary. The next, *bam*, my whole body jerked forward like I'd been yanked by a goddamn chain around the ribs.

I stumbled through the apartment door and down the stairs without touching them, gravity bending, snapping, dragging me like a dog on a leash. I hit the sidewalk with a growl and found her standing on the street corner, arms crossed, chin high.

"Are you testing me?" I snapped, barely restraining a snarl as I came to a hard stop just a few feet from her.

She shrugged, completely unfazed. "Wanted to see what happens if I walk away."

"You know what happens."

"Well, now I know-know." She smiled all innocently.

I stared at her. Unblinking. She stared back. Smug. *Little freak.*

"Don't do that again," I said flatly.

"I'm going to do it again."

"I will snap your ankle if you try."

"I don't think you can."

I growled, quiet and guttural. She grinned. Was she enjoying this? Was she really pushing me, testing me like I was some new cursed object she wanted to see spark? I took a step closer. She didn't back away.

"You're playing with fire, Opal."

Her smile wavered slightly, but she held her ground.

"Let's just go," I growled, sick of the games, the stalling, the pink.

I dragged a hand through the air and ripped the void wide open. My shadows surged forward to obey, hissing, curling, eager for the taste of movement. Obedient, for once.

"Where does he live?" I asked, already stepping toward the breach.

"Oh no," she said, backing up like I'd waved a knife at her. "We're not doing that again."

I blinked. "What."

"How about we take the train?"

I stared at her.

"You don't want to put me on a train, Final Girl," I said, voice lethal. "I promise you that."

She raised a brow. "Why? Scared of enclosed spaces?"

"No. I'm scared of what happens when someone breathes too loud, and I snap their spine in front of a toddler." She hesitated, clearly trying to decide if I was kidding. I wasn't.

"And what if I don't tell you where he lives?" she asked, eyes gleaming with something dangerously close to confidence.

She was testing again. Always testing.

I growled, taking a slow, heavy step toward her. "Opal."

She didn't flinch. "So you can't read my mind," she said, like she'd confirmed a theory.

I laughed, cold, sharp. "No. I'm just very good at reading people, and right now, you are taking liberties you can't afford." She crossed her arms. Smiled. Gods, that smile.

"Well, come on, killer," she said. "Let's go for a walk."

That *bitch*. That clever, insufferable, absolutely doomed little bitch. I let the void close behind me, shadows snapping shut like a jaw.

"Fine," I muttered, brushing past her. "But if someone so much as looks at me wrong, I'm setting a building on fire."

"Noted," she chirped, falling into step beside me, and so we walked. The god of death on a leash, and the girl stupid enough to hold it.

CHAPTER 5

Opal

I still didn't know what he was. Or *who*. And that bothered me more than I wanted to admit. He hadn't told me his name. Not even a fake one. Just smirks and barbed sarcasm, threats dressed like jokes. I knew this much: He was dangerous. *Very* dangerous.

The skull he'd painted on my wall was more than vandalism. It was a signature. A *warning*. I'd seen that mark before on late-night news segments. Wherever it showed up, people died. Sometimes one. Sometimes a dozen. And in some cases, entire buildings of people just gone, dead.

The official story was always something human. A gang. A cult. A network of ritual-obsessed serial killers. No one had ever been caught, and no one who saw it ever lived long enough to explain what they'd seen.

I glanced at the thing walking beside me: He appeared calm. That was the worst part. He was calm like a storm cloud before it split open the sky. Like if this world went up in flames, he'd just light another cigarette, watch it burn, and laugh, probably.

He didn't act like a person.

He acted like a *god* . . . And maybe he was one.

He certainly *looked* like one. All sharp edges and slow blinks, tattoos like scripture scrawled in ink, bone, and ivy. A body sculpted by violence and apathy. A face that belonged on an altar—if altars were allowed to scowl.

But gods didn't flick cigarette ash into skull-shaped incense holders. Gods didn't sleep like corpses. Gods didn't glare at subway seats like they were contemplating murder. Still . . . I wasn't sure. Maybe he wasn't a god. Maybe he was something else. Something older. Angrier. Tired of being prayed to. Tired of being feared—or in love with it.

And here I was, walking beside him like I hadn't felt his hand around my throat and still asked if he was okay. Because I wasn't brave. Or strong. Or particularly honest with myself. But I *was* kind. Maybe not everyone would've let him stay. Most people wouldn't have looked at him and seen lonely tucked behind lethal, but I had. Even if I shouldn't have. That was the scariest part of all.

The guilt crept in around the edges as we approached the MARTA station. A quiet little ghost whispering, *Hey, maybe don't commit a felony today.* We were going to Lucian's house. While he was gone. Without telling him.

I pulled out my train card and tapped through the gate like a good little citizen. Behind me, he jumped the gate. Of course he did. Landed like a shadow in a hoodie and grinned at me like committing crimes was his cardio.

"I could've bought you a Breeze card," I muttered.

"I could've let you die in the mud," he said, stretching like a cat that hated everyone.

"Okay, yeah, but you did try to kill me at least three times," I snapped back.

He smiled, wide and eerie. "Consider it a compliment. No one has ever survived the first attempt."

We boarded the train, and he immediately plopped down on the bench like it had personally offended him. Like he was mad it hadn't come with a throne and incense. He sprawled out with all the subtlety of a war crime, legs stretched into the aisle, arm draped over the backrest like he was waiting for someone to challenge him.

Everyone on the train gave us a very, very wide berth. One guy looked up, caught a glimpse of his face, and immediately decided the floor was fascinating. Like *Wow, linoleum! That's crazy.* A woman got up and actually switched cars. A kid blinked at him and started crying. Someone sneezed and then visibly regretted it.

He didn't even blink. Just stared at the floor like it owed him money and muttered, "I hate this."

"Public transit or humans in general?" I asked, clutching the pole and trying not to look like I'd brought Satan to brunch.

"Yes," he said flatly.

Lucian's street was exactly the way I remembered it: quiet, tree-lined, stupidly symmetrical. Like it had been manufactured in some suburban utopia factory, shipped in neat boxes, and assembled with matching porch lights and HOA regulations.

"Which one's his?"

I pointed to the slate-blue colonial halfway down the block, perfect paint, perfect windows, perfect wreath on the door.

He stared at it. His eyes narrowed, and his jaw twitched. A flicker. Like something deep inside him didn't *like* the place.

"You okay?" I asked, watching his expression tighten.

He blinked once, slow. "Fine."

He didn't sound fine.

"So," I said, shifting my weight, "do we knock politely or . . . ?"

He shot me a look. *Right.* We weren't doing polite. We weren't even doing *legal.*

He strode toward the side of the house like he'd done this a thousand times before, and he probably had. He inspected the windows with all the care of someone judging architectural sins.

"You coming, or are you just here for the guilt trip?" he called over his shoulder.

I jogged to catch up, hoodie sleeves pulled over my hands like they might protect me from consequence.

"This is breaking and entering," I muttered.

"Only if you get caught," he replied and pulled a shadow from his sleeve like it was a crowbar.

That shut me up.

He slid the window open like it had been waiting for him. No creak. No resistance. Just . . . surrender.

He looked around, unimpressed.

"Figures," he muttered. "Rich boy aesthetic with all the soul of a tax return."

"Can you *not* insult my boyfriend while we're committing crimes against him?"

He glanced at me. "I haven't even *started*."

He disappeared into Lucian's room like a bloodstained ghost with no respect for boundaries. I stayed downstairs, gnawing on my thumbnail and trying not to think about what I'd let him do.

This is fine, I told myself.

Normal.

Definitely not a felony.

Eventually, I heard drawers opening. A cabinet slammed. Something hit the floor.

"I swear to god," I muttered under my breath and headed upstairs.

He was in Lucian's room, standing in front of his dresser with a look on his face like he'd just discovered what human mediocrity smelled like.

He rummaged through the top drawer of the nightstand, expression deadpan. Then he froze and pulled out a box of condoms. My face went *nuclear*.

"Oh my god," I choked. "Put that back."

He held the box between two fingers. "So, this was the plan? Very romantic."

"It's not like that!"

He glanced between me and the nightstand. "Mmhmm."

My cheeks burned hotter. "It's just, people have stuff like that, okay? It doesn't mean—"

He dropped the box back into the drawer with a dull *thud*. "I don't like him," he said casually, as if he were commenting on the weather.

"You don't *know* him," I shot back, too defensive, too fast.

He turned to me, eyes cold, unreadable. "I don't *need* to know him."

I swallowed hard. "Where's the book?"

He flopped onto the bed like he wasn't halfway through looting my boyfriend's childhood bedroom. "No book."

"You didn't find it?"

"Oh, I found *plenty*." He glanced over his shoulder with a crooked grin. "Just not the one we're looking for."

I crossed my arms. "You're unbelievable."

"I'm bored."

"And *petty*."

"I am a little petty," he said, running a hand down his arm absently.

He stood up and opened the closet next, thumbing through Lucian's perfectly hung shirts like they were a personal insult.

"Gross, everything's so . . . pressed." He started shoving hangers aside. Then his hand stopped. At the bottom of the closet, half-buried beneath a forgotten pile of sweaters, lay a bone-white mask. He crouched, plucked it free, and held it up to the light. Smooth. Expressionless. The kind of thing meant to erase whoever wore it.

He turned it over in his hands. Inside, faint sigils shimmered, thin as spiderwebs, curling around the edges like veins.

"Where did you say he got that book again?" he asked, voice unreadable.

"Family heirloom. Why?"

He didn't answer. His eyes flicked once more over the symbols, then dropped the mask back into the dark.

"Uh-huh." He kept digging, as if it didn't matter, like he couldn't be bothered to care what kind of cursed shit my boyfriend was hoarding. He tugged a black shirt free, Lucian's shirt. A vintage band logo, faded from years of bragging about where he thrifted it. Without hesitation, he stripped off his ruined hoodie and pulled the shirt over his head.

I just stood there.

Watching.

Speechless.

He rolled his shoulders, adjusting the fit. He looked . . . God help me, *good* in it. Too good. Comfortable. Relaxed. Like it belonged to him now. "You're wearing my boyfriend's shirt," I said, voice dry.

He collapsed into a chair next to the window and stared at me like I'd said something adorable. "Correction: You *had* a boyfriend. I don't think he qualifies anymore. Not after ditching you to die in a graveyard while screaming like an extra in a horror movie." He stared at me for a long beat. No smirk this time. No sarcasm. "Break up with him."

The words landed hard. Too blunt. Too fast.

I blinked. "What?"

"You heard me, break up with him," he repeated, tone flat. "He's a waste of space."

"Wow," I muttered. "You should really start a couples counseling channel."

He ignored that and leaned backward in the chair, elbows on the back of the chair, Lucian's stolen shirt riding up just enough to show a sliver of inked stomach. "Ask yourself," he said, voice even. "Why would he take *that* book with him. Out of everything in this house. Why that one?"

I crossed my arms tighter. The morning air felt colder suddenly, like the breeze had teeth. "I've known them since I was a little kid," I said, trying to keep my voice steady. "They're perfectly normal. There's no way they actually know what that is."

"Normal people don't keep books like that, Opal. They don't pass them down."

"They didn't know," I insisted, even as the words started to wobble. "Lucian thought it looked cool."

He scoffed, rubbing a hand down his face. "Yeah. Sure. Just your everyday decorative blood tome, hanging out in the attic between the Christmas lights and grandma's ashes."

"Okay, you don't have to be so *dramatic*."

He turned to me, eyes hard now. "I'm telling you something's off. I've felt it since we got here. There's a stench on this place, and it's not just his overpriced cologne."

My stomach knotted, and we didn't talk much on the way back. I hugged my arms tighter around myself as we walked. The sky was cloudy now, dull gray and heavy, like the city was holding its breath.

He seemed calmer. Less irritated. Almost bored again. That didn't make me feel any better. He kept pace beside me with that eerie, too-smooth walk. Occasionally, his gaze flicked toward strangers we passed. Not with curiosity—more like assessment or calculation. A bored predator scanning the herd for weakness. Not because he needed to eat, but because the habit had never died.

Then I saw her, an old woman, small and hunched, like time had pressed her down one year too many. A pale-blue cardigan hung from her shoulders like tissue paper. She looked like she weighed less than her purse. He veered toward her. Not fast. Not sudden. Just . . . inevitable. Like he was answering a summons only he could hear.

"Hey," I said, slowing. "Where are you going?"

He didn't answer. Didn't even glance back. He crossed the street with calm certainty, footsteps light, hands in his pockets like this was just another Wednesday.

The woman looked up. Saw him coming. She smiled like she knew him. Like she'd been *expecting* him. My heart tripped. He raised one hand, fingers outstretched. A touch. Barely that. And the moment his skin met hers, she dropped.

No warning, no sound—just gone. She crumpled like a puppet whose strings had snapped mid-scene. My scream tore out of me before I even felt it rise. He flinched, turned toward me, reflex more than reaction, and bumped into a man behind him. Mid-thirties. Suit. Expensive shoes. Earbuds in. Didn't even notice what he'd walked into.

"Watch it, asshole," the man barked, shoving his bare arm as he stepped off the curb.

He never saw the bus. The sound hit harder than the impact. My vision blurred, ears ringing as the world came apart in slow motion. The man flew, arms pinwheeling, his briefcase spinning off into traffic. Someone screamed, tires shrieked, and horns bled into each other.

My knees went weak. I clutched the nearest streetlight, air burning in my lungs. I couldn't look at the bodies, but he didn't even flinch. Didn't check for a pulse. Didn't see the carnage.

He disappeared into the shadows like a thing melting and reappeared next to me.

Hands in his pockets. Jaw slack. Blank eyed. I backed up instinctively, heart hammering. His voice was flat. Empty. "Had to make sure it wasn't more than just you."

My blood turned to ice.

"What?" I whispered.

He glanced down at me like I was a puzzle missing too many pieces to be worth finishing. "The bond. The rules," he said. "I needed to know if they still applied. If I could still . . . do what I do."

"And now you know?" I asked, breath gone ragged, throat thick with something too close to fear.

He nodded once. Simple. Clean.

"Yeah."

That was it.

Yeah.

Like he hadn't just ended two lives in under sixty seconds.

Like this was a test.

I couldn't speak. Couldn't move. Could only watch him, this strange, impossible creature in a stolen T-shirt, standing under a pink sunrise like nothing had happened.

He blinked slowly.

"You gonna cry?"

"No," I croaked, though I wasn't sure that was true.

A crow dropped out of the sunrise like a piece of night that had forgotten to leave. It landed on the bent parking sign beside us and cocked its head, bead-black eyes fixed on him. The air went cold. The street noise thinned like the city was holding its breath.

He didn't look at me. He looked at the bird. "You there, reaper. Come here."

The crow hopped down to the hood of a car, then the curb, then the toe of his boot. The shadow at its feet thickened, stretched, unfolded into a woman like ink learning how to be human. She straightened, brushed imaginary dust from a dark suit, and bowed her head.

"My king."

My heart jerked so hard it knocked my breath off course. *King? King of what?*

"Do you have paper?"

"Of course, my king."

My mouth was dry. I stared at him, the same man who'd smoked in my living room and stabbed a stuffed animal for fun, while he took the paper and pen like a bored CEO signing off on something beneath him.

He hadn't told me his name.

He hadn't told me anything.

Now, someone was shape-shifting in front of me and bowing like we were in a gothic fever dream, and he was casually handing out death orders like it was just any other day. I couldn't breathe.

"Take the souls," he said, scribbling something fast and mean on the page. "And take this to the Devil. Only him, Juliana. No one else."

The Devil.

He didn't say *a* Devil. Or *some* Devil.

He said *The*. As in . . . *the* Devil.

Like he knew him. Like they had meetings. Like he had access. I felt my knees wobble. I stepped back, hand reaching for the lamppost like it could hold me steady.

He was all business, all bite now. He wasn't only used to this. He *belonged* to it. The Devil. Hell. Souls. Kingship. What had I summoned? The pressure in the air curled around me, thick as gravity, and my ears rang. He wasn't a ghost, he wasn't a demon, he wasn't something that crawled around in the dark. He was someone. A *king*. Of where, exactly? Of *what*?

Juliana turned slightly, her gaze flicking toward me. Not unkind but assessing. I felt suddenly *small*. Not cute-creepy or pastel-haunted or YouTube-weird. Small in a cosmic way. Like a mortal who had wandered too close to a divine fire and now had to pretend they were immune to burns.

He still hadn't looked at me. Still hadn't offered me so much as a sideways glance of explanation. He handed off the message like it meant the difference between worlds.

And maybe it did. And suddenly, it wasn't just the shadows I feared. It was what *he* was. When I wasn't looking, he moved. Barely a shift in weight, the subtlest tilt of his body, but it was enough.

Juliana's gaze, which had flicked to me again in that quiet, unreadable way, was now blocked, his frame directly between us. Not aggressive, not obvious . . . deliberate.

"Sir, that mortal is staring at us?"

"Mine. Irrelevant. Just ignore her." His voice came low, intentional. "And Alistair?" Just two words, but they cut through the space like a blade.

Juliana hesitated. She hadn't hesitated before, not with the Devil, not with Hell, but *that* name made her pause. Her posture stiffened. Her gaze dropped for a breath, like she was choosing words she didn't want to say.

"Gone, sir," she said, not meeting his eyes. "They say he was killed."

He went still. Not the dramatic kind of stillness. Not the human kind. This was the stillness of an ancient mechanism jamming. The air around him seemed to hold its breath.

The muscles in his jaw twitched. His hands, so often casual, loose, tucked into pockets, curled at his sides like they were remembering violence.

"That's impossible," he said, but it came out more like a warning than denial. A promise wrapped in disbelief.

Juliana didn't respond. Her silence spoke more than any excuse could have. He exhaled through his nose, sharp and fast, the sound short-circuiting something under my skin. *He cared.* Not performatively. No, whoever Alistair was, he actually cared about this person. He turned away slightly, pacing two steps, dragging a hand through his hair like he wanted to tear something out by the roots. Shadows writhed at his heels, pulled tighter to his skin, as if echoing something internal, something spiraling.

Then he stopped. Shoulders set. Expression carved back into ice. "Yeah, well," he muttered. "You can't exactly trust the rumors in Hell, now can you?"

"No, sir," Juliana said immediately, bowing her head.

But I was still staring at him. Because for a moment, I'd seen something human crack through the divine detachment. Not weakness. Not grief, even. It had shaken him. I couldn't stop wondering who Alistair had been to him—ally, family, rival, something else?—and what it meant that his death had shaken the unshakable. He turned back toward Juliana, already rebuilding the mask.

"Alright," he said. "Take the souls and take this to the Devil. *Only* him, Juliana."

She nodded. "Understood."

Her body folded inward, feathers erupting black and gleaming, and she collapsed back into the form of a crow.

She fluttered once and soared silently into the sky, wings cutting through the clouds as she circled around once over the sidewalk where the bodies still lay, and then she was gone.

It was just us again. Me and . . . His Highness.

He opened that damn rip in reality again. A slash through space, black and writhing, like the world itself wanted nothing to do with him.

"Sorry, sweetheart," he said, voice deadpan. "I know where you live now. So, we get back *my* way."

Before I could protest, he grabbed my wrist and yanked. The sidewalk vanished, and suddenly we were back in my room. The pink walls. The clutter. I stumbled backward, breath catching, and collapsed onto the bed, my legs folding like paper, my heart still trying to decode what the hell had just happened. It thundered inside my chest, wild and uneven, like it didn't trust me to survive the next few seconds.

"So . . ." I said, voice a broken thing. "You're some kind of reaper, right?"

The shift in him was instant. Like a switch flipped somewhere ancient and buried.

His eyes snapped to mine, cold, flat, *lethal*.

Like I'd said something offensive in a language I wasn't fluent enough in to understand.

He stalked toward me, slow and deliberate, each step a threat disguised as grace. The air thinned as he moved, like even oxygen didn't want to get too close. My lungs screamed. My skin buzzed. The room *shrank* around him.

Then he climbed onto the bed. Not like a lover but like a curse or a sleep paralysis demon that had decided it didn't feel like waiting for nightfall. His limbs folded around me like a cage, one hand braced beside my hip, the other near my shoulder, until he was so close I could see the fine crack of an old scar near his temple, the faintest smudge of soot under his jaw.

So close I couldn't think. Couldn't *breathe*. My heart stuttered, sharp and frantic, like it was clawing at my ribs to escape without me.

"You really want to know, don't you?" he whispered. His voice, low, dark silk pulled tight over knives, slid down my spine like a cold hand. He smiled, and it wasn't kind.

"It's eating you alive," he murmured. "The not-knowing. The *what the fuck are you* of it all. You can't stand it, can you?"

I couldn't speak.

"You know, it's bad," he continued, voice soft but scalpel sharp, "that out of everything you could've dragged from the void, you ended up with the worst option."

He leaned in closer, so close I could feel his breath on my cheek, cool and wrong and minty.

He was a heartbeat away, and I hated how my body reacted. How it lit up under his gaze. How my blood boiled beneath my skin. How I wasn't backing away. My body was a traitor. A stupid, shivering, heat-flushed traitor.

He lifted one hand, slow, like he had all the time in the world, and brushed his fingers against the little vine plant growing in a pot beside my bed. It curled and blackened. *Dead.* Just like that.

He didn't look away from me. Not even for a second. "I'm Death, Opal," he said, voice soft. Final. "You trapped Death." He smiled a wide, toothy grin. Not soft or reassuring but predatory.

He sat up slowly, smooth and deliberate, his weight shifting so I was pinned beneath him. His legs straddled my hips. His hands slid up my arms. Cool fingers. Casual cruelty. He wrapped around my wrists and pressed them into the mattress.

"You afraid yet, Final Girl?" he murmured, eyes locked on mine.

I wanted to say yes. I wanted to say *fuck you*, but my mouth wouldn't move. Because the truth was worse than fear. The truth was, I'd never felt more alive—and he *knew* it.

"You can call me Death," he said, voice like a tomb sealing shut. "Because you are not getting my name."

His eyes locked on mine. "And trust me, Opal," he murmured, lips brushing the space just beside my cheek, breath ghosting over my skin like frost, "you don't want it."

CHAPTER 6

Cain

I decided to stop playing with my food. I rolled off her and flopped onto the bed like I owned it, which, in a way, I did now. The mattress dipped under my weight. Too soft but still *so* much better than that sad excuse for a recliner she'd been keeping me in.

I stretched out, hands behind my head, taking up more space than I needed. She sat rigid beside me, still pressed against the headboard like it might protect her.

Her pulse was pounding, loud. The way her little heart was fluttering was almost as good as the hunt.

Different but good.

There was something electric about it, the tension of prey that didn't know it should be running. Something different enough that it made me want to lean in again, just to see what she'd do. I didn't. Instead, I got comfortable, and she watched me like I might lunge again. *Smart girl.*

I let my eyes close for a second, just to soak it in. I was still bound. Still stuck in this pink, bone-filled nightmare with a girl who smelled like vanilla, marshmallows and grave dirt.

I fell asleep. Time slipped away, *I* slipped away, into the kind of sleep that wasn't sleep. Not really. I never dreamed. I *rotted*.

When I came back to, it was with a sharp inhale, like surfacing from a grave. My lungs remembered how to pretend first. Then the rest of me. My eyes snapped open to her face, pale and calm, staring back at me from across the room shrouded in a pink glow. She sat at her desk, legs tucked under her, hoodie sleeves pulled down over her hands and knees.

"Shit," I muttered, voice dry and rough.

I sat up slowly, feeling the stiffness in my limbs. The telltale ache of a body that had been dead for too long. I looked at her. "How long was I out?"

She didn't blink. "Four days."

Fuck.

I wiped a hand down my face, brushing away the dried cracks in my skin. "I'm sorry."

She smiled at me, tired and faint. "It's okay." She added, quiet and casual, "You were right. You get used to it."

Something hit me right in the center of my hollow chest. The way she said it. Like it was normal. Like this was just . . . life now.

I looked at her sharply. "And you slept . . . where?"

She blinked and shrugged, meeting my eyes. "Next to you."

"So, you just . . . slept next to my rotting corpse for four days?" I asked, tilting my head, a grin crawling across my face.

She flushed, looking away.

I let out a soft laugh. "Oh, sweetheart, you're fucked up, aren't you?"

The blush deepened, blooming across her cheeks like spilled wine, and it was fucking *adorable*.

She spun her chair, turning her back to me like it might protect her, pulling her knees closer to her chest. That ridiculous oversized pink hoodie swallowed her whole, and she looked like the world's softest, stupidest creature—and somehow more dangerous than half the demons I'd ever dealt with.

"Lucian comes back tomorrow."

Right. The boyfriend. The one who'd left her bleeding in a cemetery with nothing but shadows for company and hadn't once glanced back.

I should've brushed it off. Should've smirked, rolled my eyes, said something biting and cruel. But instead, something shifted in my chest. A small, uninvited knot, coiling between my ribs like a bad omen. And I didn't like it. I didn't like that his name on her lips bothered me.

I sat back on the edge of the bed, bones aching with the kind of wear that wasn't physical. Arms folded across my chest, scowl tightening across my face. I didn't want her . . . I wasn't *here* for her. I was here because of a spell. Because of bad Latin, spilled blood, and a girl who didn't know how to be careful with things that bite *hard*.

I was *trapped*. That was all. So, why did the sound of his name taste like rot? Why did the idea of him coming back, touching her, smiling like he belonged here, like he deserved her—why did that make me want to commit murder?

I rolled my shoulders and stretched, arms lifting above my head, vertebrae crackling like dry branches underfoot. The bed creaked beneath me, a whisper of warning she didn't hear. She was still turned away. Still talking about him like he mattered. All of it, noise. I didn't care. Wouldn't.

She talked about him like it meant something, and for reasons I couldn't name, it made me want to burn his house down. Slowly. Starting with whatever shelf held that dumb framed photo of them on the beach.

"I thought you were smarter than that," I said, voice razor edged.

Her head snapped up, eyes narrowing. "Excuse me?"

I didn't answer right away. Just stared back at her, gaze steady, unreadable, jaw clenched.

I should've let it drop. Should've smirked and gone back to pretending none of this mattered. But I didn't. Because the truth was, I hated the way she said his name. I hated that it still tasted sweet on her tongue, that it hadn't curdled in her mouth the way it had in mine. I hated that he got to be the one she remembered while I was still sitting here, in her space, in his goddamn shirt.

"I mean," I said, tone drawn out and deliberate, "after everything, *he left you*, Opal. He ran the second things got messy and didn't even look back."

Her mouth pressed into a line. "You don't know the full story."

"I know enough," I snapped, sharper than I meant to. "He bolted. You bled. I caught you. End of story."

Her eyes flared. "You make it sound like I owe you something for that."

I leaned forward, elbows on my knees, shadows coiling tight around my shoulders. "You don't owe me anything," I said, quieter now. "But maybe don't romanticize the guy who left you to die in a graveyard."

She swallowed. Hard.

I watched her and hated the way her fingers curled in her sleeves like she was retreating. Like maybe part of her knew I was right. Then the smell hit me, a mix of rot and decay. Sour death clinging to my skin like it belonged there. I brought a hand to my neck, grimacing. Flesh still softening in places, patchy and wrong. Opal didn't say anything. Probably didn't want to hurt my feelings . . . Too bad I didn't have any. "I need a shower," I muttered.

Nearly four days, and I could smell myself. That wasn't something I was used to. When you've outlived your nerve endings, scent stops mattering. But this? Even *I* was offended.

I stood, watching her out of the corner of my eye. She didn't look at me. Just pulled her hoodie tighter around herself like maybe she'd finally caught the scent too.

I closed the door behind me. The bathroom was small. Cramped. Pink. Of course it was. But it had hot water, and right now that was the only thing in the world I wanted.

I peeled off my clothes. The mirror was fogged, but I could still see myself. Still see what I was. Not human. Not corpse. Not anything the world had a proper name for. I stepped into the shower and let the water hit me. It was burning hot, and it felt . . . good. I tilted my head back and let it run over me, soaking my hair, washing away the scent of decay and grave dirt.

It wouldn't fix anything, but it could drown things out. The tension in my chest. The leash pulling me back. The fact that some bright-eyed, bone-collecting mortal girl had somehow tethered death like a dog. It all melted away for a moment.

My hands braced against the tile, breath steady even though I didn't need it. I'd slept longer than I should have. Longer than I ever let myself. It had been . . . nice—really nice. I hadn't hated it, and worse, she'd stayed right beside me the entire time.

Curled beside something that had technically stopped being human a long time ago. Wrapped in blankets and shadows like they were the same thing. As if it didn't matter that the thing next to her was wrong in all the ways that mattered.

Like she'd already begun to accept it. Accept *me*. And the worst part? I hadn't wanted to hurt her when I woke up. Not really.

I turned the heat higher in the shower, let the sting climb my spine, let it etch into me like penance. Because thinking about her, about how close she'd been, how easily she'd let herself sleep beside Death, it did something to my chest. It stirred something I hadn't let surface in ages, and I didn't like it. I didn't want softness or comfort. I didn't want her. I was Death, and Death didn't feel.

I stepped out of the bathroom with steam coiling behind me like smoke from a fresh kill. The towel hung low around my hips, hair still dripping, cold water trailing paths along my ribs and down the curve of my spine. I could feel each drop like a countdown.

She turned in time to catch sight of me and let out a startled squeak that was almost a yelp. Actually squeaked. She spun so fast she nearly took out a stack of books with her hip. "Oh my *god*! Warn me next time!"

I smirked, slow and unbothered. "What, never seen a corpse in a towel before?"

She didn't answer. Just scrambled to her dresser and dug through layers of cotton and chaos like she was defusing a bomb. Her shoulders were tense, her movements jerky, like proximity had short-circuited her brain.

Then she turned, face flushed and stubborn, and shoved something toward me. "Here," she said quickly. "You can wear these."

I looked down. Bright, *unapologetically* pink Hello Kitty pajama pants covered in tiny white kittens. I stared at them. The shadows around my shoulders stirred, thickened, darker than the steam that still clung to my skin. I felt them curl around my neck, caress my face, and shadow my eyes.

"You have *got* to be fucking kidding me."

"They should fit!" she chirped, far too cheerfully for someone with a death wish. "We can wash your clothes tonight."

I glanced at her, then at the pants, and back again, and for a split second, I wanted to kill her. Forget the spell. Forget the leash. Just end her, let the pants burn, and salt the ground they touched.

But instead . . . I took them through gritted teeth. Dead eyed.

"This doesn't leave this room," I said.

She grinned like she'd won a chess match she wasn't even playing. "No promises."

I stepped forward. She stepped back. Another step, and her spine met the wall with a soft thud. Her eyes widened, breath caught halfway to spoken thought. I looked like a fucking nightmare in a purple towel, shadows clinging to me with silent fury. *Stupid girl.*

"You think this is funny?" I growled, voice low, the edges frayed with threat.

She didn't blink. Didn't look away. Her grin widened. "Hilarious, actually."

I braced both hands on the wall beside her head, boxing her in. Leaned in close enough that I could feel the warmth radiating from her skin, close enough that her breath stuttered across my collarbone. Her heartbeat kicked, wild and fluttery. Panic, yes, but not just panic—curiosity too.

My shadows curled up one of her legs like vines twisting around a trellis, slow and possessive. She stiffened. Her eyes widened, mouth parting slightly as the air in the room thickened to syrup.

I didn't look away. Not when I dropped the towel. Not when I stood there, bare, every line of my body sharpened by steam and silence, daring her to look, daring her to flinch. She didn't. Instead, she held my gaze. Her throat bobbed as she swallowed, but her gaze never left mine. Still watching, I reached down, took the pajama pants, and slid them on, slow and deliberate. Like a challenge.

The fabric clung to me awkwardly, bright and ridiculous and so deeply unholy on my frame that even the shadows recoiled slightly, confused. The corner of my mouth twitched. Her lips parted, and in that breathless moment between us, something ancient stirred. Something impatient and *hungry*. I closed the distance between us.

And then—wings.

A rustle behind me. The air stirred like a breath held too long. Shadows peeled back from the corners of the room, uneasy.

"My king."

The voice was soft, velvet-like. I turned my head slowly, jaw already clenched. Crow stood a few feet away, half-materialized from darkness, his cloak shimmering like oil slicks underwater. The eye contact he avoided was deliberate. Too deliberate. Like he already regretted interrupting whatever scene he'd just flown into.

Which, unfortunately, was this one:

Me, bare-chested, clad in offensively pink Hello Kitty pajama pants. Her, pinned beneath my arms, oversized hoodie slipping off one shoulder, bare legs tangled in shadow. Her mouth was parted. Her breath hitched. Her hands still braced against the wall like she hadn't decided whether to shove me off or pull me closer. The space between us wasn't air anymore. It was a live wire. A loaded gun in my hand. Which, let's be honest, was never a good thing.

She blinked up at me, cheeks flushed, pupils blown wide like she wasn't entirely sure what she'd agreed to and maybe didn't care. She had gotten comfortable. Too comfortable. and I . . . still hadn't moved.

Crow cleared his throat delicately, still not meeting my eyes. Respectful, supposedly. But I caught the edge of his mouth twitch. The bastard was trying not to laugh. I stepped back. Slowly. Deliberately. Letting the space stretch like a blade between us. Letting her feel the absence like a cold snap.

"Crow." My voice came out clipped.

He bowed again, a model of composure, but his composure was always just a disguise for something ancient, blood soaked and lethal underneath. He was my most loyal shadow, my most unpredictable weapon, and he was enjoying this too much.

I turned to face him fully, jaw locked so tight my molars creaked. His eyes flicked briefly toward the pajama pants and away again quickly.

I knew that look. Mockery, restrained by sheer will. I closed my eyes. Took a long, homicidal breath. Then forced it out between clenched teeth.

"Give me just one moment."

I turned slowly to look down at myself. Pink Hello Kitty pajama pants. Glitter-print kittens smiling up at me like they knew exactly what they'd done.

Fuck. My. Life.

Crow had seen me like this. Me. The end of all things. The void wrapped in bone. Wearing kitten pajamas. I could burn kingdoms to ash, and this moment would still haunt me.

I ran a hand down my face. "I will kill you if you say one word."

Crow didn't blink. Didn't flinch. His voice was calm, even. Murderously polite. "Wouldn't dream of it, my king."

Liar.

Opal let out a muffled laugh behind me.

I turned enough to glare at her, sharp enough to cut marble. "This is your fault."

She shrugged, hands raised in mock innocence, hoodie sleeves falling over her fingers like a child trying to feign harmlessness. "You looked cold."

I wanted to strangle something, preferably her, but instead, I stood there and braced myself to hear whatever the hell else had gone wrong in my absence. Because at this point? Why the fuck not.

"I'm glad to see you are safe," Crow said, voice smooth as ever, cultured, pleasant, and just a hair too even.

His lip twitched again. That fucking lip twitch. His white hair fell over his brow as he inclined his head, those glass-cut eyes flicking toward the girl behind me. He looked at Opal, and I didn't like the way he stared at her. Not because it was lewd, but because it was lethal. I didn't want to know why that made my hands curl into fists. Didn't want to examine why her name had started taking up space in places I hadn't let anyone ever touch.

I pushed forward instead and waved a hand toward her like she was the punchline to some divine joke I hadn't quite laughed at yet.

"I've been bound," I said flatly. "By *this* mortal."

Crow cocked his head. "A witch?" he asked.

I laughed, bitter and low. "I fucking wish." I pinched the bridge of my nose and exhaled hard, steam still curling off my skin. "She's a paranormal investigator."

Crow blinked again. No emotion. No reaction.

Just: "Too bad."

I *knew* that tone. It was the one he used before killing something he thought I wouldn't miss. The shift happened fast—too fast. I turned, but not fast enough. The scythe was already forming. It bloomed in his hand like smoke hardening into steel, and then it *moved*, a blur of silver, arcing straight for her throat. No hesitation. No words. Just *execution*. My perfect assassin, right where I didn't want him.

I moved faster, fueled by inhuman speed. The kind I hadn't used in eons. The kind that hadn't been called upon since the old gods still bled kings for sport. One second, she stood there, stunned. The next, my body was in front of hers. The scythe shrieked as it met the flat of my palm. Divine metal met divine bone, and the sound it made tore through the room like a banshee's wail. Sparks lit the air. My skin cracked.

Pain bloomed like a second heartbeat, but I didn't let go, and Crow froze. Shock flickered across his otherwise impassive face. And me?

I stared at the blade. At *my* hand holding it back. What the fuck was I doing? I should've let him do it. I *would've* let him do it, days ago. Would've stood back. Would've laughed. Would've told him to make it quick. But I didn't. I'd stepped between her and death.

Me.

The one who *was* death.

What the hell was that?

Even Crow knew it was wrong. I saw it in the way his brow tightened, just barely. Saw it in the way he didn't pull back right away. He wasn't sure who I was in that moment, and neither was I. There wasn't a being in existence I wouldn't kill if the equation demanded it.

Except maybe my brother, and even *that* line hadn't held. Not forever. Crow lowered the scythe slowly. His expression reset, but something in his posture didn't. Tension lingered at the edges of his calm, and that . . . concerned me.

I could feel her fear. The way her body had gone rigid, spine pressed tight against the wall, shoulders locked, breath held like it might shield her from me. Like if she moved, even slightly, I'd forget which side I was on and finish what Crow started.

Her heartbeat thudded beneath her skin, wild and stuttering, a rhythm carved from pure, primal instinct. Survival. It drummed into the air between us like war.

And fuck, it was music.

Blood slipped down my palm in slow, lazy rivulets, hissing faintly as it hit the floor. Divine steel always did sting. Crow stepped back, his blade dissolving into shadow with practiced grace. He wasn't afraid, but he was *wary* now. Watching me differently. Like he'd seen something he couldn't explain.

"She bound you," he said at last, his voice cautious, balanced like a blade. "That makes her dangerous."

"No," I growled. "It makes her *stupid*."

"Same thing," he replied, a smirk threatening his lips.

I turned my head slightly, voice dropping into a warning so low it barely vibrated the air. "Don't touch her again."

The words left before I could stop them, and the moment they did, I hated them. They sounded like a command. Like something *real*. Crow's stare sharpened. A flicker passed through his eyes. Not confusion . . . *understanding*. Recognition. Of what, I wasn't sure yet, but it was enough.

"Understood," he said, bowing his head slightly.

I turned back to her. She was still pinned to the wall like prey, pretty, eyes wide, breath caught halfway to a scream she hadn't decided to let out yet. I spun and pulled her toward me without thinking. My hand slid to hers, blood slicked, burning, and wrong. I felt her heat. The softness of her skin. The way she froze again but not out of fear this time.

Shock. My blood smeared across her fingers like a brand. Like a *claim*. Crow took several steps back. His eyes flared. His breath caught. He looked at our hands... touching, then to me, then to her, and back at me, and then he perched himself on the chair. His eyes locked on Opal with *fascination*.

"How?" he breathed. His voice had changed. No longer smooth but raw. Rattled.

He blinked again, slower. A double take. Then another.

"How is that possible?"

I didn't answer. Because I didn't know... because I was still holding her hand, and I could *feel* her. Really feel her. The pulse. The warmth. The trembling confusion she was trying to bury under bravado. She wasn't just alive. She was touching *Death* and not dying, and I liked it. Too much. More than I should've. More than I could fucking afford to.

My eyes cut to Crow, still watching, still stunned, still teetering on the line between reverence and concern. I gave a half-smile. Crooked. Tired. "I know," I said, squeezing her hand once before letting go. "Weird, isn't it?"

CHAPTER 7

Opal

I woke to the low thrum of hushed voices, guttural, rhythmic, ancient. Crow and Death had been up all night. Whispering in some dead language that scraped the walls like teeth on chalkboard, voices too low to make out but too sharp to ignore. Not human. Not meant to be heard by anyone with a pulse.

I blinked against the early gray light, rolled over, and reached for my phone, my last fragile thread to normalcy. The screen burned white in the dark, casting a soft glow against the bed.

A message.

Lucian: *Hey, can I see you today? We need to talk.*

My chest warmed. Giddy. Stupid. God, I missed him.

It felt wrong to say that out loud in this house of bones and shadows, but it was true. After everything, after the blood and the grave dirt and the monsters sleeping in my tiny-ass apartment, he was still *familiar*. Safe. Golden-boy charming in the way that made people trust him without knowing why.

And right now? That felt like a lifeline.

I typed back, fast: *Sure, babe, and hey, can you bring that book? I want to take a closer look at it.*

The dots flickered for a few seconds. Then came the reply: *I'll meet you in 45.*

I smiled to myself, heart skipping in that naive, fizzy way it always did before things went horribly wrong.

"I can't wait to see him," I said aloud, mostly to myself. "I miss him." Across the room, a chair creaked, and I froze.

He was seated in my gaming chair, lounging like some undead prince exiled from heaven, shirtless and barefoot, a cigarette smoldering between two fingers. The smoke curled around him like a lover. Shadows clung to him like they knew better than to let go.

But now? Now his posture had shifted. It was subtle at first but quickly grew lethal. His shoulders tensed. Jaw locked. The flicker of a muscle jumped beneath his cheekbone. He didn't speak. Just scowled at me. Which wasn't unusual. His resting face was eighty percent scowl, twenty percent threat of biblical annihilation.

But this—*this*—was different. This wasn't bored contempt or general disdain for humanity. This was sharper. Meaner. Like I'd said something offensive in a language I didn't know I was speaking.

I met his eyes. "What?"

He didn't answer at first. Just exhaled slow, smoke curling from his mouth like a warning. Across the table, Crow cocked his head slowly, the motion too precise. Too serpentine. Crow's eyes flicked to him, then to me, then back again. A small, knowing smile crept across his face, unnerving in its elegance.

"Don't," Death said, tone flat and razor thin.

Crow held up both hands in mock surrender. "Not a word, my king."

I turned back to him. "Seriously. What's your problem?"

His eyes met mine, flat black, bottomless, but the usual edge of apathy was gone. "I'm just trying to wrap my head around it," he said slowly, voice dry. "The guy leaves you to die, ghosts you for days, and *that's* the one you're giddy to see?"

I blinked. "He didn't know what was happening."

"He didn't *care* enough to find out." Death leaned forward, elbows on his knees, cigarette dangling from his fingers like a dying star. "You miss him? Really?"

He gestured vaguely toward the air, toward the ceiling, toward the idea of *Lucian*. "That's who you want right now?" There was venom in his voice now. Barely veiled.

"I didn't say I *wanted* him," I snapped, heat creeping up my throat. "I just said I *miss* him."

His mouth twisted. "You don't miss him. You miss the version of you that *he* let you be. The digestible one. The nice one with cute eyeliner and a sanitized obsession with the afterlife."

"Fuck you," I whispered.

Crow shifted in the kitchen doorway, and he smiled that eerie, wrong smile again.

He didn't look at Crow. He was still staring at me. Still unreadable. "I'm just saying," he muttered, flicking ash into the skull-shaped incense holder on my desk. "For someone who collects bones and sleeps beside a corpse, you've got *terrible* taste in men."

I sat up straighter, the heat rising from my throat to my cheeks, angry now. "And *you*," I said, voice cutting through the quiet, "act like *red flag* is your entire personality."

Crow let out a sound—half-cough, half-choke—from the kitchen.

The guy just blinked once. His mouth twitched. Not a smile but close enough to be dangerous.

I changed three times. Nothing felt right. Too much pink. Too casual. Too *me*. So I defaulted to what he liked, what Lucian was used to. Soft curls, pinned just so. Neutral makeup. A cropped sweater he once said made me look "approachable." My jeans tight in the right places, but not too much. Polished. Effortless. Pleasant.

I even held the perfume bottle in my hand for too long before finally misting the air with the one he said reminded him of summer. Light. Clean. The kind of scent that didn't make people think about blood or dirt or graveyards. I looked in the mirror. Smiled. Practiced it. Not the full one. Not the unhinged one I sometimes wore in thumbnails when talking about hauntings. No, this one was quiet. Nice. Forgivable.

I wore the version of myself he liked best. The version I'd designed like a brand: soft-spoken, pretty in the right lighting, curious enough to be charming but never unsettling. Not *too* morbid. Not *too* real.

I told myself that maybe he just felt guilty. Maybe he wanted to explain. Maybe he regretted leaving me there, bloody and alone in that cemetery like discarded footage from a film he didn't want to finish. That was the lie I wrapped around myself like armor. Thin, shining, hollow.

Behind me, I felt his stare before I saw it.

He stood in the doorway like a shadow that had forgotten how to be part of a body. Silent. Still. Watching. He looked at me like I'd just taken a blade to myself and smiled while I bled. Like the thing I was pretending to be *offended* him. Like he hated it. His gaze scraped over the soft curls. The perfume. The sweater. The carefully placed smile. And he didn't say a word.

He didn't have to. Because the judgment in his silence was louder than any insult he could've thrown. I stepped outside before I could decide, heart tapping wild and traitorous beneath my ribs. He was already there.

Leaning against the railing at the bottom of the stairs like a yearbook photo polished for re-election. Hands tucked in the pockets of his letterman jacket, blue and white, worn just enough to feel nostalgic but not faded. His golden hair caught the light, artfully tousled. Blue eyes bright and open, like summer skies and good intentions.

Lucian. Still familiar and smiling, but now it felt too precise, too *curated*. I smiled. "Hey."

"Hey," he echoed, posture casual as always, like he didn't know he was about to take a match to my chest and walk away whistling.

I stepped down slowly, each stair colder than the last. Somewhere between the second and third step, a prickle ran up the back of my neck. A strange, involuntary shiver.

"You didn't bring the book?" I asked, forcing brightness into my voice like it would protect me.

Lucian glanced down, rubbing the back of his neck in that rehearsed, boy-next-door way. "No. I, uh . . . forgot."

My smile dimmed, but I kept it up. "That's okay. We can grab it later, if you—"

"Opal," he said, cutting in. Gentle. So gentle it hurt.

My stomach dropped.

"I wanted to talk because . . ." He hesitated. Eyes scanning the sidewalk, searching for an escape route. "Things feel . . . different now."

My breath stalled.

And then, another chill, a *presence*. I didn't have to look to know. He was there. In the shadows, watching. Lucian felt it too. I saw the shift in his posture, the flicker of unease in his eyes. He glanced past me toward the building, jaw tensing like someone had just walked over his grave.

"I think maybe it's best if we go our separate ways," he said, too quickly now. The words falling out like he needed to get them over with. "With law school getting tough and filming all the time, it's just a lot, you know?"

There it was.

"Lucian . . ." I said, but my voice barely made it out. "Why?" I whispered.

"I don't know," he muttered. "Everything's changing. I think we're on different paths now."

Paths. Like we were majors in a university catalog, not a story that spanned a childhood.

I said nothing.

The air around me felt thicker now. Pressing in from all sides. Lucian shifted again. Nervous. Restless. He didn't understand what he was feeling, but I did. Death was close, and he wasn't happy.

"I'm sorry," Lucian said, avoiding meeting my eyes.

I nodded. Because what else was there? He leaned in and kissed my cheek. Light. Thoughtless. A ghost of affection rather than the real thing. And then he turned and walked away. No fire. No tears. Just soft footsteps fading against concrete.

I stood there in my carefully chosen outfit and sprayed-on nostalgia and stared at the place he'd just been.

Cain

I watched from the shadows, which were curled tight around me like a second skin. She didn't know I was there. I didn't need her to. I saw everything.

Lucian was already waiting outside when she stepped through the door. Punctual. Polished. Pretty boy draped in a letterman jacket like it was armor forged from privilege. His hair was golden in that effortless way that made people trust him. His smile, too perfect. Practiced. The kind that belonged on toothpaste commercials and campaign billboards. Dimpled charm. Daddy's money. The subtle, quiet confidence of someone who'd never had to earn anything but praise.

I hated him instantly. I didn't even understand *why* at first, but the second I laid eyes on him, something in me coiled. Sharp. Instinctive. Uninvited. Then I saw her, Opal . . . but not. She wasn't the girl who talked to shadows like they listened. Wasn't the girl who'd stared me in the eyes while my body flickered between decay and bone and dared me to be worse.

No. This version?

She was dressed in compromise. Polished hair. Floral perfume. Cropped sweater. She wore *his* version of her like a costume. Too soft. Too clean. Too careful. And it pissed me off. I wanted to claw it off her face, not because it wasn't beautiful, but because it wasn't hers. *She did all of that for him.*

Then he broke up with her.

Didn't even have the guts to say why. Just stood there, stammering nonsense about "paths" like she was a damn elective he no longer had time for. He kissed her cheek like a ghost and walked away.

Like none of it mattered. Like *she* didn't matter. And the second his back was turned, the shadow that was me hissed. I didn't follow him. I didn't *need* to.

Because he'd already done the only good thing he was ever going to do. He let her go.

And I would never—*never*—say it out loud, but I was glad.

The moment she started back upstairs, head down, hands in her pockets like she could hide inside herself, I slipped in behind her. Quiet. Close. She didn't notice. The second the door shut, I ghosted through the apartment like smoke.

She disappeared into the bathroom, probably to wash his kiss off her cheek like it was a stain. I went for the bedroom and rummaged. Drawers. Cabinets. Under the bed. I wasn't looking for anything in particular, just needed to *erase* the version of her I'd just seen.

But what I found? Well . . .

Some things were expected; others, not so much. Lacy black lingerie tucked into a side compartment, tags still on. Lip glosses and thick, silver-chain necklaces. A tiny bottle of perfume shaped like a coffin. A massive, monster-themed dildo.

I shook my head then slowly shut the drawer. I didn't need to know *that* much about her, but damn if it didn't make me smirk. Still, that wasn't what I was here for. I opened her closet. Pushed aside the curated outfits, the pretty little masks, the carefully arranged color schemes and found it. *Her* hoodie. Oversized, over-washed, worn to shit and then worn some more. Faint scent of coffee and vanilla and something vaguely like cemeteries.

I grabbed it. Shut the drawer. And by the time she came out—face red, eyes dry—I was sitting in the recliner again. Waiting. The hoodie in my lap. I didn't say anything.

Just held it up and let the question hang between us.

"You're not wearing *that* again," I said, voice flat.

She blinked. "What?"

I tossed it to her. "Next time you walk out that door, you go as *you*. Or you don't go at all."

She caught it on instinct. Held it like it might bite her. Like she didn't understand what it meant yet. But she would. Because I wasn't letting *that* version of her walk out again. Lucian liked soft girls in cropped sweaters. Me? I wanted the one who kept bones in glass jars and slept beside a corpse.

"You went through my stuff. I—I guess you saw what happened," she said, voice barely above a whisper.

I nodded once. She leaned on the counter like it might hold her up, fingers curled tight around the edge. Just enough tremble in her hands to make my jaw tense. "He didn't even bring the book."

Of course he didn't. I stepped closer before I could stop myself. One stride. Two. She didn't flinch. Didn't look at me.

I could still feel it, just under her skin. The tension. The sadness she was too proud to cry through. That quiet ache people got when they weren't surprised someone had hurt them. They were just surprised how much it *still* hurt. And I hated it, hated seeing her like this. Not because she was weak.

But because I didn't know how to make it *stop*.

This wasn't my realm. This . . . comforting shit. I was the consequence, not the cure. The ending, not the hand someone held in the middle of the storm.

But I tried. In the only way I knew how. "His loss," I muttered.

Her breath caught, then let out again on a shaky laugh. Barely there, but I heard it. She didn't smile, and I didn't either, but I stayed right there.

A foot of space between us. Close enough that my shadows could have touched her if I let them. Close enough to feel the warmth radiating off her skin like it was something I wasn't supposed to want.

She wasn't mine. Not by choice—by fate, but she sure as hell wasn't *his* anymore. Still, my guard slipped just a little, and I hated that too. This softness I felt creeping in. Because human grief had never been my problem. Not once in the millennia I'd been dragging souls across the threshold.

But her? Standing in that hollow quiet?

She made *me* leave a few inches of air between us like it mattered. Like I thought space might soften the blow. I stayed anyway.

While I was busy standing there, hovering too close, caught somewhere between saying something and just being near her like that might be enough, I didn't notice the letter. It had been sitting on the counter the whole time. Black wax. Pressed with Hell's seal. Meant for me. Crow had set it there for me before he left.

I didn't see her pick it up. Didn't hear the soft crackle of parchment as she turned it over in her hands, innocent and curious and utterly doomed.

Didn't feel the shift in the air until it was too late.

She said it.

My name.

"Cain."

The sound cleaved the room in half. I froze. Everything in me locked down like a machine slamming into shutdown, every nerve, every muscle, every breath. Stopped. Dead. It wasn't magic. It was law. Her voice wrapped around it, soft and small and unknowing, and it hit harder than any blade ever could. Like she'd licked her thumb and pressed it to a nuclear code.

I stood there, spine rigid, chest refusing to rise, eyes wide. Unblinking. And she saw it. Saw how one word, that single syllable, her breath passing over it, could break me in ways nothing else could.

The air between us thrummed with a pressure older than stars. Like something sacred had been cracked open, poured out, and left hissing on the floor. She didn't even realize what she'd done. Not yet. Didn't realize the kind of power she held now. Because that leash, the invisible tether that bound me to her the second she pulled me from the earth? It had just cinched tighter. Now, she didn't just have me. She *owned* me. All she had to do was speak one word, my name, and any command, I would obey, whether I wanted to or not.

"That's your name, isn't it?" she asked quietly. "Cain?"

So small. So casual. Like she hadn't just torn open the last thing I'd ever called *mine.* I ground my teeth. Felt it in my jaw, tight, cracking, molten. Pressure raced down my spine like a fuse being lit, crawling under my skin, setting my bones alight with rage.

I didn't answer. Because yes, it was my name, and yes, now she had it, and all I wanted, in that moment, was to murder something slowly. First person that came to mind? *Pretty boy.* Golden hair. Letterman jacket. The one who'd kissed her like she was a chapter he'd finished reading. The one who threw her away with clean hands and a smile. I wanted to peel him apart. Carefully. Intimately. I wanted him to know it was me when I broke his ribs one by one and shoved the dust of his spine into his lungs.

She flinched but held my gaze. Which, of course, only made it worse. Because the part of me that should've wanted to punish her?

Didn't.

I turned away before the leash could yank tighter, pacing like a caged thing too old to remember how to play docile. Shadows twitched at my heels, restless and sharp. "I need a fucking cigarette," I muttered, shoving open the back door hard enough to make the frame groan. The screen slammed behind me like punctuation.

The night air was cold. Biting. The kind of cold that tries to convince you you're alive. Didn't work on me. I dug into my jacket pocket, fingers twitching with the memory of nicotine.

Empty.

I stared at my hand like it had failed me. *Betrayal.* A tiny paper cylinder, gone. Somehow, it was the last straw.

"Fuck me," I hissed, dragging both hands through my hair like I could scrub the static out of my skull. Behind me, the door creaked again. Light footsteps.

Then her voice. Quiet. Awkward. Trying. "You, uh . . . ran out?"

I didn't answer.

She stepped up beside me, not quite close enough to touch but close enough that I could feel her warmth edging into my space like a dare.

"I have something," she said, rummaging in the front pocket of her hoodie. "It's dumb. You'll probably hate it." She held it out like a peace offering. Pink. Of course it was fucking pink. A vape pen. Strawberry cream, if the stupid glittery star sticker and pastel lettering were to be believed.

I stared at it like it might bite me.

"What the hell is that?"

"Just try it."

"No."

"Come on. One hit."

"I don't do cute candy clouds, Final Girl."

She raised an eyebrow. "You don't do *anything*. What do you have to lose?"

That shut me up. I yanked it from her hand with a growl. I lifted it. Glared. Inhaled. And—froze.

Strawberry. Real strawberry. Ripe, red, summer-warm. Cream. Smooth. Sweet. It didn't turn to ash. Didn't fall flat on my tongue like everything else. It was *there*. Taste . . . *I could taste it*. I pulled back slowly, staring at the pen like it had just rewritten the laws of the afterlife.

"Holy shit."

She grinned. Full. Bright. *Opal*.

"Right?"

I took another drag—slower, deeper. Still there. The sensation rolled over my tongue like silk and memory.

"I can taste it," I muttered. "Why can I taste it?"

She shrugged, casually powerful. "Don't ask me. I don't make the rules."

I stared at the vape like it might start glowing. "I need more of these."

She *laughed*. Not the nervous kind. Not the brittle kind she gave Lucian. A real one. Spontaneous. Bright as blood under moonlight. And it did something weird to my chest. I looked away before I could figure out what.

"Strawberry cream," I muttered, shaking my head. "Figures the first thing I taste in a millennium would be fucking strawberry cream."

"Could've been worse," she said. "Could've been pumpkin spice."

I groaned. "Blasphemy."

She bumped her shoulder into mine, barely a touch, and for once, I didn't move away. Didn't threaten. Didn't tease. I just stood there. Smoke on my breath. Warmth at my side, and the taste of something I didn't understand still lingering on my tongue.

Like maybe, for the first time in a very long time, I wasn't completely dead.

We stood there in the half-light of the back porch, silence stretching easy now. Not heavy. Not sharp. Just quiet. She was still looking at me, waiting for the next shoe to drop, the next snarl or threat or snap, but it didn't come. Instead, I pulled another drag from the stupid pink vape and sighed like it was holy.

Then I glanced at her. "Let's go for a walk."

She blinked. "A walk?"

"Yeah." I stepped off the porch, shadows curling at my boots like they were stretching after a nap. "Fresh air. Morbid vibes. Emotional damage. You know, all the essentials."

She tilted her head, suspicious. "You hate walking."

"I hate *people*. Walking's fine."

She followed. Of course she did.

By the time we hit the end of the block, she was beside me again, shoulder close, hoodie sleeves pulled down over her hands like armor, and I didn't say where we were going. She didn't ask, but when the cemetery gate creaked open and the moon poured silver across rows of stone like spilled salt, she smiled.

"Seriously?" she asked, voice lighter than it had been all day. "This is your idea of cheering someone up?"

"Got a better one?"

She shrugged. "Fair."

I led us past the usual headstones, polished granite, a few statues too eroded to read, crypts older than both of us combined. She walked like she belonged there. Like she could slip between the living and the dead without apology.

"I used to bring snacks here," she said. "Do picnics. Ghost stories. Little séances."

I glanced at her. "Necromantic brunch dates. Adorable."

"Goth girl picnic energy," she countered, grinning.

We found an old bench under a tree that had no business still being alive. The roots curled up from the dirt like they were trying to escape something. Moss had made a home in the cracks. The whole thing reeked of bad decisions and worse endings.

I sat, and Opal dropped beside me, legs swinging slightly. Her knees bumped mine.

She looked around. "So, what now?"

"Now?" I said, dragging the last inhale from the vape. "We do absolutely nothing."

"No death threats?"

"No."

"No lectures on how fragile and temporary my soul is?"

"Nope."

She leaned her head back, eyes fluttering closed. "Wow. You *are* softening."

"Watch it," I said, eyes narrowing. "I'll shove you in a mausoleum."

She laughed again. Quieter this time. It sounded like it belonged here, and for the first time in a long, long time . . . I didn't want to be anywhere else.

Chapter 8

Opal

I wasn't okay. Not even close. It had been two weeks since Lucian broke things off. Cain mostly stayed quiet, helping in small ways, but Lucian's absence felt like a pit in my chest, like a stone lodged in my throat. His words still echoed—*things feel different now*—and they did, but maybe that wasn't all bad. Because I was starting to feel different too.

The part of me that used to smooth things over for the benefit of others, that softened her edges to fit in the box someone else built for her—she was tired. Dead tired.

She'd powdered her face and curled her hair and tucked herself neatly into someone else's favorite version of her. She'd survived on compliments like crumbs. *Cute but not weird, quirky but not creepy, smart but not confrontational.* She'd convinced herself she was loved because she was easy to categorize, not because she was herself.

And now? Now all of that felt like a performance I couldn't get back into costume for. And that version of me? She'd bled out in a cemetery the night Lucian left. What was left was something raw and restless. Maybe it was time to be a little feral, a little unhinged, and a lot more me.

I was still grieving. Still cracked down the middle. But I was brave in a new, stupid kind of way. Brave like watching a death god out of the corner of my eye, lounging in a chair, wrong in a hundred different ways. Cain was shirtless . . . again.

Chain-smoking my pink strawberry cream vape like it was his divine right, legs hooked over the back of the chair, arms draped lazily. His head dangled toward the floor, hair a black tangle of chaos brushing the hardwood. Every few seconds, he let out a low, ragged sound in the back of his throat, somewhere between a groan and a moan.

Like it wasn't just nicotine; it was physical pleasure—it was sex.

I hated how my body reacted to him, like it just left all sanity behind. The sounds he was making, the way he was laying there sprawled out, were doing something to me. I was supposed to be grieving my relationship, not wanting to inch closer to the literal incarnation of death just to see if I affected him too.

I sat cross-legged on my bed, pretending to scroll through my phone while my brain did backflips and my body absolutely refused to listen to logic.

This wasn't safe.

He wasn't safe.

My pulse was already skipping toward him like it didn't care. Like danger was just another word for interesting. Because Cain didn't feel like a threat anymore. He felt like a dare.

I needed a distraction. So, stupidly—recklessly—I said the next words out loud: "I want to get to know you."

He froze mid-drag.

Paused.

Then he twisted, slowly, upside-down head tilting toward me. He stared from beneath half-lidded eyes, smoke curling from his mouth like a threat.

"You're out of your mind," he said.

I shrugged. "Probably."

He rolled the vape between his fingers. "You already know the important stuff."

"Do I?"

"I'm bound to you. I'm Death. I vape now. What more do you want? My zodiac sign?"

"Sure," I said, lips twitching. "What are you, Scorpio sun, eternal torment moon?"

He snorted. "More like arson ascendant."

I laughed, and he watched me. Really *watched* me. His smile faded. The humor didn't leave his voice, but something behind it *softened*. "Careful," he said. "You're starting to sound like you like me."

"Maybe I do."

A beat.

Then: "You shouldn't."

"I know."

Another beat. Slower this time.

He turned right side up, legs dropping to the floor in one graceful, fluid motion that betrayed how fast and dangerous he really was. The shadows curled around his feet like they'd been waiting for him. He didn't cross the room, didn't touch me, but the air felt heavier now.

"Getting to know me?" he said, voice low, amused. "That's not curiosity, Final Girl. That's a slow suicide."

I held his gaze.

"I think I'm past fearing death."

His eyes darkened, but not in warning. His legs stilled. He tilted his head just enough to give me a wicked smirk. "Terrible idea."

"Probably."

He took another drag. "You're grieving. You want attention. You're making bad choices."

"You're the worst choice I could ever make."

"Accurate."

I paused, chewing my lip. "Still, I want to know more."

"You want a distraction, Little Ghoul?" he said, voice dark silk.

I swallowed.

"Yes."

He stopped in front of me, towering, tattoos in harsh relief in the warm bedroom light. He bent down just a little. Just enough.

"I'll give you one." He smiled, sharp, slow, and *so* not comforting at all.

"But just so you know . . ."

I blinked up at him.

"I *am* the kind of distraction that gets people killed."

"And I'm the kind of girl that hangs around after," I said, heart thudding as I met his eyes. "So try me."

That crooked grin stretched wider across his face, amused and dangerous. Like I was a spark, and he was already planning the fire, gasoline in hand. "So," he said, circling me with just enough distance to make it feel like a game. "Have you figured it out yet?"

He paused behind me, voice closer to my ear. "Who I am?"

I turned to face him, lifting my chin. "That was easy."

He quirked a brow. "Was it?"

"Yeah." I shrugged. "Death. Cain. That *is* your name, right?"

For a split second, his entire body froze. Like every muscle went stiff. Like the very *sound* of it locked him in place. Weird . . . Too weird.

"Yeah . . . and?" he asked.

He threw himself onto my bed like a corpse collapsing into a coffin, arms spread wide, head tilted toward the ceiling, toward me. His legs hung off the side, one foot kicking lazily like he didn't have a care in the world.

"Cain," I repeated slowly, watching him.

"Mm," he hummed, eyes closed. "Don't say it like that. Sounds like you're trying to summon me."

I rolled my eyes. "That ship's sailed, remember?"

He grinned without opening his eyes. "Unfortunately."

I sat on the mattress and nudged his leg with my knee. He cracked one eye open.

"I'm serious," I said. "There's something else. Every time I say your name, it's like . . . reality twitches."

"Yeah," he said softly. "It does, that."

"Why?"

Cain blinked at me, slow, unreadable. Then he said, with that same wicked smile, "Because names have power, Little Ghoul. And you just so happen to own mine."

His head tilted back, hair spilling over his face, his lashes low as he stared up at me like I was either his next meal or a mildly interesting puzzle.

He took a long drag from the vape and exhaled slowly. Then he glared at it. "Empty," he muttered, like the betrayal of a tiny pink cartridge was personal. He tossed it onto the floor without ceremony, the soft *thunk* of plastic against hardwood the last sound in the room.

Now I was the only thing left to entertain him, and I was starting to regret that. Because the way he was looking at me now? Like he had nothing better to do than watch me squirm? Yeah. *That* was dangerous.

I fidgeted, heat rising in my body, my cheeks, places I didn't want to name. I tried to deflect, but my brain filled the silence with something worse.

His name.

Cain.

Not just a name. A story. The *first* story. The first sin not whispered in temptation but carved into flesh. Could he be . . . *that* Cain?

The beginning of bloodshed. The brother-killer. I stared at him, something ancient and electric twisting in my gut. He smirked, slow and cruel, but not without amusement.

"You're thinking too loud."

I swallowed hard. "Tell me I'm wrong."

His smile widened, showing just the *hint* of teeth, and he didn't say a thing. He didn't have to. Because in that one silent moment, I knew. *He was.* Not a metaphor. Not a poetic nickname. *The* Cain. The first murderer. The one who walked away from the garden and never looked back.

He moved. Like shadow. Like something unraveling. No sound, no warning. Just that slow, deliberate shift from stillness to motion. Every inch of him humming with threat. Every step carved from inevitability. My breath hitched.

This wasn't grief anymore. This wasn't about Lucian. This was adrenaline, fear, and *something else*. A thrill that slid through my body like a drug. Cain stopped in front of me, towering and still. I had to tilt my head just to meet his eyes. I was still sitting on the bed, cross-legged, hoodie bunched low over bare thighs. I felt small. Soft. Ridiculous.

His fingers reached out, brushing the hem of the hoodie. Just a graze. Just enough to make me stop breathing.

"I already know you, Little Ghoul. More than you know yourself," he said almost sweetly.

"What does that even mean?"

"Let's start with this," he murmured, gaze lifting to mine. "This thing you do, hiding behind a photoshopped version of yourself. Playing harmless. It's bullshit."

I stared at him.

"What?"

"You think wearing his perfume and his smile makes you the girl he wanted," he said. "But that version of you? The one you keep dressing up in sweaters and politeness? She's already dead."

His voice dropped lower. Nearly a whisper.

"I saw who you really are when you pulled me out of the dirt."

I swallowed, throat tight. "And who's that?" I asked.

He leaned in, close enough to share breath. Close enough for my pulse to stammer and my skin to light up like kindling. "You're the girl who called Death and didn't flinch." His eyes flicked to my lips. "The girl who slept beside me like it was normal." His lips didn't quite touch mine, but the *threat* of it was louder than any kiss. "This is a bad idea," he whispered more to himself than to me.

He didn't move. Didn't pull back. Didn't offer me space or salvation. If anything, he leaned in closer, a beat too long, a breath too far, and fuck, I wanted to close the distance.

"Say my name again," he murmured. "Like you mean it."

My lips parted on instinct. No fear. No second thought.

"Cain."

The name unspooled between us like a lit fuse. He made a sound, low, rough, primal. Somewhere between a sigh and a growl. It clawed its way out of his throat, and I felt it in my ribs, down my spine. His eyes fluttered shut, lashes dark against high cheekbones, and for a moment he looked like something reverent. Something starved. Like I'd just fed him.

He tilted his head back, exposing the long, inked column of his throat. The cords of tension there. The flutter of something fragile beneath centuries of armor. When his eyes opened again, everything inside me stopped, Not black, not empty, not pits or voids or the absence of light. *Galaxies.* They were *color.* Swirling, dying stars behind glass. Blues and purples and golds that didn't belong in this world. They weren't eyes. They were constellations. The final flicker of suns devoured by time.

The universe wasn't just staring at me. It *was* him. Infinite, cold, and beautiful. I sucked in a breath, my chest rising nearly against his. He watched me like he was starving for something he didn't know how to name.

"Again," he said, voice roughened, wrecked. A single word pulled from the deepest part of him.

I should've said no. Should've pushed him back. Remembered what he was. *What I was dealing with.* The weight behind every funeral. The end of all things. But my mouth betrayed me.

"Cain," I whispered, and this time, I meant it. All the way to my bones. His head fell back, and he exhaled like it *hurt.* Like he hadn't breathed right in centuries, and I'd just reminded him how.

"I like," he said slowly, eyes still shut, "how my name fits in your mouth."

My pulse fluttered stupidly.

"I like how you *say* it," he added, softer now.

He stilled, gaze locked on mine, something unreadable flickering behind the stars in his eyes.

And then, he drew in a breath and blinked. Just like that, the spell between us snapped. "We still need the book," he said, voice sudden and jarringly detached. Like none of that had just happened. *Asshole.*

I blinked, my heart still trying to claw its way out of my chest. "What?"

He picked up the empty vape from where he'd tossed it on the floor earlier, flipping it between his fingers.

"And these," he added casually, like I wasn't currently experiencing cardiac arrest. "I need more."

"Oh . . . okay. Sure," I stammered, brain short-circuiting, pulse still hammering.

He smiled at me. *Smiled.* Like he hadn't just reduced me to emotional shrapnel with a fucking glance.

"I had Crow bring my car," he said, stretching like this was the most normal morning conversation. "No more trains, okay?"

He eyed me, clearly waiting for some kind of gratitude or approval. I blinked again. "You have a *car*?"

That did it. He rolled his eyes so hard I was surprised he didn't pull something. "Yes. I have a car."

"What kind?"

He didn't answer right away. Just headed for the window, bare feet silent against the floorboards. I saw it outside through the glass.

A black Mustang. Growling with power, even parked. The paint was a matte black, like night itself had been skinned and wrapped around the frame. The windows were tinted darker than legally acceptable. The rims were custom, black with blood-red trim.

I turned back to him. "You drive a black Mustang?"

He looked *thrilled* with himself. "I think it's funny."

Of course he did. He opened the door with a little flair, tossing his keys in the air and catching them one-handed.

"The four horsemen and all," he said, motioning to the black beast of a Mustang parked outside. "War, Famine, Pestilence . . . and me." He glanced back at me over his shoulder, smirking. "But I don't do pale colors. Or pastels, for that matter." His eyes slid down to my sweatshirt: pink, oversized, obnoxiously soft. He raised a brow.

I crossed my arms. "Well, *I* think you looked good in those Hello Kitty pajamas."

He stopped in his tracks. Turned slowly and smiled. Not the sweet kind of smile. The kind that was all sharp teeth. "Keep it up, Little Ghoul," he said, voice sharp, "and you won't like what happens next."

I felt it in my bones. The promise there. And something in me, the reckless, aching, still-heartbroken part, *liked* how it sounded. I wanted to push those buttons just to see what he would do, what threats he would hurl my way. He was creative with those threats, after all.

But I just raised a brow. "What are you gonna do? Haunt me?"

He stepped in close, just enough to darken the air between us.

"I'm already doing that," he said, grin widening.

"Why do you even have a car? Can't you just blip yourself wherever you want?"

"Yes," he hissed. "But I like driving, and I like my car."

I held in a laugh and got in the car.

The car ride was . . . *shockingly great*.

Cain—Death, whatever—had an actual playlist. It was good music too. Gritty alt-rock, dark pop, punk. Heavy bass, haunted lyrics, the kind of stuff that made you want to drive through the night and maybe sin a little.

We didn't speak for the first few songs. Just nodded along. Comfortable. Familiar in the way only two deeply messed-up people could be.

At some point he cracked a window and said, "I could get used to this."

I didn't know if he meant the air. The music. The car. Or *me*.

Our first stop was a vape shop. Cain practically sauntered inside, shirt still a little wrinkled, tattoos out, black boots echoing across the tile floor. I swear the temperature in the room dropped five degrees.

He held up my pink vape and said, "More."

The guy behind the counter blinked like he was being robbed. "Uh . . . flavor?"

Cain pointed. "Strawberry cream. Cherry. Vanilla. Something dark. Surprise me." He pulled out a black metal card. No numbers. No logo. Just *void*. The register didn't even blink. I stared at him.

He smirked. "No limit."

Of course not. As we walked out, he handed me one of the vapes, unwrapping his cherry one with the excitement of someone opening a coffin full of gold.

"Everything you own is black," I said, teasing.

"Better than pink," he replied, glaring at my hoodie.

I raised a brow. "Is your toilet paper black too?"

He grinned, slow and devilish. "Wouldn't you like to know."

I blinked. "Wait . . . Do you have a place? Like . . . a house?"

He shrugged. "More like a fortress."

"Are you serious?"

"Castle, technically. The entire town is haunted."

I stared at him, not sure if I should take him seriously or not. He just sucked on the vape and grinned through the curl of cherry-sweet smoke. I hated how curious I was.

I tugged my sleeves over my hands, shoving them into the front pocket of my hoodie. It was starting to get chilly, and my fingers felt like icicles.

"Do you ever miss it?" I asked. "Being . . . human?"

He huffed a laugh that wasn't really an answer. "I miss food and sex."

That caught me off guard. I turned to say something smart, but he was already looking at me, smile lazy, eyes burning like some secret I wasn't ready for. He laughed harder, sharp and bright, the sound cutting through the stillness. That was when the air changed, when movement caught my eye.

Three silhouettes at the end of the block.

At first, I thought I was imagining it. The streetlight blinked, and for a second, they were just shadows. Then the shapes solidified, too familiar to mistake: hair flashing like a blade. Gloss and malice wrapped in a bubblegum jacket. A camera strap slung across a chest.

My stomach dropped.

Of course it would be them. Nyxie, Lyric, and Thane.

CHAPTER 9

Opal

I hadn't seen them in weeks, mostly because no one had replied to my texts the night Cain appeared or after Lucian broke things off, but here they were. They were bunched together and laughing like my world hadn't been turned upside down in the last several weeks.

Nyxie's hair was bubblegum blue now, twisted into two too-perfect braids, Thane had oversized sunglasses on despite the overcast skies, and a new designer bag was slung over Lyric's shoulder like it had been casually placed there by fate, not paid TikTok unboxings.

They hadn't changed, and I . . . I wasn't sure who I was anymore. I also didn't know if we were even still friends—or a team, for that matter. What did all this mean for my channel?

I tugged at my sleeves, oversized cuffs swallowed in my palms. The pink hoodie was mine. Really mine. Not a borrowed aesthetic or a curated brand. Just soft. Safe. A little spooky, a little feral, messy . . . like me.

"Opaaaal!" Nyxie's voice was sugar-soaked.

Lyric followed. "Oh my god, where have you *been*? We've been worried *sick*."

Worried. Right.

Thane adjusted his glasses and gave a short wave.

Cain shifted slightly, exhaling a cloud of cherry-sweet smoke into the space between us and them. It curled like fingers clawing at the air. Nyxie blinked at him like she'd just noticed the six-foot-four problem leaning against a blacked-out Mustang like sin incarnate. Her lips parted. Her eyes dragged over the tattoos. The boots. The shadows.

Cain didn't so much as glance at her. Just exhaled another slow cloud of cherry vapor, his eyes fixed on me. He didn't look at them, not really, but I could tell he'd already sized them up, cataloged their tells, clocked their intentions. "Friends of yours, Opal?"

That voice. Rough velvet that was still somehow painfully apathetic.

I nodded, if only to make the moment move along. "Yeah. Sort of."

Lyric tilted her head. "Ooookay," she drawled. "He's hot."

"Also right here," Cain muttered, deadpan.

He didn't smile, but he didn't walk away either. Just leaned on the Mustang, shadows coiled at his feet.

I shifted awkwardly. "This is . . . Cain."

Cain raised two fingers in something that might've been a wave if it hadn't looked vaguely threatening.

Lyric blinked. "Cain. Right." She glanced between us. "Sooo . . . Is he, like, a *thing*?"

Cain didn't say anything, but he *did* reach across the few inches between us, pluck a loose thread from the hem of my hoodie, and roll it between his fingers like it meant something. Like *I* meant something. My throat dried out.

"I'm . . . not sure what he is," I managed, voice small.

"Fair," Cain murmured, still watching me. "Neither am I."

Nyxie gave me a look. Pity dressed in pink rhinestones. "We heard about Lucian," she said gently. "You must be devastated."

"I'm fine," I said quickly.

"You don't *look* fine," Lyric added. "But it's okay. We get it. Breakups are hell."

Cain made a disgruntled noise.

"What was that?" Lyric asked, blinking.

He cocked his head. "Just thinking."

"About what?"

"Breakups." His tone was too smooth. Too sharp. "They're only hell if you lost something worth keeping."

Nyxie blinked. "Excuse me?"

I could practically hear the alarms in the back of my skull going off, but it was already too late. Cain smiled. Slow and sideways. A dagger wrapped in charm.

"I mean," he drawled, still twirling that loose thread from my hoodie, "I've only known Opal post-Lucian, and let me tell you"—his eyes flicked up to mine, that grin going sharper—"whatever that guy left behind? He was a fucking idiot."

My stomach did a very unfortunate backflip.

Lyric scoffed. "So you *are* a thing."

Cain didn't answer.

He didn't have to.

He *looked* at me, and it wasn't some performance for them. It wasn't exaggerated or forced or even smug. It was worse. Honest. Raw. Like I was the only person in the world who existed.

I opened my mouth. Nothing came out.

"Ohhh," Nyxie cooed, clapping her hands together like this was a soap opera and she'd just been handed the next episode. "Well, that explains why you've been MIA."

"Has she?" Cain asked, idly inspecting his nails. "Or were you just not looking?"

Nyxie blinked, unsure if that was shade.

Lyric changed tactics. "There's a haunted house tonight, Ironside. It's supposed to be legit terrifying. You should come."

"You should bring your boyfriend," Nyxie added with deliberate casualness. "We'd *love* to get to know him."

My mouth opened, and Cain moved. One hand curled around my wrist and pulled me gently, firmly, back against him. My spine met his chest, the leather of his jacket cold against the soft cotton of my hoodie.

"Cain—" I started.

"Shhh," he murmured at my ear, low enough that only I could hear it. His breath ghosted down my neck like a promise. Or a threat. "Let them wonder."

I stiffened, heart hammering. He wasn't smiling anymore. Just watching them, calm, casual, and absolutely in control.

Nyxie blinked, her lashes fluttering like static. "Perfect," she said too brightly. "See you both tonight, then."

Cain nodded once. Slow. Like a verdict.

Lyric tugged her sleeve. They turned, walking off in a swirl of designer perfume and unspoken judgment. As soon as they were out of sight, I twisted in his grip, shoving lightly at his chest until I was facing him. His hand stayed on my waist, barely there, like he was humoring me.

"What the hell was that?" I hissed. "Now they think you're my boyfriend!"

Cain didn't flinch. Just raised a brow, unbothered. "And?"

"And I didn't say that!"

"You didn't say no."

"Because you *grabbed* me!"

"How else are you going to explain why we're always together?" he spat.

"I could have said you were my cousin or something."

"Like that would have worked." He laughed, getting way too close to me again. "A cousin wouldn't get pissed when other people try to put their hands on you."

I paled. "What is that supposed to mean?"

He took another step forward, closing the distance between us, his lips nearly on mine. He was so close I could taste him, and my heart leapt into my chest as my breath stalled and brain overheated.

His grin curled. "You liked that, huh?"

I smacked his chest. "Cain, focus!"

He caught my wrist, gentle but firm, and held it just long enough to make me forget what I was saying. Then, he let go.

"They're going to run back and tell everyone. People are going to *talk*."

"Good."

"Good?!"

He exhaled cherry vapor, eyes on mine, lazy and dangerous.

"Who gives a shit what they do? It'll make them stop treating you like a broken toy. I fucking hate that." He flicked the vape into the air, caught it. Tucked it into his pocket. "And I *like* being the bad idea in your life right now."

I was still trying to form words when Cain tilted his head and said, voice gone low and sharp:

"If they want something to talk about . . . I'll fucking give them something to talk about."

He pushed off the Mustang and started walking toward the passenger door. Paused. Cain flicked his keys like a coin toss. He stopped in front of me, close enough that the air tightened.

"Terms," I said quickly, before the moment could swallow me. I held up a finger. "No ripping holes in reality unless someone is actively dying."

"Define actively."

"Bleeding a lot."

"Be more specific."

"Arterial."

He smirked. "Cute."

"No murder," I said, breathing through it. "Even if they deserve it."

He stared at me like I'd asked him not to blink. "You drive a hard bargain, Final Girl."

"My turn," he added, stepping closer until the car found my back. He touched the side of my throat with one finger. Not hard, just there. "You stay within ten steps. You let me pick the exits. If you want me, need me, say my name and I'll come."

"Like a dog?"

"Like a gun," he said, almost gentle. "Loaded and pointed wherever you want."

I should've walked away. I nodded instead.

He smirked. "We should look like we like each other."

"We don't," I said.

"Fake it," he said and slid his palm to the small of my back. It wasn't possessive. It was a brand. He shrugged out of his jacket, black, heavy, warm, and dropped it over my shoulders. The weight settled like permission I hadn't asked for and didn't hate.

"Oh, one more thing," I said. "Don't get arrested."

He smiled. "No promises." He adjusted the jacket and opened the car door. "Now let's go. I guess you're gonna want to change?"

I opened my mouth to argue, then shut it. Because . . . he was right. I was already cataloging outfit options that felt more like armor and less like camouflage.

He saw it. Smirked. Bastard.

"You know," he said, voice darker now, quieter. "It's October, Final Girl, but I think it's time you stopped wearing *costumes*, huh?"

That one landed hard, and I stared at him. Because he wasn't just talking about clothes, and I had to admit he was right.

I stood in the middle of my bedroom, staring at the closet like its contents might bite me. The clothes hanging there didn't feel like mine anymore. They were curated, approved, pastel, politically neutral. Girlfriend clothes. Homecoming-court clothes. *Lucian's world* clothes. I'd been doing this so long that nothing really felt like me anymore.

I didn't know what to wear now that I wasn't trying to be palatable.

"You good?" Cain asked from the bathroom doorway, leaning against the frame like he *belonged* there, like he hadn't just declared war on my social life with a single smirk and an insinuation.

I didn't answer.

Didn't have to.

He took one look at my face and sighed.

"You're spiraling."

"I'm thinking."

"Same thing," he muttered.

Before I could argue, he crossed the room in three long strides, crouched at the foot of my closet, and started rummaging through drawers like he lived here. Like this wasn't completely unhinged.

"Excuse me—what are you—"

"Fixing it."

"You can't just—"

"I *can*," he said, holding up a stack of clothes from the pit of my closet like it owed him money. "And I am."

"I don't even remember buying those."

"They were buried under two polos and a cardigan that smells like a senator's wife." He tossed more clothes on the bed. "No." Another shirt flew past me. Then another.

"I forgot I owned half of this stuff," I said, amazed.

Then he stood, and I forgot how to exist.

He was already dressed. All black, of course. Tight shirt stretched over muscle like a threat, like he knew exactly what it would do to anyone with working eyes and wanted the consequences. Silver chains hung low against his collarbones, glinting with every lazy movement. Rings covered his fingers. His boots were worn and laced like he'd kicked down the gates of Hell just for the vibe.

It was obscene, unfair. He looked like a sin I hadn't committed yet, and I was even more distracted than I was before he decided to help. He caught me staring. Of course he did.

"What?" he asked, deadpan.

"Nothing."

"Uh-huh." He tossed a skirt at me. "Pick something that makes you feel dangerous."

"Dangerous?"

"Yeah." His gaze dragged over me, slow and deliberate. "You're going into a haunted house with people who think they still own pieces of you. You want to play nice, or you want to haunt *them*?"

I hesitated, then reached for a top. It was black, soft but sheer. The stomach was covered by sheer mesh, and it was edgy, dangerous. It was totally different from the pastel cardigans and light-colored slacks I had hanging in my closet. Still, I grabbed a pink cardigan to go over it. After all, it was getting cold with the October weather. I paired it with the leather skirt—short, high-waisted, unapologetic—and combat boots.

I added smudged eyeliner. Lip balm. A little glitter on my cheeks like stardust, like war paint, and I let my hair fall in wild, loose curls down my back. When I stepped out of the bedroom, Cain was sitting on the arm of the couch, flipping his butterfly knife open and shut like it was a nervous tic. Click. Flick. Shine. Click.

He looked up and stilled. The knife stopped moving. His gaze dragged over me like smoke, slow, heavy, burning at the edges. Like he was memorizing something sacred. Or dangerous. Or his. His jaw ticked once, and his shadows stretched lazily in my direction.

"Well?" I asked, suddenly nervous.

He stood and walked toward me like he had nothing better to do than ruin the mood of every man in a five-mile radius. He didn't touch me. Just circled slow and predatory. Then he leaned down, close enough for his breath to ghost across my shoulder. "Now *that's* a haunting."

My pulse skipped.

"I look ridiculous."

"You look like you stopped pretending." His voice dropped. "I love it."

I crossed my arms, trying not to squirm under his stare. "We're not actually dating, you know."

He leaned in closer. "Don't tell *them* that."

CHAPTER 10

Cain

I shouldn't have looked. Told myself that three goddamn times. Eyes on the road. Hands on the wheel. *Focus.*

When she walked out of that bedroom wearing leather, mesh, and combat boots laced like she was marching straight into war, I forgot how to breathe. Not that I needed to, but still.

She looked like a death wish wrapped in pink glitter and bad choices. Like the version of herself she buried to make other people comfortable had clawed its way out and sat down in my passenger seat just to watch me ruin centuries of self-control.

She shifted, adjusting her skirt like she wasn't trying to kill me. Like her thighs weren't doing irreparable damage to my self-control. My cock twitched, rude and uninvited, like a defibrillator had gone off between my legs and brought it back from the fucking grave.

I flexed my jaw. Tightened my grip on the wheel. Thought about nunneries and grandmas and the statistical likelihood of crashing this car on purpose just to avoid the reaction my body was having right now.

She didn't even notice. Didn't see what she was doing. Or maybe she did, and that was worse. Maybe she was doing this on purpose.

"Seatbelt," I said.

She reached for it slowly, eyes still on me, and she missed the latch. I leaned across her. Clicked it into place. Close enough to smell cheap vanilla and something feral underneath. She stilled. I didn't. I tugged once to check the lock, then draped my jacket across her thighs like it was nothing. Like I wasn't covering a distraction that could end civilizations.

"It's cold," I lied.

She smirked like she knew.

I put us in gear. The Mustang growled like it wanted blood. We pulled out. The city slid by in smeared neon and brake lights. She tucked a curl behind her ear like she didn't know that that tiny move could end civilizations if I let it.

"You keep looking at me like that," I said, voice dry, "and we're not making it to the haunted house."

She blinked over at me, wide-eyed. "What?"

Innocent or pretending. Either way, it pissed me off. I dragged my tongue over my teeth. She watched my hands instead. The rings. The blue veins that only show up when I remember I'm supposed to have a pulse. "You dressed like that on purpose?"

Her brows knit. "Like what?"

Like my problem, I wanted to say. Instead: "Like you want me to start fights in parking lots."

She grinned. Evil. "You're the one who said I should look dangerous."

"I didn't say look like a fucking death row fantasy."

She laughed. A real one. Bright and careless. I hated how much I liked it.

"Besides," she added, "if we're going to pretend to date, I might as well look the part."

My stomach dropped a little at that word. *Pretend*. Right. This was a bit. A game. A costume party built on trauma and mutual contempt. Fake dating. That's what this was. A cover. A tactic. Everything with her was pretend, fake, and I hated it with every fiber of my being, but I could calculate romance like a murder.

She curled her fingers on the cushion of the seat like she needed something to hold. I put my palm up between us without looking. Offer, not order. She slid her hand into mine like she was testing a myth. Our fingers laced. My rings bit into her knuckles; she didn't flinch. I drove one-handed, human on purpose.

"If I do this"—I squeezed once, light, a code—"It means play along. Smile if you can't think."

"And if I do this?" She rapped her nails twice against my palm.

"Means I'm about to be stupid," I said. "And you're telling me not to."

She snorted. "Useful."

I turned up the volume, distracting myself with distorted guitar and messy, bleeding vocals. Something angry. Something loud. Something human.

She went soft against the seat. Not sleepy. Settled. Our hands were still threaded. I kept it that way because I was a liar. Because it steadied the part of me that wanted to curb stomp anyone who looked at her too long. Because the bond purred when her thumb did that absent, careless stroke over my index knuckle that made me believe in gods I hated.

She hummed along. I didn't know if she liked the music or just didn't care that I was playing it loud enough to break something in my head. She rested her head on the window like she wasn't completely rewriting the rules of my existence just by being near me.

I took the last turn. Ironside bled out of the dark like a bad memory that had learned how to sell tickets. Floodlights. Fog. Screams that weren't real trying to sound like they were.

I should have let go of her hand. I didn't.

Gravel spit under the tires. I killed the engine. The silence after the Mustang's growl felt like a dare. She glanced down at our hands, then at the gate like she remembered we had to be people again.

I was starting to understand something terrible. I could live forever, reap gods and monsters, tear kingdoms down with a whisper, but I would *not* survive her. I was the end of everything, the goodbye no one was ever prepared for, but I couldn't bring myself to say goodbye to her. I wouldn't even if it ended me.

Opal

The Ironside Asylum rose out of the dark like a towering skeleton of crumbling bricks and peeling paint, draped in webs and lit from beneath in a fever-dream palette of sickly green and blood-red.

The entrance was flanked by two rusted clown heads, mouths wide open like they were screaming. The gate creaked as we stepped through it.

Bonfires crackled across the field, surrounded by folding chairs and nervous laughter. Food trucks lined the far edge, pumping out clouds of delicious-smelling smoke. Monsters wandered freely: zombies, ghouls, someone in a bloodstained straitjacket. A girl in stilts and clown makeup giggled as she loomed over a popcorn stand. There were photo ops, carnival games, a lopsided Ferris wheel turning too slowly.

There were people everywhere. College kids, couples, screaming children, influencers posing with skull props and twelve-dollar slushies. The fall air bit down, crisp, cold, laced with the sweetness of kettle corn and woodsmoke.

Cain walked beside me, hands in his pockets, combat boots thudding against the gravel like he was bored with gravity itself. He looked like a god made flesh, draped in all black. I couldn't stop looking at him.

The way his sleeves clung tightly to his arms. The way his shoulders filled the darkness of his shirt like a threat. The way he scanned the space without *really* looking, like the only thing worth seeing here was already beside him.

He didn't belong here, and he wasn't pretending to. I checked my phone. Just a half-charged battery and a message from Lyric: *Almost there.*

Cain glanced down at the screen. "Are they ditching you again?"

"No," I said automatically and a little too quickly.

He didn't push. Just leaned back against a tree near the corn maze, arms crossed over his chest, eyes tracking movement like a predator watching a field full of prey.

I rubbed my arms against the chill, unsure if it was the wind or *him* making my skin tighten. "They're coming," I added. "Soon."

Cain made a noncommittal sound. "Great."

I shifted beside him, pretending to scroll, pretending not to look. It was so damn hard not to stare at the sharp line of his profile. The way his jaw flexed. The chain tucked beneath the edge of his collar. The ringed fingers that tapped against his bicep like they were counting the seconds until he could start a fight. People were looking. I didn't blame them . . . Fuck, *I* was looking.

I still flinched when I heard: "Opal?"

I turned. A guy stood a few feet away, tall-ish, pretty eyes, the kind of boy who probably smelled like aftershave and expensive hair products. I blinked at him, not immediately placing the face.

He smiled. "Sorry—this is weird. I just—I love your videos. The ghost hunting ones? You did that cemetery series with the spirit box and the candles and stuff?" His hands moved when he talked. Nervous energy. "You're Opal Grey, right?"

"Oh," I said. "Yeah. That's me."

"You're even prettier in person." His grin turned sheepish. "Sorry. That came out weird."

"It's okay," I said, smiling politely.

Behind me, I felt the temperature drop a few degrees. Cain hadn't moved, but the shift in the air was *physical*.

The guy didn't seem to notice. "Anyway, I just wanted to say I'm a big fan. If you ever need someone to help shoot something . . . Or, you know. Coffee?"

Cain stepped forward. Not by much but enough for his shadow to fall across both of us like a storm cloud.

The guy blinked and glanced up. "Hi?"

Cain didn't answer. Didn't smile. Just looked him over like he was debris. Then he slid an arm around my waist. Possessive. Cold. Calculated.

"She's busy," Cain said, voice cold and final.

The guy held up his hands. "Right. Got it. Sorry." He backed away fast, blending into the crowd.

Cain's hand lingered at my hip for a second too long, flexing.

"You're insufferable," I muttered under my breath.

"Wrong," he said, smug. "I'm effective."

"You didn't have to do that." Before I could argue more, a shriek cut through the noise.

"OPAAALLL!"

Nyxie. Clomping toward us in chunky platform boots and a skirt made of what looked like cobwebs, glitter, and tulle. Lyric wasn't far behind, already halfway through a drink with something bubbling in it that resembled a witch's potion, green and foamy.

Nyxie threw her arms around me like she hadn't ghosted me for a month. "You look *so* cute! Oh my god, this outfit is scary movie meets sexy corpse bride. I'm obsessed."

Lyric, though, Lyric had locked onto Cain. Her lips curled in slow appreciation. "Well, *now* I understand the disappearing act."

Cain arched a brow. "Excuse me?"

She tilted her head. "I'm just saying . . . if *I* had this at home, I'd go dark too."

I bristled, suddenly becoming too aware of the face I was making at her comment. Cain didn't even look at me. Which somehow made it worse. He smiled at Lyric. Not big. Not warm. Just sharp enough to cut.

"I get that a lot," he said casually.

Nyxie made an approving sound. "God, you two are hot together."

I looked away, heart stammering. This was fake. A bit. A charade. *Fake, fake, fake*, I repeated in my head.

The corn maze wasn't scary. Not to Cain, anyway. He walked a few paces behind the group like he was judging the whole production, hands in his pockets, boots crunching lazily against the gravel. Every time a scare actor popped out of the corn—clowns, zombies, one very aggressive scarecrow—he didn't flinch.

He laughed. *Jerk.* I was too busy trying not to pee myself whenever someone popped up.

I was also busy pretending everything was fine. That Lyric wasn't slowly twirling a strand of her hair around her finger while throwing him sideways glances. That Cain wasn't completely ignoring her as they walked a pace behind us.

I stayed a few steps ahead, eyes on the path, pretending not to notice the way Cain's voice dropped lower when he talked to her. Pretending not to hear Lyric giggle. Pretending not to wonder if she was better at playing fake than me.

By the time we stumbled out of the maze and into the firelit chaos of the field again, I needed air. "I'm gonna grab a drink," I said to no one in particular, because no one was paying attention to me. *Awesome.*

Cain didn't look up. Didn't follow.

Just kept talking to Lyric, that same infuriating smirk still tugging at the corner of his mouth. I headed toward the drink tent. It was just a few feet away, but every step felt heavier than it should've.

The line was short. I didn't even look up, just focused on the chill in the air, the fake screams in the background, the way my heartbeat was louder than it should be.

"Hey," said a voice behind me.

I turned.

It was the guy from earlier. The one who'd recognized me. Still pretty. Still a little nervous. He held up his hands like a peace offering. "Didn't mean to get you in trouble back there with your boyfriend."

"You didn't," I said, managing a smile. "We're just—" I paused. "It's complicated."

"Got it." He nodded toward the booth. "Let me get this one."

I hesitated, then nodded. *Why not?* Cain didn't care. This was fake. All of it. I owed him nothing. The guy ordered for both of us, something warm and cinnamon-spiced. I kept one eye on the maze exit. Cain was still there . . . still talking to Lyric.

She was laughing now, head tilted, and he was smiling. Not his usual cold grin. Something softer. I looked away.

"Here you go," the guy said.

I turned back toward him just as he held out the drink . . . and a folded slip of paper tucked underneath.

My fingers closed around both.

"What's this?" I asked, already knowing.

He smiled. "In case you ever get tired of complicated."

CHAPTER 11

Cain

I was driving her insane, and it was *adorable*. The stomping. The huffing. The tight set of her jaw, like she wanted to scream but couldn't figure out how to do it without handing me the win. She could pretend all she wanted, but she wasn't convincing me.

She'd muttered something about getting a drink and stalked off toward the tents, shoulders tight, arms crossed, like she might actually combust if Lyric laughed at one more joke that she told.

I let her go. Because watching her be jealous? It did something to my chest I didn't have a name for.

I stayed leaning against the fence post near the maze entrance, boots planted, arms folded, careful. Always careful. No skin. No accidents. Touch was still a loaded gun, and I wasn't in the mood to kill a stranger for brushing my wrist. There were a lot of people here, which made me hyperaware of everything around me.

Lyric, bless her clueless little soul, kept trying. She talked with her hands, laughed too loud, tried to brush her shoulder against mine. I didn't flinch, but the shadows stirred behind me. I watched Opal in that practiced way that looked like I paid her no attention at all. She didn't look back, but I could feel her mood across the field: tight, brittle, cracking under the strain of things she wasn't saying. It pulsed off her like static.

Then *he* appeared. *That guy.* The one from earlier. The one who looked at her like she was ordinary. I watched him walk up. Still smiling. Still alive . . . for now. But if he laid so much as one fucking finger on her in the wrong way, I would end him.

He leaned in, and I tracked every inch between them. She didn't pull back. She *smiled.* My grip tightened around the wood railing, and I heard it crack. I felt my pulse sharpen in a way it hadn't in centuries.

She let him order for her, and then, he handed her a drink and a slip of paper. She took both, and I couldn't move. I watched her slide the paper into her pocket like it wasn't a lit match, and every part of me that solved problems with funerals woke up. Our code had said no murder, no scenes, hands to myself. So, I took a breath and let the boy keep his heartbeat for one more night.

She was the only one I could touch without consequence. The only thing on this cursed planet I could hold without it turning into empty silence, and she was standing there, pocketing some idiot's number like it meant nothing. Like she wasn't mine. Of course, she had no clue about any of that. I was going to have to fix that, wouldn't I?

Lyric said something beside me, her voice high and syrupy. I didn't respond. Opal was laughing now, quiet, soft, just for him. Lyric was still talking. Something about horror movies. Or her ex. Or maybe it was me. I wasn't listening.

Something inside me snapped. I walked away mid-sentence. Left Lyric mid-breath, her mouth still open, one hand frozen mid-flirt. Her voice rose behind me, surprised, offended . . . but I didn't look back. She didn't matter. Not now. Not ever.

My boots cut through the gravel with purpose, shadows licking at my ankles like they wanted permission to do something worse. I pulled my expression into something calm. Civil. A smile, maybe. Something that could be mistaken for polite, if you weren't paying attention to the eyes. Menace poured off me like a warning.

He looked up as I approached. Paused. The smile faltered just a little.

"I'll take it from here."

He blinked. "Uh. Right. Cool."

He backed off with the awkward stumble of someone who didn't know he'd just been spared. I stepped beside her, close but not touching. Not yet.

"Getting real cozy, aren't we?" I murmured, voice a shade too casual.

Opal didn't answer right away. Just blinked up at me, lashes fluttering like her thoughts were trying to rearrange themselves before she let them out.

I didn't wait for her to speak. I turned back toward the firelit field, toward the rest of the group, Lyric now scowling, Nyxie obliviously sipping something pink and overpriced.

"Let's go," I said over my shoulder. "You're missing the fun." I adjusted the sleeve of her jacket that was slipping off one shoulder and pressed my hand to the small of her back.

The others clustered at the edge of the vendor strip, chattering about the next attraction. Someone mentioned the mirror maze.

"Ooooh, let's do it!" Nyxie squealed, practically bouncing in place.

"Totally," Lyric said, tone too sharp, eyes too pointed. "It'll be *fun*."

They all started drifting toward the maze's glowing archway, neon flickering around a cracked mirror frame, warped reflections laughing back at us. The music was warped carnival, low and off-key. The entrance looked like a funhouse swallowed by its own curse.

My stomach turned, sour and restless like something clawing from the inside. Heat crept under my skin, my pulse hammering once, twice, then fading again. Wrong. All wrong. I couldn't get sick now—and my body didn't *have* a pulse. Not like this.

I forced myself to keep walking, biting down hard on the inside of my cheek. The coppery taste of blood pooled on my tongue. She didn't need to know I was seconds from doubling over, shadows flickering sluggishly at my heels.

Not here. Not now. Get it together.

Opal lingered beside me, unsure for once.

"You coming?" she asked, eyes searching mine.

I smirked. "Wouldn't miss it."

She went first, pulled along by Nyxie, laughing, her silhouette disappearing into the maze entrance with the others. I watched her vanish, and then, I heard it. *Just around the corner.*

"Yeah man, you wait and see. I'm taking that chick home with me tonight."

At first, I ignored it.

Just background noise. Another idiot trying to impress his friends by pretending he was dangerous. Then—

"Opal's gonna be on my dick before midnight."

I stopped breathing. Didn't turn. Didn't react. Not yet. I pressed my head to the wall. Listened again. Someone was there. Watching, waiting. And they weren't watching the mirror maze. They were watching her. *My girl.*

"She's got that scary-ass boyfriend with her," another voice said, laughing. "There's no way in hell she's going with you."

And then:

"I just need to get her alone and grab her."

My vision narrowed. The world tilted. Static buzzed under my skin, and then . . . *then* he said it.

"No one said she had to be willing."

A laugh. I saw red. It started in my chest, slow and molten. Spread through my limbs like acid. *Sorry, Final Girl, but your safety beats our code any day.* My hands curled, knuckles cracking. The shadows behind me rose, uncoiling like something *starved*, knowing it was about to be fed . . . and just in time. I needed this kill more than I was ready to admit to myself.

Opal's laugh echoed behind me, still soft, still unknowing. I stepped forward and dissolved into the shadows. The light bent around me, swallowing my outline. The darkness opened for me like it had been waiting. *Like it missed me.*

They entered the maze. So did I. And this time, I wasn't her fake boyfriend. I was Death.

I followed closely as they fumbled along, their laughter fading with each misstep. I laced my shadows between them, quiet, strategic, a creeping divide. One wrong turn here. A flicker of motion there. My darkness pulling him further from the others. Further from *her.*

He wasn't making it out of this maze alive.

He bumped into mirrored walls, cursed under his breath, stumbled back, confused. The mirror maze should've been easy. A child's puzzle. Cheap thrills. But *Death was playing now*, and the game had leveled up.

I rewrote the paths beneath his feet. Bent light around corners. Twisted angles into lies. Every time he thought he was turning toward the voices, he went deeper inside. I watched the panic begin to bloom from the darkness, small at first. A curse. A nervous laugh. A glance over the shoulder.

Then a stumble. Then a pause. He was alone now . . . *mine now*. Far enough from his friends. Still so close to Opal that I could hear her laugh in the distance. This maze wasn't that big, but it was big enough to bury one more secret. I rematerialized. Right in front of him. My body unfolded from shadow, my reflection exploding across every mirror, twenty versions of me in every direction. All of them still. All of them staring.

His breath caught. *Good.*

"Hey," he said, too loud. "What the fuck—?"

I didn't answer. I tilted my head instead. Slow. Precise. All twenty of me did the same.

"W-we were just joking," he stammered. "It was a joke, man. Just—just drunk talk."

"No one said she had to be willing."

I spoke his words back to him. Let them settle. Let them decay in the silence between us. His face drained of color.

"Wait—I didn't mean—"

"I know," I said, stepping forward. "You didn't mean a single fucking word you said."

He ran. Of course he did. Stupid, panicked limbs flailing through the narrow corridors, lungs dragging air like it might save him. He turned right, then left, then *slammed* into a mirror hard enough to rattle the walls. The glass didn't break, but his nose did, blood spraying across the surface like a smattering of red punctuation.

He screamed. It echoed and echoed. It made me smile—it really did. Every direction, every mirrored face looking back at him, none of them his. They were *mine*. Twenty reflections of me watched him stagger. All with different expressions. Some smirking. Some grinning. Some with a straight face and eyes hollow as graves.

"Not that way," I said softly, though my lips didn't move. Only the reflections spoke.

He turned and ran again. Another hit. More blood. A dislocated shoulder. He bounced off the maze like a broken puppet, palms slapping against glass, breath coming in high, wet gasps.

"Almost had it that time," I said, voice dragging behind him like silk dipped in ash.

"W-what do you want?!" he screamed, wild eyes darting to shadows that kept shifting behind the glass.

My grin widened. The kind that made mortals cry and demons piss themselves.

"You know what I want."

The maze pulsed, every mirror vibrating like it had a heartbeat. My shadows twisted through the corridors now, tall and impossible. They danced just out of reach, changing the turns, closing every exit, folding the maze in on itself like a trap being sprung.

He hit another dead end and turned, sprinting full speed into mirrored glass, harder this time.

Crack.

His shoulder popped back into place. Blood splattered again. He was crying now. I could *smell* the terror on him, salty and sweet.

"Keep trying. Maybe you'll get away," I said, my voice suddenly behind him.

He whirled. Nothing there. Then left. Then right. Everywhere he turned—*me*. Sometimes with teeth. Sometimes with bone. Sometimes just a shadow grinning from behind the glass. He screamed again, hoarse and raw.

Then he ran. Full tilt. No plan. Straight into me. Warm breath and cold skin. He hit my chest like a wall. Froze. I glanced down at him, tilted my head, leaned in just enough to taste the fear leaking out of his pores.

"Boo," I whispered, and he dropped. Like his strings had been cut. No scream. No second chance. Just dead. I stepped over him, quiet, composed, the way death always is when the job's done. My shadows peeled back like curtains, and the maze opened before me.

I walked out alone. The night was still going, bonfires burning, laughter rising, sugar in the air. The group was gathered by the game booths, Opal leaning against a picnic table with a drink in hand.

"Hey, where were you?" she asked, smiling up at me, all soft light and easy affection like she hadn't just been inches away from the kind of death most people didn't walk past.

I shrugged, lazy and hollow. "Got lost." Stupid, I know.

"Come on, it wasn't that hard." She laughed. A scream tore through the night. Real. Sharp. Wet with the kind of panic that never belonged in a place like this.

That was fast.

"Damn," Thane said, turning toward the maze. "They're working *hard* tonight."

"Sure," I replied. Flat and careless, because I couldn't say the truth. No one screamed like that for fun. No actor hit that pitch. Someone just found the body I left behind in a nest of broken glass and blood-smudged mirrors.

"I want my fortune read!" Nyxie chirped, already pulling Opal's sleeve. "There's a psychic tent over here, come on!"

"Wanna go?" Opal asked, tilting her head at me.

I nodded. Nothing like a phony psychic to tell me love is in my future. We walked together, the crowd thick and unaware. The scream had faded beneath the buzz of music and laughter and caramel smoke, but security had noticed. Two men in polos and earpieces were already moving, eyes sharp, voices low as they rushed toward the mirror maze.

I lingered behind the group. Opal's laugh floated back to me, and I should've looked forward. Should've cared about what lay ahead. But my eyes drifted left. Back toward the maze. Fuck, I was hungry, and not for any mortal food. One kill was a drop in the ocean for me, and someone had pulled the plug about five weeks ago.

My shadows still curled around the exit of the maze like satisfied wolves. The air still stank of blood and fear and the last breath of a man who'd thought he could touch something that was *mine*.

The curtains to the psychic tent parted for us. Gold and black. Tacky. Reeking of incense and candles made in a factory. Opal was already inside, sinking into her seat, smiling like she believed, even for a second, that fate was something she could ask questions of. When I followed her in, I *felt* it.

That shift. That ripple in the air that only happens when something ancient walks into someplace it shouldn't. The tent didn't just smell like incense anymore. It reeked of knowing. She wasn't a fake.

She stood the moment I stepped through the curtain, chair scraping across the floor, medallions clanking against her shawl like windchimes caught in a storm. Her face went bloodless. Eyes wide. Locked onto me.

Like she recognized a predator in the skin of a man. *Perfect.* I smirked. "What's someone like you doing in a place like this?"

Then I dropped into the chair at her table, lazy and sprawling, every inch of me screaming *danger* without lifting a finger. She didn't sit. Not at first.

Just hovered there, trembling slightly, like the table between us might save her if things got bad.

"Impossible," she whispered.

I grinned wider. "Not hardly."

Thane snorted behind me. "She gonna conjure some ghosts or what?"

"Yeah, like we *paid* for," someone added.

I didn't look up at them. She did, just briefly, remembering she had an audience. Then, slowly, she lowered herself back into the seat. Her fingers hovered over the deck, trembling like she knew they were about to say something she'd regret.

She pulled a card, a single card, and flipped it. The Death card. I smiled. Not the kind people liked. Not the kind that meant anything good.

The card lay between us, sword crossed with a rose and a skeleton atop a pale horse frozen mid-step, riding forward through a sea of ruin. Her breath caught. I leaned in close enough to see the sweat pearling at her temples. Close enough that she could smell the grave dirt clinging to me beneath the leather and smoke.

"Go on," I murmured. "Tell me what it means."

I let her stare at the card, at me, at the terrible little joke the universe had played by letting her pull *that* card for *me*.

Her voice cracked when it came. "You shouldn't be here."

I leaned back, slow and smiling. "Yeah," I said. "I get that a lot."

Her lips moved, silently shaping the word *impossible* again. She looked like she was putting it together, but again, we had an audience.

I just shook my head.

"No," I said simply, voice low, final. "Some fortunes are better left unsaid."

And then, because the mood had gotten a little too serious, and because I was feeling generous, I snapped. Not my fingers. Just my will. The shadows in the corners thickened. The candle flames blew sideways.

A rift split open behind me, *thin*, like a crack in reality, wide enough for *things* to pour through. Spirits. Cold wind. Wailing that didn't come from any speaker. Faces pressed to the inside of the veil, screaming without mouths, eyes glowing with grief and fury and endless want.

The table shook. The cards scattered in a whirlwind. The temperature dropped ten degrees. Still, I sat there, smiling like this was a party trick. Opal's friends *lost it*. Nyxie screamed first, though it came out half-giggle, half-shriek. "WHAT THE—NOPE."

Thane was already backing toward the curtain, laughing nervously. "This is too much, nope, no, thank you—"

Lyric knocked over a chair trying to follow them out, face pale, mascara already smudged, and just like that, they were gone. Gone with nervous laughter trailing behind them like perfume, not sure if it was real or not but smart enough not to wait and find out.

Opal hadn't moved. She was still beside me. Still breathing. Giggling.

And I—I was laughing quietly to myself. Who knew? Tonight might actually turn out to be *fun*. I stood. The shadows peeled off me like reluctant silk.

The psychic stared, frozen in place, shoulders stiff, fingers clutching the rim of the table as if it might keep her anchored to this world a moment longer. "Who are you?" she whispered.

The words trembled, barely formed. As if saying them might make something *real* that couldn't be undone. I turned halfway back, just enough for her to see my smile: not kind, not cruel. Just *true*.

My eyes flicked to the table. One card remained. Pinned to the table despite the wind and chaos.

Death.

Still face up.

Realization washed over her face in slow, colorless waves. She looked at the card, then at me, then back again, like the truth was too big to fit in a single glance.

"Until we meet again," I said, voice lazy and slow, like we were old friends parting after drinks.

"Thanks for a fun night." I winked, and with that, I stepped back into the dark. The tent curtain fluttered closed behind me.

CHAPTER 12

Cain

Opal was smiling at me. That half-crooked, too-real smile that always made my chest ache in ways I didn't understand. She was laughing. It was stupid and soft, and for a moment, the night felt suspended in that sound. And then, she *swayed*. Just a little.

Her smile faltered. Her lashes fluttered like her body couldn't keep up with itself. Her lips moved around a word that never made it out, and then she dropped.

Fast.

My reflexes were faster.

I caught her before she hit the gravel, her weight limp in my arms, head lolling against my shoulder like her bones had forgotten how to hold her up.

"Opal," I said, voice sharp as I gave her a tight shake. No response. Her eyes were unfocused. Pulse frantic. She wasn't drunk, she hadn't had any alcohol. No, she was *drugged*.

My entire body went still. Dead fucking still. I could feel it in her, whatever chemical had hit her bloodstream. Bitter. Synthetic. Not enough to kill, but enough to control. That *bastard*. The drink. That *fucking drink*.

If he wasn't already dead, I'd kill him again but slowly this time. Bone by bone. My grip tightened on her. The shadows responded instantly, surging up around us like a shield, blocking the world from view. I didn't care who saw. Didn't care who screamed. But they hid us all the same.

This was mine. She was *mine*, and someone had tried to take her from me. I cradled her closer, one hand against the back of her head, breathing in the vanilla and marshmallow of her skin. The scent that was Opal, even now, *especially* now. I stood, and she didn't stir. Her head was heavy against my chest, breath shallow, lashes fluttering with effort. One wrong step, and I'd raze this place to ash.

I turned toward the field.

The screams had started up again, real ones this time. Not the haunted-house kind. Sirens cut the air while red and blue lights spun through the crowd. The authorities had finally found the corpse I'd left cooling in the mirror maze, and now, the alarm was being raised. Voices barked through radios. Police pushed through the crowd, already cordoning off sections of the field with tape.

Good. Let them panic. Let them run. I walked straight through it. Out from the shadows. Into the light. Carrying her and *daring* someone to say a word.

No one did.

Because something in me was too still. Too focused. I looked untouchable, unstoppable, and I *was*. People turned, saw me, and looked away fast. They moved but not toward me. Not *for* me. Like some instinct deep in their bones screamed *don't interfere. Don't get close.*

I walked past a cop shouting orders into a radio. He glanced at me, froze, and said nothing. The crowd parted like instinct knew better than reason, and ahead of me . . . her *friends.*

Nyxie, Lyric, and Thane clustered near the barricade. Wide-eyed and grinning. Their phones were out, recording the scene. Not worried about Opal. Not *looking for her.* Just filming. I fucking hated them.

"Is that a body bag?" Thane laughed, angling his camera.

"Get the light on her face," Lyric said, flipping her front cam.

None of them had noticed she was gone. None of them noticed me. I could've been carrying her corpse, and they wouldn't have known until it showed up in the algorithm.

I kept walking. Didn't stop. Didn't speak. Because what could I say? I'd already taken one life tonight. Though I was starting to think I should've taken three more. I was certainly craving more, needed more.

I laid her gently in the passenger seat. She didn't wake, just curled slightly, instinctively, her hand fisting the hem of her pink jacket. I slid into the driver's seat, gripped the wheel, and didn't bother with the speed limit.

The shadows took care of it, wrapped around the car like smoke made sentient, cloaking us in something primal. The tires screamed against the asphalt, a blur in the dark. Streetlights bent as we passed. Cameras blinked and missed us entirely. Death was on the road, and tonight, Death was *angry*.

I got her home. Back to her ridiculous, stubborn, tiny-ass apartment, her pink fortress, lined with fairy lights and bones and too many ghost plushies to count. I carried her inside, arms steady, jaw tight. She didn't wake, didn't even flinch when I nudged her bedroom door open with my foot and laid her down on the bed like she was made of something breakable.

She wasn't. She was the strongest goddamn thing I'd ever met, but still, I was careful. Brushed her hair out of her face. Let my hand linger a second too long.

She was going to feel like hell tomorrow, and I was already starting to feel like hell myself. Denying myself what I needed to survive for her sake wasn't going to last much longer, and I wasn't sure I was ready for that. She certainly wasn't. I wasn't ready to lose her, for her to look at me like the monster I truly was.

Whatever cocktail that asshole had slipped into her system wasn't meant to kill, but it *was* meant to erase memory. To soften the world. To make her pliable. Easy.

If I hadn't been there tonight . . . If I hadn't followed . . . If I hadn't noticed . . .

She wouldn't have had a tomorrow, and that thought . . . that single thought. It lit something inside me that I didn't have a name for. Funny, isn't it?

If all this hadn't happened, she might have died tonight. No one touched her now. Not unless they wanted to stop breathing. Not unless they wanted to disappear screaming into the dark.

I stood there in the glow of her string lights, staring down at the only girl on this cursed earth who could touch me without turning to ash, and thought:

You're mine.

Opal

I woke up drowning in static. There was a throbbing behind my eyes, like something had been scraped out of my skull with rusty spoons. Light knifed into my eyes and sounds came in half a second late, like the world was buffering. My mouth was dry, tongue sticking to my lips like sandpaper, stomach churning with something sour.

The room spun when I sat up. My bed tilted. My cardigan felt too abrasive against my skin. I blinked at my phone, buzzing with unread notifications, dozens of texts, missed calls, flashing headlines stacked on top of one another.

The news banner caught my eye first. "Man dies of a rare, undiagnosed congenital heart defect at a local haunted house."

Below that: A name. A photo. I knew that face. Not well but well *enough*. The guy from the drink stand. My hands started shaking, and one name flashed in my mind.

Cain.

I glanced up, and there he was. In my kitchen, sleeves pushed up, silent as ever. He was pouring water into a glass like it was the most normal thing in the world. Like he hadn't ripped someone out of it. Was it because he was jealous? That couldn't be it. Right?

He walked over and held the glass out without meeting my eyes. I took it, fingers trembling.

"Did you do this?" I asked, voice barely there. I turned the phone toward him. The headline glared back at us.

His expression didn't shift. Not even a little.

"Yes," he said. Flat. Icy. Final.

God, what had I done? Taking him out like he was a normal person and not Death himself. I'd caused someone's death. That thought sank, forming a pit in my stomach. Cain stared at me, watching, analyzing me like he always did.

A pause stretched between us, taut as a pulled thread. Then, he spoke. "But not for the reason you think." He sat at the edge of my bed, just far enough not to touch.

I stared at him. "Then why?"

He looked at the floor just for a second. Just long enough for the shadows to move around his jaw like smoke.

"Because of how you feel right now," he said.

I blinked. "What?"

His eyes lifted to mine. "Opal," he said slowly, "he drugged you. That drink he bought you had a roofie in it."

The world tilted. Cain's voice stayed level, measured, and *deadly*. He braced me with his hand, and I couldn't tell if my reaction was a result of the drugs or the information he'd just given me.

"I overheard him and his friends," he went on. "They were laughing about it. About what they were going to do to you. Joking. Bragging."

He exhaled once through his nose, barely audible but obviously furious all the same. "So yes. I killed him."

The words hit like a slap. Not just because of what he'd done but because of what had *almost* happened. He watched me for a moment, jaw tight, then looked away.

"I brought you home," he said, voice lower now. Quieter. "Carried you."

His fingers curled slightly at his sides like the memory was still too close. "Drink some water." The words were bitter and tight. It wasn't a request. I reached for the glass, throat dry, but before I could raise it, he turned again, sharper this time. Angrier.

"Why were you even talking to that guy?" He didn't wait for an answer. "This." He yanked the scrap of paper from his jacket pocket and held it up like it was evidence in a trial. Like I'd committed some great betrayal instead of just accepting a free drink and a smile.

I looked away. Because I *had* talked to him. Had smiled, had considered calling him. "You were flirting with Lyric all night," I muttered.

His lips curved into something between a smirk and a snarl. "Only because you look cute when you're jealous."

I crossed my arms, heat rising in my face before I could stop it. "I wasn't jealous."

He arched a brow.

I glared. "We're not really dating, remember?"

He nodded once, cold and sharp. He stood facing away from me. "Right." He paced a slow, tight circle like the walls of my bedroom were suddenly too close, like he needed movement or he'd explode. Then he stopped, back turned, voice tight. "Until we break this bond . . ." His head turned back over his shoulder, eyes dark. "Don't do that again."

I scoffed, incredulous. "So, you want me to be *fake loyal* to our *fake relationship*?"

He turned fully now, eyes locking on mine, no smile this time. Just fire and his usual intensity. "Only if you want dead boyfriends," he said. "And I don't mean like me." His voice dropped. "*Dead*-dead."

My mouth went dry again. Why was that *hot*? Like, clinically—*textbook*—I should be terrified. He'd just threatened to kill anyone who so much as flirted with me. Not metaphorically. Not in a jealous boyfriend way. In a *death is my job, and I'll end your bloodline* way. My pulse, however, didn't seem to care about ethics. It just skipped. Then sped up. Then pounded so loud I was half-convinced he could hear it. I knew he could . . . But would he think it was just fear?

I crossed my arms tighter and looked anywhere but his face. Because the worst part? He was *serious*, and it kind of made me feel safe. Which was probably the most fucked-up part of it all.

"I need something for my head," I muttered, voice hoarse from too much silence and not enough sanity.

Cain turned, his eyes snapping back to me like he'd just remembered I was breakable.

A diversion.

A distraction.

Something—*anything*—to keep my heart from leaping out of my chest and hurling itself at him. Something to stop me from asking if he meant it. If he'd really kill for me. If he already had, and if this was turning into something more than just a cover.

"It's killing me," I said, rubbing my temples like pressure might erase the thought of his mouth saying *dead-dead* like it was a promise.

"Where?" he asked.

A simple question, but it sounded like a threat.

I shook my head. "I don't have anything here."

My legs swung over the bed, hitting the floor with more force than necessary. My body ached like I'd been hit by a bus.

I needed air. Now . . . Before he decided to kiss me or kill me. I wasn't sure which would be worse. Or better. My head really was pounding.

He watched me for a second longer than he should have, expression unreadable, shadows curling behind him like they were listening in.

The sun was too bright. It clawed across the windshield like it had something to prove, painting sharp lines across my lap and Cain's knuckles as he gripped the wheel with the kind of calm that usually came just before violence. His sunglasses were perched on the bridge of his nose, eyes hidden, expression unreadable. The Mustang purred beneath us like it was bored with the speed limit.

My head throbbed, a dull, echoing ache behind my eyes, as if my brain were still trying to boot up after being forcibly shut down. My stomach curled around nothing. More than anything, I was confused. *He killed for me.* To protect me. But he didn't care about me—not like that. My mind wandered as I gave him sideways glances. He was still beautiful, dark, and so out of my reach that the things I was considering couldn't possibly be true.

Cain didn't speak. He never did in the morning unless prompted. Just shifted gears like he was waiting for the world to give him permission to destroy something.

The corner pharmacy came into view, tucked into a strip mall like an afterthought. He parked like he hated the curb. Threw it into park with a jerk of his wrist. Got out without a word.

I followed, pulling my hoodie tighter even though the morning wasn't cold. The automatic doors opened with a hollow whir, swallowing us into that fluorescent purgatory of bleach and pharmaceuticals. A place where people came to fix headaches and refill anti-anxiety prescriptions, pretending their lives weren't collapsing quietly in the parking lot.

Cain didn't browse. Didn't ask what I needed. He walked straight to the counter like he was owed something, and somehow, the guy behind the register knew. Said nothing. Just moved.

I stood too long between the gum and the greeting cards before the smell of floral cleaning supplies turned the inside of my skull into static. I needed air, so I pushed through the doors. The street outside was quiet in the way only mornings can be, slow, sleepy, still waking up.

That's when I saw them. Nyxie first, bubblegum-blue hair pulled into a high ponytail, phone already halfway to her face like she was filming something she hadn't even lived through yet. Then Thane, coffee in one hand, phone in the other, wearing last night's eyeliner like war paint.

And then . . . Lucian.

I stopped moving. He was standing beside Nyxie, too close. Hands in the pockets of his too-perfect jeans, mouth tight. Nyxie noticed me first.

"Oh my *god*." She gasped, stepping forward with a little twirl. "*Opal!* What a *coincidence*!"

Lucian's eyes found me immediately, blue and sharp and furious.

Thane gave me a little wave. "Hey girl, you okay? You kinda dipped last night."

Lucian didn't say anything. Just stared. His eyes flicked over me, landing on the bruised shadows under my eyes, the hoodie Cain had tossed over me, the faint shake in my hand.

We both muttered awkward, useless "hi"s. Mine came out thin and strangled. His didn't sound much better. The door to the pharmacy hissed open behind me. A rush of air followed, sharp and unnatural. Too cold for the season. Too cold for *reality*.

It slid over my skin like fingers made of frost, but no one else reacted. No one else noticed.

Except me.

Cain stepped out like a shadow dressed in bone, shoulders square, jaw tight, the plastic bag in one hand and a bottle of water in the other. His boots were deliberate on the concrete, not loud but final. I didn't turn. I didn't have to. He towered over me, and I could feel his glare on the back of my neck. He held out the meds and water. I took them without a word, finally glancing up at him. His face said everything I needed to know.

He hated everyone here, but he especially hated *Lucian*. Cain didn't even look at me as he handed over the bag. His eyes were locked on my ex like Lucian had been personally engineered to piss him off. His mouth twitched. Not in a smile. In the kind of movement you make when you're picturing what someone's teeth would look like scattered on pavement.

Lucian tensed.

It was subtle, the flex of his hand in his pocket, the way his jaw locked, but I saw it, and worse, Cain saw it too. I saw how close he was standing to Nyxie. Her body angled toward his. His wasn't angled away. A silent admission.

"Wow," Lucian finally muttered, his gaze flicking to Cain's hand still hovering near mine. "That was fast."

Cain's head tilted slightly. "You mean *efficient*."

Lucian gave a low, bitter laugh. "Right. You barely know her."

Cain smiled now.

Not sweet. Not sharp. Just enough to bare teeth. Just enough to silence the birds in the trees.

"I know *enough*."

Lucian scoffed. "Do you?"

Cain didn't move, but the air around him did. The shadows leaned closer. The temperature dropped to an unnatural degree, and when he spoke again, it wasn't loud. It didn't have to be.

"I know she doesn't actually like her coffee sweet. Just creamy enough to hide the bitterness she pretends isn't there."

He took a step closer, and Lucian flinched but didn't move. "I know she names her stuffed animals. Always something old-fashioned at first, like Mortimer or Theodore, but she renames them after two weeks when she decides they've 'earned' it."

Cain's voice stayed even. Low and terrible and true.

"I know she collects real bones, not just thrift store junk she tells her friends about. Human skull on the bookshelf, raccoon femur in the corner. The real stuff, the stuff that matters to *her*, she hides."

Lucian blinked.

Cain didn't stop.

"I know which hoodie's her favorite. The sherpa one. Pastel pink. It's ugly. She knows it. She wears it anyway when she feels like a ghost in her own skin."

His voice dropped further, gentler now but somehow more lethal.

"I know how she smiles when she's lying. I know the sound she makes when she's falling asleep. I know she hums when she's anxious, and it's always the same four-note pattern."

He shifted his weight and nodded toward the street.

"And I know *you've never even been in her room*."

Lucian froze.

Cain let it settle. Let it *sting*.

"She told you it was messy, didn't she?" he said, almost lazily. "Told you she was embarrassed. Told you it wasn't a big deal. But the real reason?"

Cain's eyes flicked up, and suddenly, they weren't stars anymore. They were mirrors.

"You didn't fit."

Cain's words landed like a blade, and I could feel the tension ripple through Lucian before he even opened his mouth.

"We just always went to my place because it was bigger. That's all."

His voice was tight. Defensive. But I heard it. The crack in his voice. The thinness behind the words. He wasn't talking to Cain anymore.

He was talking to *me*. Trying to rewrite history while we were all still standing in it. I didn't say anything.

Cain stepped forward once, slow, deliberate, the way someone might circle prey already bleeding.

"Oh," he said, low and cold, "you mean the place with the white carpets, glass tables, and no trace of her anywhere?"

Lucian's jaw twitched. "She liked coming over."

"No," Cain said. "She made herself small to fit in your world, and you called it compatibility."

I felt the words like a slap I wasn't ready for. Lucian flinched, and Cain still didn't stop. No, he was going for the kill.

"Let me guess," he went on, voice still calm, still terrifying, "you liked her best when she looked polished. Quiet. Pink but not too weird. Cute but not *creepy*."

"That's not fair," Lucian snapped. "You don't know anything about us."

Cain smiled, sharp and mirthless. "No. I just know *her*."

His hand lightly brushed against mine then, but it was enough to silence everything else. Enough to make the blood rush to my face and my pulse scramble into something unsteady and too aware.

Lucian's eyes followed the movement.

Nyxie shifted beside him, uncomfortable now, arms crossed like she wanted to say something but didn't know which side she belonged on.

Lucian's mouth opened like he had a comeback, but Nyxie cut in first.

"You know," she said, flipping her hair with the practiced carelessness of someone trying to weaponize innocence, "I don't think they're actually even dating."

"Yeah," Thane chimed in with a shrug. "You guys didn't even touch last night. Let alone kiss."

The air sucked out of my lungs. Fuck, they'd figured it out. That was fast.

Cain turned his head slowly toward me, expression unreadable, but *something* coiled behind his eyes. Something ancient. Something *starving*.

Then he looked back at Lucian. It was too quiet. That kind of loaded silence where the air felt thick with expectation, where every breath sounded louder than it should. All of them were watching. Waiting.

Lucian with that tired, bitter anger that always lived just under his skin. Nyxie with her eyes sharp and smug, like this was a game show she was *winning*. Thane, oblivious but amused.

I could feel Cain behind me. Not just the heat of his body or the steady rhythm of his breath, but the weight of his restraint. Tension wrapped around him like a chain pulled too tight. I felt his shadows coiling around me like at any moment they were ready to snatch me away into the darkness.

He didn't move toward me, but when he spoke, it was low. Coiled. Almost amused. "Sounds like they want a show, Blossom."

My stomach flipped. He was teasing. Daring me. Like a snake uncoiling to see if I'd flinch. And I *should* have let it go. Should've rolled my eyes, said something sarcastic, played it cool. That's what fake girlfriends did. They didn't tremble when their pretend boyfriend's voice dropped an octave. They didn't imagine what it would feel like to have him actually mean it.

He leaned in, his eyes flicking toward my lips like a dare. This was too much, I was going to break, my pulse was hammering too fast to track. My breath stalled as he closed the distance, a slight smile forming on his lips. He was teasing me, so close but miles apart. "What'll it be, Blossom?" he whispered.

My body betrayed me. "Cain," I whispered back, soft and stupid and trembling, "kiss me."

The moment the words left my mouth, something snapped. I felt it. A pulse deep in my ribs. Like a string pulled past its breaking point. Something inside me shuddered, then fell silent. It was like the feeling I got calling his name but so much more intense.

Cain stilled.

For one breathless second, he didn't move at all. He just stared at me, like the world had tilted and no one warned him.

Then—he moved. Not like a boy leaning in for a kiss. He moved like a storm answering a summons. His hand came up, fingers curling around the side of my neck, not gentle but careful, like he knew what he was capable of and was restraining himself by inches. His fingers tangled in my hair as he pulled me closer, swallowing my gasp.

His mouth crashed into mine, and the world fell apart, because he *devoured* me. There was no hesitation. No slow build. No sweet exploration. Cain kissed me like he was starving, like I was the only thing keeping him tethered to the earth. He kissed me with his entire body. His mouth was hot and demanding, lips bruising, teeth nipping like he was trying to make sure the memory of this was burned into my bones.

My hands clutched at his jacket, and I didn't even remember moving. His other arm snaked around my waist, pulling me into him like I was a possession he refused to let go of.

I gasped against his mouth. He *groaned* into mine.

The air shifted. I heard Nyxie choke on a laugh. Thane muttered, "Oh, shit." Lucian's mouth opened on my name—soft, almost sorry—then shut hard. Entitlement won. Because Cain was kissing me like no one else existed, and worse . . . I was kissing him back. *Really kissing him.*

When he finally pulled back, his breath was ragged. His eyes, those endless, impossible galaxies, blazed with something feral. His thumb brushed my lower lip, slow. Possessive. Real.

I had no idea what I'd just done or how I'd done it. Cain's thumb moved to my cheekbone, slow and unsteady. It wasn't casual. It wasn't for show. It was painfully tender.

I could still feel his mouth on mine. My lips still tingled with the sensation of him. Traffic hummed. A bird dared a trill. My mouth tasted like cherry vapor and something I refused to name. Everything else fell away. The noise. The people. The past. It was just him, and me, and the wrongness of how *right* it had felt.

Then—*yanked*.

Suddenly, I was stumbling backward, spine snapping straight, the world jerking out of place. I nearly tripped, would've hit the pavement, if not for the tight, brutal grip at the back of my hoodie, Cain's hoodie. The one he'd wrapped around me. The one that still smelled like him.

I twisted. Lucian's fist was knotted in the fabric, jaw clenched, face pale with rage.

"What the *fuck*, Opal?"

The words hit like a slap. Cain's name was still on my tongue. My heart still hadn't slowed. Lucian's eyes burned—not sad, not hurt. *Entitled.* Like I owed him answers. Like *he* had been the one I'd kissed in front of a crowd.

"Let go," I said, my voice quiet.

"What the hell is this, some kind of joke? You think this is funny?"

He hadn't noticed Cain move.

Hadn't seen how his expression had shifted from devouring to *deadly calm.* Lucian hadn't felt what I felt, how the air had turned again, thicker now. Electric. Wrong. Lucian was too busy throwing a tantrum to realize he'd just pissed off the one thing you never want to know your name.

He had no idea he was standing at the precipice of something *final.* That the hand he'd used to jerk me back, the fingers still twisted in Cain's hoodie, had just signed his own death sentence.

But I knew. I saw it. In Cain. In the stillness that snapped over him like frost. He wasn't shouting. Wasn't snarling. Wasn't storming forward with fists clenched and fire in his eyes. No. That would've been *safe*. That would've been *human*.

Cain didn't rage. He calculated. His body moved like a shadow, too smooth, too controlled. Like a blade sliding free of its sheath. Like the idea of violence was no longer a question but a promise that only needed a name.

And Lucian? Lucian still had no idea he was about to die.

"You think this is funny?" he spat, dragging me a step back, too focused on me to see Cain shift. "You think this is *real*? You're not like this, Opal. You're not—"

Cain just *appeared*. One moment he was a step away, the next, Lucian's wrist was empty. My body was free. The hoodie slipped back into place across my shoulders, and I was tucked into his arms like something holy. His eyes met mine with a silent question. *Are you ok?* I nodded, and Lucian finally turned—and *froze*.

Recognition hit all at once. The name. The way Cain's features flickered under the light just for a second. His cheek hollowed like bone. His jaw more skull than flesh. His eyes black galaxies churning behind skin too ancient to be called young.

His mouth opened, but no words came, and Cain was already mid-motion, fingers curling like they were about to close around his throat and *end it*.

"Cain, stop!"

His name left my lips before I even knew I was saying it, and he *stopped*. Every muscle locked. His body seized like someone had pulled a string too hard and broken the mechanism beneath.

I felt it again. That *snap*. The bond humming at the base of my spine, yanked taut. Power laced into my voice without my permission. Cain's name was a *command*, and Death had no choice but to obey.

He turned. Slowly. Mechanically. Like something rewinding. His eyes lifted to mine, and for the first time, I saw what I hadn't wanted to admit. Not anger or hate but *sorrow*. The kind that didn't belong in someone like him. The kind that said, *You just figured it out, didn't you? That you own me.*

Lucian was still backing away. Breathing hard. But I wasn't looking at him. I was looking at Cain, and he looked *wrecked*.

CHAPTER 13

Opal

Cain slung me into the car like I weighed nothing. The passenger door slammed with a sound that could've shattered bone. He stalked around the front, every step vibrating with fury, and when he dropped into the driver's seat, he gripped the steering wheel so tight his knuckles went white.

He didn't look at me, not yet, but the air inside the car felt *wrong*. When he turned, his eyes were galaxies again, but this time they were made of fire and wrath. "Don't you *ever* do that again."

I swallowed hard. I knew he couldn't hurt me, not physically. The spell made sure of that. But god . . . he looked like he *wanted* to, and that also didn't stop the feeling that he could ruin the rest of the world and make me watch.

I hadn't meant to do it. I hadn't even known I *could*, not like that, but the second I'd said his name, really said it, with that tone, that command . . . I felt it. The pull . . . the *power*. Now I understood why he guarded his name like it was a loaded gun. This spell didn't just bind Death to me. It made him *mine*. I had complete control over him. That was the most terrifying thing I'd ever known.

"You're going to pay for that," he added, voice feral and vibrating, before jamming the key into the ignition.

The engine roared to life. He peeled off into the street, tires screaming, leaving Lucian and Nyxie tangled together in the rearview. Good. They deserved each other.

I turned to him, fury bubbling up beneath my skin. "Why did you *do* that?! You didn't have to start a fight."

"And you didn't have to make me kiss you. Guess we're even."

My blood went cold. I'd made him do that? Instead of admitting anything, I deflected and snapped, "You had no right to just show up and ruin my life!"

He turned his head and gave me a look that could kill gods. "You were ruining your own life, Opal. Not me."

I opened my mouth. Closed it again.

"You really think they *cared* about you?" he asked. "Those people weren't your friends."

I sniffled, chest tight, and shook my head. "Yes—"

"No."

He cut me off. Sharp. "You remember how you thought I could read your mind when we first met?"

I nodded slowly.

"They were *not* your friends."

The words crackled through the car like thunder, and the worst part? I believed him. Because I'd felt it too. Nyxie's hand in Lucian's sleeve. Thane's camera. How none of them had seen me fall. I curled my hands in my lap, suddenly cold despite the heat between us. And Cain? Cain was still seething but quieter now. Simmering, maybe.

The car ride was quiet, and not comfortably so. Cain hadn't looked at me since we left. Hands tight on the wheel. Jaw clenched. Muscles coiled like he was trying not to explode. I stared out the window, trying to breathe through the chaos spinning in my chest.

The truth was echoing in my skull. I had told him to kiss me. Not asked . . . told. And he had. Not because he'd wanted to, but because he'd had to. The thought made me sick.

I glanced over at him. "So . . . I could tell you to do anything?"

He didn't flinch. Just nodded once, sharp and bitter. "You say my name first, then tell me what to do. Out loud—and mean it. If you wobble, it slides right off." He sighed. "People usually want me to kill for them," he said, voice even.

"Use me as a weapon. A threat. A way to get what they want." He finally looked at me, and his eyes, god, those eyes, were calm in the way oceans were calm before they dragged you under. "Whatever you tell me to do, Opal . . . I won't have a choice."

I swallowed hard. "That's . . ."

"Yeah," he said, gaze snapping back to the road. "That's why I didn't want you to know."

I shook my head, the guilt rising fast. "I would never—"

"I know," he cut in, his voice quieter now. Calmer. Like it cost him something to say the next part.

"That's why . . . out of everyone it could've been"—he paused, jaw flexing like he was fighting the words—"I'm glad it was you."

I glanced at him. He wasn't looking at me, but his lips were pulled into a hard line. His profile was all sharp lines and celestial rage, like someone had carved him out of mythology and set him loose with tattoos and attitude.

And for just a second, he looked at me too. Our eyes met. I blushed. Hard. "I'm so sorry I made you kiss me," I said quickly, heart pounding. "I didn't know, I swear. I didn't mean to—"

He blushed. Actually fucking blushed. That smooth ivory skin of his turned just a little pink, like those damn Hello Kitty pajama pants.

He turned back to the road quickly. "I don't want to talk about it. I know you had no clue what would happen."

I grinned. Couldn't help it. Because . . . yeah. It had been nice. Better than nice. That was the best damn kiss I'd ever had.

"It was—"

"Opal," he cut me off, and his voice dropped low.

I didn't stop.

"Oh, come on, Cain. You can't just ruin me in front of my ex, blow my mind, then pretend like it was no big—"

He swerved. Sharp. Sudden.

The car jerked off the main road, tires squealing as he pulled onto a shadowed side street framed by blackened brick and twisted trees. He threw the car into park with one smooth motion and turned toward me. His eyes were glowing.

Stars, galaxies, and final judgment burned behind his lashes like the cosmos was bleeding through.

I shut up.

He leaned in, slow and predatory, one arm braced on the back of my seat, the other lazily gripping the gearshift like he wasn't two seconds away from flipping the whole damn car over with me still inside.

His presence wrapped around me like smoke. Hot. Heavy. Impossible to breathe through.

"You think this is a game?" he murmured, voice low enough to crawl along my spine.

I swallowed hard. My thighs squeezed together entirely on instinct. His mouth hovered near mine, too close yet not close enough.

"You made me kiss you," he whispered. "You commanded me."

His voice dipped even lower, just above a growl.

"And I'm going to make you pay for that."

My breath caught.

"You—What does that mean?" I asked, throat dry, body traitorous.

He grinned then.

Wicked. Slow. Like a match dragged over sandpaper.

"You'll find out."

I shivered.

He didn't move. Didn't blink. He just dragged his gaze down to my lips, my throat like he was already imagining how . . .

"You like teasing me, Final Girl?" he whispered.

"I—" I blinked, brain misfiring. "I mean—"

"Because I promise," he said, leaning in so close his breath brushed my ear, "when I start teasing you back . . . you'll beg."

I was going to combust. Die right there in his fucking car. Not from Death. From Cain. And the worst part? I wanted to. This man was going to bring me to my knees. I just knew it.

He finally leaned back like he was letting me breathe again. The glow in his eyes dimmed to a slow burn, but the tension didn't leave. Cain shifted gears and swung back onto the road like we hadn't just nearly combusted in a parked car.

"You okay over there, Little Ghoul?" he asked, voice smug and satisfied.

I rolled my eyes. "I *hate* you."

He smirked. "No, you don't."

I crossed my arms and stared out the window, trying not to melt into the seat. I blinked and looked out the window again. This wasn't my apartment. This wasn't *anywhere near* my apartment.

"What the hell—"

That's when I saw it: Lucian's house. Big. Clean. Pretentious. Cain shifted in his seat, unbothered, already reaching for the door handle.

"Stay here," he said, voice casual.

"Wait . . . *What are you doing?*" I half-shouted.

He gave me a look like I was the dumb one in this conversation. "Pretty boy is still back in town. I'm getting the book."

I blinked at him. "Pretty boy?"

"Shut up," he grumbled, slamming the door behind him. "Before I actually do decide to kill him."

I watched him walk toward the house like he owned it. Like it wouldn't matter if there were a hundred locks or a guard dog or Lucian himself standing on the porch with a baseball bat. Cain didn't knock. Didn't creep. He just vanished into the shadows like smoke.

I sat back in the passenger seat and let out a huff. After a second, the window rolled down just enough, and his voice slipped back in like mist, making me jump.

"By the way . . . What did the spell look like?"

I blinked. "What?"

"The page you used. The one that did this."

"Oh." I tried to remember. "It had . . . a skull inside a sun, I think. I got blood all over it. I don't remember much else. That night was kind of chaotic."

He didn't say anything. Just gone. He really wanted that book so badly, to end this . . . us. I was a fool. I was pretty sure I was misreading every signal he was throwing my way. He was back in under ten minutes. No breath. No hair out of place. He slid in, shutting the door.

I stared at him, wide-eyed. "Well?!"

He reached into his jacket, pulled out something wrapped in old fabric, and dropped it into my lap. "I got the book."

Adrenaline tightened my fingers around it. "That fast?"

"Locks are for the living." He stared through the windshield for a long beat. Not his usual simmering, ready-to-snap tension. This was different. He didn't look at me right away. Just stared out the windshield like it had answers.

"There's something you should know," he said finally, voice quiet. Not soft. Just . . . careful. He looked up at me, and something in his eyes made my stomach twist. "That house was warded."

My brows pulled together. "Warded?"

"Yeah." He nodded slowly. "Not amateur hour, chalk-scribbled-on-the-door kind of crap. Heavy-duty shit. Deep. Old." He shifted in his seat, visibly uncomfortable.

Which was *terrifying*, honestly.

"Dark shit," he added. "Stuff I haven't seen in a long time."

I laughed nervously, trying to shake the chill creeping up my spine. "Okay . . . What does that mean?"

He didn't answer right away.

Just looked at me. Eyes unreadable. Finally, he said, "Opal, I want you to stay away from Lucian."

My throat went tight. "What? Why?"

He shook his head. Just once. Firm. "Just stay away from him. Okay?"

"I've known Lucian since I was five years old," I said, shaking my head. "He couldn't hurt a fly."

Cain laughed, but there was no humor in it. He leaned forward, jaw tight, voice dropping into something more feral.

"You think that means anything to me?" he snapped. "You think I care how long he's been playing the golden boy?"

I flinched.

He ran a hand through his hair, muttering under his breath before slamming back against the seat. "Gods, you're so *stubborn*."

"I'm serious, Cain. He's not like—"

"*Just listen to me on this one thing*." His voice cracked like a whip. "Just *once*."

I opened my mouth. He didn't let me speak.

"I swear to every god I've ever outlived," he growled, "if you don't—if you keep fucking around with whatever *that* is—I'll get you a new skull for your collection."

I blinked, stunned. "What?"

He looked at me. Dead serious. Flat and furious. "A *pretty* one."

My heart stuttered. Because he meant it, and not in the sweet, let-me-bring-you-some-curio-shop-gift way. He meant freshly carved and still warm. Lucian-shaped.

"Cain—" I tried, but his jaw locked, and he looked out the windshield again. Conversation: over.

The road unspooled like a vein. Cain kept us in the left lane just to bully the horizon, one hand loose on the shifter, the other welded to the wheel. Streetlights strobed through the cab, painting his knuckles and the ridge of his throat in a golden glow. I tucked his jacket tighter around me, the book heavy in my lap like a sleeping heart.

"Head?" he asked finally, not looking. The word came out like it was annoyed with itself for caring.

"Still pounding," I admitted.

He dipped two fingers into the pharmacy bag, tore a blister pack without glancing down, and held out the tablets and water. I took them. Our fingers didn't touch.

"Drink," he said.

"I am."

"All of it."

I made a face and finished the bottle. Petty victory flared in his eyes, quick as a match-strike, then was gone.

We hit a red light. The Mustang idled like a threat was coiled under the hood. A couple crossed in front of us, hands linked, laughing. Cain's gaze slid to the glass, caught their reflection, then returned to the light. Something in his jaw eased, then tightened, hard enough to whiten his knuckles again.

"You okay?" I asked, and it wasn't about the light.

He let out a small, disbelieving sound. "Ask me that when your blood isn't ringing in my head like a dinner bell. When you feel better."

I tried to ignore the part of me that liked being his problem. "About earlier," I said, voice careful, "the name thing. I won't—"

"You'll use it if you need to." He kept watching the light. "That's the point. Just don't confuse want with need."

The signal turned green. He didn't move right away. The cars behind us didn't dare honk. Then he slid us forward with silk-smooth menace, as if the city needed to apologize for existing.

He took a route I didn't recognize, backstreets where the streetlamps were out and the pavement went from municipal to maybe, alleys that felt like secrets. Twice he cut around a slow driver by slipping between a delivery truck and a shadow that shouldn't have had depth. The world bent a little to let him through. It made my teeth ache. It also made me feel weirdly safe.

"Seat heater?" he asked abruptly.

"What?"

He pressed a button. Warmth bloomed under my thighs, and I hated how grateful my bones felt. He pretended not to notice me melting into the seat. Gentlemanly cruelty.

"Thank you," I muttered.

"Don't make it a habit," he said, but it wasn't sharp.

A song came on, low bass, a woman's voice like smoke and broken glass. I reached to turn it down. His hand shot out, catching my wrist in warning, then let go before the spell could think about waking up.

"Leave it," he said. "It keeps me civil."

"You have layers," I said. "Like an onion."

"More like an explosive." He flashed a grin that didn't reach his eyes.

We passed the river; fog hugged the black water like it was whispering secrets. Cain watched it for half a second too long. "You ever going to tell me what you saw in there?" I asked, tipping my chin at the wrapped book.

"Later," he said, which meant "not in the car with the night listening." He flexed his fingers on the wheel. "You're changing."

I startled. "Excuse me?"

"Not the cute rebellion," he said, vaguely disgusted, vaguely fond. "Under the skin. You said my name today like you were born knowing it. That's . . . new."

"Is that bad?"

"For who?" He let the question hang, then added, quieter, "We'll figure it out."

A pothole appeared; the Mustang floated over it like physics had taken the evening off. I watched his profile in the dash glow: killer's mouth, saint's eyelashes. I hated him for being beautiful. I forgave him for it immediately.

"Look," I said. "About the kiss—"

"Opal," he warned.

"Shut up," I said, and his brows lifted, amused. "I know it was the spell, but if I ever . . . if we ever do something like that again, I don't want it to be because I said your name like a command."

He was silent long enough for my stomach to knot. Then: "Good," he said simply. "And it won't."

Oh. Okay. Great. My pulse did something humiliating.

We turned onto my street. The building felt smaller than usual, like a toy model of a life I wasn't sure fit anymore. Cain killed the engine and the night pressed in, soft and damp and curious. Somewhere down the block, a dog barked once and then thought better of it.

He didn't move. Neither did I.

"You still mad at me?" I asked the windshield.

"For stopping me?" His mouth twitched. "Yes." A beat. "For using my name? Yes." Another beat. "For needing to? No."

Chapter 14

Cain

Opal stood, yawning, mumbling something about needing the bathroom. I didn't really hear it. Or if I did, I pretended not to. Because my eyes were on the book in front of me and my mind on the torn scrap already in my pocket . . . the spell.

Ripped from the book the moment I'd stepped foot into her ex's picture-perfect, morally bankrupt family home while she wasn't looking.

A flash:

Lucian's study.

Framed diplomas, perfectly dusted shelves, a fireplace that had never seen a real fire. The book was on the highest shelf like they didn't even know what it was they *had*. But I did. I knew it the second my fingers had brushed the spine. The air *changed*. Warped. Smelled like old bone and betrayal.

It opened too easily. Like it wanted to be read. Old, ancient, evil things like that often did. The binding spell had been on a dog-eared page, ink smudged like it had been touched too many times. Or too recently.

This book was about as real as they got, filled with dark, ancient shit. Then the sensation hit—a pull. The kind that would have kept lesser demons and spirits locked out of this place completely. I tasted the magic. It was black and bloody. Not something an amateur could pull off. The wards made even me uncomfortable and that . . . that said something.

I didn't hesitate. I ripped the page from the spine. Folded it twice and stuffed it into my pocket like a stolen secret and walked back to the car like I hadn't just made a decision I might pay for.

Now, back in her bedroom, I held that same scrap between two fingers. The ink was darker in this light. Redder. Bolder. Like it remembered what it had done.

My thumb dragged over the sun sigil, the skull at its center etched in a hand that knew exactly what it was binding, and beneath that . . . *Cainum.* Dog. It wasn't Latin. It looked like it. Cainum. Close enough to count, close enough to cut.

She didn't even mean to. Didn't even try. But the magic didn't care about pronunciation. It cared about names . . . and mine? Mine had rung through that cemetery like an oath. A command.

Instead of summoning the beast, a hell hound, she'd summoned *me*, and now I was tied to her. Not just in proximity or energy, but in *will* . . . now, willingly, I'd killed for her. I'd stopped because she told me to.

The worst part? Some sick, snarling part of me *liked it*. Liked the leash. Liked the voice that could call me back from the brink of insanity. Liked her. I wanted her in more ways than I should.

I folded the spell again. Tucked it back into my pocket. I'd have it when we needed it. If ever. But now? Now I'd bought myself a little more time.

I sat still for a moment, the page from the book tucked safely into my pocket, the weight of it both a victory and a problem. I'd bought myself time . . . *But why the fuck did I want it?* My chest thudded once, an ugly, human thing, and I pressed a hand to it, scowling at the treachery of my own body. That wasn't supposed to happen. Not anymore. My Mark burned faintly like it had been stirred awake, already hungry.

I picked up the cherry vape she'd left near the pillow to distract myself and took a slow drag. Sweet. Artificial. Fucking amazing.

It reminded me of something. Not the flavor, but the *idea* of it. The color. Cherry blossoms. Like the ones curled around my tattooed ribs, inked in black and soft rose, crawling through the bones and skulls etched across my skin. *I had cherry on my tongue, blossom on my mind.*

I swear she'd been made to fuck with me personally. Like she was *mine*. That thought, it was a problem. A dangerous, *rooting* kind of problem. That possessiveness had no business blooming in a body like mine, but it already had roots. I'd figured that out last night, when I'd killed that bastard for even thinking he could have a piece of her.

It had to be the magic, the spell, the leash, something. Because otherwise I'd have to admit—No. No. I didn't want to admit it. I didn't want her to *see* it.

Not what she did to me. Not the way I burned every time she looked at me. Not the way I wanted her close and hated the idea of anyone else even touching her. My mind drifted back to today.

Lucian?

That motherfucker filled me with *rage*. More so after flipping through the margins of that book. After seeing the handwriting, the added lines. The intent behind the alterations. Someone had meant to weaponize that spell, and someone had given it to *her*.

She came back into the room and *stretched*. Arms up. Back arched. And her shirt—her fucking shirt—rose with her, dragging up her legs.

No shorts. Just a glimpse of bare thighs. Curved hips. That ass. Oh, she had to be doing this on purpose. *Testing me again.* My cock went rock hard.

Always testing me, aren't you, Final Girl? My fingers twitched against the armrest. I wanted to grab her. Bend her over the bed and remind her exactly what kind of creature she'd summoned.

She caught me staring. Her eyes met mine, wide, curious, almost innocent. Almost. And I glanced away first. She stretched again, longer this time, and looked right at me while she did it. Not innocent. Measured. A tiny, satisfied tilt to her mouth that said she'd clocked the wreckage and decided to press on the bruise.

Fuck.

She flopped onto the bed like she hadn't just shattered my entire nervous system five seconds ago. One leg bent, the other stretched, her oversized T-shirt just barely covering enough to keep me functional. The hem rode up over her hip, exposing the creamy curve of her thigh, lit softly by the bedside lamp, the edge of a ghost tattoo with flowers peeking out like it knew exactly what it was doing.

Gods. She was fucking perfect. This creepy, soft girl who didn't even blink at the god sitting just feet from her. She was so goddamn tempting. I had tasted her . . . and now I needed more. I glared at the ceiling. The floor. The chair leg. *Anything but her.*

"You know," she said, voice light, teasing, "now that you've got the book back . . . you'll finally be rid of me soon."

My jaw locked. There it was. That word again. *Gone. Done. Free.* I snapped before I could stop myself, just a crack, not a break, but sharp enough to make her flinch:

"Is that what you want, Final Girl?" I said.

She sat up a little, startled. "W-what?"

"To be rid of me."

"N-no, I—" she stammered.

I leaned back in the chair, the shadows curling around me like armor.

"Too bad," I said, letting it settle. "Because I've got bad news for you."

She blinked, confused. "What do you mean?"

"The page you used?" I said coolly. "It's gone."

Her body stilled.

"What?"

She lunged for the book, flipping frantically, her fingers trembling as she searched, and there it was: the torn edge. A ragged scar where the spell had once lived. Her face paled. For half a heartbeat I almost told her. Almost. Then the old instinct—deny, delay, protect the advantage—snapped my mouth shut like a trap.

"But I—it was right here—" she looked up at me, wide-eyed.

I just shrugged. I let her sit with it. Because *yeah*, I had it safe in my pocket. But she didn't need to know that. Not yet.

No . . . I was thinking. Thinking about *her*. About this bond. About the way my name sounded in her voice, the way she kissed me like it meant something, the way her eyes sparkled every time she tested me.

I was thinking about telling her things I hadn't said aloud in centuries. Things about *what* I really was. *Who*. How far would she really go? If she knew? If I gave her the truth? Or worse . . .

If I gave her *me*.

Opal clutched the book, still turned to the torn edge. Like if she stared at it long enough, the spell would come back. Like this whole thing could go back to *before*.

It couldn't, I wasn't about to let it.

"Cain?" she pressed, eyes searching mine. "Why would someone take it?"

I exhaled slow, cherry-sweet vapor clouding the air between us. "Lots of reasons," I said finally. "Power. Knowledge. Control."

I leaned forward a little, elbows on my knees. "Maybe someone wanted to use it for themselves. Maybe someone wanted to keep it from being undone."

Her eyes narrowed. "But I'm the one who used it."

I just nodded. Exactly. Her gaze sharpened, suspicious now. "You don't seem that surprised."

I smirked, slow and tired. "I've seen a lot of things, Final Girl."

"But you haven't seen *this*," she whispered. "You told me. This wasn't supposed to work."

I leaned back again, head hitting the chair like gravity had finally won.

"No," I said quietly. "It wasn't."

I stared at the ceiling, bored with honesty, then did something I shouldn't. "You know I kill people by touching them, right?" The words came out flat, scalpel sharp. I wanted them to cut. I liked watching her flinch.

Except, she didn't.

Opal's head snapped up, eyes too wide, too alive. "Yeah?" she said carefully.

I didn't look at her. Couldn't. She was cross-legged on the bed, the book open between her thighs, pink hair falling down her shoulder like spun sugar. Fragile.

Stupidly soft. Everything about her screamed alive in a way that made my teeth ache.

I forced my eyes to the wall, to the shadows crawling across the plaster. Focus. Stay still. Don't grab. Don't ruin it.

"I can't control it," I said. "It's not a curse I flip off when I'm in a good mood. Not a weapon I draw when I want to make a point." My tone was detached, but my chest was tight. My hands flexed once on my knees.

Silence. Her silence. Always pulling the truth out of me like hooks under skin.

"What . . . does that mean?" she whispered.

My jaw clenched. Talking about this felt like chewing glass. "I kill everything I touch," I said, quieter now. "Whether I want to or not."

My fingers dragged through my hair, harsher than I meant. Starving. Wanting. I hated how the confession shook loose something raw in me.

"There's no exceptions," I went on, sharper now. "No gloves. No safe zones. No romantic loopholes. Touch equals death. End of story."

I finally looked at her, and it was a mistake. She was watching me like she saw more than I wanted to give, and I hated how my voice cracked when I said, "Until you."

Her breath caught. I saw it, felt it. Like her lungs were stitched to mine.

"If we break it," I rasped. "I'll never touch you again."

Her throat bobbed. "And if we . . . don't?"

Her voice was small—careful but steady. Brave in a way that scraped something deep inside me.

"I don't know," I admitted. The words tasted like blood. "This isn't normal. Not a hex, not a contract, not some sigil. It's new. Wrong. Wild. And you—" My voice faltered. My gaze dragged over her, cataloging every detail like it was carved into me. "You don't have an end. No expiration date. No clock ticking down."

The thought rotted in my gut. Would she live forever? Stop aging? Or would she decay slowly, skin sagging, body collapsing, while I stayed the same?

The truth ripped out of me before I could stop it. "Immortality isn't life. It's the longest death sentence anyone's ever written."

The air between us thickened. The lamp hummed.

Then, she moved.

Her hand brushed my arm.

My body went rigid, head falling back like the touch burned. Heat slammed through me, crawling down my spine, curling into the ache I'd buried for centuries. My breath stuttered, feral, caught between a growl and a groan.

I shouldn't let her. I should shove her away. But I didn't. Couldn't.

Her other hand joined the first, dragging up my arms, across my shoulders. My pulse—fuck, my pulse—hammered, a beat I hadn't listened to in decades. My whole body shook with the effort of not snapping, not crushing her against me just to prove I could still feel.

A groan ripped out of me. Uncontrolled. Raw. The sound of starving too long.

"I told you," I muttered, shaking my head, voice fraying. "No one can touch me."

She was already climbing into my lap. Soft thighs pressing into mine. Shirt hem brushing bare skin. Her weight settling against me like temptation made flesh.

My hands clawed into the chair arms, wood splintering under the strain, because if I touched her back, there would be no coming back.

For a second, I let myself imagine it anyway. My hands on her. Her pulse in my grip. The heat. The taste. The ruin.

I hated myself for wanting it. I hated her more for giving it.

But gods help me, I wasn't pushing her away.

"Cain . . ." She breathed my name like it meant something.

And my cock throbbed. I was fucked. So goddamn fucked.

"Can we talk about today?" Her fingers trailed around my neck, brushing my jaw, and my whole body buzzed with it, every nerve screaming to pull her in and lose myself completely.

"No." I forced the word out and opened my eyes. She was fucking beautiful and in my lap. Her lips were pouty and bruised from my kiss earlier. I couldn't stop myself. I reached for her neck and drug her down till her lips met mine just to see what she would do. To test it. My breath fanned over her lips as I whispered. "Is this still fake for you, Final Girl?"

She closed her eyes and shuddered but didn't answer. That's when I saw it. Something moving outside the window. I turned my head, jaw tight, heart pounding.

Lucian was standing across the street. Watching us. Right through the glass. Stone-still. Eyes wide. Face like he'd seen a ghost. Of course he'd be here. The wards would have screamed when the book crossed the threshold.

Or worse . . . me. I smiled darkly, slow and sharp. I bet he wanted his fucking book back. *Oh, you wanna play, fucker? Fine. I'll play.*

My hand slid up to her jaw, fingers firm but careful, tilting her face to mine like she already belonged there, and then I dragged my tongue—slow—from the hollow of her throat up to the soft, perfect curve just beneath her jaw.

She gasped, then moaned. Gods. The sound shot straight through me, raw and needy and so fucking pure it made something ancient curl in me. The sweetest fucking sound I'd ever heard. She couldn't help but grind into me, making my cock throb with need.

My girl.

But I had to stop this before things became even more complicated. She still hadn't seen him. Didn't know Lucian was watching. Didn't know he was getting front-row seats to the part of her he would never touch again. And I wasn't about to let my girl give him anything else.

I hovered over her lips, close enough to kiss, to claim, to ruin, and watched her eyes flutter, breath catching, lips parted like she was begging for it. Instead, I leaned in and whispered, low and smug and full of venom:

"Blossom . . . I think you have company."

Her eyes widened, snapped to the window. And just like that, she scrambled off me, face flushed, shirt tugged down, heart pounding. *Adorable.*

I smirked. Leaned back. Arms over the chair like a king in his throne. Lucian was still there. Still watching. I tilted my head and gave him a lazy, knowing wave.

Enjoy the show, golden boy. Because that? That was just the trailer.

CHAPTER 15

Cain

I stood up, rolled my shoulders, cracked my neck. Time to end this little show. "Put some pants on, Opal," I muttered without looking at her.

I could feel her scrambling behind me like a startled kitten, tripping over her own shame while *he* stood out there like some lovesick ghost haunting the sidewalk.

I grabbed the book off the desk, spine still warm from my hand, and headed for the door. The air outside hit like ice, cool and heavy and silent. Two a.m. It was the witching hour, and Lucian was standing right there, across the street, hands in his pockets, trying to look like he hadn't just been caught spying on us like a pervert.

I stepped into the glow of the streetlamp and let the door slam shut behind me. He stiffened.

Good.

I held up the book in one hand, giving it a little wave like I was auctioning it off. "Looking for this?"

Lucian's face twisted in confusion. I tossed the book, and not gently. It smacked him square in the chest, and he stumbled back, arms catching it awkwardly.

He looked down at it like it had bitten him. "How the fuck did you get this?"

I smiled, slow, sharp. The kind of smile meant to cut. "Did you really think you could hide it from me?"

Something clicked. His hands trembled as he held the book, too surprised. He hadn't even known it was missing. No. He'd come here for her. He just hadn't expected me.

Too late, pretty boy. Your ghost haunts the wrong house now.

I rolled my shoulders, tension buzzing like leftover static. My body begged for violence. Needed it. Her touch still lingered on my skin, soft, deliberate, devastating, and I hated him more for ever having it first.

He'd had his chance. He'd left her, and I? I don't let go of what's mine.

"You lost your shot," I told him. My voice was flat, almost bored, but the promise underneath it was a knife's edge. "I don't give second chances. She may not know it yet, but . . . she's already mine."

Lucian's face twisted. No masks this time. No polished smile. Just anger. Ugly and real.

The book dropped to the pavement with a dull thud as he lunged, fury rolling off him in waves.

I let him.

Let him swing. Let him believe he could land a hit. Because Lucian had no idea who he was aiming at, and I wasn't about to tell him. Better to watch him figure it out.

His fist cut through empty air when I slid into the shadows. One second, flesh and bone, the next, smoke. I was gone.

Darkness curled around me like it recognized its master, and why wouldn't it? I was the cold breath at the nape of people's necks. The whisper in the hallway at midnight. The reason children hid under their blankets when the lights went out.

I reappeared behind him and whispered, "So close."

He spun, wild-eyed, chest heaving. "What the hell are you?"

I crooked my head, eyes narrowing. "Better question: What the hell are *you* mixed up in?"

He froze. Just for a second, but I saw it. That twitch in his jaw. That guilt.

I smiled, cruel and knowing. The shadows thickened at my feet, spreading, hungry. "You think I don't smell it on you? The rot clinging to your soul? You've dipped your hands in something dark, pretty boy. Blood, magic, cults, whatever the hell it is, it reeks. She deserves better than that."

His fists clenched, knuckles white. "That's why I left her." His voice cracked, raw. "To protect her from it. From me. From what I was becoming."

For once, I almost believed him. Almost.

"At least you did one thing right," I said flatly. "One redeemable feature in an otherwise pathetic résumé."

I let the words sink in, sharp as razors. Then, I leaned closer, shadows curling like smoke at my shoulders. "But don't make the mistake of thinking that it buys you anything with me. Or with her."

Lucian's face hardened, eyes flicking toward Opal's window. His lips parted like he wanted to explain, to beg, to fight, but he didn't.

He whirled and tried again, missing again. I didn't do it for *him*. One touch from me, and he'd be a corpse on her front lawn. No, I did it for *Opal*. Because she didn't need blood on her hands tonight, not even his, and because I'd promised.

Lucian glanced around, chest heaving, panicked now. "What the fuck are you?!"

I stepped out of the shadows again, just a few feet away. Smirking. Calm. Watching him come undone.

"You can't just waltz into her life and *claim* her!" he shouted, voice cracking with something too close to desperation.

I huffed. "You *abandoned* her," I said, the words low and heavy. "You left her for dead." He tensed, and I leaned in. "Left her with *me* all bloody and gift-wrapped in a cemetery like a sacrifice just for me," I whispered. "And I liked what I saw. All pretty and sweet and so very alone."

He spun, fists raised, teeth clenched.

"She's not yours!" he snapped. "Whatever the fuck you are, *stay away from her!*"

"No," I said, voice smooth as the smoke that curled from my lips. "I don't think I will." I smiled, the kind of smile you only give someone *after* they've already lost.

The words hung sharp in the air as the shadows stirred, thick as tar. They bled along the pavement, pooled across his shoes, then blanketed him in black. Lucian stiffened, body jerking as if the night itself had swallowed him whole.

He clawed at it, panic splintering across his face. He couldn't see. Couldn't breathe. My shadows pressed in, curling down his throat, stroking his skin like icy fingers.

I stepped forward, calm, letting the nightmare wrap him tighter. "I'm not smoke. I'm not illusion. I'm every monster you ever thought hid under your bed." My voice was low, cold, absolute. "And now you know why people are afraid of the dark."

I snapped my fingers, and the shadows peeled back, hissing as they slipped into my skin. Lucian staggered, coughing, chest heaving, panic written all over him. For a second, he just glared at me. His jaw hardened, his hands shook as he wiped his mouth, fury masking the fear.

"You think you're better than me?" he spat. "You think you can just take her, and I'll stand here watching? Whatever the fuck you are, you're worse than anything I've ever touched. Worse than the blood. You're evil." His voice cracked, but he forced the words out anyway. "And I'll get rid of you."

He glanced at the book lying on the pavement. His gaze lingered too long. Heavy. Meaningful.

Ah. There it was.

I tilted my head, a smile curling slow across my lips. "Going to use that, pretty boy?" I asked, voice a velvet taunt. "Crack open a grimoire you barely understand, hope it bites me before it eats you alive?"

Lucian's glare hardened, but the flicker of guilt betrayed him. He didn't know what he was doing. Not really.

"You won't last," he said, jaw tight. "I'll find a way. I'll use it if I have to. You don't belong here."

I stepped closer, shadows curling lazily around my ankles like wolves stretching after a long nap. "You're right," I said flatly. "I don't belong here. But neither do you. And the difference is"—I leaned in, close enough for him to feel the cold radiating off me—"she chose me anyway."

Lucian flinched, fury clashing with something like grief. His fists clenched, shoulders trembling.

I smirked, cruel and certain. "You think I'm evil? You're dead wrong. I'm not evil. I'm inevitable."

I didn't need to kill him tonight. Just to let him know. To show him what hunted in the dark.

"I think I'll stay," I said casually. I turned my head just enough to catch the outline of her slowly appearing on the porch, framed in soft lamplight. She had changed into a black tank top and ripped jeans that were clinging to legs that had been wrapped around me not long ago. She looked like defiance. Like temptation made flesh.

Like *mine*.

Lucian moved fast. Like he was going to be the hero. Like he was going to *save* her.

"Opal!" he shouted. "Get away from him. He's not human!"

Nope. Just *fucking* no.

He ran like he planned to come between us, to *touch* what was mine, and there was no fucking way I was letting that happen. The shadows curled around me like smoke, and I let them take me. One heartbeat, and I was *there*. My arms around her, my breath at her ear, pressed to my chest, warm and steady.

Lucian skidded to a stop.

Too late. Always too late.

Opal looked up at me, heart racing under my palm. She didn't flinch. Didn't pull away. She just whispered, "I know."

Then the world *ripped*, and we disappeared into the dark. Together.

Opal

We appeared in Cain's car. Same black leather, same shadows pressed into the floorboards. He was gripping the steering wheel like it had personally offended him. Jaw tight. Tattoos flexing across his arms with every twitch of muscle.

He was pissed. *Raw* in all the wrong ways, and maybe all the right ones too.

"I need to get away from him before I actually kill him," he muttered, the words vibrating through the silence. He sighed like murder was just another bullet point on his to-do list. "I don't think you'd be happy with me if I did."

I didn't respond, because he wasn't wrong, but also because part of me wasn't sure *how* I felt about it.

He started driving.

Three a.m.

The city was glowing: neon signs, street lamps, low jazz bleeding out of a cracked bar door. Everything felt unreal. Like we were between worlds.

We didn't talk much after that. Just drove. Let the road unravel under us while music poured through the speakers. Some of my favorite songs played—haunted indie ballads, slow and sad, mixed with gritty rock he seemed to like too. I noticed the way he hummed under his breath. Off-key. A cherry vape passed between us like a peace offering. We didn't say it aloud, but something was shifting.

We weren't just girl and ghost. Not just the one with the leash and the monster on the other end. It was becoming something else. More than friends. More than summoned and summoner. Still dangerous. Still way too complicated. But there was a pull now. Like gravity or fate but probably both. Neither one of us was brave enough to defy it.

Maybe I was still stupid, maybe I'd still end up dead, but I wanted to see where this would go. Cain pulled off the main road, weaving through alleys until we stopped downtown.

The lights were soft here. Pretty. Shimmering against puddles from some forgotten rain. Without a word, he got out of the car. Quietly, I got out of the car and joined him. He was standing on the edge of the street, leaning against the car, shoulders tense, eyes fixed upward like he was studying the stars.

There were no stars tonight. Only the reflection of a thousand windows blinking back at us. A skyscraper towered above, lit from within like a vein of light carved into the dark. He was still sucking on that damn cherry vape, shadows curling at his heels like loyal pets.

I bumped him with my hip. Playful. Testing. Trying to ease the tension I could *feel* coiled under his skin. He didn't flinch, but his hand found my waist. Firm, warm . . . and then—we were gone.

The wind shifted, and we reappeared at the top of the building. I stumbled, and it felt like the wind caught me. The spire rose above us like the crown of some long-dead god, humming with static and electricity. The city sprawled out in every direction, alive, flickering, golden.

Cain leaned on the railing, his profile sharp against the skyline. The wind played with his hair, tugging strands across his face like they belonged to it.

He didn't look at me.

Just stared out at the world like he'd seen it a million times and was still trying to decide if it was worth the trouble. He looked like something forged in fire. Dark and eternal and beautiful. Smoke curled from a face framed by moonlight and the neon glow of the city below.

His breathing was ragged.

I could feel it before I heard it, the rise and fall of his chest just inches from mine, too fast, too heavy. Like holding back had become something *violent* in him. Like the only thing keeping him from falling apart was *me*.

"Tell me not to touch you," he said, the words a low snarl threaded with desperation. His hands were clenched at his sides like it took everything in him not to reach for me. "Tell me to walk away. Give me one reason—one fucking reason—and I'll go."

His voice cracked near the end. Not with weakness. With *restraint*.

My throat burned. My heart beat too fast, too loud, trying to climb out of my chest.

"I can't," I whispered.

My whole body trembled with it. The air between us snapped tight. Cain flinched like the words had physically hit him. Then, his jaw locked. His voice turned sharp, almost *frayed*.

"Then *say it*."

The words fell between us like a blade, but I couldn't. I couldn't lie either. I couldn't pretend I didn't want his hands on me, his mouth, his *everything*. I couldn't act like I hadn't already let him in, under my skin, into my blood, past every defense I swore I'd keep.

So, I stayed silent, and in that silence, he stepped closer. His lips hovered over mine—not quite touching, but so *close* I could taste the promise there. Smoke and shadow and something ancient clawing its way up from whatever dark pit he called a soul.

Finally, he broke the silence. "Is this really what you want?" he asked, voice rough. It wasn't bitter. Wasn't mocking. Just . . . tired. Like he didn't understand *why*. Like he didn't think he *should* be wanted. Like he was *begging* for a reason to stop.

I stood beside him, heart racing so fast I could barely draw a breath. He still hadn't looked at me, but I could *feel* it. Building between us. Buzzing under my skin, in my ribs, in the space where our bond pulsed, alive and ready. Like the air right before lightning strikes.

"I don't know what this is," I said softly, echoing the words he'd once thrown at me in the dark. "But I'm falling, Cain."

His eyes lifted and *god*—something ancient glared back, but also . . . something human. So human it hurt. His mouth opened like he might deny it, might lash out, but I didn't stop.

"Even if it's too soon to name it," I whispered, voice cracking, "even if it kills me . . . I'm falling for you."

He stared at me for one long, agonizing beat, and he did the last thing I expected. He took a step *back*. Shoulders tight. Chest heaving. Like he was *terrified* of what I'd just given him.

His voice came out broken. "Tell me to leave." He shook his head, jaw trembling. "Tell me this is just the bond. That it's magic. That it's fake. That we just need to break this spell and be done. Please, Opal." His hand hovered at his heart. "Because if you want me the way I want you—if this is *real*—I won't be able to stop."

I smiled at him. "We both know I'm not that smart," I teased, and he gave me a half-cocked grin. The wind caught the strands of my hair and tugged them like it was trying to carry my words away, but I didn't take them back. He nodded. Just once. That small, heavy nod that said *I hear you. I feel it too.*

Then: "Do you trust me?" he asked, stepping closer.

I didn't hesitate. "Yes." His eyes searched mine for a beat longer, and then he pulled me close. Hands firm at my waist, dragging me flush against him so quickly I gasped. The city lights disappeared behind his shadow.

His lips hovered just above mine, *just* close enough to feel, not close enough to taste. I pressed in, lips parting instinctively, but he pulled back, grinning. That grin. *Wicked.* Like this was a game. Like *he* was the prize. His breath brushed my lips, and every time I moved, every time I tried to close the gap, he shifted, just out of reach.

"No fair," I whispered, chasing his mouth.

He laughed, dark, low, amused. "Isn't it?" His fingers slipped under the hem of my shirt, rough hands skating over bare skin. Up my sides. Down my back. Pulling. Pushing. Guiding.

My knees nearly gave out. My heart beat so hard I could feel it in my throat.

"Do you trust me with your life?" he murmured, voice velvet-wrapped danger.

I nodded, breathless. "Yes."

His nose brushed mine. Lips grazing. Unbearable.

He whispered, "Then you should know what it's like . . ." His hands slid up my arms, sending shivers chasing his touch. "To *date* Death." And before I could answer, before I could *beg* . . .

He gripped my arms and kissed me. Deep and hard and desperate. He devoured me. This man wasn't gentle. He didn't kiss like he was afraid or shy. He kissed me like I was everything, like he wanted to destroy me with just this kiss.

And then . . . he *pulled*, hard and sharp. Toppled us both over the railing of the building, taking me with him. And we *fell*.

The world dropped out from under me. The wind screamed past my ears, my stomach shot into my throat, and my scream never made it out. Because Cain's mouth was *still on mine*.

We were falling.

The city spun in blurs of neon and night around us, skyscrapers slicing upward like jagged teeth, but all I could feel was *him*. His lips devouring mine like this was his last moment on Earth. And maybe it was. Maybe that was how Death kissed.

Like the end.

My arms wrapped around his shoulders on instinct, because if I didn't hold on, I'd come undone. Not from the fall. Not from fear. From *him*.

His tongue slid past my lips, and my breath hitched. There was nothing gentle about it. This wasn't some soft, testing kiss. This was war. It was him telling me without words that I'd chosen this. That I was *his*.

My fingers curled into his shirt, clutching, grounding. The wind roared past us, but he was calm. *Unbothered.* Like gravity didn't apply to him. Like the air *belonged* to him.

In that moment, falling through the sky with my lips crushed to his, every nerve lit like a fuse, I realized something terrifying and true. I wasn't scared. Not of him. Not of this.

I felt *alive* like I never had before, and as the city screamed up to meet us, I kissed him harder. Because if I was going to fall . . . it was going to be with Death.

Then suddenly, we were gone again. No crash. No impact. No death.

Just air, and Cain catching me like I was falling out of nothing. One second, I was plummeting through the sky, heart in my throat.

The next?

I was curled in his arms, cradled against his chest like I weighed nothing, like I *was* nothing compared to the force of him. His body was warm and unshakable.

I looked up at him, dazed, blinking hard, and before I could say anything, before I could breathe, he leaned down. Not for a soft, slow, asking kiss. He slid his tongue into my mouth like he *owned* it. Like he owned *me*. And I let him.

God, I let him.

Because this wasn't some boy with a big credit line and a pretty car. This was *Death*, pressing me into him like the world could fall apart around us and he wouldn't flinch.

My body melted. I forgot what words were. He kissed me like he was drowning in me, and I let him pull me under. When he finally pulled back, his eyes were glowing again.

Smug, hungry, and wild.

I didn't notice when he moved, only that the next second, I was back in the car, breathless and shaking, heart stuttering like it was trying to restart.

Cain slid behind the wheel, cool and unbothered, like he hadn't just rewired my soul. I sat there, wrecked, completely obsessed, and utterly, hopelessly *his*.

CHAPTER 16

Cain

The car was quiet. Like the air hadn't caught up to what we'd done yet. She sat curled in the passenger seat, still catching her breath, pressing her thighs together like she could trap whatever I'd just awakened inside her.

And fuck, I could feel it. The tension, the heat. The pulse in her neck fluttering like a live wire. Her skin flushed, mouth still kiss-bruised, heart still racing. And all of it was mine.

I rested my hand on her thigh. She jumped just a little. That didn't stop me. My thumb started moving, small, slow circles. Rhythmic. Thoughtless. She pressed her thighs tighter. Like she was trying to contain it. Contain me. *Good luck with that, Blossom.*

I felt her swallow. Watched her try to breathe normal again. I smirked. Turned down a side street. We were almost home when something shifted in the air. I stilled. Pulled the car into the lot like nothing had changed, but my body had already gone cold. The shadows were shifting around me as I stepped out of the car without a word. I didn't wait for her to follow, I just took the stairs two at a time. Her door was ajar.

No.

I shoved it open. Her apartment was torn to shit. The place looked like a homicide scene without the courtesy of a body. Drawers yanked, shelves smashed, bones scattered like confetti at a funeral. Her articulated cat was shattered across the floor. Her pink hell had been gutted.

I didn't even have to guess. Lucian. Fucking Lucian. I was crouched on the floor when she walked in. One hand cradling what was left of her articulated cat skeleton, delicate ribs cracked down the center, tail snapped.

"Oh my god . . ." she whispered, freezing in the doorway. She stepped past me, eyes sweeping across the carnage.

Photos knocked off the wall. Pages from her notebook torn and scattered. Clothes strewn across the floor like someone had tried to strip her identity out of the space.

"What happened?" she asked, voice tight.

I stood, cat bones still in hand, scowling like it would make the answer any less obvious.

"I'll give you one guess," I said, voice flat.

Her eyes met mine. I crossed my arms. "Can I please just kill him already?" I asked, only half-joking. She side-eyed me like she wasn't sure if I meant it. I did.

Eventually, I couldn't hold it in anymore. I leaned against the doorframe and asked, flat out, "What did you ever see in that guy anyway?"

She paused, kneeling by a stack of bent photos, and gave a half-assed shrug like even she didn't know anymore. "He was . . . familiar."

"Familiar?" I echoed, incredulous. "That's it?"

"I don't know," she muttered. "Maybe I just got used to him."

I stared. That wasn't an answer. That was a coping mechanism. I stepped closer, arms still folded.

"I mean, really," I said, tone sharper now. "Was he just that good in bed? Massive cock? Magic tongue? What was it?"

She looked away, flushing. "He was . . . okay."

I blinked. Then I laughed. Low. Deep. A little cruel. "Just okay, huh?" I whispered near her ear, breath hot. "Good to know." Because me? I didn't do "okay." I was fully planning on counting the number of times she orgasmed, planning on seeing exactly how much she could take before she broke, on seeing how loud she could get.

She was still kneeling, trying to sort through the wreckage, pretending she wasn't trembling from the way I'd looked at her. My Little Ghoul, trying to play ghost with the god in the room.

I leaned on the wall, arms crossed, and let a slow, wicked grin curve across my face. She glanced up and she knew. Knew exactly what that smile meant.

Trouble.

"Little Ghoul," I said, voice smooth as a mortician's suit and feral underneath, "I'll make you come so hard you forget how to pronounce his name."

She backed up one careful knee-shuffle, a laugh catching like silk on teeth. Her eyes flicked to mine. *Play or run? Gods, please run. I like the chase.*

"You think I'm joking?" I took one predator's step forward.

She tried to recover. Put some sass in her tone. "Please . . . Everyone knows that's not a real thing."

I stopped mid-step. The grin slipped from my face. I tilted my head, studying her.

"What's not real?"

She shrugged, a little too casual now. "Girls don't actually . . . you know. Come. That's just something people say."

I stared. Blank. Then—laughter, but there was no humor in it, just disbelief.

"Let me guess," I said. "Golden boy was your first. Told you that, didn't he?"

"Maybe I'm just broken," she said, half-laughing, half-pleading. "Lucian said some girls are."

"Broken?" I echoed, voice low. A dangerous calm. "No, Blossom. You're not broken. You were lied to."

Her laugh faltered.

I stepped in close. Real close. So close my shadow climbed over hers. "That idiot wouldn't know what to do with a woman if the instructions were carved into her skin." My voice dropped, a rasp against her mouth. "You're not the problem. He is."

I brushed a thumb under her chin, coaxing her gaze up to mine. "You think the fault's with you? That your body forgot how to feel? No." I leaned in, close enough that my breath shivered across her lips. "It's waiting for the right hands. The right mouth. The right death to wake it."

Her breath hitched. The tremor in her throat told me she heard it, what I wasn't saying. That I'd make it right. That I'd make her *remember*.

"Pathetic," I whispered.

Not her. Him. Fucking disgrace. I reached out, fingers brushing under her chin, tilting her face up to mine.

"You don't even know what you've been missing," I murmured, voice like smoke wrapping around her spine. "But that's fine." My thumb brushed over her hipbone, under the hem of her shirt, tracing circles against bare skin that twitched under my touch. "Because I'll show you, Blossom." I grinned. "Not gently either," I said, letting the words lick across her skin. "Not kindly. You won't get romance from me, Blossom." My other hand slid around her waist, pulling her to me. I was done playing pretend.

I kissed the corner of her mouth. Not sweetly. Not softly. Just enough to make her ache for the rest. Another inch. My lips grazed her jaw. Then her neck. My breath hot against her pulse. "I'll ruin you."

She whimpered, and gods, that sound. That sound was mine now.

"I'll make your body remember me. Long after you forget how to speak."

Her legs buckled slightly, but I caught her. Held her firm. "You'll come on my tongue. On my fingers. On my cock. Until the only thing you can say is my name." Her lashes fluttered. I let her see my teeth. "Still think it's not real?"

She held my stare, and the smirk lit. "Prove it."

Oh, Final Girl. Bless your wicked little heart.

"I'll tell you what," I growled, my teeth grazing the delicate skin of her neck. She shivered, her breath hitching as I nipped sharply at her pulse point, leaving a mark that would bruise by morning. "I'll make you a deal." My hand slid down her waist, fingers digging into the soft curve of her hip. "If I can make you come with just my tongue, I get whatever I want. If I can't, you get whatever you want."

She laughed, that fucking laugh that made my cock twitch in my pants. "I can already make you do whatever I want, remember?" she teased, her voice dripping with that smug confidence that made me want to ruin her.

"Oh, I haven't forgotten," I snarled, nipping her neck hard again. "I still need to make good on my promise to make you pay for that." That shut her up. She pushed at my chest, testing. I pushed back, firmer, until the backs of her knees kissed the mattress. "You're mine," I warned, voice low. "No backing out now."

"Not gonna happen, killer," she teased, but I could hear the tremor in her voice. She was trying to play it cool, but her body was already betraying her.

"Sounds like a challenge," I said, my lips curling into a wicked smile. "I'll tell you what," I purred, my hands moving to the waistband of her pants. With one solid yank, I peeled them off, leaving her bare and exposed.

I didn't wait for her response. My mouth was on her in an instant, my tongue licking a slow, torturous path up her slit. She gasped, her hips bucking against my face, but I held her down, my hands gripping her thighs with bruising force. Her pussy was already wet, her arousal dripping down her thighs as I teased her clit with the tip of my tongue.

"Fuck," she gasped, her voice breaking as her fingers clawed at my scalp, pulling me closer, deeper. Her hips bucked against my face, but I held her down with a firm grip on her thighs, pinning her to the bed.

"Go ahead and fight it, Little Ghoul," I growled against her thigh, my voice dripping with menace. "It's still going to happen." I sucked her clit into my mouth, swirling my tongue around it in tight, relentless circles. Her moans turned into desperate whimpers, her body writhing under my touch as I pushed her closer and closer to the edge. She tried to pull away again, but I tightened my grip, my fingers digging into the soft flesh of her thighs as I held her in place.

"Cain, please," she begged, her voice trembling with a mix of fear and desire.

"Just don't come," I interrupted, my voice dark and commanding. "That's all you have to do. Prove me wrong." I sucked harder, faster, my tongue working her clit with a precision that had her screaming my name. I could feel her orgasm building like a storm, ready to break, but she was still fighting it, still trying to hold back, and that only made me more determined to make her come.

Her body tensed, her muscles tightening as she tried to resist, but it was no use. With one final flick of my tongue, she came undone. Her scream echoed through the room, raw and primal, as her orgasm ripped through her like a fucking earthquake. I pulled back, licking my lips as I looked up at her, a wicked grin spreading across my face.

"Cain," she whispered, soft as silk, "don't stop."

The command slid into me like a key turning a lock. Power snapped tight throughout my body, and I had to brace a hand on the mattress to keep from shaking apart. I could feel her feel it, the way the air changed, the way the shadows went still like they were listening for more orders.

"Fuck," I breathed, and she laughed, because she'd wanted that reaction. She stretched under me on purpose, slow and languid, clocking my wrecked control, and pressed on the bruise.

I crowded closer, mouth teasing, never quite giving. "You want more?"

Her fingers curled in my shirt. "Cain," she said again, throatier, bolder now, "more."

It hit harder the second time. My will slid, obedient, into the groove of her want. I was still the blade, but she had the grip and angle. I kissed her like surrender was a language and I was fluent, like she'd called me up from the dark and I was grateful for the work.

I rose like a predator claiming its kill, my cock already straining against the confines of my pants, hard as fucking steel. I didn't waste a second. My fingers fumbled with the zipper, the sound of it tearing open like a gunshot in the silence. My cock sprang free, thick and throbbing, veins pulsing with the need to bury myself deep inside her.

I didn't give her a chance to recover, didn't let her catch her breath. My hands gripped her hips, fingers digging into her soft flesh as I lined myself up with her dripping cunt. She was still quivering from her last orgasm, her pussy begging to be filled. I didn't hesitate.

I drove into her like a coffin nail, my hard length stretching her wide, forcing her to take every inch of me. She gasped, her back arching off the bed, but I didn't stop. Her nails clawed at my arms, leaving angry red marks, but I didn't care. Pain was just another way to claim her.

I leaned down, my breath hot against her cheek as I grabbed her jaw, forcing her to look at me. "Open your mouth," I commanded, my voice low and dangerous.

She hesitated, her lips trembling, so I didn't wait. I hooked my thumb into the corner of her mouth, prying it open before sliding my tongue inside. She tasted like desperation and submission, and I fucking loved it.

Her body betrayed her as she tightened around my cock and came again, her moans muffled by my mouth, but I wasn't done. I wasn't even close. Her tits bounced with every thrust, her nipples hard and begging for attention. I reached down, pinching one between my fingers, twisting it just enough to make her whimper.

"You're mine," I snarled, my voice rough with need. "Every fucking inch of you belongs to me."

Her eyes were glazed over, her body limp except for the way she clenched around me, trying to milk every drop of pleasure from me. I could feel my own orgasm building, a tight coil of heat in my gut that threatened to explode. I grabbed her hips harder, pulling her onto me as I fucked her deeper, harder until I was buried to the hilt.

"Come for me again," I demanded, my voice a harsh growl. "I want to feel you fall apart on my cock." And she did. Her body convulsed around me, her screams muffled by my hand over her mouth. I followed her over the edge, my cock pulsing as I filled her with my cum, marking her from the inside out.

When I finally pulled out, she was a trembling mess, her cunt still twitching, my cum dripping out of her. I leaned down, licking a stripe up her neck before biting down hard enough to leave a mark.

"Mine," I whispered against her skin, my voice dark and possessive. "Forever."

I lay back against the mattress, chest rising and falling in slow, steady pulls, the shadows around us finally quiet.

She didn't say anything. Just shifted closer, slipping under my arm like it was natural. Like I hadn't just ruined her on every level and whispered promises I had no right making.

Her fingers curled against my ribs. A sigh against my skin, and then she did it: She nestled into me like I was safe. Like *I* was something good. I should've moved. Should've pushed her off. But I didn't.

I wrapped my arm around her, pressing my nose into her hair and breathing her in like she was the only thing keeping me tethered to this cursed fucking plane.

I hadn't meant to fall asleep, but she was there, and I was so tired. Not from the sex, but from a life that had been lived too long without her. So, I closed my eyes.

And let her have me.

Voices. Arguing. Opal's voice first, sharp and upset . . . but then someone else. *His* voice.

My breath came in a hard, dragged-in pull. I sat up fast, the world slamming back into focus like it had been waiting for me to rejoin it. I was still naked. Still in her bed.

Still surrounded by the scent of her on my skin and every nerve in my body humming like I'd been plugged into a live wire. But the second I heard his voice again? That pleasant afterglow? *Gone.*

Lucian. Fucking Lucian.

I reached blindly for something, *anything*, and of course, the first thing my hand landed on was those *goddamn* Hello Kitty pajama pants. Her pants. Pink. Cartoon kittens. Glittery bow detail. I stared at them like they might bite.

Fuck it.

At this point, I didn't know where my clothes were, what day it was, or how long I'd been asleep, but I knew one thing . . . That piece of shit had no business being outside *her* door. I shoved the pants on, still half in a daze, my teeth already grinding.

"Please, Opal," Lucian said, his voice full of that fake-boyfriend sincerity. "I wasn't thinking straight."

Bullshit.

"I just have some personal stuff I'm dealing with," he continued. "I thought space was the right move, but I was wrong."

Wrong doesn't even begin to cover it.

Opal's voice came next, smaller than I liked. Too soft. Too careful.

"Lucian . . . It's too late."

No.

No, no, no.

That wasn't my girl. Not the one who flirted with Death, who commanded me, who bled in graveyards and wore scars like crowns. Not the girl who looked me in the eye and teased. That voice didn't belong to her.

"That thing isn't even human," he snapped. "It could be dangerous."

Thing? Could be?

I stepped into the doorway.

No shirt. No shoes. Just six feet of ancient death wrapped in fucking *pink pajamas*. Lucian turned and *froze*. His face drained of color like someone had hit a dimmer switch.

His gaze dropped: chest, abs, bruises down my throat, claw marks on my arms and chest, and yeah—the pants. He gave me a once-over, and I watched the exact moment his brain tried to process all the ways he'd already lost.

Then he looked at her. Saw the marks. My marks. Her swollen lips, her bruised throat. The way she was standing like she wasn't sorry. Yeah. I was proud of my work.

I crossed my arms slowly, letting the tattoos stretch over my skin like serpents waking up. "Problem?" I asked, voice low, lazy.

Like I didn't already have a dozen different ways to ruin him ready to go. Lucian didn't answer. He couldn't. He was too busy realizing he was staring at the fucking end of the line, and it was wearing kittens.

"Opal, just step away from him. Slowly."

Lucian's hands were up like I was a wild animal that might bolt or bite. Honestly? Not a bad instinct.

I cocked my head, shadows curling lazily up my forearms like smoke come to life. They coiled around her too, slow, familiar, possessive, and she didn't flinch. Didn't move. Didn't even blink. *Good girl.*

"She's not afraid of me," I said, smiling without warmth. "You should be asking why that is."

"She's not *thinking clearly*," Lucian snapped. "You clearly have some kind of *hold* over her. We can figure this out—"

I laughed. Sharp and cold. Like broken glass in lungs.

"Oh, I *do* have a hold on her," I said, stepping in front of her with the casual confidence of someone who couldn't lose. "But I think it has more to do with my tongue than any magic."

Opal went *scarlet.*

"Cain," she hissed under her breath, smacking my arm with wide eyes.

I laughed. *Worth it.*

Lucian looked like he'd swallowed a knife. "You're disgusting," he snapped, fists clenched.

"And you're boring," I said with a shrug. "Which is worse?"

Wings rustled behind me. Crow. Of course. He always had perfect timing. Bastard loved the drama.

He held out a letter without a word, and I took it, still watching Lucian from the corner of my eye. I cracked the seal, unfolding the parchment.

A wedding invitation. Already checked for a plus one. I almost laughed. It hit me. I turned to Opal, flicking the invitation with two fingers. "I think space is exactly what we need."

Lucian tensed.

Opal blinked. "What?"

I grinned.

"Blossom," I said, stepping closer, "you want to come check out my place for a bit?"

She looked between us, between the trembling ex-boyfriend in his letterman jacket and the immortal creature wearing her *fucking pajamas*.

I saw it click behind her eyes. She nodded. "Yeah. Yeah, actually . . . I do."

Lucian looked like he might explode. "You don't even know what he *is*, Opal!"

"You're right," she said quietly. "But I know what you are."

Oof.

I bit my lip to stop the grin. Almost. I slung an arm over her shoulders and turned us toward the stairs.

"That's right, Blossom," I murmured in her ear. "Big castle, servants, all of it, and yes . . ."

I glanced back at Lucian. Smiled, slow and vicious.

". . . the toilet paper is black."

She snorted. A breathy, almost embarrassed sound that was *so* her. I didn't look away. *It was time my queen saw her kingdom*, and the way she looked at me, wide-eyed, dazed, already half-daring—yeah. She was ready. I met her eyes again and gave her a look that said exactly what I was thinking.

Come with me. Come inside so I can remind you who you belong to, so I can take you apart again, piece by trembling piece.

She blushed. Soundless. Color bloomed in her cheeks like blood in water, and I wondered, how many times could I make her fall apart for me? Three? Four, last night? Maybe more. I'd lost count.

Might've gotten more if I hadn't been so damn eager to—*tch. Focus.* I stepped forward, reaching for her.

"Seriously, Opal," Lucian snapped behind us. "Don't do this."

Gods, he was like a gnat. Persistent. Loud. Completely insignificant. I didn't even look at him. I just turned, hooked one arm behind Opal's knees and scooped her up, bridal-style, smug as sin—*and nearly doubled over from the pain.*

Fuck.

Opal gasped. "Cain?"

I tightened my jaw, holding her closer so she wouldn't see the twitch in my expression.

Not now. Not in front of *him*.

My head spun for a second, a ripple of something sharp clawing under my ribs like someone had jammed a divine needle straight through my sternum.

My curse was deciding to rear its ugly head.

CHAPTER 17

Opal

Cain dumped me onto the mattress like I weighed nothing and immediately bolted for the bathroom. *Not* exactly what I was expecting. I blinked, still dazed, still half-caught in the way his arms had felt around me, until I heard it.

The unmistakable sound of him throwing up. Not just once. Violent, guttural, like his body was rejecting something it had no right to contain.

I sat up fast, eyes darting toward the bathroom door. Crow stood by the window, hands tucked neatly behind his back, expression unreadable. We exchanged glances. Even *he* seemed worried. The moment Cain emerged, I knew why. He looked . . . wrong.

Pale—paler than usual. A cold sweat clung to his skin. There were dark hollows under his eyes like bruises that ran bone-deep, and a thin smear of blood painted the corner of his mouth.

He looked like death, and not the untouchable, cocky version I was used to. This was the real thing. "Cain," I said, rushing to him.

He wavered on his feet. I caught his arm, tried to brace him. He didn't shake me off.

"How long was I asleep?" he asked, his voice low, cracked.

"Three days," I said hesitantly.

He turned to Crow, who was already moving toward us.

"You've been here *nearly two months*, sir," Crow corrected, his tone measured but tight. "How many lives have you taken?"

Cain sat down hard on the bed, like standing had become dangerous.

He swallowed.

"Three."

Crow's brow furrowed. "Three hundred should be fine," he said, already turning back toward the window. "Lucian is leaving."

Cain didn't respond. Didn't move. I glanced back at him just in time to see his head drop into his hands. "No," he muttered. "Just three . . ."

His fingers dug into his hair. Shoulders curled forward. Chest rising too fast, like he couldn't get enough air into lungs that probably didn't need it in the first place. He looked up at me with a pleading look in his eyes, a look I'd never seen him wear, and it scared me.

I sat beside him. Careful. Quiet. "Cain?" I asked, afraid of the answer.

He looked away from me and muttered through his teeth, "It's not supposed to hurt like this."

Crow watched from the window. Like he knew there was nothing to say.

Cain lifted his head. His eyes, normally endless galaxies, were dimmer now, ringed in gray. His voice cracked at the edges and smudged red. "I haven't fed."

"Fed?" I echoed, pulse ticking up. "I thought you couldn't eat?"

He laughed once. Dry. Cruel. At himself. "I don't eat. I don't sleep. I don't breathe." A pause. "I *take*. That's my nature. My duty. My curse."

The words hung in the air like smoke. "I have to end lives, Opal," he said, meeting my eyes with something that looked a lot like shame. "Not because I want to. Not for fun. But because if I don't . . ."

He gestured to himself, shaking, sweating, too pale even for him. "This happens."

"How many do you need to—?"

"Hundreds," Crow answered for him. "Sometimes more."

Cain sighed, low and bitter. "I've been pushing it. Too far. Too long."

"You didn't want me to see," I whispered.

He didn't deny it. He just stood. Slow. Unsteady, but taller again. Stronger now that he'd said it out loud. "You wanted to know what I am, Final Girl?" He didn't wait for my answer. "Time to find out."

The room darkened, shadows curling like smoke at his heels. He held out a hand. "Come with me."

"What happens if I don't?" I asked, voice shaking.

He tilted his head. Smiled that dangerous, broken smile. "You don't have a choice, and I need to reap in volume to fix this."

"How many is volume?" I asked, voice shaking, afraid to know.

He didn't answer. His silence told me everything. *It was a lot.* He reached for me, cool fingers brushing my cheek, too gentle for someone about to become an instrument of mass destruction.

"Stay close," he said. "No matter what you see, do not run from me."

My skin prickled. "And if I do run?"

His mouth curved, slow and cruel. "If you run, I'll chase you," he whispered. "And you won't like the version of me that catches you."

The shadows rose around us like a tidal wave, and then we stepped into the rift.

We stepped out into an empty warehouse yard. The concrete was cracked with weeds filling the gaps, and the windows had been shattered long ago. It looked like the kind of place the world had forgotten, and for good reason. Cain stood still for a moment, the wind tugging at his hoodie, his shoulders hunched beneath the weight of something I didn't yet understand.

Then he turned, cupped my face in both hands. His fingers were cold, *shaking*, and then he kissed me. The kind of kiss that steals your breath.

"What was that for?" I whispered, eyes wide, heart hammering.

He looked at me like I was the only thing he didn't want to lose. "Because after this," he said, voice rough, "you might not want to kiss me again."

I didn't know how to respond.

He looked *worse* than he had before—paler, shadows deeper under his eyes, like something inside him was unraveling. Cain rolled his shoulders back. Popped his neck and smiled. That *smile*. Cold, sharp, deadly, and too wide.

"This has been something of a pet project for me lately," he said, gesturing toward the warehouse. "Usually I bring . . . someone else. A friend. But tonight, it's just you and me."

He glanced sideways at me. "As long as you're bound to me," he said, stepping closer, "you can't be hurt. You can't die. You're safe, even if someone gets close enough to *think* about doing something stupid to you."

His voice dropped, nearly a whisper. "They won't get the chance."

I swallowed hard. "Cain—"

"Don't speak." His eyes lit faintly. Stars flickering in dying galaxies. He walked forward, shadows curling around his boots like they were guiding him. His spine straight. Eyes dead ahead. A can of spray paint dropped from his pocket. Clattered once on the ground.

He caught it mid-roll, kicking it back up into his hand. He turned to me, smiling like a wolf in the middle of a blood moon. "Don't use my name in here," he said. "Just call me Death."

He shook the can once, then knelt at the back of the warehouse, right where the metal siding dipped into crumbling brick. In seconds, he painted a skull. Dripping. Grinning. His mark.

"Claiming it?" I asked.

"Always." He stood. Passed me the can. "Your turn."

I blinked at him. "My . . . What am I supposed to do with this?"

He just raised a brow. So, I crouched and felt stupid. The spray paint hissed. I painted a crooked little ghost beside his skull. Fat, lopsided, with outstretched arms and little "x" eyes.

Cain looked down at it. Smiled. That rare, *real* smile. The one that reached his eyes and made the stars burn a little brighter behind them.

"Perfect," he murmured.

Then, he pulled a knife. Not flashy. Not gilded. Just cold steel. Matte-black handle. Balanced in his hand like he was born to wield it.

I swallowed. "Can't you just touch them?" I asked. "Kill them that way?" He twirled the blade once, the edge catching the light in a flash that made my stomach flip. "Where's the fun in that?" His voice had changed. Not cold. Not quiet. *Controlled.* He was dialing something down. Or maybe up. I couldn't tell.

"Stay close," he added, sliding the knife down his sleeve. "Remember, we only have about a hundred feet before we start running into problems, and just so you know, these men deserve what's coming." Then he turned and burst through a set of twin double doors like a storm made of bone and blade.

Cain stalked into the room like the apocalypse come to collect, black shadows dancing at his heels, that knife spinning in his hand with surgical elegance.

And me? I followed. Because that's what you do when you've tethered yourself to Death. Oopsie.

The first scream didn't shake me. It *froze* me. Like someone had grabbed my spine and slammed it in a freezer. Like the sound had bypassed my ears and carved itself straight into my bones.

Cain had entered the warehouse like an artist, not a soldier. Not a god but a *composer*. A genius on a stage no one saw coming. The men didn't run. Not at first.

Not until the second body dropped, twitching, arterial spray painting a jagged arc across the concrete. The knife hadn't even slowed down. He flipped it once, reversed his grip, and caught the next one in the gut behind him like it was nothing.

The blade sang. That was the only way to describe it. It wasn't just a weapon, it was a voice, and Cain was the mouthpiece of something ancient, something terrible, something *beautiful* in the way wildfires are beautiful when you're miles away and haven't realized the wind is changing.

Some of them dropped instantly. Throats slit. Jugulars split. No ceremony. Others?

He lingered. He watched the light leave their eyes like he was drinking it in.

Cain tilted his head and smiled. My knees nearly buckled, and still—still—I couldn't look away. He was fucking grinning that too-wide grin. Like he was high on the taste of ending lives. Like this was his opera, and every scream, every drop of blood, every gurgling breath was part of the symphony.

He moved with grace, impossible grace, spinning and pivoting and striking like he could *see* the end of time and was choreographing toward it.

It was . . . horrible—and magnificent. I hated the part of me that thought so. Because even as the blood sprayed, even as bodies dropped, even as he carved something into the chest of a man with a slow, brutal drag, I felt the adrenaline spike in my veins like lightning. My body knew. Every part of me knew. I should be *running*.

He was covered in blood now, chest rising with exertion, that grin still carved into his mouth like it had never belonged anywhere else. Then, he *laughed*. Low. Unhinged. Wild. Like the end of the world was the punchline. He turned, just for a second, and looked at me. Eyes shining like galaxies caught fire. And in that moment, I felt it. The danger.

His boots echoed against the concrete. Slow. Inevitable. He twirled the knife once, blood flicking in a lazy arc through the air. Then licked it.

His tongue dragged up the side of the blade like it was a lollipop, casual, unhurried, *hungry*.

He was still smiling, watching me. "You gonna run, Final Girl?" he purred, daring me, like he wanted it.

I didn't answer. Couldn't. Because the way he said it, low and intimate, like he was already inside my thoughts, shot *ice* down my spine and heat right behind it. The kind of burn you didn't come back from.

"Do it," he whispered.

My breath stalled in my chest. My heart screamed.

I *ran*.

Not because I thought I could get away, not really, but because I *wanted* to. Wanted the chase. I wanted him. I couldn't change his need to kill the way I couldn't change my need to breathe.

The air in the warehouse yard was cold. Wet concrete and rust-scented wind slapped my face as I ducked through the cracked doorway, nearly tripping over a fallen beam.

Behind me—*laughter*.

Low. Joyful. A little unhinged. Like he was having the time of his goddamn life. He was perfectly keeping pace, just close enough not to trigger the bond but far enough away to make me think I had a chance.

"Faster, Blossom," he called. "You're not gonna make me *work* for it, are you?"

I sprinted behind a stack of old pallets, breathing hard. My pulse pounded like war drums in my ears. He shouldn't have sounded like that.

So *giddy*. So *alive*. But he *was* alive. On fire. Death, come to dance. I crouched low, hand over my mouth, heart thudding. A shadow passed. I peeked . . . nothing. I blinked. Swallowed, and then—"Boo."

I screamed.

Cain grinned. He was *right there*, face streaked with drying blood, eyes glowing with galaxies that didn't blink. He looked like something out of a nightmare.

I bolted again. This time, I laughed. Just a little. A broken, breathless sound I hadn't meant to make, but god, it slipped out like truth. Because this was *madness*, and part of me liked it.

The sprint. The high. The predator behind me who could've caught me at *any time* but hadn't. Because this wasn't a hunt. It was *foreplay*. Courtship, Cain-style.

The shadows lunged ahead of me, slithering like fingers pointing which way to go.

"Almost caught you, sweetheart," he growled from somewhere too close behind.

I veered. Slipped behind a shipping container, breath ragged, cheeks flushed. This was insane. This was *us*. I didn't know how much longer I could keep running, if I even wanted to.

Maybe that was the point. Because every time he got close . . . every time his fingers brushed the air just behind me, I burned a little more.

I barely made it around the corner before a shadow surged ahead of me—wrong angle, wrong timing, *he was already there*. Cain stepped out of the dark like he *was* the dark.

I skidded to a stop, chest heaving, mouth open on a gasp I promptly forgot how to take. My back hit the wall behind me. He was blocking every exit. He smiled, and it was *feral*. Like he'd tasted blood and wanted something sweeter now.

"End of the line, Final Girl," he said, voice syrup-slow, glinting with the kind of danger you didn't walk away from unchanged. "You run real pretty, you know that?"

My legs were trembling. Not from fear, not . . . exactly.

He peeled his hoodie off as he stalked toward me. The shirt underneath followed, landing on the floor in a wet heap. A show. He stepped closer, the knife still in his hand. His body lit in blood and moonlight and menace, muscles slick with the aftermath of the hunt.

Tattoos crawled like vines up his arms and throat, ink shimmering faintly where the blood hadn't dried yet. He looked like a god who had crawled out of hell, taken one look at the world, and decided to burn it down, and he wanted *me* next.

"You like being chased, don't you?" he asked, voice velvet and gravel.

I tried to shake my head, but he pointed the knife at me.

"Don't lie to me. I can tell when you're lying." My breathing gave me away. My stare. My pulse hammering against the base of my throat like a warning that had turned into a *want*.

"Yes." The words came out shaky and weak, and he grinned.

He moved closer. Close enough I could see the flecks of crimson drying on his jaw. His eyes burned like twin supernovas, wild, hungry, *mine*.

"Say it," he whispered, caging me in with one hand against the wall beside my head. He brought the knife up to my throat.

"What?" I breathed.

"That you wanted it."

My skin prickled. My knees wobbled. His fingers ghosted up my waist, slow and possessive, until they curled at the base of my spine. He ran the knife down the hollow of my neck and to my breasts. He was a predator, high off the kill, and I was his prey, cornered, trembling, and fucking ready.

His blade was still there running up my neck, sharp enough to raise goosebumps, deliberate enough to make my breath stutter. My heart thundered against my ribcage like it wanted to throw itself at him. Cain's eyes didn't waver. Didn't blink.

He was *buzzing*, high off the hunt, lit from the inside out with a vicious sort of euphoria. The kind that came only after bloodshed. The kind that said *I won*.

And I—I had *never* seen him like this.

The knife traced upward, dragging slowly along the curve of my collarbone, gliding over the fragile line of my throat until it rested at the underside of my jaw.

I tilted my chin up. Offered it. His eyes flicked to mine. Something *broke* in them. A sound left his throat, low, animal, reverent. Not quite a growl, not quite a moan. Just a *need* made audible.

"You wanted this," he rasped. "You *ran* from me."

"Yes," I breathed, heat flooding my skin.

"You don't run from me," he growled against my skin. "Not unless you want to be *ruined*."

I gasped, digging my nails into his back, clinging to the monster I'd summoned and wanted and *craved* like a sickness.

"You already did," I whispered.

He laughed, low and broken and dangerous.

"Then I guess I'll finish what I started."

His mouth crashed into mine. He consumed me like he was starving, like the taste of me was the only thing that could burn the blood off his tongue. His lips were punishing, biting, devouring, desperate. Tongue slick and greedy, hands gripping my waist like he was holding onto sanity by a thread.

The knife pressed tighter against my jaw—not enough to cut, just enough to remind me what he was.

What I'd chosen. He kissed like he was marking territory. Like the game was over and this was his *victory*.

My back slammed harder into the wall. His hips pinned me there, every line of his body carved from chaos and want. He kissed me until I forgot my name. Until the only word I remembered was his.

Cain.

His free hand tangled in my hair, tilting my head further, taking more. His lips dragged across my cheek down to my throat, where his breath scorched the place the knife had been.

His fingers trailed down to my thigh slowly, tenderly, sending shivers up my spine. They hooked under the hem of my skirt, and with one sharp tug, my panties were gone, shredded into nothing but scraps of lace. The cool air hit my core, making me gasp, but Cain didn't give me a moment to recover. He grabbed me by the hips, lifting me like I weighed nothing, and slammed me back against the wall, his mouth finding mine again.

My hands were gripping his shoulders, nails digging into his skin as he pressed himself against me. His cock, hard, thick, and already leaking, was grinding against my clit, making me whimper. He was relentless, ruthless, and I fucking loved it.

"You wanted this," he whispered, his breath hot against my ear. "You wanted me to catch you. To fuck you until you couldn't walk. Until you were nothing but a limp, writhing mess on my dick."

The worst part of this all? The part I couldn't admit out loud? I did. I fucking did.

He didn't wait for an answer. His lips crashed into mine again, swallowing my moans as his tongue invaded my mouth. He pulled away just long enough to spit into his hand, the sound crude and obscene, before wrapping his fingers around his cock. He was desperate now, his strokes rough and frantic, as he lined himself up with my entrance. I could feel the heat of him, the way he pulsed with need, and I wanted him inside me more than I'd ever wanted anything.

"Say it," he demanded, his voice a dark, menacing growl. "Say you want it."

"I want it," I gasped, my voice trembling. "I want you. Fuck me, Cain. Please."

"Bad girl." He smiled. With one brutal thrust, he was inside me, filling me to the hilt. I cried out, my nails digging into his back as he started to move. He fucked me like he was trying to break me, each thrust deeper, harder than the last. My body was shaking, my legs wrapped around his waist as he pounded into me, the sound of skin against skin echoing through the room.

"Fuck," he grunted, his voice rough with desire. "You feel so damn good, Blossom. So tight, so wet."

I was losing myself in him, in the way he moved, in the way he claimed me. My orgasm was building, coiling deep in my core, and I knew I wouldn't last long. He was relentless, his pace never slowing, his cock hitting that spot inside me that made me see stars.

"Cain," I moaned, my voice breaking. "I'm close. I'm so close."

Then he did something that made me scream. He reached down between us, his thumb finding my clit and rubbing it in tight, fast circles. It was too much, too fast, and I couldn't hold back. My orgasm hit me like a tidal wave, crashing over me, making my body convulse around him. He groaned, his hips stuttering as he followed me over the edge, his cock pulsing as he spilled himself inside me.

We stayed like that for what felt like forever, his forehead pressed against mine, our breaths mingling in the air. I didn't want to let go, not yet. If I did, I was afraid I'd lose him. Maybe forever, by the way he was looking at me.

CHAPTER 18

Cain

She was still wrapped around me. Body trembling. Skin flushed. Nails still buried faintly in my back like she didn't want to let go . . . or didn't know how to yet. I didn't move. Not because I couldn't. Because I didn't *want* to.

She was weak in my arms, breath hitching like she'd barely survived something . . . and maybe she had. Me.

I had been inside her. Still was. I should've pulled back. Should've said something. Instead, I buried my face in her throat and just breathed her in. Vanilla. Marshmallow. Cherry. Blood. Okay, the blood was me, and probably the cherry too, but the smell was intoxicating.

She had run. Not because she was afraid of me. She still wasn't afraid of me. That much was clear. She hadn't been afraid. Not when I killed. Not when I chased. Not when I caught her and showed her exactly what kind of monster I was. And still—*still*—I didn't know how long I could keep her.

My hands curled tighter around her thighs. I didn't want to let her go. Could we stay like this forever?

She shifted faintly. A soft sound escaped her lips, part sigh, part aftershock, and I felt it again. That sharp twist behind my ribs. Not hunger. Something worse.

I pulled back slowly.

"You saw me," I murmured, voice catching in my throat. "All of me."

Not just the kiss. Not just the skin and heat and hunger. The *other* parts. The broken parts. The blade, the blood, the beast that tore through men like they were paper and then kissed her like she was a prayer I never should've learned.

She blinked slowly. Met my eyes. Didn't flinch.

Fuck.

That made it worse. I'd rather she screamed. Shoved me away. Glared at me like the monster I was. Instead, she looked at me like I was still *him*, the one she whispered to, trusted, the man she *chose*.

"Say something, Final Girl," I said, my voice fraying at the edges, sharp with self-loathing.

She smiled. Faint. Crooked. "You already know."

My body locked up. "No," I said, too fast. Too raw. Too fucking *afraid*. Because I *didn't* know. Because if I let myself believe, if I *hoped* for a second that she still wanted me after this, it would *break* me if I was wrong. I buried my face in her neck. Not out of lust. Not out of triumph. But because I couldn't bear to look at her when she realized the truth. When she finally saw what I really was. "Say it," I whispered. Begging now. My voice wasn't even my own anymore. "I need you to say it." I hated how I sounded, small and cracked open.

My hands trembled where they held her. Her breath hitched. Her arms wrapped around me like I hadn't just killed for the thrill of it. Her fingers curled at the base of my neck like I was still worth touching.

"I'm still yours, Cain," she said softly. "You didn't scare me off." She pulled me closer and kissed my jaw.

My knees nearly gave out. I exhaled a sound that didn't belong in this world, half-wrecked, wholly inhuman. Not a sigh. Not a sob. Just the echo of something that had been locked inside me for *centuries* breaking loose. I clutched her tighter. I held her like she was the only thing standing between me and the abyss, and for once, the abyss wasn't winning.

The men in that warehouse? They weren't enough, and there were still other matters here to attend to. They were just the first drop in a storm I'd been holding back too long. I needed more.

Fuck.

"Our night's not over," I said, low and quiet. "Not yet."

She didn't answer. Just nodded, slow. Still dazed. Still mine.

My hands lingered longer than I meant them to. Not because I was sentimental, but because I knew the second I stepped away from her, I'd want to start all over again.

"Get up," I said. "We're not done."

She blinked at me, legs still loose and trembling. "What do you mean?"

I didn't bother explaining. I just grabbed her hand and started walking. If she wanted answers, she could keep up.

The air shifted the deeper we went, less blood, more decay. The kind of stink you couldn't fake.

She wrinkled her nose. "What is this place?"

"Take a wild guess."

The hallway turned sharp, and there they were.

Dozens of cages were sprawled out one by one in the dark. Girls were crammed inside them like inventory. Some unconscious, some crying, some just staring at the wall like they'd already decided not to come back from this. Opal stopped walking. Her breath hitched like it had caught on barbed wire.

"Oh my god."

"Save the prayers," I muttered. "They're not listening." Her hand found my arm again, like she needed something solid to hang onto.

"This is why . . ." Her voice was shaking now. "This is why those men—why you—"

"Deserved it?" I finished for her. "Yeah. No shit."

She looked at me like she was seeing me for the first time. I didn't like it.

"You thought I was just killing for fun."

"Weren't you?"

"Fun. Justice. Same difference, some nights." I shrugged. "Don't pretend this shit wasn't earned."

Her eyes swept the cages again. The girls. The chains. The filth. "How long have you been doing this?"

"Since a friend dragged me into it," I said. "He didn't even know what we were walking into. I figured it out first. Let him think he had the moral high ground. But I didn't stop swinging either."

She was quiet. Processing. Like she wanted to paint me in a different color now. I didn't let her. "Don't romanticize it, Little Ghoul. I didn't do it to save them. I did it because it pissed me off. Because I *wanted* to kill something that deserved it for once."

"But they're alive now," she said. "So, what now?"

"Now we open the cages."

"And after that?"

I looked around. At the rusted chains, the rot in the corners, the kind of evil that didn't scream anymore, because it had gotten too used to the sound.

"Then we burn this place to the fucking ground."

Opal was the first to kneel, but she didn't wait to be told how. "Help me with the blanket," she said, handing out towels and instructions like an anchor.

I glanced down at her and met her eyes. "You be soft, Blossom. I'll do this my way." I kicked the first lock in. It wasn't dramatic. It wasn't heroic. I was never going to be anyone's hero. The metal gave way with a sharp crack, like it had been waiting for someone mean enough to finish the job. The girl inside flinched. Curled tighter in the corner of the cage. Her eyes were wide, glassy, already halfway to someplace else.

I crouched. Met her stare. Flashed a smile. Not a kind one.

Not the type you offer someone to say *You're safe now.* She flinched. I couldn't help the way I made people feel; it just came with the territory.

"You're free," I said, voice flat. No sugar. No softness.

She didn't believe me—smart girl. Behind me, I heard Opal's breath catch. She moved differently than I did, slow, careful, like a bird afraid of startling something. She dropped to her knees beside the girl, her hands open, her voice warm. "It's okay," she said, brushing hair gently back from the girl's face. "We're here to help you." Her tone was everything mine wasn't: gentle, deliberate, and *human*. I didn't do human. While she soothed and reassured, I moved to the next cage. Steel met my boot, and another lock snapped.

The girl inside was crying, quiet, controlled. Like she'd been punished before for making noise. "Out," I said. "Door's open." She didn't move.

I didn't coax or kneel. I wasn't here to earn their trust. I was here to destroy whatever made this place necessary in the first place.

Opal followed closely behind me. Her hands reached for the girl like they belonged there. "You don't have to be afraid anymore," she whispered. "You're not alone."

I watched her fingers stroke trembling shoulders, brush tears off dirt-streaked cheeks. She was softness in a space built to crush it. I was bone and blade and rage in a hoodie. But somehow, we worked.

"Is anyone hurt?" she asked, scanning the cages with wide eyes that looked more furious than afraid. "We'll get you out, I promise."

One of them, young, couldn't be more than fourteen, raised a trembling hand. Her eye was swollen shut, lip cracked, one arm held too carefully to be unbroken.

"She needs help," Opal said, glancing at me.

"She'll get it."

I kicked in another lock, another cage. Finding another girl too frozen to move.

"You could be gentler," Opal murmured when she returned, voice tight as she kneeled beside the girl.

"Yeah," I said, kicking in the next door. "I could. But I'm not."

She didn't argue. She just kept being the softness to my sharp. The mercy to my violence. The hands that held while mine had already broken. We didn't make sense. She talked like a lullaby and smelled like sugar and carried her kindness like a shield she refused to put down. I was cold breath and rot. Old bones in borrowed skin. A nightmare she should've run from a long time ago.

And yet, she moved beside me like we were pieces meant to interlock. I didn't pretend to deserve her, but I didn't stop her either, because she chose this, chose me.

Opal stood in the middle of them now, barefoot girls in torn shirts and haunted eyes circling her like she was their last soft place. She knelt when they couldn't stand. Let them lean on her when their knees gave out. Whispered things that cracked through the silence like the first birdsong after war.

I stood back and watched her do what I couldn't. She reached for a girl with red welts on her wrists and tucked a filthy blanket around her shoulders like it mattered. Like anything could make this better.

"Authorities will be here soon," I said, cutting into the moment. My voice felt louder than it should've, slicing clean through the tenderness she was building like a wall. "Crow sent an anonymous tip. Fake witness report. Should be lights and sirens in five."

Opal turned toward me slowly.

Her eyes met mine, and for a second, I thought she might cry. Not because she was weak, but because she still gave a shit.

"You . . . you called it in?" she asked.

"I'm not dragging half a dozen broken girls through the Veil," I said. "Figured human trauma needs human help. Crow usually makes the call."

"That was . . . thoughtful," she said.

"It was efficient," I corrected.

I didn't linger in the moment. Didn't hold her gaze. Just turned and walked. The storeroom was where I left it. Dark. Reeking. Stacked with drums of chemicals.

"Where are you going?" she called after me.

"Cleanup."

She followed. I heard her shuffle to catch up, saw her nose wrinkle at the burn of fumes, at the scorch marks on the wall where something had already tried to catch fire and failed.

I flicked the Zippo open. Flame bloomed, bright and beautiful.

"You don't have to burn it," she said. Her voice was low now. Not afraid—*tired*.

I tipped a drum. Liquid splashed across the floor.

"Yeah," I said. "I do."

She didn't argue. Just stood there and watched as I dropped the flame. It caught immediately. Slow at first. Then fast. Flames racing over the floor like they couldn't wait to devour something. We walked out together.

The night air hit hard. Cold, wet with dew. The girls were out now, clustered beneath a dead tree near the road, shivering in silence. Opal's steps slowed. Mine didn't. She turned back, walked toward them, eyes soft again, arms open. One girl burst into tears the second Opal touched her. Another threw herself into her arms like she'd been waiting for permission to fall apart.

Opal held them. Whispered again. Ran shaking fingers through their hair and kissed one girl's forehead like it meant something. She gave them back pieces of themselves I didn't know how to hold, pieces I could only break.

I stood under the trees and waited. Watching. Not because I was impatient, but because watching her be *good*—it hurt more than anything I'd done tonight.

She came back eventually.

Her mascara was smudged. Her sleeves were soaked. Her jaw was clenched like she was holding the world in her mouth and trying not to scream.

"You okay?" I asked.

Her answer was honest.

"No."

"Good," I said. "Means you still have a soul."

She let out a half-laugh, half-sob and wiped her face with the sleeve of my hoodie.

"Do you?"

"Debatable."

Behind us, the warehouse roared. Flames cracked the night sky open like a curse fulfilled. Sirens whined in the distance, drawn by the stink of gasoline and justice.

"Where to now?" she asked.

"I need a little more," I added, voice rough in my throat. "And then I'm taking you home."

Another nod.

"My home." I pressed a kiss to her neck, soft this time. Not the claiming kind. Not the kind meant to bruise or bite. Just something that said *Hold on to me. Don't give up just yet.*

Then I gathered her up bridal-style. I didn't trust her legs yet. I did a pretty good job of wrecking her, and if I was being honest with myself, I didn't want to let go. The rift opened with hardly a breath, shadows parting like old friends. I stepped through, and the world changed.

We emerged in a quiet village carved into mountains in Nepal. A place folded in fog and prayer wheels, tucked so far into the earth it felt like time forgot it. The air was cold. Clean. Still.

Except for the illness. A slow fever moving like smoke through the town. Quiet deaths. Peaceful ones. But still mine to take. I set her gently on a low stone bench carved beneath a prayer flag canopy. "Wait here." She didn't ask questions.

She just wrapped her arms around her knees, watching as I moved into the shadows. I took twelve. Twelve breaths. Twelve heartbeats. Twelve souls that passed gently, with a whisper and no pain. I didn't make it violent. I didn't *need* to. She had seen enough of the monster I was tonight. She didn't need more.

I returned to her quieter. Steadier. Still not full. Still not *right*. But the edge had dulled for now. The pain was gone; my stomach settled. This would last until we figured something out, a *method*, an *agreement*. A way to make this work without breaking her in the process.

Because the balance had to be maintained, and I couldn't keep starving myself just to make her think I was a good man.

CHAPTER 19

Cain

She was exhausted, and I laid her in my bed. Carefully. She didn't stir. Just curled into the pillow like she knew she was home. The blankets swallowed her, soft as fog and dark as a sinner's last breath. I stepped back and let her be. I tried not to stare too long.

My room, my whole *world*, looked like something stitched from nightmares. All brutal lines and gothic spires, iron and bone carved into every arch. African bloodstone pillars stretched to vaulted ceilings, and the bone chandelier overhead was made from femurs and skulls. Everything was black.

The windows were tall and narrow, overlooking the Fields of Mourning, miles of long grass blowing in a directionless wind under a sky that shifted from pale gold to a bruised, unnatural pink the closer it bent toward the Kingdom of Hell. Our kingdoms were separated by Purgatory.

No one lived in Purgatory, not really, not the way mortals understood it. Souls rejected by both Heaven and Hell wandered those ruins. Demons slain in rebellion. Angels cast down and left to wither. I didn't claim them. I didn't *touch* them. That wasn't my place. But the city behind my castle? The City of the Dead? That was mine. Reapers lived there. Ghosts. Spirits too far gone for redemption but too sharp to fade. All manner of psychopomps. They answered to me. I didn't ask them to. They just did. I was Death, and I had never needed a crown. Never asked for it.

I sat on the mattress, back to her and listened to the wind moan softly through the tower. "Welcome home, Final Girl," I whispered.

The candles guttered when Crow appeared, like even the flame knew better than to shine too bright around him. He leaned against the doorway, white hair falling in uneven strands across his face, eyes that cold shade of blue that looked borrowed from winter itself.

"She's asleep," I said.

"I can see that." His voice was even, but something sharp lived under it. "You look worse."

"I've been worse."

Crow's mouth tightened. For a beat his calm thinned, and something else, something sharper, slid behind his eyes. It was the split I knew by heart: the scholar and the killer sharing the same skin. Crow crossed the room, boots whispering over the black stone. He studied the circle burned into the floorboards near my desk, the remnants of the last attempt. Ash and chalk, both useless.

"Still nothing," he said quietly.

I didn't answer.

"We tried the salt and the rune," he says, voice low, practiced. "It held for an hour. The ointment slowed it, barely.

He crouched, tracing a finger near the sigils, not touching. "The bond is weakening you."

"I know."

"Then let me end it."

I turned fast, the word coming out more growl than breath. "No."

Crow's gaze flicked up to meet mine. Calm. Annoyingly calm. "Cain." He said my name like it was a weapon. "This is not working."

"I said no." The word cracked through the dark like a whip. She shifted in her sleep behind me, and I froze. We both did. "Quiet."

Crow stood, straightening his coat, his reflection ghosting in the tall black mirror. "You're not thinking clearly," he said in a hushed voice.

I swallowed the ache in my throat. "She's the only thing I can touch without the world breaking apart."

His expression softened just slightly. "If the bond breaks, you get better."

"And I lose her."

Silence fell heavy between us, filled only by the low hum of the wards and her breathing from the bed.

Crow's voice came quieter now but still edged with steel. "You're trying to hold a burning house with your bare hands."

"Then I'll burn. I'll take as many lives as I need to so that I can sustain us both."

He sighed, dragging a hand through his hair, the silver strands catching faint candlelight. "I'll keep looking," he said finally. "But you can't hide this from her forever."

"I know."

"She'll notice."

"She already has."

Crow hesitated at the door. "If she wakes and asks what's wrong—"

"Tell her I'm fine."

He almost smiled, that tired, knowing look he got right before giving up on an argument. "Liar."

She stirred before the sky changed. Not fully pink yet, just gold light spilling through the thin, vertical windows. I'd been watching her for an hour.

I was sprawled along the chaise across from my bed, one boot dangling lazily off the side, the other still on. She moved again. This time slower, dragging herself up from the nest of obsidian sheets, her hair a wreck, her T-shirt hanging off one shoulder and clinging to her torso. She blinked, and then she looked around.

She peered at my bed, which was draped in layers of darkness like a tomb built for comfort, and her eyes caught the large chandelier of bones above us. She didn't say anything at first. She shifted and ran her fingers across the velvet blanket like she was making sure it was real. Then her eyes landed on me. I sat up slightly, resting my arms on my knees. "Morning, Final Girl."

Her lips parted. "This is your room?"

"Mmhmm." I dragged the vape from my lips, exhaling a slow cloud toward the rafters. "Welcome to my home."

Her gaze flicked past me again, toward the balcony and the endless sky beyond it. "It's . . . not what I expected."

I raised a brow. "Not black enough?"

She actually smiled. "No, it's very on brand."

"Good." I stood slowly, shaking off my other boot and crossing the room, barefoot and bare-chested, shadows curling along the floor behind me like loyal dogs. "Didn't want to disappoint."

I crawled into the bed slowly, each movement purposeful. She blinked at me, lips parting, just as I slid over her, pressing her into the mattress. Not hard, not rough, just . . . *there*. A promise in my body, in the way I caged her with my arms.

Her breath caught, but she didn't pull away. My hand slid behind her neck, fingers curling against her skin as I pressed in and kissed her, soft and slow this time. No teeth. No chase. Just mouths brushing in a way that felt dangerously like comfort.

When I pulled back, she looked up at me with those too-honest green eyes. I brushed a curl from her cheek, letting my fingers linger. "I don't know how you pulled off that spell," I added, thumb grazing the hinge of her jaw. "But you did." A pause, and I meant every word of what came next. "And I don't think I want to change it."

She opened her mouth, maybe to argue, maybe to ask. I didn't let her. "Shhh. Just think about it," I said, barely above a whisper. "You. Me. Like this. Forever."

I kissed her again, slower, deeper. A question and a warning. Because what I wanted? Was her. All of her. Forever might not be a curse anymore.

"Now get up," I murmured against her lips as mine curled into a grin. "You have a kingdom to see."

She blinked up at me, still dazed and a little breathless. I rolled off her, sitting at the edge of the bed, raking a hand through my hair as the shadows coiled around my forearms.

"Wait, you're serious?" she asked, her voice thick with sleep and disbelief.

I looked over my shoulder, grinning. "You think I'd bring you to my castle and not show off a little?"

She stood, brushing her skirt down, hair a mess and lips still swollen from my mouth. She was chaos in a pink T-shirt, and she was beautiful.

The Deadlands were gray, filled with soft wind that never stopped blowing but never led anywhere. Cold ground, no sun, but the people here made their own color. Paper lanterns strung above the walkways. Spices and incense curling from open market stalls. Music made from memory, threading through the streets. Colored flags and ribbons wrapped around bare, leafless trees.

Every eye turned to us. Not because she was mortal, though that was rare. No. They stared because of *me*. Because I was walking hand in hand with a living girl like she *meant* something. Like she was mine—and she was. *Gods*, she was. They knew it already, even if she didn't. I caught the stares from passing reapers, black-robed for their assignments, hoods pulled low. They paused, bowing slightly as we passed, but I could feel the questions humming under their skin.

Ghosts drifted nearby, translucent but solid here in the Deadlands, hovering behind lantern-lit stalls and skeletal trees. They blinked at her like she was a myth. Something warm in a place where warmth was legend. One of them reached out and touched the sleeve of her hand in disbelief. She smiled—of course she did—and the ghost *laughed* like it had forgotten how.

I don't think she realized what this walk meant. That every step we took was a declaration.

A claim.

That Death, the untouchable one, the destroyer, the inevitability, was holding hands with a girl who smiled at ghosts and slept next to corpses like they were cats.

I knew what this would mean. The word would spread through my city like wildfire through a dry field. Death had chosen, and she? She might be queen. If she said yes, of course . . . It was a lot to spring on someone, but I knew what I felt.

She didn't belong here, but the city already loved her. It didn't matter if she was mortal. The wind curled around her like it wanted to protect her. Ghosts watched her like a miracle. She was becoming something, *someone*, I couldn't unchoose.

"You're making a scene, my king," a voice murmured behind me.

I turned.

Crow stood at my shoulder, though here, in his human form, he wore a long black coat and gloves, his white hair falling over his crystal eyes.

He looked past me at Opal and then back. "You're serious about her," he said. It wasn't a question.

I didn't answer. Just took a drag of my vape and exhaled smoke.

"She's changing things," Crow added. "We feel it. The city feels it. Hell, even the psychopomps have been whispering."

"She's not a threat," I muttered.

"That's not what I'm afraid of," he said, deadpan. "Sir, numbers are dropping fast and—"

I shot him a glare. "You have something to say, Crow?"

He met my eyes, no fear, just truth. "She's not like us . . . but she's not *not* like us, either. Whatever she is . . . it's growing, and it's affecting the balance."

Opal was spinning with a ghost child now, his little translucent arms stretched wide as she twirled him like they were dancing in a sunlit garden, not the middle of a city made of death. I didn't smile, but I wanted to. She wasn't mine by title yet, but this place? This city? It was watching—and it already knew.

The Queen of the Dead had arrived.

Opal

We walked back slowly. Hand in hand down the obsidian causeway past drifting spirits and the bowed heads of reapers and shades.

They looked at me like I *meant* something. Like I was more than the mortal girl who'd accidentally chained herself to Death. They bowed when we passed. Called me "my lady." I didn't know how to respond to that.

It wasn't bad, it just felt . . . surreal. Like stepping into a dream painted in grayscale and shadow, but finding yourself the only thing in color. Pink, to be exact.

The City of the Dead was beautiful in a way most people would miss. It was full of stark contrast. Brutal architecture, yet soft soul. There were no flowers, but fabric banners danced between towers like whispers. No sunlight, but lanterns glowed with warm light. It was *alive* here. More alive than anywhere I'd ever been. And somehow, I fit. I was bright and wrong, just like the rest of this place.

We stepped through the castle gates, tall slabs of bone and blackened glass that groaned like they knew I was coming.

Cain didn't say anything. He didn't have to. His words were already doing circles in my head, wearing grooves. *"I don't think I want to change it."*

I stepped toward the bed and crawled onto the black sheets, letting myself sink into them. Cain watched from the corner of the room, his jaw tight like he didn't want to scare me off. Like he wasn't sure how to ask me to stay without *asking*.

I laid back, staring at the bones overhead, their shadows dancing like constellations. Maybe this was madness. Maybe I was spiraling into something I wouldn't come back from. But honestly? What was the harm in trying this out? We had time—forever, maybe.

I turned my head. "Cain?"

He glanced up. Eyes that could slice bone, suddenly uncertain.

Softly, I asked, "What happens if I don't want to break the spell?"

For once, he didn't have a blade of sarcasm ready. Didn't sneer or deflect. He just . . . froze. The shadows at his shoulders stilled, like even they were waiting for the answer.

When he finally moved, it was slow. Careful. Reverent in a way that scared me more than his violence ever had, like he was approaching something sacred. Like *I* was sacred.

"I have no fucking clue, Blossom," he said at last. His voice was low, rough, honest in a way Cain rarely ever was with anyone. The admission cracked something open in him. I saw it in his eyes, that flicker of fear, of want, of a hunger that had nothing to do with killing.

"But we can figure it out."

The words cost him. I could hear it in the way his jaw tightened, like honesty tasted like blood.

I looked up at him, breathless, still half-tangled in his sheets and the weight of everything he'd just handed me—the truth, the city, the choice.

"So . . . we're winging this," I said, trying for lightness.

His mouth twitched. The smile that broke through wasn't his usual sharp, wicked slash. Not the grin he wore when shadows curled and blood dripped fresh. This one was crooked. Real. Dangerous in a way that had nothing to do with death, and everything to do with him letting me in.

"Fuck yeah, we are." Then he kissed me. It wasn't punishing It wasn't possessive. It was warm, slow, just a little shy, like he couldn't believe I was still here. Like he couldn't believe I wanted to be.

For a second, he broke. I felt it in the way his hands trembled where they held me, the way his breath caught like he was choking on relief. He was starving, desperate, undone, and if I pushed, I could've broken him open completely. But then the mask slammed back down, and he pulled away, and the softness vanished under sharp angles and bad intentions. A grin crawled across his face, crooked, cocky, the grin of an arsonist who'd just discovered a new way to set the world on fire. Like I'd given him hope, and he was already sharpening it into a weapon.

"Wanna come to a wedding with me?" he asked, already stretching—*nude*—like the concept of shame didn't exist in his vocabulary.

Which, honestly? It probably didn't.

He arched his back like a cat, arms over his head, all muscle and ink and unbothered beauty. Just standing there like the actual apocalypse with bed hair.

I blinked. "A *wedding*?"

"Yup." He popped a vertebra, cracked his neck, and yawned like I'd just asked if we were out of cereal. "Somehow I got volunteered as best man."

I stared. "You? *You* got volunteered?"

"Don't look at me like that, Blossom." He smirked, totally unrepentant. "Apparently I'm charming, and I was volun-told."

"You're psychotic."

"Same thing."

I narrowed my eyes. "Whose wedding could possibly justify dragging *you* into a tux?"

His grin stretched wider. "The Devil's."

I blinked again.

"Oh. Yeah. That tracks."

He bent down to grab the vape off the nightstand, still completely naked, like modesty was beneath him and probably had been since the Bronze Age.

I was still reeling. "You're going to Hell," I said slowly.

"Technically we're already in Hell." He took a drag and exhaled cherry smoke like a slow curse. "Dress cute."

I groaned.

He grabbed my hand—still naked, mind you—and tugged me toward the tall cathedral-style window that arched above his bed like something out of a gothic fever dream.

"C-Cain—" I sputtered, dragging the blanket with me and trying *very hard* not to look directly at him.

"Relax, Blossom," he said, utterly unbothered, as usual. "You've seen all of me already." He smirked, planted a bare foot on the stone ledge, and pointed out into the vast, strange landscape beyond.

"Yeah, but not while *giving geography lessons*."

"See that?" he asked. "Where the sky turns pink, way off in the distance?"

I followed his finger, gaze sliding past endless deadlands, mourning fields, and long stretches of soft gold wind that blew unceasingly.

Far, far away, the skies were bleeding peach and crimson, like the world had caught fire.

"That," he said, tapping the glass with one knuckle, "is the Kingdom of Hell."

My breath caught.

He said it like it was the most normal thing in the world. Like he was pointing out the neighbor's backyard.

"We're neighbors, kinda," he added, flashing a grin over his shoulder. "Not exactly a block party situation, but close enough." I blinked at the soft horizon and then back at the *very nude* man beside me. "And there"—he pointed to an ominous mist—"is Purgatory . . . Never go there." He moved his finger, pointing at a large canyon. "And never go in there. You won't come out of either," he said, deadpan. "Ever."

"This is the weirdest relationship I've ever been in."

"I hope it's your last," he said with a shrug, turning back toward the bed like he hadn't just casually pointed out Hell while standing fully exposed to the universe. "I'm very good at ending things."

I pulled the blanket tighter.

"He made me." Cain's voice dropped—low, like it hurt to say it out loud. I turned to face him, wrapped in one of his dark sheets, watching his expression shift. The playful gleam was gone now, replaced by something heavier. Older. I watched as he draped himself back over the chaise tiredly.

"The Devil and I . . ." He looked out the window again but not like he was admiring the view this time. Like he was *remembering* it. "I was his first deal."

"He made you Death?"

Cain nodded once. "To save humanity."

That was *not* the sentence I'd expected to hear before brunch.

My brow arched. "You're telling me the Devil created Death to save us?"

He laughed, but there was no humor in it. Just tired weight. "Funny, right? But yeah. There was too much suffering. Too much war. Humanity had made a mess of things . . . again. The gods had voted to scrap the whole species, wipe the slate clean."

"And he stopped them?"

"He made a trade," Cain said. "One soul. One immortal. To carry the burden of death and end all suffering so no one else had to. And that soul was me."

I didn't know what to say. My mouth was open, heart thudding like it was trying to fill the silence. He turned to me, finally. Eyes dark and endless but not cold.

"I'm not some natural force," he said. "Not divine. Not demonic. I was human once, and I gave that up."

"To save us?"

"To buy you time," he said simply. "To give humanity a chance to be worth saving."

I stepped closer, the weight of what he said settling in my chest like a stone.

"Do you regret it?" I asked quietly.

He shrugged, but it didn't look casual. "Some days I think I should've let the world burn."

"And today?" I whispered.

He looked at me, and for the first time, I saw it: The grief. The ache. The thousand years of being alone.

His voice was barely audible. "Today . . . I don't."

"I knew a bit of the story," I murmured, heart catching in my throat as pieces started to click into place.

"Cain and . . ." I hesitated. Then said it. "Abel."

His jaw tensed. A slow nod. "I was the first murderer," he said, voice stripped of bravado now. No smoke. No swagger. Just truth. "The first to create death." The words hung there like ash in the air. He glanced away, dragging a hand through his hair like it might pull the past from his skull. The sheet twisted in his grip like he suddenly felt cold.

"That angered God," he went on. "The deal I made with the Devil . . . it *infuriated* Him. That I'd choose Hell over Heaven. That I'd barter my soul for a world He was ready to abandon."

I sat on the bed, not saying a word. Letting him speak.

"He cursed us both," Cain whispered. "Me . . . and the Devil. One became the ruler of what God forsook. The other . . . became what he feared."

He swallowed hard, eyes distant.

"I've been Death ever since."

My voice came out softer than I intended. "And your brother?"

He was silent a long beat. Then: "He became the first demon."

I didn't move. Didn't breathe.

Cain's eyes found mine. Haunted. Still burning with something centuries old and never forgiven.

"Abel . . . doesn't remember me," Cain said softly.

He wasn't looking at me but somewhere past me, eyes clouded like the memory was too sharp to touch.

"He doesn't even know who he is."

My breath caught.

"When demons are reborn, it's with a clean slate. That's how the Devil designed it. No past. No pain. Just . . . whatever purpose they're given."

I watched him, trying to imagine it—what it meant to walk through eternity while the person you loved most wandered in the dark, not knowing your face.

Cain swallowed hard. "It was to protect him. From the memory, from what I did, and maybe . . . maybe it was to protect *me* too." He rubbed his chest absently, like something still hurt there, something old. Something buried too deep to name.

I stared at him for a long moment, the words dancing in the silence between us, too heavy to ignore. Finally, I just asked it.

"The deal," I said sharply. "What was it? What did you *get* in return for giving up your soul?"

He looked up at me, and this time, he didn't hide.

"I asked that Abel would live forever," Cain said, each word deliberate, reverent. "That nothing, *no god, no demon, no force in the universe* could ever hurt him." His voice dropped lower. "That he'd be safe. Always. Under the Devil's sworn protection. Untouchable." A beat passed. Two. "And if anyone ever broke that part of the deal . . . the contract would be void."

I met his gaze, breath shallow. "And what happens then?"

Cain's eyes darkened. His jaw tensed like he didn't want to say it, like even after all this time, the truth still tasted bitter. "God saw to it that I could never stop taking souls," he said slowly. "It's the one part of the curse that's never bent. Never quieted."

His fingers flexed like he was remembering what it felt like to rot, like the sickness from a few nights ago still lingered in his bones. "You saw what happens if I try."

I swallowed. Nodded.

He exhaled a breath that sounded like the world cracking. "But what most don't understand," he continued, "is that I'm not just the collector." He looked up at me, voice gaining weight with every word.

"I hold all the power of where those souls go. *How* they get there. Every gate opens with my hand. Heaven. Hell. Purgatory. Even the ones that don't have names." A pause. "Think of my kingdom like a merchant kingdom," he said, gesturing faintly toward the window. "No deal? No souls. No flow. No currency."

I sat perfectly still, feeling the pieces slot together.

"And if there are no souls," he continued, "the other kingdoms? They start to starve. Their gates run dry. Their powers dwindle." He looked at me again, and this time there was no trace of a smile. Just Death in his full, ancient, merciless truth. "They fight. They war. They fall. Balance collapses. The universe begins to unravel."

My breath hitched.

He nodded. "Eventually, everything . . . *ceases to exist.*"

A long silence stretched between us. Cain leaned back, resting his weight on his elbows, gaze pinned to the ceiling like he could see the cosmos fracturing above it.

"All that . . . just because I wanted my brother to live."

"And he's the biggest asshole I've ever known," Cain muttered, dragging a hand through his hair like the memory physically hurt.

I blinked at him. Then raised a brow.

"Bigger than you?" I asked, tone flat, unamused.

His head snapped toward me, brow arching with theatrical offense.

I snorted. A full, real sound. Couldn't help it.

The corner of his mouth twitched. "Careful," he said, that gravel-smooth voice dropping lower. "You're still in my bed, Blossom."

"And you're still wearing nothing but sarcasm and that scowl."

He glanced down at himself, made no effort to move, and just said, "Comfortable."

I rolled my eyes. "You know, most people put on pants for emotionally scarring conversations."

"Most people," he said, sitting up slowly, shadows curling across his spine like they missed him, "don't wake up in bed with Death."

I wanted to be annoyed.

Instead, I bit back a smile. "You're impossible."

"I've been called worse."

"You *are* worse."

And that? That got a proper grin from him: half-feral, half-amused, and completely Cain.

CHAPTER 20

Cain

She really had no idea what she was doing to me. Sitting there on my sheets in a T-shirt that was too big for her, eyes all playful innocence, poking the monster like she wanted to see what would happen. I'd given her a kingdom. She gave me a fucking heartbeat.

Now she was smiling at me like I wasn't three seconds from dragging her back under the covers just to see how many times I could make her scream my name.

Instead, I stood and stretched like I hadn't just peeled open my entire past and laid it out for her inspection. She watched and didn't even try to look away this time. Good girl. My grin slid sharp across my mouth when I caught her staring. I had no business letting her look at me like that.

"What, never seen Death in the flesh?" I teased, sauntering toward the armoire like I had all the time in the world.

Her throat bobbed. Cheeks pink. She flopped back onto the bed with a groan. "God, you are the worst."

Something snapped in me.

In two steps I was on her, shadows curling across the sheets like eager hands. She squealed and shoved at my chest, but I caught her wrists, pinning them above her head.

"The worst, huh?" I growled, nose brushing hers. "Say it again."

Her laugh tangled with her breath, reckless and sweet. "You *are*—"

I kissed her before she could finish. Hard. Starved. Like I hadn't tasted anything real in centuries—and I hadn't.

She kissed me back just as desperately, legs hooking around my waist like we were both drowning and this was the only way to breathe. Neither of us could stop. Not when her pulse thundered under my tongue, not when my shadows hissed and coiled, dragging across her skin like they wanted her too.

Every time I tried to pull away, she pulled me closer. Every time she gasped, I chased the sound like it belonged to me. It was reckless. It was fucked. And it was inevitable. By the time I dragged back, panting against her mouth, my hands shook with the effort not to keep her there, not to drown myself in her.

Her smile was dazed. Wild. "See? The worst."

I huffed, trying to wrestle the crack in my composure back into a grin, sharp and cocky. Pretend the moment hadn't gutted me. But the truth was written all over me, raw and dangerous. She couldn't keep her hands off me and I—I couldn't stop reaching for her either.

"Cain?" Her voice was soft.

"Get dressed," I rasped, pressing my forehead to her shoulder. My skin burned cold against her warmth, and I hated how much I needed it. "You're gonna need something to wear."

She stiffened, just for a second, then flushed all the way down her throat. "Oh. Right. Clothes . . . for Hell."

I smirked, but it cracked, jagged at the edges.

Her fingers brushed my jaw, steady, unafraid. "You're pale."

I cracked one eye open. "I'm always pale."

She gave me that look, the kind that said *don't bullshit me*.

"No, I mean—paler. Than usual."

That shut me up. My hand clenched the sheet hard enough to tear. Shadows hissed at the edges of my grip, restless. She saw too much.

"We need to go back," she blurted, sitting up straighter. "You're sick again. You need to—"

"No." I caught her wrist, not rough, just final. "We're not going back there."

"But Cain—"

"I said no." My voice cracked through the air, harder than I meant it to. I exhaled slowly, shoulders tight, swallowing down the black creeping into the edges of my vision. "Not until the wedding. Not until I have to."

She watched me. Quiet now. Concern bleeding from her eyes like it might cut me open if I let it.

"It's okay . . ." she whispered, too soft. Her hand slipped into mine, warm and mortal and steady. The kind of steady I'd never been.

"I don't want to see you get sick because of me," she said. "You shouldn't have to push yourself like this."

I hated feeling weak. Hated the shake in my hands, the chill in my skin, the way the shadows twitched like they could smell the cracks forming in me. I wasn't supposed to break. Not in front of her.

I didn't look at her. My gaze stayed locked on the floor like maybe the shadows would swallow me before I admitted it out loud.

"I'm Death, Blossom," I muttered, forcing apathy into place in my voice like armor. "This is what I do."

"Yeah, well . . . Maybe it doesn't have to be."

Her fingers laced through mine. Gods, she was so Opal about it. Too damned sweet and so stubborn. Like she didn't know she was trying to stitch together something made from rot and razor blades.

I forced a laugh. "You think I want this?" I asked, teeth gritted. "To kill? To rot from the inside out when you don't?"

She blinked. Didn't look away.

"I didn't fucking ask for it," I added. Quieter now. "But that's the punchline, isn't it? Nobody asks to be the monster."

"I know," she said.

"Do you?" I snapped, a little too fast. "You see me bleeding, and you think that makes me broken? Human? It doesn't."

"No," she said, steady even now. "It makes you real."

I turned my face away. Jaw tight. Breathing worse than useless. "I don't *need* anything," I muttered. "Don't need comfort. Don't need softness. I just need to keep going."

She brushed her thumb across my knuckles. "I'm not offering comfort," she whispered. "I'm offering *me*. Someone to share the weight with. Even monsters get tired."

"I'm not tired." Lie. "I'm used to this."

She tilted her head, studying me the way prey shouldn't. "You're shaking."

Fuck. I glanced down. My hands weren't steady. My skin pale, even for me. I yanked them back, shoved them through my hair. "Don't do that."

"Do what?"

"Look at me like that," I spat. "I don't want your pity, Opal."

"Good," she said, voice quiet but solid. "Because I don't pity you. Just let me help."

I paused. "Let you help?" I scoffed. "What—you gonna hold my hair next time I puke?"

"No. I'll hold you."

The words hit harder than they had any right to. So stupid. So simple. I stared at her. At the girl who should've run from me weeks ago.

"You're not scared?"

"Terrified," she said. "But it's a little late for second thoughts, don't you think?"

I watched her like I was watching the edge of a knife. Beautiful. Dangerous. Something that would tear me open if I let it. *Fine. Fuck it.*

"I need more," I admitted, feeling a little defeated. "Soon."

"Then let's go," she said. "Whatever you need, I'll come with you."

"You know this means you're stuck with me, right?" I murmured, brushing a strand of hair from her cheek. "Forever?"

"Yeah," she whispered, pressing a kiss to the corner of my mouth. "I know."

And fuck me . . . I *wanted* that. I needed it. Her. This. The *idea* of not doing it alone. I'd spent centuries pretending I was fine in the dark. Maybe it was time to admit that I wasn't.

"Come on, then," I said, voice back to a growl, burying what had just been cracked open like it hadn't happened. "We've got souls to collect."

She sat up, pulling on her boots with a smile that was full of mischief. "Where to?"

I grinned, the kind of grin that meant trouble. The kind of grin that promised fire and blood and maybe a little fun if you weren't on the receiving end and were a little fucked up in the head. I slipped my hand into hers like it was the most natural thing in the world even though I still wasn't used to being allowed to touch at all.

I led her down a corridor, shadows snaking along the walls, guiding us like they knew where we were headed before I did. Massive double doors loomed at the end, carved with symbols she couldn't recognize.

She slowed. "What's this?"

I pushed the doors open with both hands, wood groaning, and the answer swallowed her whole. A kingdom of weapons stretched floor to ceiling. Spears older than empires. Blades that still stank of wars long buried. Rifles polished to gleaming death. Crossbows, axes, scythes, an arsenal stitched from every age humanity had ever bled through. The weapons on the wall ringed a large sparring mat with practice dummies.

The air itself smelled of iron and history. Opal froze on the threshold, caught between awe and horror. Her green eyes reflected all the steel on the walls.

"Holy shit," she whispered.

I leaned against the doorframe, watching her drink it in. "Impressed?"

She turned, incredulous. "Disturbed."

I chuckled. "In my book, that's just another word for impressed, Blossom."

She walked in slowly, fingertips trailing across the hilt of a sword taller than she was. "You've . . . kept all of this?"

"Kept?" I scoffed, stepping in after her. The shadows curled around the racks like guard dogs on a leash. "I don't keep. I collect. Every soul leaves something behind. Sometimes it's a weapon. Sometimes it's a scar."

Her hand stilled on a chipped battle-axe from the Viking era, and I saw the way her breath quickened. I prowled closer, lowering my voice until it wrapped around her like smoke. "This is who I am, Opal. Death doesn't just take. Death *remembers*. In my own way."

She shivered, though not entirely from fear.

I grinned again, wicked and diabolical. "Pick one."

Her head snapped toward me. "What?"

"Pick a weapon," I said. "If you're coming with me, you're going to need something."

"You said I was immortal?"

I nodded and let the words bleed out slowly. "Yes . . . But just because I can't hurt you doesn't mean someone else can't, and take it from me, it fucking sucks having to heal from something that should have killed you."

Her eyes darted over swords, rifles gleaming under shadowlight, blades that could split bone with a whisper. She walked past all of them, humming under her breath like she was browsing a thrift store instead of my museum of murder.

I leaned against a rack of spears, watching. Waiting. She walked the racks like she was window-shopping. Then she reached up, fingers brushing against a small silver hilt. She pulled it free and held it to the light, a tiny dagger with roses etched down the blade. The kind of thing a lord's daughter might've kept hidden under a pillow sometime during the French Revolution to feel brave at night.

She turned, holding it up with both hands, grinning. "This one."

I stared. Then barked out a laugh. "You had your pick of history's finest, Blossom, and you chose the letter opener."

"It's cute," she said, all mock innocence.

"Cute?" I echoed, shadows twitching at the word like they didn't know if they should strangle her or applaud.

She twirled the dagger in her palm—badly—and nearly dropped it, then caught it again, cheeks pink but chin tilted high. "What? Not everyone needs a giant death scythe. Sometimes less is more." She eyed me.

I shook my head, smirking. "You're ridiculous."

Her smile widened. "You love it."

"Yeah, Blossom," I said, stepping closer, brushing my knuckles down her jaw. "I do."

Her breath hitched, eyes flicking between my face and the dagger. "Good. Because it's mine now."

Midnight. My favorite hour. The alley bled color, neon pinks and toxic greens dripping down wet brick, graffiti layered thick over itself until the walls looked like screaming collages. Spray paint cans rolled under my boots. Our tags were now covering the other many layers: my skull, her ghost. The stink of piss, burnt plastic, and blood money hung heavy, cut only by the tang of motor oil that had been spilled on the concrete.

This was no backstreet gamble where I was hoping to find some straggler to end. No, this was gang territory—a drug ring hub, to be exact. A nest for career criminals with rap sheets longer than my shadow. Murderers. Traffickers. Parasites who sold ruin in plastic baggies and let it chew holes through the city, through families. The kind of men who thought they'd beat the system because the system was too scared to crawl into alleys like this.

But me? I wasn't the system, and I wasn't fucking afraid.

The first one stumbled out of the door, drunk, knife tucked in his belt. His hands still smelled of powder and cash, and the stains on his shirt weren't from tonight. He'd slit throats before for smaller sums than the roll in his pocket.

He blinked at me once. "Hey!" he yelled. "Who the fuck are you? What are you doing here?" Then my shadows struck, curling up his throat, jerking him off the ground. His feet scrabbled against brick until the life ripped out of him, a light only I could see. I swallowed it whole.

Alive. For a second, I felt alive.

The second kill was faster, meaner. Chain in his hand, scars on his arms from the fights he'd started but hadn't finished. He came rushing out of the building after the first guy quit screaming. His teeth gleamed gold, his laugh mean. He'd killed a man once for looking too long at his girl. I saw it still clinging to him like perfume.

He swung. I didn't even try. I caught the chain in midair, twisted it like a noose, and cracked it around his head, pulling down hard. His skull cracked against the pavement before his soul tore loose. It slid down my throat like whiskey, hot and mean.

More poured out of the building, three this time. Mafioso wannabes, leather jackets with greasy collars, guns tucked in waistbands. One with knuckles split from beating a kid half to death for not paying up. One with a watch worth more than the mother he'd left rotting in a nursing home. One who carried the smell of burned rubber and screams. I knew what hit-and-run guilt looked like when it stuck to a man.

They wanted to fight? Good. I liked a fight.

Opal stiffened behind me, her hand going for that ridiculous little dagger in her waistband. I grabbed it from her before she even cleared the sheath. One flick of my wrist, muscle memory, instinct, and it lodged in his carotid. Pink roses carved into silver glinted under the neon glow as the man dropped.

Opal gasped, then snorted out a laugh she couldn't hold back. "You did *not* just kill him with *that*."

I grinned, teeth sharp. "Blossom, I could kill a man with a breath. Be grateful I made it entertaining."

The last two charged. My body didn't even bother asking me what to do. It just did a sidestep, shadow snare, soul rip. One pointed his gun at Opal, the muzzle flash painting her in red light for a heartbeat. I wanted to tear him apart just for thinking of hurting her. The shadows obliged, breaking his arm before I even thought it.

Their souls bled into me, rich and hot, fuel for the engine I'd been pretending wasn't running on empty. My veins thrummed. My lungs filled.

None of it mattered half as much as her. Opal stood there, bathed in neon glow and the ghosts of killers, her little hands gripping nothing now because I'd stolen her toy. Her chest rose and fell, quick but not panicked. Not terrified but alive, watching me like I was putting on a show choreographed only for her.

I killed them with muscle memory, but my focus never strayed from her. Her pulse, her breath, the way her eyes locked on me and didn't flinch, even when the shadows hissed and the bodies hit concrete.

I wiped my mouth, shadows curling around me like smoke after a fire. "See?" I said, grinning sharp and mean. "Effortless."

She shook her head, muttering, "You're insane."

I laughed. "Did you just figure that out?"

She swallowed and shook her head. Part of me was starting to think she actually liked it, like maybe she was just as fucked up as I was.

We were almost clear of the alley when another one stepped out of the doorway. Greasy hair, rotting teeth, eyes glassy from whatever cocktail he'd shot into his veins. A straggler. A parasite who hadn't learned to run when his friends started dropping like flies.

He looked at Opal. Not me. Big mistake.

"Well, well," he slurred, lips curling into something between a sneer and a snarl. His eyes dragged down her legs like slime down a drain. "Pretty little slut. Bet she tastes sweet. You sharing or just keeping her for yourself? I'd love a taste."

My shadows surged before I did, coiling up his body. One tendril snapped around his jaw, locking it shut with a brutal *pop* of cartilage.

I moved in, slow. Deliberate. Let him see me. Let him *know* he fucked up. "You want a taste?" I asked softly, almost gently. "You want something of hers on your tongue?"

I pulled a rusted pair of pliers off the nearby tool bench, still crusted with blood from gods-knew-what, and slid them into the air like a scalpel into a surgeon's hand.

"Alright," I whispered. "Let's start with that tongue."

He thrashed, eyes going wide, trying to scream behind clamped teeth. The shadows held him in place like iron. The pliers didn't hesitate. They slipped past his lips, forced between his teeth, found their target.

I didn't yank it out fast. I twisted, then ripped. The muffled shriek that escaped him was wet and gurgled, panic and agony blending into something animal. He tried to breathe, to sob. I didn't let him.

I shoved the mangled thing back into his mouth, deeper, deeper still, while his lungs spasmed and his hands clawed at his throat like he could undo it. "Choke on it," I said.

His face turned purple, veins bulging as he collapsed forward. Still convulsing. He wasn't dead yet, but I wasn't done. One boot to his head did the trick. His soul tried to peel free, too late, too slow. I caught it mid-scream and tore it from his body like lint from a suit jacket. It went down hot and sticky. I wiped the blood off my fingers with his shirt and looked at her. "Anyone touches you," I said, voice as sharp as the edge of a blade, "they don't get to live long enough to regret it."

Opal's breath hitched, but she didn't flinch. Not from me.

She just whispered, steady, "I know."

CHAPTER 21

Opal

We landed in what had once been a designer boutique in Milan. Now it was . . . closed. Or rather, *Cain-ed.*

The place smelled faintly of mothballs and dust. Dresses hung in rows of muted colors, safe colors, black, gray, navy. The kind of colors that didn't draw attention.

Cain leaned on the wall near the entrance, dark hoodie pulled low, arms crossed, every line of him screaming *Don't look at me.* Shadows slid around him like smoke curling up a candle's throat. He looked carved out of midnight.

I'd spent most of my life trying to match that kind of silence, slipping into whatever skin would make me less noticeable. The safe girlfriend. The cool, ironic YouTuber. The girl who played along with Nyxie and Lyric's influencer antics, even when they grated my nerves like glass.

Standing here with him like this, I realized he wasn't blending in. He wasn't hiding. He *was* the darkness in the room, and he didn't care who noticed.

"Pick something." His voice was flat, practical, like this was nothing more than an errand. "Black, preferably. You'll blend in. No one in Hell's gonna look twice."

He reached into the rack like he was pulling a weapon and shoved the hanger toward me. "Something like this." It was a long, black, satin gown, the kind of thing you'd wear to a funeral if you wanted to look expensive while mourning. Sharp, sleek, elegant. Perfect for Cain's world, but not mine.

I held it up between us, trying to picture myself inside it. Cold fabric against my skin. Shadow draped over shadow. Another costume. "You really think I could pull off a funeral gown at a wedding?" I asked lightly.

Cain's expression didn't shift, but the corner of his mouth twitched like the ghost of a smirk. "It's not a funeral. Yet."

I should've rolled my eyes, tossed the hanger back, and taken the easy route. That's what I'd always done. Blend in. Adapt. Keep the peace. But something in his tone, sharp, mocking, *watching*, made me want to be defiant, be me.

For a second, I saw the tiniest crack in his armor, like he was bracing for me to choose the black dress, to confirm what he already believed about me—that I'd always play it safe. That I was just another human pretending to be brave.

I slid the hanger back onto the rack. "No."

Cain's gaze flicked toward me, a smile sliding onto his face sharp as a blade. "No?"

I pushed past him before I lost the nerve, weaving through the racks until I found it: the explosion of color I hadn't even realized I'd been craving. Pink. Layer after ridiculous, ruffled layer of tulle. A corseted bodice, heart-shaped neckline, sleeves blooming with flowers so oversized they looked obscene against all the beige and black.

I grabbed it, undressed with a glance to make sure that Cain wasn't in eyesight, and wrestled into the fabric. I spun back toward him, grinning before I even realized it. "This one."

The silence that followed was thick enough to choke on. Cain's eyes dragged over the dress like it had personally insulted him. His jaw tightened. Shadows licked at his boots.

"You'll stand out," he said at last, low and dangerous.

"Exactly." My voice wavered at first, but then steadied, louder, braver. "Why would I want to blend in?"

The words hit me as hard as they hit him. Because I'd been blending in my whole life, and for what? To be liked? To be safe? To keep myself from being abandoned? The truth was, I'd been abandoned anyway—by friends, by a family that never really saw me. But I was still here . . . still breathing, still me.

Cain just stared. His face gave nothing away, but his silence felt like an earthquake. He wasn't used to people opposing him, not like this.

I twirled once with the pink monstrosity clutched in my hands, defiantly laughing at his scowl. "What? Afraid the big bad Reaper will be caught escorting Barbie to Hell?"

His lips curved. "Final Girl," he muttered, voice rougher than I'd ever heard it. "You wear that to the Devil's wedding," he said, "and I'm going to have to start a war."

I tilted my head. "Over a dress?"

He stepped closer.

"No," he said, all quiet menace and promise. "Over you."

Cain ran a hand over the crushed flowers on the sleeve and down my chest. Slow.

Reverent.

His fingers ghosted just above the curve of my breast, not quite touching, but close enough that my breath hitched. His eyes didn't leave mine, not for a second.

"You look like something that doesn't belong in this world," he murmured. "And I mean that in the worst and best ways."

"Flatter me more," I said, but my voice had that telltale shake, the one he always caught.

He smirked. Dragged his thumb lower, just beneath the bodice.

"Don't need to," he said. "I already got you half undone."

His knuckles brushed along my waist, then back up to toy with my shoulder.

"I should destroy this," he muttered, almost to himself.

"Because it's pink?"

"Because it makes me want to bite."

I gasped, but he was already pulling away, stepping back like he hadn't just unraveled me with a sentence.

"We've got a wedding to crash," he said, tossing me a wink over his shoulder. "Better hurry up, Final Girl."

Cain walked over to a rack, plucking a black suit from the hanger like he'd been born in it. The fabric was dark, rich, tailored, way too nice for a condemned building full of forgotten dreams and broken glass, but that was Cain for you. Death in a tux.

Then—because of course he did—he started stripping.

Right there.

No hesitation. No shame. Just pulled his shirt over his head and let it fall to the floor. My cheeks went up in flames. "Seriously?" I squeaked, trying to look anywhere but the sharp cut of his hips and the ink that sprawled across his skin like a map to my personal hell.

"What?" he said casually, kicking off his boots, then his pants. "You've seen it all, Blossom. Don't start getting shy on me now."

"That was different. That was . . . private."

He smirked. "And this is efficient."

I covered my eyes. "Cain."

"You really going to pretend you didn't just ride me like your life depended on it?"

"God," I groaned into my hands.

He chuckled. Low. Dark. Pleased with himself. "Look, if you're gonna be Death's date to the Devil's wedding, you better get used to a little scandal."

"I don't think you'd ever qualify as a *little scandal*."

Cain laughed again and slid the jacket on. It fit too well. Like it had been stitched around his sins. When he turned around, his eyes found mine and held.

"What do you think?" he asked.

I tried to breathe.

"You look like trouble."

He grinned.

"Good."

We were about to leave when curiosity got the better of me.

"Hey," I said, tugging gently on his sleeve before he could open a new shadow gate. "If no one can touch you without dying . . . how did you get tattoos?"

Cain paused, lips twitching at the corners like he wanted to laugh. He smiled, that crooked, cocky, I-know-something-you-don't grin that always made my stomach tighten.

"It's magic, Blossom," he said, rolling his shoulders lazily. "Glamour."

He raised his hand, and before my eyes, his skin shimmered like smoke over ink. The tattoos rippled . . . and vanished. All of them faded away like fog burning off morning glass.

My jaw dropped a little.

"You mean they're fake?" I asked, scandalized.

He shrugged, totally unbothered. "I just like them. They look cool."

I blinked. "You gave yourself glamoured tattoos. For fun."

"Of course I did," he said, deadpan. "What else am I supposed to do between plagues and mass extinctions?"

I shook my head, trying not to laugh. "You're unbelievable."

Cain flashed me that feral little smirk again. "And yet, here you are, voluntarily dating Death. Maybe you're the one that's unbelievable."

He flicked his fingers, and the tattoos slid back into view like ink soaking into paper. "Ready, Blossom?" He reached out a hand, and I took it and didn't let go.

"Let's crash a wedding."

"I thought you were invited," I said, raising a brow as his shadows coiled tighter around us.

He turned to me, face void of emotion.

"Shhh."

I laughed. "Technically . . . aren't you the best man?"

He scowled like I'd accused him of something unholy. "Details."

"Uh-huh. Pretty important detail, don't you think?"

He stepped closer, gaze dropping to my lips before flicking back up to my eyes. "Blossom, I've crashed my own funeral before. You really think a wedding's going to stop me?"

I blinked. "Wait. You had a funeral?"

"A couple," he said with a shrug. "They got boring after the second one, but this"—he gestured toward the rift starting to open beside us, firelight licking at the edges—"this should be fun."

"Define fun."

Cain's grin went sharp. "The Devil. A forbidden bride. A gathering of immortals who all hate each other. Assassination attempts. Maybe a dance floor."

I blinked. "Wait, what was that middle one?"

"C'mon, Blossom," he said, already grabbing my hand. "Let's make a scene."

The grin stayed in his eyes long after he'd stepped back. It was a laugh that sounded like a warning and, somehow, comfort. When the rift sighed open at his elbow, the moment cracked like thin glass, and we stepped through.

The rift closed behind us with a soft hiss, and I barely had time to register the massive bookcases or the scent of old parchment before I was pressed against a shelf, breath stolen, dress hitched.

Cain's lips crashed into mine, urgent and hungry, fingers trailing up the slit in the tulle like he already knew what he wanted and didn't care if he got caught getting it.

"Cain," I gasped, heart in my throat, thighs already trembling, as he pressed me into a bookshelf.

"Shhh," he murmured, his breath warm against my cheek. "Baby, don't use my name like that."

He kissed down my jaw, hand curling around the back of my thigh, lifting it to hook over his hip.

"That's a powerful thing," he whispered, voice dipped in smoke and promise.

A throat cleared behind us. Cain let my leg down slowly.

I turned, and whatever breath I'd been holding since Cain's lips left mine left in a ragged, stupid little sound that wasn't quite a cry or a laugh. The Devil stood there, long, slow, immaculate, like a man who'd stepped out of legend and found the lighting convenient. His black coat hung off him like he'd been painted in absence.

It hit me like cold water. Not logical fright—something older than reason. A pressure behind my sternum, like someone pressing a palm into the hollow of my ribs and asking me to make peace with a predator. I knew the legend was meant to make me wary, but knowing wasn't the same as feeling this animal, bone-deep dread.

Cain didn't flinch, didn't bow, didn't do the social dance. He simply looked at the Devil like a man might look at a neighbor who'd wandered into his kitchen to steal a loaf of bread: familiar annoyance, a little fondness, a shrug of "this again."

"Breathe," Cain said, voice flat and meant only for me.

Cain's hand closed over mine so hard I tasted it on my tongue. His thumb pressed at the heel of my palm, and his voice was a low tether. "Don't," he said, simple and absolute. "It's his curse, Blossom. You feel it because you're human. He makes people feel afraid."

He shifted, stepped so that his body was between me and the Devil, facing me. Close enough that his smoke and mint scent steadied me more than his words did. "He's not dangerous," he added. "He hates what he is, most days. He's . . . complicated. He's decent enough about the things that matter. He won't hurt you."

"He knows you are important to me," Cain continued, audible only to me. "He'll respect that. He'll protect you because I asked. Because of the bargain." His breath warmed my ear. "Trust me. I'm worse than he is."

Trust was a risky currency with Death, but the fear the Devil cast didn't make Cain flinch, and the steadiness in Cain's voice steadied something in me. I lent him the fraction of faith I had left and let my fingers curl around his. The cold that clung to me lost some of its bite.

"Nice to see you too," the Devil said, dry amusement curling across his mouth. "Though I was expecting you at the front door. Not making out with your plus one in my office."

"Pit stop," he said, turning back around, completely unapologetic, flashing that wicked grin that made my knees weak and my soul question its morals.

The Devil's mouth twitched. Cain stepped to my side, shadows curling lazily around his fingers like they were waiting for something to burn.

"This is Opal," he said, like it meant something. "Opal, this is Damon, the Devil and also my best friend."

Damon studied me, really studied me, then nodded once. "Welcome to Hell, my lády."

"For safety reasons," Damon said, turning slightly toward me with that devilish calm, "I think it's best if we just call her *Lady Death* tonight."

Cain nodded once. "Agreed."

I blinked between them. "Wait—am I in danger?"

Cain turned to me, his smile a little too wide, a little too sharp. All menace wrapped in charm. "Not after they see you on my arm." He leaned in, lips near my ear. "No one would *dare*, but let's keep that name to ourselves tonight too, huh?"

"One more thing," he said, and Cain stilled. "About your brother."

Cain's head snapped up so fast I felt the air shift. "What about him?" he growled. "He's gone missing. I expect you had something to do with that?"

Damon grimaced. "He tried to kill my bride and overthrow me," he said, but the word "tried" felt smaller than the sentence deserved. "He's gone too far."

Cain frowned, until Damon moved forward and dropped something into his palm. A stone that was small and blood-red. Pulsing faintly like it remembered being alive.

Cain stared at it, frozen.

"He's safe," Damon said, his voice clipped with a strange tension, "but locked away."

"He's no longer welcome in Hell," he added, voice darkening. "And he knows the truth now about who he is, about who you are to him."

"I'm sorry for the trouble he caused," Cain said quietly. "He can be a bit . . ."

"*Prideful?*" Damon finished, glancing back with a knowing look. "I'm familiar."

There was a beat. Then, unexpectedly, the Devil softened. "This changes nothing between us," he said, heading for the door. "You are still my closest friend."

Cain didn't speak. Not right away. He stared at the stone, then slipped it carefully into his pocket like it weighed more than the world.

"Thank you," he said at last, rough, quiet, but real.

Damon only nodded.

CHAPTER 22

Cain

The stone in my pocket burned like a brand. Abel, my brother and my curse. Now sealed into a prison small enough to fit in my palm.

I stood in Damon's study long after the Devil himself left the room, shadows breathing slow and silent around me. They curled along the floor like waiting dogs, itching for a command.

Opal stood across from me, watching, waiting, breathing the same sharp-edged air, but she didn't press. She didn't ask. She just stayed close, a warm weight pressing in beside me.

Gods, I needed that.

"You okay?" she asked after a long beat of silence, voice soft like it might spook me.

I shook my head. "No." Honesty was a strange thing. Bitter and clean. But she made it easier. I turned to her, to *Opal*, and for a moment, everything else quieted. Her hair was a little messy, her lips still red from where I'd kissed her like the world was ending.

"What now?" she asked.

I didn't answer.

Just stepped toward her.

Her eyes widened slightly, but she didn't flinch away from me.

Good girl.

I brushed a knuckle down her cheek. "Now," I whispered, "we play nice."

She blinked. "You?"

I smirked. "For about five minutes, maybe six."

"You're a menace."

I tucked a curl behind her ear and pressed a kiss to her temple. "Takes one to love one, Blossom."

Her heart skipped, and I *heard* it. Like a drum against her ribs. And mine? That long-dead thing in my chest? It remembered how to beat.

For her.

Only her.

My girl.

"Come on," I said, offering my hand. "Let's go crash a wedding."

The grand hall of Hell was built for spectacle.

Black marble stretched beneath our feet, veined with molten gold. Chandeliers spiraled from the vaulted ceiling like something alive. Every immortal in the Under Realms was seated in their twisted little section, reapers, devils, demons, drakes, all of them. Every single one of them turned when we entered. Eyes followed us. Mouths parted in disbelief. Whispers spread like sparks on the wind.

I didn't blame them. It wasn't every day Death showed up to a royal wedding with a mortal girl in pink on his arm.

Opal didn't shrink. Not even once.

She walked beside me like she belonged there. Like she ruled the room just by breathing in it. Head high, eyes wide, that faint little smirk dancing at the edge of her mouth like she knew exactly what kind of chaos she was causing.

Gods, I loved that smirk. Loved that girl.

I led her down the aisle between rows of curious onlookers, my hand firm around hers, until we reached her seat, first row, right side, just behind the Devil's family.

"You sure you're good?" I asked.

She tilted her head. "You mean aside from the fact that I'm sitting in literal Hell, in a flower bomb dress, surrounded by monsters?"

I lifted a brow.

She smirked. "Totally fine."

I bent down, brushing my lips against her knuckles. "If anyone looks at you wrong—"

"They'll die?" she finished.

"No. *I'll get jealous.* Then they'll die."

She laughed quietly, and I wanted to bottle the sound . . . But duty called.

I released her hand reluctantly and turned toward the altar, toward Damon. He stood at the end of the aisle in full regalia: black suit, wine-red tie, long coat trailing behind him like a cloak of shadows. His expression was unreadable, but there was a glint in his eye that said he'd seen the stir we'd caused.

"Smooth entrance," he said under his breath as I joined him.

I shrugged. "Could've been flashier."

"You're the only person I know who can make *death* look like a romantic gesture."

I let my eyes flick back to Opal. She was watching me, chin on her hand, legs crossed, utterly calm.

"She's not a gesture," I said quietly. "She's the decision."

Damon didn't comment.

Didn't need to.

He just adjusted his cufflinks and said, "Let's get this over with before someone decides to start a war over your little statement piece."

"Let them try," I murmured.

Then the doors opened again, and the hall fell silent.

Carmen, Damon's bride, stepped into the room like a reckoning, cloaked in black lace and crimson veils, her hair braided with thorns, her eyes steady and bright blue, a strange light that didn't belong to this realm or any other shining from them. Her dress rippled like liquid night, corseted and stitched with runes that glimmered when the light hit them just right. Her power was quiet, but no one missed it.

Especially not Damon. His eyes never left her. Not as she passed rows of dignitaries and demons. Not as her heels clicked against the obsidian floor like war drums. Not even when the firelight made the edges of her veil look like burning coals.

He only moved when she reached the dais. One step forward, and his face split into that damn smile, the one only she ever got. They joined hands.

The officiant said words. Ancient ones. Words in languages that twisted around your spine and pulled at the parts of you you'd forgotten you had. Vows that echoed beyond life and death. Promises that burned through time.

But Damon?

He ignored most of it.

He only had eyes for her.

When the final vow hung heavy in the air, the Devil leaned in so close no one else could hear, and whispered something into Carmen's ear.

Her eyes widened for a fraction of a second, and then she smiled. Not a soft smile. Not , *that* smile was wicked. That smile was ownership.

And I'd bet my blades I wasn't the only one who noticed.

The officiant turned to me.

"Rings?"

I stepped forward, stone-faced, and handed them over.

Two twisted bands. Gold and black. Intertwined like smoke and thorn. Fused in the fire of a kingdom that never forgot. Damon took one. He slid it onto Carmen's finger. She took the other and slid it onto his.

When he kissed her, when the veil dropped and the room broke into unsteady applause, it wasn't delicate or polite. The Devil's wife didn't flinch. She kissed him back like she was born to it, and just like that . . . Hell had a queen.

The hall transformed. Where vows had been spoken in low, ancient tongues, now music thundered, dark and rich, stitched with a pulse like something alive. The chandeliers flickered with blue flame, casting long shadows over velvet-draped tables. Goblets brimming with things that shouldn't sparkle. Laughter sharp enough to wound.

I stepped down from the dais and offered my Little Ghoul my hand.

Whispers swirled like incense, trailing behind us as we walked arm in arm into the Devil's ballroom.

"Lady Death."

"She's mortal."

"She can't be."

"They say she *bound* him—"

"She *commands* him."

"She's the reason he's been smiling."

I could feel them watching, and I didn't give a single fuck. I leaned down, lips ghosting the shell of her ear.

"They're talking about you," I teased, my voice quiet but no less wicked.

She looked up, cheeks flushed. "No shit."

I smirked. "Does it bother you?"

"A little," she said. "But mostly, I think they're scared."

I laughed. "They should be."

We reached our table. Opal settled into the black-velvet seat, adjusting the layers of tulle around her hips. I stayed standing, one hand on the back of her chair, letting my presence curl around her like smoke.

She leaned toward me, voice soft, just for me.

"Do you know what Damon whispered to Carmen?"

My grin stretched, crooked and sharp, the kind of grin that always made her breath stutter. "His true name," I said, brushing a pink curl off her shoulder like I had the right to. "It's a powerful thing to have, Blossom."

I cut my gaze across the room. Damon lounged on his throne, bone and gold carved like sin had commissioned it. One arm draped around his queen as if she'd always belonged under it. The sight made me itch. Not because I envied him, but because I understood.

"And do you know it?" Opal asked. She wasn't looking at Damon. She was looking at me, like she already knew the answer but wanted to hear me say it. Like I was a riddle wrapped around a blade.

I tilted my head back toward her. "I do."

Her breath caught, pink lips parting. "How?"

I leaned in close enough our noses brushed, close enough she could feel my smile ghost against her mouth. "It was part of our deal."

She didn't ask what deal. Smart girl. My Final Girl.

"You're dangerous," she whispered.

I kissed the corner of her mouth, soft for once. Just enough to make her eyes widen. "You knew that going in."

She rolled her eyes, but the curve of her lips betrayed her. "I just didn't know I'd like it so much."

That made me laugh. Low. Satisfied. The sound scraped out of my chest like smoke and fire, because fuck, she was wrecking me and didn't even know it. I leaned in, closer still. I could smell the faint wine on her breath, the heat of her skin still clinging from earlier—from me. My hand curled around the back of her chair, knuckles grazing the bare strip of skin between her shoulders.

She tilted her head like she was going to ask me something. So I gave her an answer instead. No hesitation. No shame. "Do you know how badly I want to fuck you in that dress?"

She choked on her drink.

The sound was everything: messy, unpolished, human. Her eyes went wide, green shot through with surprise, and pink rushed across her cheeks like sunrise bleeding into a graveyard. My cock twitched behind the safety of black tailored pants.

I grinned slow, sharp. I didn't give her space to think. Just let her flounder while the entire room blurred into shadow. Because right now, I only cared about the way her thighs pressed together. The way her teeth worried her bottom lip like she was trying not to smile.

"Death . . ." she warned, voice trembling but not afraid. Never afraid.

"Shhh." I dragged my fingers up her spine, slow, deliberate, until she shivered under my touch. "You wore pink. You knew what you were doing." I reversed the motion, whispering in her ear. "Pink is quickly becoming my favorite color."

Her laugh came ragged and unsteady. "I didn't think—"

"You never do," I cut in, letting my lips graze along her jaw, not kissing, not yet. Drawing it out until she trembled. "That's why I like you."

The music shifted. A slow song. A violin dragged out a haunting note, and I swear the bastard instrument knew exactly what I wanted.

"Dance with me," I said. It wasn't a question.

Her wine glass clinked against the table as I pulled her into me. She was warm. Too warm. A little drunk, a little giggly, and somehow more dangerous because of it. The violin wove around us, and her hips swayed against mine like temptation hadn't already been gnawing at me for hours.

Her laugh slipped past her lips and wrapped itself around my ribs like a pink ribbon I'd gladly strangle on, and she glowed. Gods, she glowed. Pink tulle and flowers blooming across her chest, her green eyes catching the light like emerald fire. My Little Ghoul, my Final Girl. Drunk on wine and adrenaline and me. Always me. Her fingers curled at the back of my neck, toying with my hair like she didn't know it made me want to ruin her right here in front of everyone.

"Careful," I warned, my mouth brushing her ear. "Keep touching me like that, and I'll take you home in pieces."

She giggled again, wrecked and perfect, not caring that we were standing in Hell's most dangerous ballroom.

"Not scared of you, Death," she whispered back.

And that, fuck, that was worse than any curse I'd ever carried. Because she meant it. Because for the first time in forever, someone saw me. Not the monster, not the reaper, not the myth. Me.

The violin still throbbed low and haunting when Opal jolted against me.

Her body stiffened, eyes wide, and before I could ask, her hand was already moving. Quick as lightning, she yanked the rose-engraved dagger from the holster strapped to her thigh, skirts swishing around her legs as if the dress itself wanted to get out of her way.

I felt it before I saw it, the shift in the air, the ripple of killing intent. I whirled, shadows flaring just as steel flashed. A demon lunged from the crowd, blade glinting as it arced toward me, and Opal, my ridiculous Little Ghoul in her candy-floss gown, drove her dagger straight into his chest.

The sound was wet, brutal, real. The demon staggered, choking, eyes bulging as he stared down at the hilt blooming from his sternum. For half a second, the entire world narrowed to her pink curls falling into her face, chest heaving, pupils blown wide with adrenaline. She'd moved without hesitation.

Fuck. I had never wanted her more.

The demon gurgled, half a laugh, half a snarl, and then Damon was there. Flames licked up his arms, curling like living things as he stalked out from behind his throne. His crimson eyes burned through the haze, molten and merciless. He didn't hesitate. Didn't pause. His hands wrapped around the demon's head and—*crack*.

The snap echoed through the hall. The body crumpled, twitching once before stilling at Opal's feet. Damon's flames burned hotter, singeing the air itself as he glared down at the corpse. His voice rolled out, low and dangerous enough to make the chandeliers tremble. "That's for making a scene at my wedding."

Opal stood frozen, hand still clenched around empty air like she couldn't believe she'd actually done it. Her dagger. Her kill.

I crouched, tugging the blade free from the demon's chest. Blood slicked the steel, dark and viscous. I wiped it clean on the dead bastard's shirt, not breaking eye contact with her.

Then I held it out, hilt first. "You dropped this," I said, voice low, a curl of pride and something darker winding through my chest. Her fingers trembled when she took it back. Opal still clutched the dagger like she expected another demon to leap from the shadows. Her cheeks were flushed, her breath ragged, but her eyes—her eyes were fixed on me.

"Why would someone even try?" she asked, voice hushed but unsteady. "You're immortal. They can't kill you."

I let out a low laugh, sharp as broken glass. "He wasn't trying to kill me, Blossom. He was trying to steal my Mark."

Her brows knit, confusion and dread tangling in her expression. "Your . . . mark?"

I lowered my voice to a whisper. "The Mark of Cain." The words tasted like ash. "The thing that makes me what I am. The thing that makes me Death." My jaw tightened. "It can be transferred. Ripped out of me and forced onto someone else."

Her lips parted in horror. "So, he wanted to become you."

"He wanted my power and throne." I met her gaze, steady, unflinching. "But I would never wish this curse on anyone, not even my worst enemy. It's mine to carry. My punishment. My burden."

For a moment, the reception hall felt too quiet. The music had stuttered to a halt. Demons whispered along the edges of the crowd, eyes flicking between me, Opal, and the still-smoking corpse at our feet.

Damon's voice cut through the silence, molten and absolute. "He would have failed."

Opal flinched as the Devil himself strode closer, fire still licking at his arms, his eyes a pitiless glowing crimson. He didn't bother looking at the body. His focus was on me. On us.

"The location of Death's Mark," Damon continued, voice carrying like a decree, "is a closely kept secret. Only two souls outside of God Himself know where it is hidden." His mouth curled into a humorless smile, all teeth and fire. "Cain is one. I am the other."

The crowd was still buzzing, low voices, the clink of glasses, the hiss of Damon's flames as they guttered out along his forearms. Eyes followed us like carrion birds, demons whispering about the human girl in pink who'd just spilled blood in Hell.

I'd had enough.

I slid the dagger from Opal's trembling fingers and tucked it back into her thigh holster, letting my hand linger just long enough to feel her shiver. Then I straightened, shadows rippling at my feet like they were restless to leave.

"We're done here," I said flatly.

Damon arched a brow from his throne, fire still glowing in his eyes. "Running so soon, Death?"

"Not running." I tugged Opal closer, my hand firm at her waist. "Removing my date before your guests decide they'd like to test their luck."

Opal blinked up at me, still wide-eyed, still processing. I didn't give her the chance to argue. I didn't care if she understood. This wasn't a negotiation. I slipped an arm under her legs. She gasped, half a protest dying on her lips as I hoisted her up like she weighed nothing. "No—" she started, but we were already gone.

The rift opened with a breath of heat and sulfur. When we landed, her fingers still clenched the fabric of my shirt when we hit the ground. Not a fist of panic, not exactly. More like a reflex, like she was making sure solid things still existed. Her chest rose and fell too fast. Her cheeks were flushed with adrenaline. Her hands trembled.

"Talk to me," I said quietly as if a loud sound might rip her open. "You okay?"

She blinked, then laughed, a thin half-laugh that sounded like a match struck and sputtering out. "I stabbed a demon," she said, like that explained everything. "So, yeah. Fine."

"I mean right now," I said. I slid my fingers under the hem of her sleeve the way a thief checks the lock on a door. Her pulse hammered under my thumb like it was trying to run. Not badly wounded. Not a ripped-out thing. Just the tremor of someone who's held a knife in a place where knives should never belong.

She swallowed, eyes going suddenly glassy. "I thought—" Her throat closed. "I thought you—"

"Don't." My voice was a low leash. "Don't tell me what you thought." I pressed my palm hard to her shoulder so she couldn't look away from me. She met my eyes, and the tremor in them steadied a fraction.

I let my fingers trail, silently taking inventory, checking the small lines of blood on her wrist, the smear on her thigh where it had soaked through the tulle. Nothing life-ending. Nothing that would ruin tattoos or make good TV. Still, blood is a language I know. I cupped the side of her face and turned it toward me so I could see her properly. Her lips were raw where my mouth had been. Her pupils were blown wide. She smelled like wine and iron and something sweet that was just her.

"You saved me," I said. Plain and ugly and true.

She blinked. "I didn't—I didn't mean to—"

"You did." I thumbed the dab of blood at the corner of her mouth and wiped it with my sleeve. My fingers shook, which I hated. "You moved faster than anyone has a right to. You put steel exactly where it was deserved. That means something."

Her breath hitched, not quite a sob. "I'm sorry. I don't even know why I—"

"You don't owe me explanations." I pressed my forehead to hers for one slow, ridiculous second because I needed to feel the shape of her. Her breath fogged against my skin. "You're reckless and glorious and a goddamn idiot sometimes, but you are mine."

She laughed once. Small. Broken. "Mine?"

"Yeah." I smiled crookedly, felt the old world tilt. "Mine."

She melted into that like it was the only map she had. The tension in her shoulders eased a fraction. Her hands found the lapels of my jacket and clutched it as if to anchor herself.

"You're bleeding a little," she whispered, suddenly practical.

"So are you." I got up, because staying still felt dangerous, and went to the cabinet. I fetched a cloth, damp with something cool and clean. When I came back she was watching me like I was about to perform some obscure ritual.

"Hold still," I said. I dabbed at the cut on her thigh, careful. She had nicked herself pulling the blade from its holster. Her skin was hot. She flinched when I touched the wound, but she didn't pull away.

"Does it hurt?" I asked.

"A little." Her voice was small.

"You did good," I told her, as if rewards were currency I could hand out. She blinked at me like I'd just paid her in gold.

"You sure?" she asked, voice brittle.

I tapped my thumb against hers, felt the tremble. "I'm sure."

There was a quiet between us after that. Not silence so much as settling dust. She leaned into me without meaning to, like gravity had remembered how to favor certain things. I wrapped an arm around her, and she let her head fall against my chest. I could feel the rapid little stutters of her heart under my ribs. Mine answered, like someone had lit a match in a room that had been dark for too long.

"Stay," she breathed.

I nodded. "You did good," I repeated. "You saved me."

She laughed once, soft and jagged. "I didn't save you. I panicked and stabbed first."

"You panicked well." I nuzzled the hollow beneath her ear. She shivered. I swallowed that sound, kept my hands steady. Her tremors stilled, and her breathing evened out. "Tell me if you want me to stop. Say the word."

Her fingers tightened in my jacket, nails warm. "I won't," she said, voice small, dangerous. "I don't want you to stop."

I let my hands travel slowly, hands that had been trained to take and bury and stand back. Tonight they hesitated, because this wasn't about owning; it was about making sure she stayed human. I slid down the curve of her back, felt the ribs hitch under fabric, and cupped the soft place at the base of her spine. She leaned into my hand like she belonged there.

She laughed, breathless and stupid and alive. "You're being weirdly tender," she said.

"Shut up." I laughed and met her eyes. "Do you want me to be gentle?" I asked, because even monsters have manners sometimes.

Her laugh was small. "No," she whispered, the single word a challenge and a plea. "Not at all."

"Good. I'm not great at keeping myself tame when it comes to you."

CHAPTER 23

Cain

I dropped her onto the mattress with enough force to make her bounce. Before she could catch her breath, the lights died, snuffed out by the shadows slithering from my skin. The room went black, thick and heavy, until it felt like she'd been swallowed whole.

I crawled onto the bed after her, slow, deliberate, looming like I was planning to devour her. Shadows slid across the mattress, cool tendrils wrapping around her wrists and dragging them above her head, pinning them against the headboard. Another crept up the curve of her thigh, teasing its way higher, stroking just shy of where I knew she was throbbing for me.

She gasped, back arching. "Cain—"

"Shhh," I murmured, pressing my body down into hers, grinding just enough to make her squirm. I buried my face in the curve of her neck, nipping and sucking until she whimpered, shadows tightening on her wrists when she tried to move. Her hips bucked helplessly against mine, caught between my weight and the darkness.

I caught her chin between my fingers, forcing her to meet my eyes in the pitch black. My grin cut sharp across my face.

"I warned you what would happen if you wore that dress." I flipped her onto her stomach, her ass in the air, and gripped her hips, my cock throbbing as I lined myself up with her dripping entrance. "Now you're going to pay for it." I rubbed the tip of my cock on her clit. "Now beg," I growled, pressing the tip against her opening, and she whimpered, her hips pushing back, desperate for me.

"Please," she whined, her voice broken, and I slammed into her, burying myself to the hilt in one brutal thrust. She screamed, her walls tightening around me, and I groaned. She was so fucking tight, so hot, so perfect.

I grabbed her hair, pulling her head back as I fucked her hard and deep, my hips slamming into hers with a rhythm that was primal, punishing. She was moaning, begging, her nails clawing at the sheets as I destroyed her, my cock stretching her, filling her, claiming her.

I reached around, my fingers finding her clit, and I rubbed it hard, fast, until she was coming again, her pussy clenching around me.

I pulled out, flipping her onto her back, and jerked myself off, my cum spraying across her stomach, her tits, her face. She panted, her body still quivering with aftershocks, and I smirked. She was fucking wrecked.

Still trembling, skin flushed, lashes fluttering like she was chasing the last breath of her climax.

I should've pulled away. Given her space. Let her breathe. Instead . . . I stayed and cleaned her up with the damp rag I still had lying beside the bed.

I slid in beside her, wrapped my arms around her waist, and pulled her to my chest like I was afraid she'd vanish if I let go.

The morning was too quiet. I had slept a few hours but woke before Opal, so I lay there, staring at the ceiling. Opal was curled beside me, one bare leg thrown over mine, her face half-buried in my chest like she hadn't just spent last night tormenting me with bare thighs and the thought of round two or three. Her breath came slow and even, dreaming, maybe.

My arm was slung around her waist, fingers twitching with the urge to pull her closer even though she was already pressed against me like a second skin.

She sighed against my collarbone, breath warm and minty like cheap gum, and I . . . I almost smiled. Almost. But then the ache hit. That slow rot in my bones. Like frostbite from the inside out. I breathed through it. Jaw clenched. Let my eyes flutter closed. *Not yet. Not now.*

I'd only taken a few lives yesterday. Enough to settle the sickness. But the tether between us was still growing stronger, and it was draining me more than I wanted to admit. If I kept pretending it wasn't affecting me, I'd end up collapsing again. *Rotting* in her bed again . . . and she'd *worry*. Again.

I exhaled slowly. Fuck. I was getting too comfortable. Too *soft*. Sleeping beside her like some mortal lover instead of what I was: a cosmic curse, the ultimate protector of the balance of the universe.

She stirred, mumbling something against my chest, and I glanced down. Her hair was a mess. She had a crease on her cheek from where she'd been squished into my ribs all night, and I swear to the Devil himself, she looked like trouble incarnate wrapped in a fucking sunrise.

I shifted, trying not to wake her as I sat up, but of course, she blinked awake, bleary and confused. "Cain?" Her voice was a rasp. She stretched, one arm flopping dramatically across my lap like she had *any* idea how hard she was making this. Literally and metaphorically.

"Morning, Blossom," I muttered.

She sat up slower, rubbing her eyes. "You *slept*."

I snorted. "Don't sound so surprised."

"You *never* sleep."

"Not true. I just—"

She cut me off. "Crash like a plague victim and then rot for days."

That made me huff a laugh despite myself. "Dramatic."

"Accurate," she said, poking my ribs. "I don't think you have supernatural no-sleep abilities. I think you have insomnia and a god complex."

I raised an eyebrow. "You trying to provoke me, Blossom?"

She smiled, lazy and satisfied. "Always."

I fucking loved that. Even now, with the first flickers of imbalance tightening around my ribs like barbed wire, I wanted to pull her closer. The sickness crept back into my bones, a cold that smelled like iron and old smoke, and my fingers twitched against her hip as if to anchor myself to something real.

Something was changing. The cycle was off. The weight of souls wasn't balancing like it used to. I couldn't tell if it was her, me, or that fucked-up spell, but the ripple was there, running under my skin.

For now, she was here, sprawled across my lap in one of my shirts, hair tickling my throat, grinning like she was looking for trouble. I was letting her, because I was selfish. For the first time in forever, I didn't want to let go, and that thought felt like a problem with teeth.

I ran a hand through my hair and checked the clock. Time folded around her, slow and soft, like the world had learned to be careful. "We need to work today," I said, watching the early light smear across her face. She blinked up at me, half-wrapped in sleep. A sleepy nod. A tiny mumble that may have been "Okay."

I arched a brow. "You sure? Because that sounded like consent under the influence of pillow."

She groaned and rolled over, dragging the comforter with her. "Five more minutes."

I sat down on the bed and tugged the blanket off her face. "Opal."

Her eyes peeked out, hair a mess, expression pure evil. "You're lucky I like you."

"I know." I smirked.

I buried my face in her neck, pressing a kiss just below her ear where her pulse fluttered. "I'm going to make you my queen," I murmured, voice dark, curling around her skin like smoke. Another kiss. Lower. "Whether you want it or not."

She laughed again, that bright, unguarded sound that always felt like lightning straight to the ribs. "You're insane," she whispered, curling her fingers in my hair.

"Absolutely, but you knew that going in and still chose me."

I coughed, and I knew it before I saw it. Blood. Bright and hot and wet against my palm. I turned, tried to stifle it, to swallow the sound, but she saw. Of course she saw.

Her joy vanished like smoke in a gale.

"Cain?" Her voice was sharper now, awake. A little scared.

I wiped my mouth, forced a smirk. "Sexy, right? Definitely one of my better moves."

"Cain—" she said, taking a more serious tone.

"I'm fine," I cut her off, throat tight. I wasn't fine. Not even close. But I couldn't let her see it. She was already reaching for me, but I stepped back and straightened. I swallowed back the burn and smiled.

"I'm ready," she said, hopping off the counter, that damn sunshine blooming in her voice like she hadn't watched me choke on my own mortality. "Let's go."

I stared at her for a long moment. Because she still looked at me like I wasn't a monster unraveling at the seams, and I knew, sooner or later, I was going to have to tell her the truth.

That I was coming undone, and she was the reason why.

Opal looked smug as hell. She was wearing my hoodie, hood up, sleeves past her fingertips, drowning in it. Her boots crunched over concrete and loose stone as she strolled through the street, pink spray can swinging like a murder weapon in her grip. She insisted on the pink this time, and I had no choice but to entertain her. The wall in front of us was pristine, curated brick arranged thoughtfully. A church—not my usual haunt but not above my reach.

I tagged my usual skeletal face, teeth bared in a sinister grin. I stepped back to admire it, dragging the back of my wrist across my mouth. Opal was still picking her spot. She finally chose a corner and sprayed her crooked ghost, "x" eyes, wobbly outline, lopsided. Absolutely ridiculous; absolutely perfect.

"Cute," I said, leaning against the brick.

She smirked and shoved her hand into the hoodie's kangaroo pocket, thumb hunting, then froze. "What's this?"

She pulled out a crumpled scrap of parchment; the edges were ragged, the ink smeared like it had been handled in a hurry. Fuck. I'd forgot that was in there.

Her eyes flicked to mine. "Is this from the spell book? Why do you still have this?"

My chest tightened, a stone where my breath should be. "It's nothing."

She unfolded it, slow and curious. "Cain—"

I took the spell from her fingers faster than a blink, fingers shutting over the paper like a trap. The scrap folded under my grip. I shoved it into my pocket the way you bury a confession in fresh dirt. "I said it's nothing."

Her brows drew down. "You didn't think I deserved to know?"

"I didn't think it mattered." The words came out small and brittle.

"Bullshit."

"I didn't tell you," I said finally, voice low, flint against glass, "because I didn't want to lose you."

Her lips parted. She reached, tentative, and pulled back as if she'd been burned. I watched her, because I'd spent too many lifetimes watching the people I let in take a step back, then another, then gone. I'd learned the sound of someone deciding to leave, and I couldn't risk hearing it with her. I should have burned the spell when I had the chance.

"I didn't know if you'd stay. If you'd choose me. If any of this"—I jutted my chin between us, sharp to keep my hands steady—"was real, or if it was just me."

Her breath caught. I didn't look at her. Couldn't.

"So, I kept it." My hand twitched against my pocket where the paper burned like an ember. "Because I wanted more time. To see if this . . . whatever this is . . . could work. If you were falling too."

Her silence dug in. It cut deeper than any blade.

"And now?" I forced a laugh that sounded like a snapped wire. "Now I can't bring myself to ever let you go. Even if it kills me. Especially if it kills me."

"What—"

I shut her down before she could pry. I wouldn't let her give me an out. "You're the first thing in centuries I haven't wanted to lose."

Her silence stretched so long I almost wished she'd scream at me, hit me, anything but look at me the way she did. Like she could see through the rot to whatever was left underneath. Then she moved. Slow. Careful. Her hand lifted, tentative, and pressed flat against my chest. Right over the place where it shouldn't beat. I stiffened. Too late.

Her eyes widened, lips parting in shock. "Your heart . . ."

The word hit like a blade to the gut. I jerked back, breaking her touch, shadows snapping up between us like a wall. My chest hammered harder, uneven, frantic, like it wanted out of me. Like it wanted her.

"No," I rasped, shaking my head. "That's not—no."

The pounding beneath my ribs stuttered, then slammed again, louder. A mockery of mortality. I've been dead a very long time, and my heart suddenly finding a steady rhythm couldn't be a good thing. It was an alarm bell ringing in a house that was already burning down.

Opal's hand hovered in the space between us, trembling like she wanted to reach for me again, but I couldn't let her.

"Don't," I snapped, though my voice shook with something dangerously close to fear. "Don't you dare."

I turned away, dragging in a breath I didn't fucking need, willing the beat to stop. Trying desperately to silence it before it unraveled me completely. I pulled my knife from my belt and headed toward the far side of the yard.

"Where are you going?"

"To work."

She followed.

The church was quiet. Wax dripped from half-burned candles along the altar, their smoke curling into the vaulted ceiling. Colored light spilled from stained glass, saints and angels fractured into reds and greens, their eyes watching. Stone saints loomed from niches, hands outstretched, frozen in blessing or warning. The faint echo of a hymn clung to the rafters like something that had died here but refused to leave.

I stalked down the center aisle, boots thudding against worn wooden floors, shadow stretching long and crooked over the pews.

At the far end of the nave, a priest stood by the confessional. His robes were immaculate, white collar cutting sharp against black, but his skin sagged, too pale, his eyes ringed in gray. He should've been gone three days ago. Still breathing. Still rotting from the inside. The balance had led me here. It was time to finish what should have been finished.

I slipped into the shadows, silent as grave dirt, and moved behind him. One swift movement, blade angled through the ribs. Clean and perfectly aimed at his heart as usual. His death should have been instant.

He gasped, staggered, but didn't fall. His hands clawed at the pew for balance, chest heaving around the knife protruding from his ribs. He turned and looked straight at me.

"Please—" he gasped.

My shadow reached for him. Nothing.

"No," I said, breath gone. "No—" I gripped his throat. "Die."

No. No, no, no. The system was broken, the balance tilting, and all because I'd had the audacity to fall in love.

My heart pounded against my ribs, uneven and frantic. My vision swam, pews bending in strange angles, the saints' faces twisting. Weakness crawled up my spine like a disease I couldn't shake. The priest wrenched free, staggering toward the aisle, a knife still jutting from his chest. He ran, robes whipping around his legs, blood dripping over the polished wood.

The pounding in my chest went wild, deafening. My knees buckled, and I hit the stone hard, the colored light from the windows splintering across my vision. Opal's voice echoed through the vaulted ceiling, breaking with panic.

Then nothing. Blackness swallowed me whole.

CHAPTER 24

Opal

Cain collapsed like someone had cut his strings. He hit the concrete with a hollow thud. "Cain?" I dropped to my knees. My palms landed on his chest, gentle, useless. "Cain—hey. Come on. Wake up."

Nothing.

His skin was wrong beneath my hands: too pale, cool as a drawer in winter. His eyelids lay slack, lips parted into the soft, stupid angle of death. If I didn't know better, I would have said he was gone, but that didn't make any sense. How the hell was I supposed to figure out what was wrong with him? How was I going to fix this?

My nails dug into his wrist. No pulse. But that was normal, right? *God, what the fuck am I doing?* I slapped his cheek once, hard enough to sting my palm. "Don't do this," I whispered. "Don't scare me like this."

For one absurd second, I thought of all his small lies, the parchment, the secret he'd kept from me. He'd risked this. He'd risked me.

Panic lanced through me, hard and bright. I needed him out of here. Now. I hooked my fingers under the back of his jacket and tried to drag him, only to find the concrete catching at the fabric. I had no idea where to go. All I knew was the memory of that demon, the one who'd tried to steal his mark, and the image of his blade still burned into my mind. He was vulnerable like this . . . I couldn't leave him on the floor for whatever wanted to finish what the balance had started. The hoodie fabric was tearing under my grip as I hauled him toward the nearest door.

Then I felt it: A rush of wind that smelled faintly of paraffin wax and rain. I felt him before I saw him, that unexplainable calm that fills your body like a drug right before the blade falls. A shadow eased down beside me.

Crow.

That terrifying, uncanny bastard—I was so glad he was here. Pale, white hair. Black coat. Sharp crystal-blue eyes that took one look at Cain and narrowed with a kind of knowing dread that I felt in my stomach.

"Were you following us?" I asked, not accusing. Just stunned.

He nodded. "The balance has been off." His voice was quiet, soft in a way that was kind. "I wanted to make sure Death was okay."

Crow knelt beside us and extended his hand but didn't touch. His fingers hovered over Cain's chest, and with a flick of his wrist, the shadows beneath Cain rippled. They moved unnaturally, like they were alive. Like they recognized Crow's call. The shadows rose, curling beneath Cain, lifting his body gently off the ground.

"We need to get him back," Crow said, standing and guiding the shadows that held Cain aloft.

"To the Deadlands?" I asked, my voice thin, my hands still shaking.

Crow nodded once. "Now."

He sliced the air with a hand, and a rift cracked open. Crow stepped through first, guiding Cain's suspended form like a shepherd to his bed.

Crow didn't touch him. He stood at the foot of the bed like a statue carved from patience, eyes hard and unblinking. Watching, not touching, as if even a breath might bruise whatever fragile thread still clung to Cain.

I sank beside the edge of the mattress before I could think better of it. My knees hit the floor, and everything inside my chest lurched: anger mixed with fear. My hands hovered, useless for a second, then settled on his head. His hair was cold under my fingers, slick at the roots with sweat that I could feel but not see in the dim light. I ran my fingertips through it slowly as if motion could anchor him to the world.

His chest didn't rise. There was no beat under my palm. My hand strained for a pulse at his throat and found only stillness.

"Has this happened before?" I asked.

Crow's jaw worked. He didn't look at me at first. Then he shook his head once, careful and final. "Not like this."

Crow began to move as if he was working through a checklist. He lit one candle, then another; the wax hissed like small, angry insects. He murmured something low, syllables I didn't know but felt vibrate in my core. Crow's face didn't change. He never let his face change. I hated him for it and clung to him for it at the same time.

"Come back," I repeated until the words turned brittle. "You can't leave like this. Don't leave like this."

Crow's voice cut through me, calm as a blade. "Don't panic. Stay with him." He crouched and didn't ask if I was okay. Instead, he assumed I would not be and set to work.

I wanted to be furious at Cain for the lies, for hiding this secret, for bringing this mess; I wanted to be furious at Crow for being too calm. Instead, my fingers worked through his hair, nails pressing into scalp, because touch was the only language I had left.

"Can you . . .Will he—" I started, because the question had to be voiced. My throat closed on the rest.

Crow looked up at me for the first time since he'd entered the room. In his eyes there was no sign of emotion, only the math of what needed doing. "I don't know," he said. "But don't move. Don't let go of him."

So I didn't. I ran my fingers through his hair. I kept my palm against the place his heart should be and pretended that the nothingness I felt there was normal.

"Do you think . . ." I started, the words scraping like glass. I couldn't get the rest out clean. "Do you think this is because of me?"

Crow didn't answer right away. He just watched Cain with those calm, unreadable eyes, the kind that measured a thing and then decided how to fix it.

Finally, slow and careful, he said what I'd already feared. "That's the theory."

A cold, silly laugh slipped out of me. I sank back until I was sitting on the floor. "Because of the spell?"

Crow nodded once. "Because of the bond."

"I don't understand how the bond is affecting him like this," I said, voice thin as smoke.

Crow glanced at me and leaned his shoulder against the window. The city lights fractured across the glass, little broken stars that made the room feel both too big and too small all at the same time.

"We've been talking, Death and I," he said. "We think . . . he gave you some of his immortality. And you gave him something else."

I blinked. "What?"

Crow dragged a hand through his white hair. His voice dropped lower, like he was lowering a curtain. "Your mortality."

"He's becoming mortal?"

"Not exactly, but he's been showing symptoms," Crow continued, eyes on Cain's still body. "Side effects. Nothing major at first, but now?" He tapped the mattress with a single, clinical finger. "Now it's bad."

My chest constricted like a fist. "So basically I'm . . . stealing his immortality?"

"We're leaning that way," Crow said. "You're not fragile the way you were. You don't age the same. Your wounds don't stay. But all that comes at a cost."

For a second I was so angry I couldn't think. He'd known what this was doing to him and still hid the spell, still let things go till he was past his breaking point . . . all for me.

"Did he tell you?" I whispered. I needed the answer. I didn't want it. I wanted to have a reason to hate Cain for hiding it, but I also wanted to know he'd warned them. That he'd tried.

Crow's mouth tightened. "He told me," he said. "He knew something was wrong. We've been working on ways to fix it without breaking the bond."

Relief flared for a breath. They'd tried. Then Crow's voice went precise as a scalpel. "We tried blood magic, rituals, throttling the ledger. Nothing has held. Each attempt weakened him a little more."

"So, what happens if it keeps going?" I forced myself to ask, my throat raw.

Crow paused a long time, like he was weighing each syllable. "Eventually . . . everything dies. Not the way it should. Not with peace. Just—stops." Crow's next sentence was small and exact. "There is one option that might save him."

My whole body went brittle. "What?" My voice sounded tiny even to my own ears.

Crow didn't look away from Cain. "Sever the bond."

The room tilted. I could feel the words like an axe lifted above my head.

"You mean—" I couldn't finish.

"Yes." Crow's voice had no flourish left. "Cut it clean. He stabilizes. He stops bleeding out, but the bond ends."

Heat rose to my face. "He'll—he'll hate me," I breathed. "He'd never agree."

"He told me not to tell you." Crow's hands stayed precise, methodical. "He begged me to find another way. I've tried. There are no other ways that don't kill him faster."

The truth hit like a corpse bell. If I wanted Cain alive, I would have to give him up. The trade was ugly and immediate: his life in return for the quiet death of us.

I could see him there in the bed, fragile and wrong and perfect, and I knew with a cold certainty that he would never give me permission to cut that thread. He would hold on to the bond if it meant keeping me; he would choose to die with me rather than let me choose the end of us.

Crow's eyes were flint. "It's the only thing I believe will save him."

I let out a sound that was half-cry, half-laughter, and I realized I'd been crying without knowing it. My hand stilled against his hair. For the first time, the bond felt like a thing I could see, a rope fraying at the center, and my fingers were on it with a knife.

"I can't ask you to—" I started.

"You won't have to ask me," Crow said. "You have to decide."

CHAPTER 25

Cain

Everything was velvet at first, soft and silent. So quiet it felt like a joke. I wanted to stay. I wanted the dark to swallow me and never spit me back out. Fingers ghosted through my hair, steady and warm. Someone's thumb dragged across my scalp, and the world liquefied for a second. Nobody touched me. I thought . . . Not like this.

Opal's name unfurled in my chest like a bell. *Opal.* The syllables were bright and ridiculous and somehow safe. She was here. Her breath near my ear tasted like vanilla and cheap coffee and the exactly wrong kind of ordinary. I wanted to open my eyes and see her grin, that stupid, perfect, trouble-making grin.

Then a voice: muffled, distant. Fog on glass. "We have to break the bond."

The sentence slammed through me like cold water. What? No. No. No. My mouth fought to form words, and my body hummed, soft and dull, like a radio searching for a signal. Feeling filtered into my body in bits. Someone dug in my pocket. Fingers found something I didn't want found.

I tried to move. The world answered in static. My limbs were lead, useless. Panic wanted to bloom, bright and hot, and I clamped it down, because burning was what I did, and this . . . this was wrong.

Another voice: Crow. Close, clinical, the kind of voice that carved things into tidy pieces. "This will be fairly easy to sever."

Not if I could help it. The thought exploded through me like a flare. I pushed. My ribs burned. It was like trying to move through honey and glass. My hands twitched; my knuckles whitened. Someone murmured—Opal, I think—pleading, small. A breath, then another, counted. The room hummed with instruments and soft curses and the smell of wax.

Crow's words are glass: "sever," "stabilize," "clean." As if love were a cable you could snip and expect no sparks.

My anger clawed through the fog of my mind, the static of my body. My jaw tightened. My hands, finally, remembered how to move. They came up, slow and arrogant, and then, like the tide answering the moon, my body detonated, and I sat up.

Glaring was the only thing I could do at first. Crow looked like he'd been carved from the same stone as always: steady, inevitability made human. Opal's face was an open wound of horror, guilt, fear, and a small, awful bravery that made my chest ache even harder.

"Traitor," I said. The word was small and lethal. It fit perfectly on my tongue.

I didn't trust the sound of my own voice. It was raw, wrong, close to breaking, but it landed. It rang in the room, and the thread of it vibrated against the place where the bond lived.

You don't sever my tether and walk away, I wanted to growl. *You don't touch that rope and expect me not to shred your hands with teeth.* The world around me was brightening into threat: tools glinting, candles stuttering like weak hearts, Crow's hands folding into the practiced motions of someone who did what must be done and never questioned the cost.

Opal reached for me, fingers shaking. Her touch was the only honest thing in the room. For a second—a ridiculous, dangerous second—I wanted to crawl into her lap and forgive every damn thing. I wanted to let the whole universe burn rather than lose the way her cheek fit under my hand. But they were talking about killing us to save me. Killing us. And it made me want to scream until my throat bled.

I stood up too fast. The room rocked. I was furious and scared and small and bigger than goddamn anything I had the right to be. Crow's eyes didn't waver. Opal looked like she might fall apart, and I wanted to tear the decision out of their hands and shove it back into the dark where it belonged.

"Don't," I said again, softer now, but with teeth. "Don't you dare. I'm fine," I told her, fingers finding her face, because touch was the only honest currency I had left. I cupped her jaw, thumb wiping the crease by her mouth the way I used to when things were easy and stupid. I leaned in and kissed her slow, like I was trying to seal the world with one stupid, selfish mouthful of her.

Her eyes didn't soften. They hardened. There was a clarity there so terrifying it might as well be a blade. The line of her mouth said she'd chosen already. I pressed harder, trying to make her forget the ledger, the priests, the way the church smelled like rust that night. Kiss after kiss, I pushed, pleading without words. "Don't," I breathed against her mouth.

She pulled back enough that I could see the set of her jaw. "Cain," she said, and the name was a verdict. "You have to." The sentence was small, exact; it landed in my gut like an order. "If you die here, there won't be an us anymore."

Something dark and delighted wanted to tear that sentence apart. Instead, I grinned, because what else did I have? "I'd rather die happy than leave you."

Opal's face folded with the kind of resolve that had no business living on someone who smelled like vanilla and bad coffee. My feet were unsteady beneath me. The room tilted and righted and tilted again. The adrenaline that had braided through me since I'd woken was bleeding away, leaving me soft and hollow. I felt like someone had unplugged the lights one by one.

"We can buy more time," I said, bargaining, because bargaining is a habit older than grief.

Opal watched me with exhaustion in her eyes, and a fierce, terrible thing I didn't want to see: readiness. Slowly, the same truth crawled across my skin to where the sweat was cooling into gooseflesh. If there was any hope that didn't require me to keep killing the rules that held the world together, we'd have to find it now. Or we'd cut the rope.

If we stayed like this, the ledger would unthread. Hospitals would go quiet. Markets, playgrounds, city streets . . . blink, and it would all be gone. It wasn't one place—it was the whole damned world that would come undone. Then Hell would catch like dry tinder: Fires that should have been eternal would flare and collapse. Heaven would fall too; spires and stained glass would shudder and rain down like rotten fruit, angels tumbling with faces like stone.

I reached for Opal's future like a blind man reaching for a hand. I expected to find lines, a path, a little flame to follow like I would with anyone else. Instead, I found . . . nothing. It was as if the tapestry that was her life had been burned away where it touched me. No thread, no knot, no name. The emptiness looked deliberate, mocking: the fates playing with a toy, seeing me panic because I wanted to stitch my name into someone else's life.

They were toying with me, and I wanted to smash something.

My knees buckled. There were two choices on the table, and both were a blade:

Keep the bond. Keep Opal.

Let the ledger lurch and pray that our glue would hold as the world creaked and broke. Watch cities go dark in an unbidden calculus: one pair of hearts for a planet of lives. Or sever the bond. It would heal me, stabilize me. The ledger would right itself. The world would breathe. But I would lose the girl who'd taught me how to feel again, how to live again. The ledger would be satisfied, and the universe wouldn't notice the hiccup, and all it would cost would be everything I loved.

The more I looked, the clearer the equation became. It wasn't moral calculus. Either I let the world slip—millions for one—or I let her go and saved the rest. The cruelty is that both felt like murder.

I made a choice with the single, terrible selfishness of someone who loved a species of people and also loved one person beyond all reason.

I would not let the world burn for us. I would not make her hold the match. I rose from the bed with all the resignation of a man walking to his own execution. My hands were steady, though my heart was splintering.

"Teach me how to do it," I said. "Show me how to cut the tether clean. I'll do it. I'll take the decision from her."

Crow's face changed in a way I've rarely seen. Not pity, exactly, but a folding in, like a page turned to the most awful paragraph. He nodded once, small and professional. "It will save you."

"It'll save everyone," I added, softer, for myself. My throat wanted to break. "It'll save her." I ran a thumb over her face and vowed, "I won't let this be over." Somehow, my voice held. It was a promise and a threat braided together. I reached for her hands, and my fingers closed around hers like iron. Her skin was warm and real and small and exactly the thing I'd burn a thousand ledgers for.

"If it's the last fucking thing I do, we will be together again."

The graves smelled the same as they had the first night: wet dirt and old stone, the faint, sour scent of long-burnt roses. Moonlight scoured the headstones, made the letters look like they were carved from wet bone.

Crow stood where he always did: precise, back straight, a silhouette that refused to tremble. He'd done the arithmetic in his head a thousand times and kept the ledger tidy for me until now. His shadow fell long and even across the ground, like a ruler laid against chaos.

Opal sat on the low wall of the cemetery, hoodie up, knees hugged to her chest. She was quiet in a way I'd never seen her: small and taut, like a thing waiting to break. Every now and then, she rubbed at her upper arm, as if she could feel what I'd lost already. Her breath made tiny clouds in the cold. I wanted to step away and come back with a different plan, because plans were always better when they didn't involve cutting your own throat.

I knew the spell was simple. I had known from the beginning, the neatness of it, how it would fit like a key in a lock. It would be fast and clean, a single line that had to be drawn the right way. Breaking it wouldn't be hard. That fact had haunted me from the first night I'd read the page.

"You sure about this?" Crow asked. He didn't need to. He knew we had to.

I pulled the hoodie off slowly and slid it over Opal's shoulders, the old comfort of possession softened by the night. She smelled like vanilla, coffee and the faint trace of my smoke. I wanted to tuck all of that inside me, memorize the exact crease in her smile, because once this was done, my memory might be all I'd have.

"Yes," I said. My voice was a thing with edges. "I'm sure."

Crow set the implements between us: a small blade that seemed ordinary and a strip of parchment inked with the spell's unmaking. He'd traced the sigils twice and then folded the paper until it sat like a promise in his palm.

"This will stabilize you," Crow said, not unkindly. "It will right the ledger. It will cost you the bond."

I watched Opal's face as the words landed. She'd already decided. The resolve in her eyes had been carved out long before we came here tonight.

I wanted to make one stupid joke, to say something that would make her laugh and undo the whole script. Instead, I crouched down so my face was level with hers. I cupped her cheek, thumb lingering by the crease near her mouth. Up close she was all freckles and the stubbornness of youth. She was unbearably human.

"Okay," she breathed. "Do it."

I set the blade against the paper, and—for a breath—the whole world narrowed to the hiss of candle wax. Crow's voice steadied me. I knew what to do . . . chant, fold, cut. The sigils began to smoke like a wound opening.

My hand trembled. Under my ribs, the bond beat like an animal, hot, hungry, alive in a way that had ruined me. The ritual bent toward its final motion. The blade hovered above the seam that kept us knotted together.

"Stop." The word ripped from me. Opal's fingers dug into mine, frantic and pleading. For one stupid, selfish second, I closed the gap between us and kissed her, hard, greedy, pouring every promise I'd ever made into a single, ragged mouthful. I tried to memorize her, to force forever into that instant.

When I broke the kiss, she opened her mouth like she was going to say something, and the next second I dropped her hand as if it had burned me. The motion was reflex, fast enough that there was no time to second-guess, no room for the bargaining that might have unmade me. Her skin left a heat on my palm that cooled quickly. The quickness of it felt like mercy and cruelty at the same time.

I didn't look at her. I set the paper flat over my sternum, felt the bond recoil under that thin skin for the last time, and swiped the blade in one clean arc.

The sound was a bell struck wrong. Light flared, then a pressure unspooled from my chest like someone unclasping a fist. The bond recoiled as if surprised and slid away, thin as smoke through my fingers.

For a second the world hung on a thread. Then Opal lunged forward, hand seeking me like she always had, automatic, frantic, forgiveness in motion. She wanted to touch me, to anchor whatever remained.

I jolted back as if I'd been branded. The movement was sharp, protective, animal. Her fingers missed my face by inches; the air between us burned with what hadn't been there a breath before. No one moved. The candles hissed. Crow's chant fell into silence.

The knowledge landed like a stone: If she touched me now, if skin met skin as it had so many times before, she would die. Not gradually. Not poetically. Immediately. Her hand trembled in midair.

"Don't," I said. The word was small and flat and full of everything I could not let happen. My voice shook despite the attempt at steel.

Opal's fingers curled, then dropped, as if someone had cut her line. A sound like a sob tore out of her. She looked like she might collapse. The light in her eyes was gone, and then, the remaining hollowness was replaced by a fragile, terrible understanding.

Crow stepped forward, gloved hand hovering as if to take up what wanted to be done. "He's right," he said, the sentence a verdict. "No contact."

I felt her inhale, the breath sharp and raw. She forced her hand back to her chest as if it had been scorched. The warmth of her palm, the thing I had used for comfort a thousand times, was suddenly the most dangerous temptation I'd ever known.

Opal's eyes burned. She tried to smile, and it came out small and broken. "You—" she started, then decelerated into a whisper. "You did it."

"I did," I said. My voice felt thin in my throat. I wanted to reach for her, to fix the look on her face, to promise impossible things. Instead, I kept my hands where they were, empty and deliberate.

She slid down until she was sitting on the stones, hoodie bunched around her knees, and wrapped her arms around herself like someone trying to hold a wound closed. The candles threw their light across her face, and in that glow, she was both the most alive and the most untouchable thing in my world.

I stared at her, and it hurt, sharp and stupid. My face did the thing I'd practiced for a thousand years: the mask, the half-smile that kept the knives from finding your throat. Inside, everything felt raw.

I get it, Final Girl, I thought, voice dead in my head. I felt the same. Felt . . . Gods, that part wasn't gone. It was sitting under my ribs like a stone, stubborn and loud. I could feel the cold sliding back into my limbs, the way my skin went papery and thin. For a moment, absurd and terrible, my heart stuttered and stopped, a clean, absolute nothing where a drum should be. Fuck. For an instant, I nearly tasted the finality of that stop.

Then the hunger hit—two kinds at once. First, the old hunger: the professional hollow that had always lived in my belly, the appetite for endings, for death. Second, something more animal: a low, constant gnaw that nothing had ever fed. It slammed into me like a physical thing, hot and ugly and demanding. I gritted my teeth until the taste of metal filled my mouth and rode it out, because the world still wanted decisions, and whining about being hungry wasn't an acceptable currency.

I leaned my shoulder against a cold obelisk, the stone damp with dew. The texture scraped my jacket through to bone; it anchored me. I watched Opal curled on the stones, and my eyes felt thick the way grief makes everything look underwater. I fished in my pocket with hands that trembled despite the attempt at indifference and pulled out a vape, more habit than sense.

"So—are you back?" she asked, looking up at me with tears slicking the rims of her eyes.

I lifted the device to my mouth like it would be a talisman. For weeks that cherry hit had been a stupid comfort: a little burn that fixed a morning, a flavor that carved space in the day where nothing else could. I inhaled hard, wanting the cherry to be a bandage.

Nothing.

Dry air and nothing. The flavor had fled the world with the rest of the small mercies.

I flung the vape away like it had insulted me. It hit the stone and skittered into the grass. "Yep," I said instead, and the single syllable was all the honesty I could afford as bitterness crawled back into my chest.

Opal's face crumpled, a knot of disbelief and pain and the small, dawning horror of the thing we'd done, and for a second, I let myself watch her unravel. My mask tightened into place; the corner of my mouth tilted a fraction to pretend. *Final Girl*, I wanted to say, not as mockery but as pact. I wanted her to hear that I felt the same fracture she did. I wanted to promise her nonsense I couldn't keep. Instead, I blinked the salt from my eyes, swallowed the rest of the taste, and let the stone hold me upright while the world reassembled without the tether between us.

Crow spoke up, flat and businesslike. "It's time to go set things right."

I lashed out before I could stop the bite in my voice. "Don't you think I know that?" The words hit him like feral dogs, loud and stupid. My jaw ached from the anger, so I shook my head and dragged a hand over my face until the skin stung. "I'm sorry," I said, softer, ashamed of how hard I'd snapped. I crouched down, close enough to Opal to be a threat but far enough that I wouldn't touch her if she reached.

"Listen to me, Blossom," I said, and the nickname came out rough and real. "This isn't over."

She looked up at me. For a second the room narrowed to the plain geometry of her face: the wet shine of her eyes, the way her lip trembled. I kept talking, because the sound of my own voice steadied me. "I'll figure it out," I promised. "One way or another. It might take some time, but I'm not giving up."

She nodded once, weak and nearly decisive. Relief loosened something in my chest, and I let myself inhale a stupid, grateful intake. Then I looked closer. You learn to read a ledger in a person's face if you live with balance and numbers long enough. The way the skin at her wrist moved. A small, pale bloom under her pulse pulled my gaze. She was literally ticking. The mortality we'd given back to her was fragile and audible if you knew how to listen.

Dread slid cold and heavy down into my stomach. The fact arranged itself into a brutal shape in my mind: three days. Three days to find a fix, or to find another kind of miracle, or to watch her time unwind in real time. My mouth went dry; the scent of candle wax and dew sharpened into metal. My hands dropped to my knees, because standing straight felt like pretending.

She had only three days left to live.

CHAPTER 26

Opal

I watched him go and didn't try to stop him.

The rift swallowed him like a pocket in the dark. He didn't look back. Death never looked back. For a moment the world held its breath, as if it couldn't figure out whether to keep moving or to honor what had just been cut loose.

I took the long way home. My footsteps sounded too loud in a city that felt hollow. It smelled like wet asphalt, old grease, and a million indifferent things that wouldn't notice if I broke. By the time I pushed my apartment door open, the pink neon strips on the ceiling were already humming like a heartbeat I couldn't hear. The apartment answered with its usual glow, soft and ridiculous and unbearably small.

For the first time in two months, I was alone.

Alone should have meant relief. It should have meant freedom and space to breathe and to be the person who used to be messy in other ways. Instead, it felt like someone had taken the outline of my life and erased the middle. The air was wrong. The chair he'd claimed sat like an accusing thing near the window. I crossed the room and stopped in front of it like a person who'd forgotten a name. The hoodie draped over the back smelled faintly of smoke and something sweet I'd come to recognize as him.

I knew I'd made the right decision. Of course I did. We'd saved . . . everything. The ledger was balanced. People who would have otherwise died kept breathing.

Farms didn't fail. Babies were still born. That was right. That was huge. It should have felt like victory.

It didn't. It felt like a hollowness that existed only to remind me of what I'd given. Lucian smashing things off the shelf—that had been performative, loud. He'd left me because he wanted something else, because he was bored, and I was safe and small. This hurt differently. This hurt clean and surgical; it was the kind of wound stitched down and left to scar inwardly. Lucian's goodbye had been an avalanche; this was an amputation.

I sat on the bed and tried to pretend I could go back to . . . this. I kept glancing at the chair, half-expecting to see him swing a knee over the arm and make a joke about me overworking the pink fairy lights. It was ridiculous to expect a presence where there was a void.

My phone screen blared: no new messages. I should have thrown it across the room. Instead, I made coffee, because habit is a small sanity. The pot hissed, and the room filled with steam that fogged the cheap poster on my wall. I sipped and realized the cup felt wrong in my hand. It wasn't heavy enough to anchor me.

Every little thing cut. The empty vape on the table. The ashtray I half-expected him to occupy. Memory is a traitor when it shows up in my hands like evidence.

I replayed that kiss, the one before he dropped my hand, and it hit me fresh like a cut. He'd chosen the world over us. He'd chosen to be the sacrificial math that fixed everything. That was noble, I told myself like a mantra, and heroic and necessary, but knowing a thing didn't blunt how much it stung.

I tried to name what this pain was, and my brain kept circling the same two words: guilt and gratitude. They fought like siblings. I was grateful that the world kept turning. I wanted to be proud. I wanted to feel like some kind of badass savior who gave up forever for everyone else. Instead, I felt guilty for being the thing he'd been willing to lose, for entering his life and requiring him to choose.

My phone pinged, and I stared down at it. Thane's message sat on my screen like a dare.

Yo. You in for the next Spooky Ghouls shoot? Abandoned hospital. A few towns over. We're thinking two days out.

My thumb hovered over the screen like it might burn. I used to live for that ping. The thrill of a weird location, the caffeine-fueled adrenaline, the way the group would get giddy about the stupidest things. My brand, my job, the thing that paid for my stupid neon lights and rent and the emergency ramen fund.

Now the idea of skulking through a place pretending terror made me feel silly. But if I stopped doing the thing that had shaped me, what was I left with? A hoodie, a grief, a hollow that echoed too loudly when the lights went out.

So, I typed out the message like my life hadn't just fallen apart.

Yeah. I'll be there. Two days.

Sent.

I decided I needed to get out of the apartment.

Retail therapy wasn't exactly healing, but it was *something*. Movement. Distraction. A chance to pretend I was just a normal girl mourning a breakup instead of a former ghost queen nursing a hole in her chest the exact size and shape of Death.

I pulled on leggings and a hoodie, shoved my hair into a clip, grabbed my bag.

Then, I opened the door and froze. A slip of paper fluttered down from the doorframe, landing like a dead leaf on the threshold.

I stared at it, throat tight. My fingers shook as I picked it up.

The handwriting was unmistakable, sharp, impatient scrawl in black ink, p's and y's like sharp knives . . . Cain.

My heart did a stupid, *stupid* little stutter.

I stepped back inside, closed the door, and opened the note.

Blossom,

I'm on it. The spell. A fix that won't break you or me. I've got a lead, and it's ugly, but I don't mind ugly.

I feel better. For now.

I don't give a damn about the world. I give a damn about you. If someone grabs your hand, I take their hand. If they look too long, I take

their eyes. If they try more than that, I take their life. I won't be neat about it.

Stay inside. Curtains shut. Doors locked. Whatever you do, don't go outside, and don't test me. Behave for me, Final Girl. Or I come hunting.

—C

I read it three times before I could breathe.

He was okay. Or okay-*ish*. Still fighting. Still trying. Still *mine*, in whatever impossible way that meant now. Only he could fit so many threats in such a short note, and it made me smile. Threats meant he cared. I pressed the paper to my chest.

But I reread the line. **"Don't go outside."** A chill crawled down my spine.

I was already halfway dressed, halfway in the mood to buy candles and crap I didn't need and couldn't justify. That one sentence rooted me to the floor. Because Cain didn't warn lightly, and I didn't spook easy.

And if *he* said not to go outside . . . ? I dropped my bag and locked the door. I sat down at the kitchen table with Cain's note still clutched in my hand.

For a long time, I just stared at it. Read it again. Memorized the shape of his words. The tilt of his letters.

He was trying. Reaching out. So, I grabbed a pen and paper. *Clever*, I thought, smiling a little. *A way to keep in touch without getting too close. Without touching.* I could do that.

I could send him something back. Leave it where he'd find it. Slip it between the cracks of this thin reality we'd pulled too tight.

I chewed on the end of the pen for a second, then wrote:

Dear Death,

I miss you in the stupid little ways. Coffee sputters, and no one swears at the machine. The fridge hums like a bored ghost. I hold up something weird, and there's no one to roll his pretty eyes.

I miss your noise. The scrape of your ring on the counter. The weight you put in a room just by breathing.

The house is too quiet. The night's behaving, and I hate it. I'm fine. Mostly. Eating. Sleeping-ish. I talk to the shadows like they're your interns.

Don't rush if it gets you hurt. I know you're out there bleeding for solutions.

I'm not shopping for a new man. Please. I've met the reaper. Everyone else feels like decaf.

Come home when you can. I'll be here, lights low, knives clean, heart open.

Don't forget to live.

XOXO,

Opal

I stared at the letter until the ink felt warm under my fingers. I folded it, neat as a bandage. It felt silly and perfect at the same time. A dead drop for Death.

Claws clicked on the fire escape. Soft. Familiar. I eased the window open, and a black shape shuffled in like it paid rent. A crow cocked its head at me, bright eyes mean and curious.

"Here to spy on me?" I laughed and held up the letter. "Special delivery,"

The crow didn't argue. It took the paper in its beak, hopped to the sill, and shot me a look that said *Don't be stupid*. Then it was gone into the wet city, and I felt a little less alone.

My phone buzzed again. The group chat had gone feral.

Nyxie: *Permits came thruuu. Doors at 11. We go live at 11:59. First-ever stream from St. Mercy. Screaming.*

Lyric: *Headlines, baby. Exclusive. I already made the thumbnail.*

I watched the screen until my eyes did that static-snow thing. St. Mercy. The abandoned hospital with the crumbling angel out front and the rumor about the morgue drawers that never stayed shut. The one I'd joked about a hundred times and never touched because something in my ribs didn't like the way its name felt.

Two days. Halloween night. A live I couldn't fake or edit. No reshoots. No cutaways. No hides. Cain's handwriting knifed through the thought.

Don't go outside.

I could feel the numbers dropping in my bones. Ad revenue had already slid. Sponsors were "keeping an eye on Q4 performance." The cemetery footage had died with the camera, and what we salvaged had . . . evaporated. I told myself files get corrupted. I told myself that all the time. The truth tasted metallic.

Another ping.

Lyric: *I queued a countdown page for IG and YouTube. It auto-posts at noon tomorrow. Pls send a clip.*

My thumbs typed before my brain caught up.

I tossed the phone onto the couch like it had bitten me and scrubbed my hands over my face. I got up and paced.

I tried to negotiate with my own rules. What if I didn't go inside? What if I ran the live from the parking lot? What if the team went, and I monitored chat from my couch with the curtains shut and my knives clean? A workaround. A loophole. Cain didn't say not to breathe. He'd said, "Don't go outside."

Except he knew me. He knew loopholes were just lies I told myself to feel clever while I made a mistake.

The apartment creaked the way old places do when they remember being trees. The AC kicked on.

The chat pinged again, this time a call. Thane. I let it ring once and answered, hit speaker, set the phone face down on the table so I wouldn't have to see myself reflected in the dark screen.

"You good?" he asked. No hello. Just that. Bless him.

"I'm . . . medium."

"Numbers are ugly," he said, soft for him. "Hospital's the fix. One clean hour and we're back on top. It's content, Op."

I stared at the door. At the slip of light under it. And then Cain's handwriting cut it in half again. Behave for me, Final Girl.

"I'll think about it," I said.

CHAPTER 27

Cain

They told me once that grief was a tidy thing, a sorrow you carried in a pocket, a stone you could learn to balance. Whoever "they" were had lied. Grief is a hammer, and I had been swinging until my arms went numb.

I'd been on the road all night. The world blurred into the same pale smear of bars: neon, barbed wire, church steeples, and skyscrapers. I killed in barns, in motels that smelled like cigarettes and detergent, in graveyards where the stones kept the wind honest. Every place I stopped had a body count by the time I left. Not because I wanted numbers, although the ledger liked tidy sums, but because killing calmed the parts of me the bond had broken. Blood was arithmetic I could understand. The ledger was stubborn; sometimes it needed a shove.

When I killed, I felt clean for a moment. Like a machine with a clogged gear: cut the bad thread, the rest spins. It never lasted. The hunger woke faster, meaner. The ledger tightened like a noose. I filled my hands with violent things to keep my head from thinking of soft things like Opal's laugh, the way she tucked a strand of hair behind her ear, the small, dangerous way she said my name.

Crow found me in a wreck of a bar with a cracked mirror and a bartender who should have quit years ago, now face down in spilled beer. He carried papers the way some men carry guns, folded and inked and heavy.

"You shouldn't have done this alone." His voice was not scolding. It was just the simple observation of someone cataloging the wreckage.

"You think I don't know that?" I said. My fingers still smelled like blood and cheap whiskey. My throat was still raw from yelling in the night. "You think I like it?"

Crow pinched the bridge of his nose, then said what he didn't want to say. "There are stories . . . buried deep. They say that thing in the pit, the old god, knows how to grant immortality to mortals."

He looked at me like a man offering a blunt instrument. "If it knows how to make Opal immortal, maybe it's worth paying the old bastard a visit."

The packet smelled like wrong choices. The description that followed was worse: a crown of bones, a mouth that eats promises. It had existed before light. Waking it wouldn't be tidy, it would be dangerous, and nobody could say how bad for sure. The not-knowing made the option itch.

"You want me to wake it?" I asked.

Crow's laugh was dry. "No. I'm giving you the option and the warning. If that god can anchor a life outside the ledger, it'll demand a price none of us can name. You're its keeper, Cain. If it stirs, you know what that means for duty."

My hands tightened on the packet. Rain hit the window like a fast drum. *"Bad decisions" is my middle name*, I thought, and shoved the packet into my jacket like contraband.

"It's not a yes," I said. "Not yet. But if I wake it, it will be because the alternative is worse than the gamble."

Crow's jaw set. "Prepare. If you go, don't dive in blind."

The Deadlands felt colder when I came back, like the stone itself had learned to hold its breath. Though maybe that was just me.

Two days. Barely. That's what I had to keep my girl breathing.

I went straight for the ancient stacks. Books crumbled under my hands, ash and dust. Black smears on every thumb. Then, one held: leather, charred corners, heavy as a promise. The script inside was older than the law. I flipped until I found it, a sigil burned so deep the paper was a wound. The Mark. My Mark.

Seeing it felt like being recognized by a mirror you didn't trust. The ink shimmered like the thing on the page knew my name by stillness. My jaw clenched until my teeth ached. Of course it knew me. Of course this started here.

The Mark tied me to the duty. It kept the pit sleeping. It also, I realized with a cold twist in my gut, pointed at the one thread that might undo everything. The old thing in the pit, the pre-light god with rules meaner than mine. A mechanic that might override the ledger if I asked the right way.

"Damn it."

Two days. The pages whispered. The decision hung in the air like smoke. My hands trembled. Not from fear but from the part of me that wanted to do something reckless, final, and cosmically stupid.

So, I did something impulsive.

Something I told myself I'd never do.

I reached for the red stone Damon had handed me at his wedding. I'd tucked it away after, like a thing that might burn. I hadn't touched it since.

Tonight, the ache in my heart was a living thing. Nothing was left to lose except the shape of my life. I took the stone from where it sat and carried it down to the Deadlands' summoning chamber. The summoning ring lay carved into the flagstones, old runes rimmed with dust and old blood.

I set the stone at the circle's center. It pulsed a deep red under my hand, like a dying sun trapped in glass. I slit my palm. The blood fell hot and honest into the runes.

I mouthed the words, because they were the only language left that might answer me. The syllables felt wrong and right all at once, ancient, ugly, older than heaven and meaner than hell.

The stone flared, and for a moment, everything went white: burning, bright, like the sun had been forced through a paper screen. My ears filled with the sound of old things turning their pages.

When the glow died away, he was there. Standing in the circle as if he'd always been part of the architecture. Tall, still, a silhouette that made the air feel less like a trap and more like a room that could hold two people. I felt less like a guardian of the balance and more like a man who had a single, terrible craving.

"Alistair," I said before anything smarter could form.

He stepped out of the light like a thing that had always belonged to shadow. Gray skin, like smoke kissed with ash. Gold-ringed eyes that caught under the chandelier and glowed faint and dangerous. Gold tattoos snarled his throat and arms in careful filigree, art with an aftertaste of violence. Horns curved, elegant and ridiculous, obsidian tips glinting. Black hair to his ears, longer than mine, neater, deliberate in a way that said he still ironed his sins before wearing them.

His smile crawled across his face slow and knowing. "Hello . . . brother."

The word landed like a match struck. I exhaled, slow, bitter. "Abel."

He stepped across the threshold of the circle, foot brushing the runed edge like a man who treats rules as suggestions. It probably didn't matter to him. Not anymore.

"Not quite, but you must really be desperate," he said with a tilt of his head.

"I am," I said.

His smile widened until it looked almost cruel. "Good. So am I."

He stood there, gold eyes amused as ever, but the ease I remembered in him was fraying, fine cracks spidering under the tattoos, a tremor in his fingers when he flexed. His horns didn't sit as proudly as in the old stories; they dipped, almost sheepish. Pride was still his armor, but the seams were splitting. He was a mess.

"You brought me back," he said, voice silk over steel. "What do you want?"

I didn't answer. Not yet. I let myself look. The scars—infernal seams that hadn't been allowed to heal properly—caught my attention. So much like my brother, but at the same time, not. He was not whole. He had been broken into a new shape and named a demon for the deal I had made. Back then I was powerless, just a mortal making a deal. He moved with that dangerous composure of someone who'd been taught to survive by being sharper than the rest. He was beautiful, wrong, and dangerous. Once Hell's weapon, just as Crow was mine, the only difference being that Crow volunteered, and he liked what he did. He hadn't been broken and remade.

Neither of us were whole.

"You've been banished," I said, quiet as a door closing. "From Hell. From the courts. From your title."

He didn't flinch. Didn't deny it. "They called it treason," he said, flat. "Free thought doesn't exactly sit well in a burning monarchy."

I let out a laugh. "You always were the rebellious one."

He arched a brow, mock injury like a practiced mask. "That's rich, coming from Death himself."

There it was: He'd always been the one to wear chaos like jewelry, but now his amusement was thinner; his pride had a new edge—defensive, raw. Pride is a crooked god. It makes you think you're untouchable—until you're not.

Silence filled the chamber in that way a room does when two dangerous things size each other up. I felt the loneliness again, centuries thick, a coat I'd never taken off. Seeing him there, some perverse, ridiculous part of me softened. Family, even found and broken, was something you noticed when everything else went quiet.

"You have nothing now," I said. It wasn't a taunt. It was inventory.

He stiffened, but only a fraction. "I know," he answered. The voice was lower, something like confession. "I know what I am. What I'm not. I was made into something cruel and beautiful and not mine, but I know the truth now."

That—truth—was dangerous. Dangerous because it suggested he could be reasoned with, bent. Dangerous because it suggested hope.

I nodded once, a small, dangerous gesture. "Then you'll start over. With me."

His smile quirked, pride and curiosity battling. "Start over?" He rolled the word like a coin. "You summon me for companionship? For family? You want *me*—Alistair—by your side? After what I did?"

"Yeah." My voice was low. The word felt like admitting a debt and lighting a match. "You're reckless, I know. You're trouble. You're pride and treason. But I'm tired of the ledger being the only company I keep. I need someone who remembers what being a bastard once felt like. Someone who can hurt and still laugh. Maybe you'll be useless. Maybe you'll burn the place down. Maybe you'll be exactly what I need."

I stepped closer to the ring, boots whispering on stone. "I'll offer you sanctuary," I said. My voice surprised me by being steadier than I felt. "In the Deadlands. Under my care. My protection. A place where no one owns you—not Heaven, not Hell, not prophecy."

The words landed in the circle, and the stone seemed to drink them in. His jaw worked as if chewing on an old regret. "And in return?"

"Loyalty," I answered, and the word tasted like iron and old promises.

He smiled, bitter and rehearsed. "I already gave that once. Didn't end well."

"This is different," I said. The truth in my chest burned. "This time you're not a soldier. You're my brother."

The single word hung between us like something sacred and absurd at once. For the first time since light had a beginning, the name felt dangerous in the best possible way.

For a flicker, he let it land. He let it mean something.

"I'll accept," he said slowly. "But I want something first."

I didn't move. The stone at my feet hummed, impatient.

"I want to remember."

I blinked. "What?"

"My human life." His voice scraped, like a key finding a stubborn lock. "Like the citizens of the Deadlands do. I want it back. I want to know who I was before . . . before Hell. Before they broke me into something they could use."

I've never cared about the world. I care about one girl and the few things that keep her alive. But this? This I could do. For him. For us. For what I used to be before the job taught me to sharpen everything, including myself.

"Okay," I said. "You get your memories. You get your name back. You get a beginning. And in exchange, you stand with me when it gets ugly."

His smile came back, smaller, realer. "It's always ugly with you."

"Good," I said. "I'm better at ugly."

I raised a hand. The room narrowed to the small, dangerous geometry of ritual, the curl of inked lines, the candle's halo, his breathing in my ears. From my palm, a thin thread of gold unfurled, and it slithered across the space between us, coiling at his sternum like a memory finding a home. Humanity.

The light burrowed in.

He gasped, his body arching, the sound raw and truthful. Flesh that had been ash-colored caught a slow bloom of warmth. Grey bled into tan like sunlight through winter fog. Horns receded, their shadow shrinking. Tattoos softened, ink loosening into pale, untouched skin. Hair darkened and fell, wilder than before. The shape of him narrowed into something lean and human—not whole, but startlingly, painfully close.

He looked like he might laugh and cry at the same time. The demon peeled back in layers until the man was visible through the cut.

When he opened his eyes, the gold was still there but gentler now, threaded with something like sorrow and humor and a kind of weary wisdom I recognized in myself. He studied his hands as if checking for a lie, then at his chest. Then he glanced up at me.

"I remember," he whispered. The words were small and fragile and immense all at once. "I remember you."

He swallowed hard. His eyes were bright with panic and relief braided together. "Damon always said his greatest mistake with me was stripping me of my humanity completely. With all the demons that followed, he left a tiny bit intact."

The truth was simple: He would be softer at the edges. He would be unpredictable in ways a demon never was He wouldn't be as cold. He wouldn't be heartless. He would feel things they'd spent centuries erasing, and that would change everything.

He looked terrified of that change and thrilled by it at the same time. His mouth opened, closed. "I—"

"Yeah," I said, because I could think of a dozen things to say, and none of them were good enough. "It'll be strange at first. You'll want to put the old shell back on because it was simple." I let the truth hang there. "But you're not that demon anymore—and you're not exactly a man either. It will take time to get used to the new angles of your own face."

His laugh trembled out of him. "I will break things," he said. "I will hurt people in stupid ways because I'll forget. I'll—"

"You'll fuck it up," I agreed. "You'll mess it up, and then you'll have to fix it. That's how you learn." I tilted my head, softer than I'd been in a long time. "But you won't do it alone."

We stood there, two ruined things with matching griefs and matching stubbornness, and for a moment the loneliness that had lived in my bones for centuries began to loosen.

Abel crossed the room with steps that sounded too light for someone who'd worn hell like armor. He moved like a man rediscovering how to inhabit himself. He reached up and took the weathered leather jacket off the peg, the one I'd worn until it was tattered. Smoke-scorched, sewn at the seams, still carrying the damp tang of graves and the kind of memory only clothes could hold.

He held it up and glanced at me, one brow lifted.

I barked a dry laugh and shrugged. "You can have it."

He grinned, small and almost embarrassed. "Thanks, big brother."

It hit me harder than it should have.

He slipped the jacket on. It draped around him as if it remembered him: The shoulders sat right, the sleeves fell like a returning familiarity. He looked . . . better. Less carved from shadow, more a man stitched back together.

I turned to the far side of the room where he leaned against the window frame, the Deadlands spilling out past him: flickering graves, wind that sounded like sighs through hollow trees. He wasn't harmless. He never had been. But he wasn't just a demon now. He had his humanity back, and maybe that meant something.

"So," I said, folding my arms. "We gonna talk about it?" The "it" was the murder. The bargain. The canyon that made a legend out of our worst day.

He didn't move. "You are Death," he said, voice like riverstone, cool, smooth, unmoved. "You did what you were born to do. What you had to do."

The sentence landed with a precision that made my chest ache less and somehow more all at once.

"I don't think we need a conversation," he added, quiet. Abel finally looked over. The pride was still there, because it always was, but humanity had put hands on it. "You've punished yourself more than I ever could."

That slid in without an edge and still cut. The old ache bloomed under my sternum like it had been waiting for permission. He was right. I was Death. I did the work. But I was Cain too, and rot sat under everything like bad wiring.

He pushed off the frame and rolled his shoulders, showman to the end. "Now. Strategy. Do we perform an elegant coup on cosmic law or improvise something vulgar and effective?"

I let myself grin back. "We start over," I said. "Together."

He nodded, solemn as a vow, then ruined it with a flash of teeth.

I sank into the stone chair and rubbed my face until the lines blurred. The guilt stayed. Quieter. The loneliness unwound a fraction and didn't fight me for it.

"So," I said, because bridges need words to rebuild, "I met a girl . . ."

CHAPTER 28

Opal

I hadn't been sleeping. The pink lights hummed, giving the apartment a theatrical glow that used to feel safe. Now they only made the shadows look emptier.

My mind kept wandering back to him. To Cain. To the way he'd kissed me like he was trying to smuggle forever into one mouthful. To the way he'd walked into a rift and not looked back. Where was he? Was he okay? Was he somewhere I couldn't reach?

I was staring at the empty chair he'd claimed, the hoodie hanging over the arm like a small accusation, when the air in the corner of the room changed.

It wasn't a sound so much as suction, a small unthreading. The lamp that hung over the kitchen flickered, and the pink lights went a hair dim, like someone had pinched the world between thumb and finger.

A seam opened in the air. Not violently, more like a mouth parting. The rift smelled faintly of smoke and candle wax. My heart did something stupid, and I forgot to breathe.

A figure stepped through.

At first, I thought it was Cain. It had to be. Same length black hair, the same sharp cheekbones, the same leather jacket with the same cigarette smell in the collar. For a breath the world stilled, and I could hear nothing but the blood in my ears and the foolish little hope that maybe, just maybe, he'd wandered back with a fix.

Then his eyes hit the light. Golden. Not Cain's tired, dark voids, not the small, wrecked moons I'd learned to read the universe in. These were bright, proud, and a little dangerous.

The resemblance stopped being comfort and started being a trick. He was the spitting image of Cain, and I didn't think I could trust that. I froze. Something in my body tightened like a wire.

He cocked his head, and that small movement, so like Cain's, made my chest ache. He smiled, and the smile was almost welcoming.

"Who are you?" I managed. My voice sounded thin, like something I'd forgotten how to use.

He cracked his knuckles like Cain did when he tried to look nonchalant and failed. Then, impossibly casual, he plopped into the chair Cain had claimed, sinking into it with an ease that made my insides hollow.

"My brother sent me," he said, voice smooth and amused in a way that set my teeth on edge. "Told me to keep an eye on you while he runs off to do something catastrophically stupid."

I took an involuntary step back. "Abel?"

The name came out like a question and a prayer. It landed on him, and he tilted his head again, considering.

"Abel," he repeated, slow, and nodded.

Something in me wanted to laugh and hate him at the same time. "You—" I started, and then I didn't know what I wanted to say. Thank you? Why him? Who gave you permission? What the hell did Cain think he was doing?

Abel leaned back, one booted ankle resting on the opposite knee. Up close he smelled like Cain but different: mint and smoke, yes, but edged with something metallic, like a coin freshly minted. The gold of his eyes warmed when he looked at me, but there was a caution there too, a quiet I didn't trust.

"He said you needed . . . company. Said not to trust me too far, but also not to let you sleep alone." He shrugged, as casual as a man can be when he's stepped out of a rift into someone's apartment. "Cain's reckless," he added. "You know this. So, I'm here to make sure you don't try to match him in bad decisions while he's out fixing his latest one."

I plopped onto the bed, arms crossed, a practiced pout. "I'm not going to do anything dumb!"

He snorts like he's heard that one before. He watches me for a beat like he's cataloging which lies I tell myself and which ones I actually believe. "You say that," he said. "That's exactly what people say before they do something spectacularly stupid."

I flipped him off without a thought. It was an old habit for when I was trying to sound sure. My fingers fumbled with the seam of the hoodie anyway. It was stupid and tiny, and he laughed.

"You're scared," he said. Not a question.

I didn't answer, because if I spoke, I'd start crying, and I didn't have Kleenex. Instead, I let the apartment make noise around us: the refrigerator humming, the lights buzzing, the city breathing beyond the window. My chest was tight. My pulse banged against my throat like I'd stuck my finger in a socket.

"Is he—" I started, voice small. "Is he okay?"

Abel's face softened for a second in a way that could be mistaken for tenderness. "He's not fine," he said honestly. "He's Cain. He's doing what Cain does. He's trying to fix things the way only Cain would try."

"Which is?" My sarcasm broke off halfway. I needed the truth, even if it killed me.

"Too loud, too proud, too quick," he answered. "And reckless as hell." Then, with a tilt that told me he knew exactly how much of that was family curse and how much was personal: "But he's trying for you."

Something small and hot bloomed under my ribs, gratitude tangled with terror. I swallowed it down. "And you? Why trust him to make you my babysitter?"

He smirked like a man who knew the exact line that would get under my skin. "Because you're the one thing that makes him softer than he has a right to be. Because he asked. Because he thinks I can keep you alive, and because he knows you'll try to take care of yourself with either dignity or chaos, and I prefer the dignity route tonight."

My laugh was brittle. "Dignity? From a demon?"

His grin broadened. "That's 'father of demons' to you, princess." He flashed me that wicked, toothy smile, his canines a fraction too long to pass for purely human, and it made the room tilt for a second.

I shoved a cushion at him, because being flirted with by a thing that looked like your boyfriend but wasn't your boyfriend felt like a new low. "Uh-huh. Cute. You seem like trouble."

He plucked the cushion from the air and dangled it like a prize. Up close he was ridiculous in the best possible way—more showman than reaper, all swagger and overconfidence. There was a chaotic electricity to him that Cain had never owned: Cain was a slow burn. Abel was fireworks in a storm. He tossed it back at me. "Trouble runs in the bloodline, princess."

"You look like him," I said. "Like, exactly like him except . . . you don't have tattoos."

Abel's face softened the tiniest fraction. He rolled his shoulders, showing me the clean sweep of skin where ink might have gone. "They gave me better fashions," he said, cocky as hell. "Also, I was unmade, remade, and then rebranded. Some accessories were lost in the process."

He patted his chest, fingers splayed over the smooth skin, and the gesture felt performative and intimate all at once. He studied his own arms like a man considering a new canvas. "This look is new," he added, voice playful. "Maybe I'll add something later. Maybe I won't. Depends on how bored I get."

I prodded again, harder this time, curiosity a knife in my hands that I didn't know how to put down. "Cain never hid what he was about. He never pretended to be anything but a walking mess with a conscience. You . . ." I trail off. "You're different."

He side-eyed me, gold catching the pink light, amusement folded over something sharper. "So, you're curious about me," he said, voice velvet and very wrong for three in the morning.

"You could say that." I folded my arms, trying to sound stern but only achieving "annoyed girlfriend." The hoodie smelled like him, and I kept sniffing it like a madwoman.

He snorted. "Curiosity killed the cat, they say." He tapped the side of his nose with a long finger. "Lucky for you, I'm less of a cat and more of a calamity."

He watched me while I tried not to squirm. There was a lightness to him Cain never had: not childish but deliberate, like someone who'd practiced charm as a weapon and found it far more effective than teeth. He toyed with the cuff of his jacket, thumb tracing a burn mark.

"I'm not the one who tried to overthrow Hell," I said, level, because if I was going to pry, I might as well dig properly.

Abel's grin thinned for the barest fraction of a second. "So, you know about that, huh?" He looked away, eyes glittering with a memory that wasn't pleasant. "Let's call it a complicated career move." He tapped his temple as if the complexity lived in his head and not his bones. "And besides, I'm not the one who needed babysitting. You are."

"Right," I said, because of course he'd say that. "I'm the problem."

He put on a whole performance then: palms up, bow of the head, voice thick with mock solemnity. "Allow me to present Abel: charming, cultured, a dash dangerous. Demonic résumé includes subverting celestial bureaucracy, dabbling in political upheaval, a brief romantic fling with several conceptions of regret." He gave a theatrical shrug. "And I just got out of a relationship."

I arched an eyebrow. "Let me guess," I said. "She left you?"

He blinked like I'd made the joke too easy. Then, with that same calm, like he was telling me the weather, he said, "No."

My laugh choked off when he added casually, "I killed her." He shrugged, but the grin died in his eyes for a fraction of a beat. "She was a snake," he said. "Not the best moment but dramatic—very dramatic." He leaned forward, elbows on his knees. "Look, moral complexities aside, I'm not here to list out my sins for you. I'm here because Cain asked. Which means you're under my protection, and I take my job very seriously. Seriously enough to murder, if the situation calls for it. But I won't hurt you. You have my word."

I had to give it to him, he had a way of saying monstrous things like people talk about the weather: offhand, practiced, and somehow almost conversational.

It was infuriating. It was magnetic. I hated that his confidence made me sit straighter.

"You do realize you're terrifying," I muttered.

"Good," he said. "Fear sharpens the room. Helps people remember to behave." He tilted his head and his smile softened—actually soft for a breath. "But I'm not monstrous for the fun of it. I was forged into a thing by other people's business. I made choices. Some ugly. Some regrettable."

"And you?" he asked, sudden, direct.

I blinked. "Me?"

"You," he repeated. "Small, ridiculous, and pink. The one who steals hoodies and smuggles chaos into his bed. You are trouble with a side of glitter, and I approve."

I was half-annoyed, half-pleased, both things that made me uncomfortable in equal measure.

"Look," he said, voice losing the showmanship for a second. "I'm not Cain. I never wanted to be. I don't love the ledger's neat arithmetic. I like flare, noise, things that smell like burnt options, but I keep my promises. Cain trusts me enough to leave you with me. That's not nothing."

He leaned back, hands splayed like a man who'd practiced owning space. "Just know, if I have to be your babysitter, I'll do it with swagger. I'll make you laugh in the wrong places. I'll also kill anyone who tries to open a rift in your living room. And if Cain doesn't come back—" He let the sentence hang, not finishing but heavy with intent.

"Fine," I said at last, and the word was caution wrapped in acceptance. "But no more casual confessions about murder."

He snorted. "Where's the fun in that?" Then he sobered like a magician lowering his wand. "Look. I'm not here to be a hero. I'm here to be useful."

He tapped his face. "Give me a reason to be terrible, and I'll promise to be terrible. Remember that, princess."

There was a pause while we both let the truth settle. He stood up and threw one of Cain's old hoodies at my face and said, "You're brooding. I'm bored. Let's go."

I peeled the hoodie off my face. "Cain said not to go outside."

Abel waved a hand like that was the least important piece of information I'd ever offered. "My brother is paranoid that something unfortunate will happen before he can fix your mortality issue." He flashed a crooked grin. "And now I'm here. You're safe with me."

I stared. He was utterly unbothered, flipping a coin between his fingers like mischief incarnate. Wild-haired and catching the kitchen light so that the gold in his eyes winked like a private joke.

He didn't wait for my permission. "Get your shoes," he added, tossing me a look that was too smug for someone currently breaking Death's very specific instructions. "We're stealing you a better mood."

Ten minutes later I was in the passenger seat of a matte-black 1970s Dodge Charger that definitely hadn't been in my parking lot yesterday.

"Whose car is this?" I asked, trying to steady the seatbelt as we peeled out.

"Mine," Abel said, drumming lazy fingers on the wheel. "Technically. I liberated it from a collector. He'll mourn it come sunrise."

"You stole this."

"I liberated it. Don't be dramatic." He flicked his coin into the cupholder and winked at me with the kind of grin that should come with a warning label.

The engine growled like it wanted the asphalt. Wind shoved the hair from my face, and the city blurred into neon. I should have felt panicky—after all, Cain was out there, somewhere nasty, and I had a demon in the driver seat who'd admitted to a cheerful homicide an hour ago. Instead, my chest loosened in a way I didn't expect.

We ended up at an arcade that smelled like cinnamon dust and old quarters, a place stuck in the mid-2000s: neon, blinking cabinet lights, the overhead jangle of a hundred half-broken machines. It was loud in the best possible way. Every beeping light felt like a tiny, defiant promise.

Abel stepped inside like a general entering a playground. He stretched, cracked his knuckles with a pretty flourish, and declared, "Stay close, little mortal."

The attendant who was in a tank top and chain shot us a bored expression. I went for the ticket counter and Abel slunk behind me, hands in pockets, eyes scanning like a connoisseur noting all the delicious targets.

He played everything like it was an instrument. Pinball machines? He knew the firmware like a lullaby, his palms rolling the flippers with an ease I envied. Racing pods? He beat the leaderboard by margins that made other players mutter. On the claw machine, he leaned in, narrowed those gold eyes, and murmured like a preacher and a pickpocket all at once. Then, he won me a pink-stuffed cow.

I don't know if he bribed the gears with charm or actually made physics feel embarrassed. One second, the claw hovered over a pile of pastel plush, the next . . . the cow. The attendant's jaw dropped.

"Ta-da," he said, pushing the cow into my lap. "For you. A token to stop you from brooding and start moo-ing."

I laughed. "You're ridiculous."

"Ridiculously efficient," he corrected, puffing up as if I'd offered him an accolade. He winked at me in a way that said he knew exactly how magnetic he was.

We were on a roll. The machine spat tickets like a glittering waterfall, and Abel whooped like a lunatic, fist punching the air. For one ridiculous, neon-streaked second his face was just a kid's again, electric and ridiculous and alive.

Then the jackpot pushed out, and the room changed. The attendant's face closed up like a safe. He came over, clipboard snapping shut in his hand. "You two," he said, voice suddenly tight, "what did you do?"

Abel glanced over casually, winked at me, and tossed another handful of tickets into the air because theatrics is his cardio. The attendant didn't laugh. He accused. "We enforce fair play here. You were pushing the machine. We had reports."

"Reports?" Abel arched a brow, leaning in with the exact charm of a man who knows how to disarm. He slid over a grin that could have sold sand in a desert. "Who reported? The prize counter or your ego?"

The attendant pointed to the camera above the cabinet with a finger that trembled. "You were manipulating the claw. Cheating's not allowed. We're . . . we're calling security."

The next thing I knew, two bored security guards in polyester were grabbing our arms with grips like cheap cuffs, and people were murmuring. It was absolute chaos.

We were escorted out with the pink cow tucked under my arm like contraband and a scattered trail of a ludicrous amount of tickets at our feet. Outside the arcade, the alley air hit like a cold slap. Abel laughed, big, breathy, the kind that made your throat unclench in the best possible way, and flung his head back. "We have been banished!" he declared, theatrical as a coronation. "A tragic exile. A victory!"

I hugged the cow like a talisman. My chest was a fizz of adrenaline and guilt. Cain had told me not to go, and I'd gone, and the world could be cracking somewhere, and I'd played a game for a stuffed animal. But the night had loosened something in me; for a few hours I'd been unburdened.

We piled into the Charger, Abel at the wheel grinning like a man who'd stolen the moon. We peeled back toward the city, tires whining a note of victory.

Back at my building, the stairwell smelled like antiseptic and cheap carpet. The apartment door opened to my pink lights humming the same stupid lullaby. He padded in, dropping the cow on the bed like a talisman, and flung himself onto the floor, still giggling at something he'd said to the attendant. He was contagious; his laughter ricocheted off my walls.

Then I saw it: a slim envelope tucked under my pillow, the paper too crisp for my messy life. My name on the front, handwriting I knew as intimately as a bruise.

My stomach dropped out of my body in one clean motion.

Blossom,

If you're reading this, I'm probably being an idiot. Don't panic—panic makes me do worse things.

Trust Abel. He owes me, and he'll keep you from doing anything spectacularly suicidal. (He will try to convince you to do dumb, fun things anyway. Don't let him guilt you.)

I'm following a lead. If I disappear, tell Crow I went to the pit. He'll know what that means, and he'll come. Don't go after me. Lock the door.

If I'm late, blame me. If I never come back, well, then you know I chose you over the ledger. Try not to hold that against me.

—C

"What's the pit?" I asked, voice too loud in the small room.

Abel's face drained the color out of him in a heartbeat. He snatched the note from my hand, fingers trembling just enough that the paper crinkled. He muttered, low and disgusted, "Idiot," under his breath, like he was both exasperated and proud.

"I have to go," he said suddenly, all movement and clean edges. He shoved the note into his jacket as if it were a live thing. "Now."

"Why?" I reached, because my feet moved before my brain did.

"To keep your boyfriend from getting himself killed. Permanently."

CHAPTER 29

Cain

I stood at the edge of the chasm, and the world felt like it had been cut out from under me on purpose. Stone fell away into a black that did not want light. This was the pit, the place the old God slept, the valley between Hell and the Deadlands where bargains went to get chewed up and spit out.

There was a calculus in me, a bone-deep accounting I'd been trained to obey. Keep the pit asleep. Keep the ledger neat. Keep the world from unspooling. Keep the souls flowing to Heaven and Hell. That was the job, solemn and cold, but there was another line running under all of that now, inked in softer script: Save Opal's life.

A rift tore open behind me. Not the polite, ceremonial kind Crow used, but ragged and smelling of vanilla and coffee. Abel stepped through like he'd been waiting for the curtain call, hair wild, jacket snagged, eyes burning gold and furious. For a beat seeing him there steadied the world. Family was stupid like that. Seeing him reminded me that I wasn't the only broken thing with hands.

"Don't be an idiot," Abel said. The words came sharp as flint. He sounded like someone ready to drag me back by the hair and the jaw if I needed it.

I thought of Opal, the smell of vanilla and coffee in her hair, the stupid crease at the corner of her mouth when she laughed, the hoodie folded across her chair like a map to everything I wanted and had no right to. She made the world bright in tiny, stubborn increments. She had taught me how to feel again, taught a man who'd long ago learned to be a machine how to live again, and I wasn't about to let that go. Her green eyes flashed in my mind, her laugh, the way she touched me like a lover and not a monster.

So, I jumped.

Abel's fingers closed the air where my sleeve had been. He cursed at me, sharp and hot, lunging forward, knuckles skimming the fabric. He was so close. He cursed again, a string of vulgar names, and reached down as if he could brute-force fate.

I didn't fall straight. I twisted backward, a slow, balletic refusal to be caught. The motion was ridiculous and precise.

"Cain—no—fucking—" he howled, voice shredding into the rift, every swear stitched with panic and something that sounded dangerously like love. I twisted enough to catch one ridiculous, impossible, infuriating glimpse of him, and Abel's mouth forming the word "idiot" like a benediction, and then the cliff swallowed the light.

The fall stretched like bad gum—long, sticky, stupid. There were no pleasing physics, no graceful arc, no thrilling wind, just a rubber-band yank through the dark. Time stretched and unspooled. Every awful choice I'd ever made unfolded in flashes, fights, murders that felt like math, and then there was her, right in the middle.

Landing wasn't cinematic. It was a fist to the lungs, a paper-tear of sound and pain. My ribs sucked air in like a desperate animal. Something in my left knee complained, and something in my shoulder sang a warning. I lay there tasting the small, stupid victory of having made the choice that mattered. Now, we would see what the cost was.

The god lay coiled in on itself like a storm compacted into a shapeless heap. Where flesh should have been was the suggestion of space, blackness folded over blackness, and it smelled of damp earth and rot.

I gave it a kick with my boot. Hard. The sole met something that was not flesh but not stone either. "Wake up, you old bastard." My voice scraped like gravel. I sounded like someone used to screaming at things that wouldn't move.

The god did not stir at first. Then the dark unrolled and drew a breath. "Who wakes me?" The voice came from everywhere and nowhere at once, hollow, cathedral-voiced, the sound of caverns trying on speech.

It righted itself like a mountain fixing its posture. Where a head should have been, a crown of bone reassembled from kings' jaws and godly vertebrae that drifted into a shape that could be called a face. The crown shivered; little bones clicked like teeth. The thing looked down at me as if I were an insect on its hand.

"I am the god of death," I said. There was a punk in my chest that wanted to laugh at the absurdity, but my voice was steady, flat, the tone you used when you listed your name on a warrant.

"Ah." The creature's tone lengthened in a way that suggested pleasure. "A dark god like myself."

"No." I shook my head slowly. "I'm the god of endings, not darkness." The words were a ward as much as a claim.

The god tilted its head in a way that snapped with a sound like dry leaves. "But you carry darkness like a crown just as I do," it said. Its finger, if it could be called that, pointed at the Mark on my chest in a way that made the air crackle. The Mark of Cain, the scar and seal I lived with, shimmered like an old wound under my shirt. I gasped and clutched at the place my Mark rested beneath my ribs.

"You carry what I am," it said. "You lock endings into bones and call them duty. I took darkness and made it a throne. We are cousins in the way the universe makes relatives: obscene, necessary."

The god's amusement rippled through the mist like oil over black water. "You're smaller than I imagined, Cain. Teeth, pedigree, all the proper nightmares stitched under your skin, but there it is, the absurd tenderness of a brief human obsession. You put a life before the ledger. That is a dangerous miscalculation." The god drew in a shallow breath, tired eyes finding mine.

"Then let me be dangerous." My jaw locked, hunger clawing at my ribs. "I'm not here to trade the world for a stall of glory. I'm here to ask."

"So ask." The god's voice moved like tides dragging a body out to sea.

"Make her stay. Make her permanent. No ledger loopholes, no polite deaths. I want"—the word shredded in my throat—"I want her to live."

The pit hummed, a throat clearing before a verdict. The shape in the dark shifted. Its sound was older than bargains. "I have the answer you seek," it whispered, each syllable an open grave, "but my help always comes at a cost."

I tapped my boot against the dirt, a defiant metronome. "Then. Name. It."

The crown clicked. "You will carry the darkness," it said, slow as a waiting guillotine blade. "Give it a new life in my stead."

The words dropped into me like iron. Carry its darkness. Be its vessel. My next breath was jagged. "Done," I snapped before panic could dress itself up as a speech. "How do I save her?"

The god laughed, a drawn-out, wet sound like something rotting underwater.

"Follow the beating compass, the key to death, the lock to life. Press it deep to bend the ledger. Give it freely to tip the scales."

Old gods loved riddles. Riddlers in bad tailoring, all of them. I crossed my arms. "What the hell kind of answer is that?" I muttered.

I turned to leave. The only thing worse than a riddle was being tempted by it.

The darkness moved faster than light. Inky hands seized my jacket, slammed me to the ground. "Not before your debt is paid, Death."

I didn't hesitate. I didn't dance with metaphors or grovel at the altar. I moved the only way I knew how: blunt, honest, quick, and lethal. I twisted and grabbed the god back.

The contact was a death sentence. The god's eyes widened, something like surprise cracking its voice. It fell with a heavy, obscene thud. The god that had slept for ages folded into itself, and the crown rolled away, spilling little fragments of fossilized kings like dice.

I glanced down at the corpse of a pre-creation titan and felt nothing saintly. I felt the thing I always felt: the clean, hungry economy of endings. I felt the mark under my ribs thud like a hammer.

"I kill everything I touch, dumbass," I said, because someone needed to tell the universe the rules. The old god was dead. The bargain, what it had meant, what it had promised... that had died too. I had killed gods before, things that were supposed to be eternal. This one was no different.

Now the only way out was up.

There were no polite rifts here, no bargains to call for help, just slick stone and the sucking black that smelled like old promises. No shadows to hide in. No shortcuts. Just the cliff and me and the small, ugly job of hauling my useless body back into a world that still expected arithmetic.

I grabbed at the rim, and the rock shredded my palms like a paper test. Skin came away in ragged ovals, my nails split, blood ran warm and slick between fingers that had strangled priests and signed death certificates with cleaner hands. I tasted iron and the sourness of adrenaline. Each hold was an argument: a fistful of grit, a bone-fingered notch, a fossil edge that crumbled under weight. The crown's fragments lay scattered like the world's bad receipts. I used them because there wasn't honor in leaving anything to be admired.

My boots slipped half a dozen times. I cursed at the cliff with the kind of profanity that was practical—short, sharp words to scare the stone into offering purchase. Muscles screamed in a language I mostly ignored.

When my fingers finally closed over the last ragged notch and my shoulder cleared the rim, everything went wrong and right at once. I hauled, a human engine with too much fuel cursed into my veins. The pull was holy and obscene: grit to palm, teeth clenched, breath a saw.

I rolled over the edge and collapsed like someone who'd been carrying houses. The world tasted of dirt and victory. My chest heaved; my palms were laced with blood. I lay there, gasping, the rim biting my collarbone where the jacket snagged, and laughed because that was what I did when things were too raw to cry.

"You are such a fucking idiot." Abel's voice rang out, half-laughter, half-reprimand. "What the hell happened down there?"

I smiled, crooked, dangerous, the kind of smile you give before you tell a terrible story over beer. "I killed a god."

He blinked. "Did you at least get any answers?"

"No." My grin stretched until it hurt. "None at all."

The joke evaporated fast. The world narrowed to the clock in my head. She had less than one day. Abel crawled over the rim and sat beside me, boots scuffing the stone. He was all profanity and that impossible confidence that made people want to believe in almost anything. Up close, the gold in his eyes looked tired in the right places. "So," he said, like a man choosing which sin to perform next, "you murdered a pre-creation god, and it gave you . . . nothing? That's almost poetic."

"Poetry doesn't buy time." I wiped my hands on my jacket; it came away red. The smell of iron was everywhere. "It handed me a riddle and offered me a bargain. Then I killed it because I don't bargain with predators who put a price on my heart."

CHAPTER 30

Opal

The apartment felt like a dressing room and a war room all at once. My laptop was a mess of tabs, archive scans, obituary clippings, amateur ghost-hunter blogs, the town's old newspaper microfilm, and a paper map of the hospital with routes circled in neon pink pen. I'd spent most of the day on research: names, dates, where the nurses used to smoke, and where, supposedly, the infants kept crying in the walls.

Tonight was Halloween, and the *Spooky Ghouls* crew had booked the abandoned hospital two towns over. It was perfect: peeling paint, a wing that smelled like old bleach and the memory of too many hands, a nursery with a cracked mobile. It was the sort of place that begged for a camera and a pink-haired calamity like me.

I cataloged my kit one last time: ring light, spare batteries, the EMF reader that Lyric swore looked legit, a roll of gaffer tape, two headlamps—because I'd lost one once. I'd packed for a shoot and for a séance and for everything in-between because improvisation had always been the safest thing I owned.

Then, I dressed for myself.

The outfit was an argument: a cropped pink leather jacket, a black mesh top with little stars stitched on it, a skirt that was half-tutu, half-combat, and boots that could kick through a boarded-up door if anyone asked them to.

I did my makeup like I was painting a warning: smudged liner, a dab of glitter, lipstick the color of cherry blossoms. I braided my pink hair back. This look was not for Lucian, not for the crew, and definitely not for anyone who wanted me to go back to safe. This was Opal. Loud, dumb, prickly Opal with a camera and a knife.

I checked my reflection until it felt like a prayer. The hoodie Cain had left on the chair smelled like him, like nicotine and peppermint, and for a second, I considered bringing it, but this shoot was my promise to myself: no armor, no apologies.

So, I grabbed a pen, scribbled a quick note, and folded it once.

Dear Death,

I'm fine. Don't spiral.

New shoot for *Spooky Ghouls* at St. Mary's.

Here's the address.

Again, totally fine.

Opal

I slid it into the crack of the door. I doubted he'd find it in time, but leaving it made me feel better. Like maybe I wasn't running off. Just . . . living. Which, ironically, felt more dangerous than anything I'd done in weeks.

It was raining. Of course it was. Perfect weather for ghosts. The metro exhaled me into rain that smelled like old pennies and wet concrete. Thane's van idled under a busted lamp, windshield streaked, wipers on a lazy loop. Lyric perched on the bumper like a neon gargoyle, already crafting the cold open in her head. Nyxie leaned against the passenger door, threading a black ribbon around the neck of a porcelain doll.

"Trigger object," she said as I approached, matter-of-fact. "From a '90s yard sale near St. Mercy. If anything's still here, Agnes will get them talking."

The doll's one good eye gleamed. I tried not to shiver. "Agnes?"

She grinned, shoving the doll toward me. "Mmhmm." The side door slid back. Lucian was inside, B-cam already mounted, headphones around his neck like an earned halo. He smiled when he clocked it was just us, no Cain, and something in his smile loosened, almost satisfied.

"Good turnout," he said lightly. "Fewer variables."

I climbed in, brushing past him to the gear bins: EMF meters, recorder mics, our recently battered spirit box, REM pod, thermal imager, laser grid pen, a pair of cat balls that blinked like tiny comets, extra batteries labeled with Sharpie. I did roll call with my hands because working steadied me: REM, check. EVP, check. SLS, check. Grid, check. Trigger object, Agnes, nestled in Nyxie's tote like a cursed accomplice, check . . . unfortunately.

Lyric dropped into the back row, gum popping. "Okay, team: intro at the ambulance bay, thermal sweep of the nursery, laser grid down the east corridor, EVP in the boiler room, Agnes on the nurses' desk. If a ghost even clears its throat, we're viral."

Nyxie peered around. "Where's your . . . mystery boyfriend tonight?"

"Busy," I said, buckling in. "With his brother."

Lyric whipped around, eyes cartoon-wide. "Wait . . . He has a brother, and you didn't tell me?"

I laughed. "Yep. They could practically be twins."

"Oh my god," she gasped, clutching imaginary pearls. "You've been holding out on me."

Nyxie watched Lucian not watching her. Lucian's smile didn't change, but the corners of it tightened. "Well," he said, almost relieved, "it's good we'll have a focused team tonight." He handed me a coffee like a gift he expected to be thanked for. "Maybe we can talk after," he added, softer. "You and me. I've . . . missed this. Missed you."

"We're working," I said.

"Work can wait for a bit," he murmured, then, louder for the van: "Safety briefing. No one wanders off. Stay in pairs." He glanced at me. "With me, preferably."

Lyric's eyes met mine. Ugh. Nyxie's smile went thin as wire.

We rolled out. Rain stitched the windshield; the hospital hunched on the hill like a rumor that had learned to breathe. In the van's hum, the gear became a choir: the EMF's tiny baseline, the recorder's red eye winking, cat balls quiet in their tray like sleeping meteors. I felt keyed up and weirdly right. This was my habitat, damp and haunted and staged. I'd done the homework: names, dates, the rumor about the head nurse who'd kept a ledger of sins.

We parked by the ambulance bay. Everyone hesitated on the same beat: ritual, terror, and the small thrill of being who we were on camera.

"Let's make some ghosts jealous," Lyric declared, hoisting the ring light like a standard.

We spilled into the rain. The cold slid under my jacket, and I liked it. Nyxie planted Agnes on the nurses' desk in the intake hall, smoothing the ribbon. Thane set the REM pod beside the doll. Its green LED blinked awake. I fixed the laser grid toward the mouth of the east corridor. Emerald light stippled the dark into a thousand points. Lucian shadowed my shoulder with the B-cam, too close for a wide, just close enough to feel like a shepherd.

"Stay near me," he said, the words soft as cotton. "It's not safe to—"

"I've been here before," I said and stepped through the grid anyway.

On cue, the EMF ticked up: 1.2, 1.6, a teasing 2.0. Lyric's voice turned silken for the cold open. "Spooky Ghouls, we have boots on the ground at the infamous St. Mercy, rumored home of—"

Lucian touched my sleeve. I moved out of reach. "After the intro," he said softly, "we should talk."

"About what?" I whispered. I didn't look at him. The EVP recorder sat on the desk, red light steady. I pressed RECORD and set it down like an invitation. "I'm Opal, and if anyone remembers Agnes, we brought her back."

Silence layered over rain. The REM stayed green.

"About us," Lucian said, voice calibrated for Hallmark. "About how we make sense. I'm glad he's not here. I never liked the . . . noise."

The EMF hiccuped to 3.1, and I felt something else tick up with it—annoyance. "Lucian," I said evenly "we're not doing this tonight."

He smiled like I'd told a joke at a fundraiser. "After," he said. "When you're warmer."

Nyxie slid me a cat ball and an eye roll. I set the toy by Agnes' porcelain feet. "If you want to play," I told the empty hall, "light this up for us."

A faint tap answered from the east wing. Lyric's brows jumped. "Hook," she whispered to camera. The laser grid shivered like heat over asphalt. An illusion, probably. Or not.

Lucian leaned in, trying for conspiratorial. "See?" he whispered. "Not safe. Stay by me."

It should have read as protective, but instead it read like positioning—who owned the shot, who owned the story. Lyric caught the vibe and pitched her voice bright. "Opal, give us your history hit. Name the nurse, give us dates. Let's feed the air."

I did what I did best: Facts like salt. Names like a map. The hospital leaned closer. The EMF ticked. Agnes smiled her cracked little smile at the corridor. The REM pulsed once, twice, flashing amber, amber, then green.

"Opal," Lucian said quietly. "Let's not antagonize it. Come back here. With me. We should . . . get back together." He said it like we were rescheduling a meeting. "We fit."

Nyxie's head turned, a slow blade. Thane's hands stilled on the tripod. Lyric's mouth made a perfect O off camera, then snapped shut.

I kept my eyes on the grid and my voice on the history, because that's what a woman does when the past wants to drag her back by the wrist. "In 1979, a strange case turned the staff superstitious," I recited steadily. "They left offerings in the nursery. Ribbons. Dolls. They say a child haunts these halls, and she likes to play with toys."

Agnes tipped. No one had touched her. The cat ball blinked once, soft blue, like a heartbeat.

Lyric didn't breathe. "We got that," she whispered, hands tightening on the ring light.

Lucian's fingers hovered again, that almost-touch, the choreography of ownership. "Opal," he said, gentling my name. "Don't be reckless."

I smiled into the dark, and it was all teeth. "I'm being myself," I said. "Finally."

The corridor exhaled. The laser points rippled. The REM squealed to red. In the camera's tiny screen, something mapped briefly where no one stood: stick-limbs, a head, gone.

We all felt it then: the shift. The hospital paying attention. And beneath that, another shift, colder—Lucian's patience with me thinning.

"Spooky Ghouls," Lyric breathed into her mic, "welcome to the part where the building starts to flirt back."

Nyxie's gaze slid to Lucian like a warning tied with ribbon.

I set the recorder closer to Agnes and, for the first time in a long time, didn't shrink to fit the room. It started as a whisper I couldn't place, like a lullaby someone sang through a wall. Then came the soft thudding on tile, too delicate to be pipes, too careful to be wind.

"Did you hear—" I began.

"EVP's still rolling," Thane said in my ear.

The sound tugged at me like a thread. It slid down the east hall, past the laser grid, and toward the stairwell with the peeling EXIT sign.

"I'm checking it," I said before anyone could vote. The ring light washed the corridor in pink white. Agnes stared after me with her one good eye.

"Opal, wait," Lyric's whisper snapped. "Pairs!"

I was already moving. Boots on damp tile, breath loud in my head. The whisper thickened into melody, nursery simple, off-key, like somebody humming. I pushed the stairwell door open, and a cold blast of air rolled up from below.

"Opal." Lucian's voice came from behind me, soft as a glove. "I'll come with you."

I didn't argue. Better a camera than a lecture. We slipped down the stairs, light skittering over flaking paint and rust freckles. Each step answered with a hollow clang that dipped into something that wasn't an echo. The song thinned, then returned stronger, close now, near the basement corridor where the floor changed from filthy linoleum to clean, old tile. A sign with missing letters still managed "M—R—GUE."

The morgue door pushed open like it had been waiting. The temperature bottomed out. The air was the kind that finds your bones, a fridge-cold that held the faint sweetness of rot under a choke of disinfectant. Light flickered because it could.

"We should bring the others," Lucian said, but he didn't call them. He followed me in.

Drawers lined the walls like quiet promises. A stainless gurney waited in the middle of the room, a sheet folded with too much ceremony at its foot. Drain in the center, a circle of darker tile like a target. My breath made smoke. My fingers tingled. The hum of the building vanished; silence leaned in.

The lullaby slid under the door, past us and behind us all at once. "Did you hear that?" I whispered.

Lucian didn't answer right away. He set the B-cam on the gurney and switched it off, cutting the live feed. "I hear you," he said finally.

I turned to face him. "You're acting weird."

He looked like the same man he always presented to the world—handsome in a press-photo way, hair that never quite moved, that tidy face donors trusted—but the wrongness I'd been feeling under irritation began to show its teeth.

"I wanted to save you from this," he said, almost conversational. "From the darkness."

A laugh jumped out of me, brittle. "We're ghost hunting in a morgue, Lucian. Darkness is the point."

He took a step closer. The morgue light made shallow hollows under his eyes. "Not this darkness," he said. "Mine."

My throat tightened. "What does that even mean?"

He smiled, small and rueful, like a man admitting a youthful misdemeanor. "I'm . . . different," he said, and the word strobed wrong in the air. "Darker than you ever knew. I wanted you out of it. You were—are—bright. Clean. You touched rooms and they softened for you."

My heart ticked faster. "You mean controlling. You wanted me contained."

"I mean safe," he said, patience thinning. "Until you went and found some-one worse, and I realized you couldn't be saved. Not from me, and not from him, either."

Understanding flickered like a bad bulb. "This is about Cain."

"It's about *you* and what you're doing to yourself." His voice sharpened; the polite mask slipped a millimeter. "You don't belong with someone like that. You don't know what he *is*."

"I do," I said. "And I chose anyway."

He flinched like I'd struck him. "He's wrong for you."

"He's *mine*."

Something in his face rearranged. The pretty-boy act didn't drop all at once; it peeled off. The careful smile held, but the eyes went flat. He stepped closer, and the room shrank around his shape.

"Leave with me," he said. "Now. We go upstairs. We tell them you're done with this. We talk. We fix us. We put you back where you belong."

I felt my spine straighten in a way that had nothing to do with bravery and everything to do with finally taking up the space my name required. "There is no *us* to fix."

The mask cracked. It wasn't dramatic. The softness drained from his face, and what was left was all calculation, bright and cold. The smile stayed, but it was all teeth now.

"You've always been stubborn," he said, and now there was no velvet at all. "It was charming when it was small."

Fear slicked my palms. My breath came higher, faster. "Lucian," I said, keeping my voice level by force. "Back up."

He didn't. He reached for my arm, gentle in the way a vise is gentle before it tightens. "I'm trying to help you."

I yanked free; nails scraped skin. "You don't get to help me."

He stepped in, and the smell of his cologne under bleach made my stomach turn. I felt the gurney's cold edge hit the backs of my thighs. Panic set up shop in my ribs, and my fingers went pins-and-needles. Somewhere above, faint and muffled, Lyric's voice called my name from a distant hallway, distant floor.

Lucian's eyes didn't move. "Leave with me," he said, one last time. "We're leaving together."

"No."

The last of the pretty fell off him. The expression underneath was terrifying, because it wasn't monstrous. It was ordinary cruelty, the kind that writes laws and calls it order.

"Fine," he said, and the word was a door closing.

He moved like he'd rehearsed it a thousand times, all easy charm and small, practiced gestures that put people where he wanted them.

One second, he was soft, the next, his hand was on my shoulder, the kind of touch that read as guidance until it wasn't. I tried to step away, but his grip tightened, polite and absolute.

Something cold and wet touched the back of my neck, and my head snapped up. He'd produced a cloth so smooth it slipped against my skin like oil. Before I could shout, he pressed it to my mouth and nose; the scent was sickly sweet, thick, syrupy chemicals under the antiseptic. The world blurred and hatched.

In that blur I saw movement, metal doors yawning open like mouths, men in robes stepping out of the body coolers as if they'd been stored there, waiting. A wireless speaker somewhere in the mist played a soft, tinny lullaby.

"Shhh," he said, his voice a soft lullaby. He kept his face close. "It's okay. Don't make this harder."

Hands closed around my wrists. Firm. Not cruel but trained. Two pairs of arms folded behind me, and ropes bit into my palms as they cinched knots. Panic flared hot and stupid, but the cloth did its work: my breath came shallow, then thinner, like a signal losing strength.

I hit the tile with my face and tasted copper and bleach. The lullaby kept going, twisted now into a siren. Lucian whispered, "Nice and quiet, Opal. Just nice and quiet."

My limbs trembled, hot and useless. I bit. My teeth found fabric and flesh, but the world still narrowed to a pinpoint of cold and a bloom of black. The camera on the gurney looked on, blinking stilled, helpless and mechanical, as everything else went black.

It was the dark that I felt first, the cold, damp floor next. Torches flickered in iron cups along stone walls, smoke licking the ceiling and coming back down in thin, stringy veils. My head pounded in a bright, stupid rhythm. When I tried to move, rope bit my wrists and ankles.

A circle of figures in dark, hooded robes ringed the room, faces hidden behind bone-white masks. Beyond them, a chalked sigil sprawled across the flagstones. One of the masks stepped forward. Hands lifted. The mask came off. *Lucian.*

He crouched so our faces were level. In torchlight, the pretty I'd once mistaken for gentleness turned precise, almost elegant. Knife-bright. "Hi, Opal," he said softly, as if saying my name kindly could rename whatever the fuck this was.

I yanked against the rope. Heat crawled up my neck. "What is this?" My voice broke on the last word.

"It's family," he said. "My legacy. We go back centuries. Priests and magistrates and men who understood order." He glanced past my shoulder at the masked faces, then back, proud. "I'm being initiated tonight, and you"—his smile sharpened—"you're our honored guest."

Ice licked up my spine. "Honored guests aren't tied up," I snapped.

"Ceremony has its . . . formalities." He smiled wide and tipped his head toward the sigil on the floor. "We're just waiting on one more."

"Who," I asked, and the word came out like a cough I couldn't swallow, "are you waiting on?"

"A demon," Lucian said, matter-of-fact. "The one you bound." His eyes glittered. "Cain."

I forgot to breathe. "You don't know what you're saying."

"Of course I do." He leaned closer, voice that of a confidant. "Ever since the day you stopped that fight, remember? You said his name, and he froze. I did my homework. Old bindings are name-work. Anchors. Beasts brought to heel." His mouth curved, pleased with his own cleverness. "You brought a dog to heel, Opal. You just didn't know what breed it was."

Rage hit so hard I almost didn't taste the fear. "He isn't—he's not mine to—"

"He will be ours," Lucian said with such calm certainty my skin crawled. "My family has always understood what to do with power. We will bind Cain. Use him properly. Direct him toward usefulness. Imagine it: wealth, influence, a cleaner world. The respect I'll earn."

"You can't," I said. My breath was coming too fast, too shallow. The torches wavered. "You don't know what you're doing. If you try to summon him, he will kill you."

Lucian's smile went small and pitying, like a teacher indulging a child who'd misread an equation. "That's why we're doing this properly. Every ritual needs an offering." He glanced toward the robed circle. "And you brought the perfect one with you when you bound him. You."

The room tilted, the ropes bit, the torches flared. "No." The word scraped against my throat. "No."

"You were always going to be part of this," he said gently. "The night you chose him, you chose this. I tried to save you from that darkness. I tried to keep you safe, keep you . . . presentable, but you kept running toward the abyss, and then"—something ugly flickered across his face, quick and honest—"then you found something worse than me."

He smiled again; all the kindness drained out of him. "So, I'll make use of the mess you made."

"Lucian," I said, because I wanted one last lie, one last chance for the man I'd thought I knew to be anyone but this. "Please. Don't."

He sighed like I was late to a meeting. "Gag her," he said to someone over my shoulder.

Hands at the back of my head. Cloth slid across my mouth. I jerked away, bit down as they tied it tight.

He stood and moved to the edge of the sigil, raising his hands. The robed circle shifted to face inward; low voices gathered like flies. Latin. Something older. Lucian began to speak my lover's name.

Cain. Cain. Cain.

Each repetition struck like a nail driven into a board. The sigil's lines smoldered. The stone under my legs hummed. I thrashed because there wasn't anything else I could do. The circle's chant lifted and fell, a tide of wrongness. Lucian's voice wove through it, patient, proud, a man who'd been waiting his entire, careful life to put his foot on the universe's neck.

In the corner of my vision: an altar table, Black-veined marble streaked with old, brown shadows. A silver bowl. A bell. A knife.

The knife was ceremonial: beauty first, purpose second. Its blade had scripture etched into it, the kind of words men used to make violence sound ordained. Lucian took it up with reverence, as if he were greeting an old friend.

Lucian knelt in front of me again and set the bowl under my chin, careful, tender, like a lover straightening a necklace. He pressed the blade's tip against the hollow of my throat.

He looked up at me, and his eyes were radiant with belief. "He will come for you," he whispered.

I shook my head, hard enough the world smeared. A muffled sound tore out of me. Salt burned my eyes. Rope bit until the pain turned the edges of the room white.

"This is how you fix things," Lucian said almost lovingly. "You make a sacrifice. You get a miracle."

The knife bit harder and the room held its breath.

CHAPTER 31

Cain

I hit the castle steps still dripping blood from my palms. Abel kept pace, gold-eyed and electric.

"What's the plan?" he demanded. "Clock's out. You should be with her."

"I'm going," I said, stripping off the torn coat and reaching for blades I didn't remember summoning. "I just need—"

The floor buckled. Hairline cracks spidered across the hall and split wide like a grin. Far below, something old screamed. A name tore the air in two. "Cain!"

We ran to the window. The horizon, where the Deadlands should slouch and keep its bad manners to itself, rippled. The pit mouth yawned wider than physically possible. A vast shape heaved itself up from the black, crowned in bone and wearing a new hunger like a fresh coat.

"That's impossible," I said, because sometimes stating the obvious is in fact needed.

"Apparently not." Abel's laugh was knife-thin. "Did you insult his lineage?"

"Yeah . . . probably."

The castle shook again; mortar dusted our shoulders. We were already deciding ten moves at once: hold the ridge, call Crow, anchor the wards, triage the ledger. Then Fate shoved its thumb on the scale.

It started in my ribs: a tug, mean and intimate. The first teeth of a summoning closed around my sternum like a chain pulling taut.

"Fuck," I hissed. "They're calling me."

Abel's face snapped to ready. "I'll take care of *that*," he said, chin tipping toward the horizon where the old god was dragging itself into a world that had not invited it. "Besides, we both know I can pass as you if I need to."

He wasn't wrong. In bad light, we were the same problem with different hair. I yanked a black hoodie off a chair and hurled it at him. "Put this under your jacket. It'll help."

He caught it one-handed, already shrugging into it with a cocky flourish that made me want to punch him and thank him in the same breath.

"Here," I said and opened my palm. Shadows moved like water pouring from a sleeve. They coiled from my wrist to his. "For a while," I told him, "they'll answer to you. Don't get cocky."

"I am literally the definition of cocky," he said, grinning, but his eyes flicked to me, gauging the pull of the summons. "Go."

I called up a spare scythe and pressed the haft to his palm. It drank in the torchlight and looked pleased about it. "Try not to die," I said.

"Hypocrite," he shot back, twirling the blade, already turning toward the window where the sky wore bones. "I'll keep the ancient nightmare busy. Go handle your fans."

The chain in my ribs yanked hard, merciless. The summoning climbed up my spine like a ladder.

"Abel," I said, because sometimes brothers deserve the real thing, "thank you."

He rolled his eyes like I'd confessed to having feelings. "Bring *her* back," he said, serious under the swagger. "Then you can thank me."

The world grabbed me by the sternum and ripped. The room hit me like a concussion of heat and iron. They dragged me up from the dark with a bad circle and worse Latin. Cult robes. Torches. Cheap iron stink. And there he was running it all like a smug little maestro. *Lucian.*

Opal was on her knees inside the ring. Her eyes found me and the whole room tilted. The sigils lit white-blue and faded to black. That ugly not-color you only see when something tries to lie to reality. The chant scraped my name out of their throats.

Lucian lifted the knife. It kissed her throat and opened her clean. Red found the offering bowl like it had been waiting its whole life. The binding woke. The chalk hissed. Power crawled up my boots and died there.

Opal's knees went soft.

I moved. The air turned thick, like wading through syrup. Binding script bit my ankles and pulled tight. It burned for the effort. Lines blistered. Ink peeled. Symbols tried to hold and broke. They were built for demons, for lesser things with collars and rules.

I was not a demon. I was the end.

I reached her, dropping to my knees. Blood warm under my fingers. But I was still . . . Gods, I was still one blink too late.

Opal's eyes found mine, wide, wet, furious, and apologetic. Her body went slack the way the living would never allow themselves to. She sagged against the ropes in a spill of limbs and pink hair, the sound small, obscene, final.

My mouth opened. The noise that came out didn't belong to language. It was animalistic. "OPAL."

My shadows cut her ropes, and her slack body fell into my arms. My knees were covered in the blood. It soaked my jeans and skinned my palms when I reached for it. I turned her toward me, stupid, gentle, the way the living always handled the dead as though tenderness could edit time. Her head lolled in my arms.

"Blossom," I said, and the word came out shrapnel-soft, like I'd bitten it and swallowed it and still tried to cradle the piece I had left. "Hey. Hey—"

Her lashes were wet. Her mouth was parted in that small, stubborn way I'd kissed a hundred times. Her fingers twitched once against my wrist.

"Look at me," I begged, and shadows climbed the walls in the shape of my knees, my grief, my stupid, helpless hands. "Look at me."

She didn't. Couldn't. The silence after a heart stopped was a doctrine. I felt it pass through me like a bell-note that would never end. I was only a conduit; I could ferry, I could tally, I could close the books—but I couldn't rewind a single second. That was the first law and the last cruelty.

So, I stood.

The spell broke like glass, and my mark detonated under my ribs, a furnace door blown open. Shadows ripped off my spine and hit the walls like a storm. The nearest acolyte lifted off his feet and folded midair, mask and bones snapping loud as cutlery. The next one went skidding, robes on fire.

Opal's blood was on my boots, my cuffs, the creases of my palms. It dried hot. It made a map of a life I would carry no matter how clean I tried to get. I turned to Lucian, and the room's temperature found a new, lower floor.

The torches bent toward the shout like grass to a wind. Every sense choked on detail: the sour stench of fear-sweat under the robes, the sweet rot of incense, the sterilized tang of old tile, and the copper flood that had been her.

Lucian stood stupidly triumphant for one heartbeat, the maskless priest at his altar, breath caught, waiting for applause. Then he saw me properly. The delight died on his face like a candle wick pinched between fingers. He tried to lift the knife again, and the shadow of my hand broke his wrist without touching it. Bone snapped with a wet pop. The blade clanged across tile and skated into the blood, writing his failure in a bright arc.

He gasped, clutching his ruin of a hand, and made the mistake of speaking. "It's—it's for the greater—"

My scythe materialized and hit the floor beside me. Behind him, robed figures scrambled, some crawling, some praying, some groping for something holy. The old scripts on their hems lit and guttered, failing in waves. Lucian's summoning had been perfect on paper, perfect in rooms where men mistook obedience for power. It failed like all their bindings failed, because they had never called me. They had only called a title. They had called Death, and I didn't kneel for anyone who wrote my name in chalk.

Opal had been the exception. She had not called my title. She had said my name and asked me to be a person. That was the violence. That was the miracle. She hadn't called me to use me, to control me. She'd called the man, not the god, and I'd answered.

"You need a lesson in summoning." My voice came out quiet and razored. "You didn't call a demon."

He staggered back, cradling his ruined wrist, breath ragged. The robed chaos froze, as if stillness could bargain.

"You called a god." I stepped over the sundered sigil. It hissed under my heel. "The god of death. Keeper of the ledger. The weight at the end of every scale. The man who turns off the lights. You invited me to a massacre and handed me the blade."

The exits went dark behind my shoulders. Shadows sheeted down across the doorways, thick, matte, absolute. Steel would have been kinder. One of the acolytes made for a side passage and hit the black like a wall. The sound his body made arcing back was a lesson in regret.

"You—" Lucian tried, voice shaking. "This is—"

"Cause and effect," I said. "You tried to leash something you don't understand. Now you get to pay the price."

The first mask flinched. I reached, and the robe folded as if the bones had chosen a different direction. The second tried a prayer. My shadow took it out of his mouth and gave him silence instead. A third lifted a brand and found it cold in his hand before the floor took his feet. When someone ran, the doors stayed closed. When someone begged, only the ceiling listened, and the ceiling did not care. Pain bloomed in pockets across the room, but I made sure every one of them knew which name had brought this on.

"Look at him," I told them as they broke. "This is your priest. This is your architect. Watch what your faith bought."

Lucian watched as, one by one, the robes thinned. They crumpled, masks split, chants guttered into small, human sounds. The air filled with iron and smoke and the ozone tang of power pushed too far. When it was quiet enough to hear the torches spit, only Lucian stood.

He backed into the last unbroken wall, pale, beautiful in that useless way rich men are when the lights go out. "You loved her," he said, as if the fact might save him. "So save her."

"Oh, now you offer a trade." I smiled without heat. "You had a bargaining chip. You chose spectacle."

He swallowed. "I—I can fix it. I can make this right. Please."

"You can make nothing right." I walked until the scythe's shadow split his shoes in half.

He squeezed his eyes shut like a child about to be scolded. "Make it quick."

"No." I leaned in, close enough to smell the starch and fear. "I've wanted to kill you for a very long time."

His fingers twitched toward the knife. Reflex. I didn't grant him theatrics. Shadows peeled off my skin like gloves, twisting around his wrist with polite cruelty. His grip faltered. The blade clattered on the tile. Iron bit the air. Her blood still streaked the edge when I bent to reclaim it, and it sang in my hand like a hymn.

I planted a boot hard on his chest.

He gasped. "Cain—"

"No," I snapped, steel wrapped in grief. "That name means nothing coming from you." I slammed the scythe beside him, shadows snapping against the floor like they wanted to chew the air.

He tried to crawl backward, eyes wide, trembling, but the shadows held him like judgment incarnate. I bent down, scythe whispering at his throat. "Look at me," I said, deliberate, venom-laced. "Feel what you've done. No charm or smile will save you now."

I pressed the blade—the one he'd used on her—to his face. His jaw clenched. I dug in a fraction, enough to mark. "You thought you could hurt her, hurt me, and walk away. Pretend you were untouchable. Pretend you mattered."

His eyes flickered, a shadow of recognition. "She mattered," I yelled, voice raw, a blade of grief slicing through the air. I slammed the scythe down, not to kill, but to pin him under the weight of the blade.

He spat a laugh that came out like a cough. "You—"

"Shut up." My scythe swung and came down in a motion that was a promise and a verdict. The blade found the space beneath his jaw. His severed head hit the floor in a wet slosh. He blinked once, and then his body followed, slumping to the side.

For a moment I watched him, as if I could read every misdeed off his face. Rage flared, but grief undercut it. I regretted that I hadn't made his death slower, but I couldn't stand the sound of his voice a second longer. I planted the haft into the floor and let the shadows curl around me.

When the last tremor faded, I wiped the scythe on the tile and let the weight of what I'd done fall where it would. It did not unmake the hurt. It did not bring her back. But it did close a door. I turned back to her.

The floor ran thick with blood. Bits of people lay everywhere. My boots found their way to the only clean thing left: a small ring of stone around Opal's hair, spared by some petty geometry of the spill. I knelt in it like it was holy.

I lifted her.

She was so light. Too light. All the fight and spark that used to make her feel like a living thing had gone slack, like a marionette with the strings cut. My arms had carried a thousand bodies but never like this. Never her. For the first time in an eternity, my eyes burned, and before I could stop it, tears slid hot down my face, carving through the dried blood on my skin.

I buried my face in her hair. The faint cherry of her shampoo, vanilla and coffee. It made me want to scream. My heart thudded against her ribcage, stubborn and loud. I cursed it under my breath.

A flutter of wings behind me. A crow . . . Of course.

I didn't even look up. My voice came out rough and shaking. "If you so much as touch her soul," I growled, "I will personally end you."

The wings faltered, then receded. Silence fell again.

"Thought so . . ." I muttered.

The old god's words rang in my head: "Follow the beating compass, the key to death, the lock to life. Press it deep to bend the ledger. Give it freely to tip the scales," and I finally understood what I had to do.

I looked down at Opal's face. Even now there was a hint of stubbornness at the corner of her mouth. It broke me open. I smiled, cracked and ugly. "I'm sorry," I whispered. "I'm so sorry . . . But I'm too selfish to let you go."

My fingers trembled as I cupped her cold cheek. "I would never have wished this on my worst enemy," I told her softly, "but you once said you'd help me carry this burden. I'm not letting you out of that promise that easily." I laid her down gently on the stone, smoothing her hair back from her forehead with shaking hands. "You gave me my heart back," I said, voice a thread. "So it's only fair if you get to keep at least half of it."

I stripped off my shirt. The air hit my skin, cold and raw. My fingers dug into her hair one last time; my forehead pressed to hers. "I'll let you in on a secret, Opal," I murmured. "My Mark, the thing that keeps me from dying, it's in my heart . . . and that belongs to you now."

I wavered, inhaled once, twice, like a diver at the edge of an abyss. My hands hovered over my chest. They were already shaking.

Then, I pushed.

My fingers slid under my ribs. Skin tore, bone resisted, pain detonated white-hot. I screamed, not a shout, but a raw, broken noise ripped from my lungs. Arms trembled; sweat poured down my temples. Blood soaked my stomach, thick and hot.

I gasped, choking on my own blood. My vision blurred, but I pushed deeper, fingers curling around my own heart, my beating compass given freely. It was slick and heavy, pounding against my palm as if it wanted to escape.

Tears fell onto the wound, mixing with blood. My shoulders shook with sobs I couldn't contain. "Stay with me," I begged her limp body, voice ragged. "Stay with me."

I tore it free. The pain flared, white stars, and my knees hit the stone. I clutched the black heart in both hands. It pulsed once in the open air, spraying across a mist of dark veins.

Then, still shaking, I reached for her. My bloody hand pressed to her sternum. I whispered an apology she couldn't hear, grateful she wouldn't feel this, then pushed through her ribs. Her body yielded; the sound was small and obscene. Her heart came free, pale and still, her blood warm on my wrists, and I sobbed again, shoulders heaving, forehead pressed to hers.

We were two animals gutted side by side. I tore mine in half. It hurt worse than the first wound, like being ripped out of myself in slow motion. Blood dripped from my chin, nose, eyes. Hands shaking, I tore hers too, gentler but no less brutal. Two halves of me, two halves of her. My dark spilling into her pale, her pale into my dark, black veins bleeding into her red as they stitched back together.

My vision swam. My teeth chattered from shock. I pressed one heart made of two halves deep back into her chest with shaking hands. Praying I could bend the ledger. "Please," I gasped. "Please come back." My palms pressed over her sternum. "Please."

Then the other heart into my own chest. The wound sealed around it with shadows. My forehead dropped to hers. I sobbed again, full body, everything shaking. "Come back, Blossom. Come back to me."

For a heartbeat, nothing. Then her lashes fluttered, and her eyes opened.

CHAPTER 32

Cain

I tore the rift open like a wound and stepped through with her in my arms. Blood still slicked her throat. The hole over her sternum pulsed black where my mark had taken root. She wasn't alive. She wasn't gone. She was . . . here. Lady Death in the truest sense, newly crowned.

Crow met us in the corridor, lamplight cutting hard edges over his face. For half a breath his composure cracked, just a hairline fracture, and then it sealed.

"No," he said, a verdict soft as dust.

"Yes," I said, pushing past. "Move."

I laid her on my bed. The shadows in the chamber crawled up the walls and held, an instinct I didn't try to stop. Opal's lashes trembled. The new heart ticked under her ribs like a fledgling learning to fly. Breath came shallow, curious. The room hummed with a frequency only dead men could hear.

"Watch over her," I said, not looking up. "And above all, don't touch her."

Crow stepped close, hands clasped behind his back like he was at a wake. "What happened?"

"She's Death now," I said, and the words tasted like iron and prayer.

He caught the edge of the bedpost, knuckles white for the span of a heartbeat. "Your Mark—" he began, meaning: the impossible, the forbidden, the thing the books only whispered about.

"Half hers," I said. "Half mine." I tucked the blanket higher over her ribs, let my thumb find her cheek. She was warm but cooling. She was wrong. She was perfect. "Watch her. I'm going to find my brother."

"About that—" Crow moved quickly for a man who preferred libraries. He paced down the hall after me. "The old god dragged Abel into the pit thinking he was you."

For a second I just stood there with blood under my nails and a ringing in my bones I didn't have a name for. I had lost Opal and stolen her back. I had killed a god, and it hadn't stayed dead. Now the pit wanted my brother because we dared to look like one another.

"Stay with her," I said. "If she wakes—" My throat worked. "Tell her I'm in the habit of making bad decisions."

"She knows," Crow said, almost kind. "Cain." I turned. He searched my face like a scholar weighing blasphemy and hope. "Don't come back empty-handed."

I nodded once. Then I ran.

The pit was where it had always been. I stood at the rim and stared down. Last time I'd jumped for love. This time I jumped for blood.

The dark took me fast, the way it does when it already knows your weight. Air bit my teeth. The smell hit first: iron, wet stone, and something sweet-rotten underneath, like flowers left too long in a vase.

I hit the bottom in a slide of sandy grit and bone dust. Two heaps appeared out of the dark: one a collapsed mountain, the old god's carcass sloughed into an outline of crowned vertebrae and rotten winter. The other was a man in a shred of a jacket, face turned to the stone.

"Abel." Panic punched my lungs empty. I skidded to him on my knees, hands in the dirt, shaking too hard to be useful.

He didn't move.

For half a second the universe went very small: his slack mouth, the smear of blood at his ear, the ruin of his hoodie. Then memory snapped my spine straight: the deal. Oldest one in the book. My first signature in Hell's ledger. If Abel hung between life and death, the Devil would have to intervene and do everything to save him.

"Come on," I hissed into the dark, to the pit, to any clerk taking notes,

He moved. "Ugh," he muttered, spitting grit from his mouth. "Zero out of ten pit. Would not recommend."

I slumped, then hauled him by the fabric of his shirt. "On your feet."

He blinked blearily at the ruin beside us, squinting at the crowned bones like he might pick a fight with what was left. "You weren't kidding," he said, voice hoarse. "It really does smell like old gods and wet socks down here."

"Can you climb?"

"Can you be less charming?" He rolled his shoulder, winced, shook out his hands. "Yes. Lead."

The wall was a shitty friend, crumbly, mean, stingy with holds. We went anyway. Fingers screamed. Boots slipped. Once, he swore and his foot went, and I had him by the collar before gravity remembered its manners. We climbed in the language of old brothers: grunts, curses, the dumb faith that the other wouldn't let go. At some point my ribs decided I was an idiot; at some later point I agreed. We kept moving.

When we finally dragged ourselves over the lip, we didn't stand. We collapsed in a heap, backs to the cool stone, chests hauling in air like bellows. The sky above the Deadlands looked closer than it had any right to. My hands were raw lace. His weren't much better.

Abel sat up first, shoving the shredded hoodie back. That's when I saw it: dead center of his chest, black and clean as ink, a mark the size of a palm. Not my sigil. Not any I liked.

I stared. He noticed where my eyes landed and glanced down. "Oh," he said lightly, but the light didn't reach his eyes. "Party favor."

"What is it?"

"Consider it a thank you note from our subterranean host," he said, fingers hovering over it without touching. "Or a bill."

"How exactly did you kill that god?" I asked, suspicion sharpening in my head.

Abel huffed, thumb tracing the new mark like he could rub it off. It didn't budge. "I don't want to talk about it," he said. "It's dead and I'm alive. That's all that matters."

"Sure," I said. "Except for the part where something old put its fingerprint on you."

"It's not your problem, Cain."

"It tried to take me," I said, pushing to my feet. Every muscle argued; I didn't care. "It got you instead. That's mine to fix."

He rose, too, rolling his neck, the gold in his eyes back to a simmer. "I'm fine," he said, clapping my jacket over my shoulder once. "Did you bring back your girl?"

I nodded, and we stood there a beat, breathing, bleeding, looking like the bad idea we've always been. Above the horizon, the castle lamps burned like patient stars.

"Come on," I said. "Crow's watching her."

"And she's . . . ?" He left the word bare for me to ruin or redeem.

"Here," I said. It wasn't an answer, but it was the only response I trusted. "Half mine. Half herself."

He grinned, wicked and relieved. "Sounds like trouble."

"Always."

The castle doors groaned like they were tired of letting us back in. We took the corridors fast, blood dried to our sleeves, grit still in our teeth, and Crow met us before the threshold of my chambers like he'd been carved there.

"She's still," he said, which was Crow for alive-not-alive.

I pushed through the doors. Opal lay where I'd left her, tucked into the dark like a secret. The shadows kept the lamps from burning too bright. She looked—gods—she looked dead.

Her skin had gone pearl-pale, lips colorless, chest a quiet thing with an unfamiliar rhythm. The hole over her sternum had sealed, but a black blush spread like spilled ink beneath the skin, shielding the wound.

I stopped two steps inside the room, something stupid and human cracking open in my chest. I hadn't prepared for this . . . The way she wasn't her and was also unbearably herself. The way the quiet around her felt too much like death at a wake.

"Well," I said, and my voice sounded wrong in my own mouth. "I . . . get it now."

Crow's gaze didn't move from her. "You should tell her what you did," he said softly, like he was offering me a scalpel. "Before the body starts to rot. I'm assuming she doesn't know."

"She doesn't," I said. The words scraped.

Abel hovered at the doorframe, hoodie torn, trying to make his grin do all the work of being fine. He wasn't. None of us were.

I crossed to the bed and sat carefully like I might spook her. The mattress dipped. Her lashes didn't twitch. I folded my hands to keep them from shaking and looked at her mouth as if it might make my sentences braver.

"How do I say it," I asked the air, the floor, the man I'd never once prayed to. "I loved you enough to make you like me. I loved you enough to curse you. I stole you back. I split the only thing that could kill me and shoved it into your chest because I could not, would not, write your name in a ledger I'm supposed to keep."

The apology didn't sound like an apology. It sounded like a confession written with blood.

"I'm sorry," I told her, thumb brushing the shell of her hand. Cold. So cold. "You asked me to let you be brave. I made you permanent instead. If you hate me when you wake, you'd be right."

Crow shifted at the foot of the bed, hands tucked into his sleeves like he needed something to hold. "She won't rot quickly," he said, clinical as mercy. "Your Mark arrests . . . processes."

"Reassuring," Abel muttered, then cleared his throat and peeled away from the door. "I'm going to—uh—borrow something that doesn't look like it died twice."

He drifted to the wardrobe like he owned the place and started flipping hangers, landing on a black shirt he'd seen me wear to war. He pulled it on over the hoodie, sleeves too long, collar a little wrong. It looked better on him, and I hated him for that.

As he tugged the hem down, the fabric shifted, and the mark on his chest flashed: a neat coal-black sigil, dead center. Bigger than before. Edged like something that bites.

"Abel," I said. Just his name. A question with claws.

He yanked the shirt into place and snapped the buttons like a man shutting a trap. "We're not doing this right now."

Crow's head tilted, curiosity knifing through the worry. "That mark—"

"It's fine," Abel said, too fast. A smile that didn't make it to his eyes. "Souvenir."

"From?" Crow's eyebrows made a precise cathedral.

"The part where your favorite demon killed an old god," Abel said brightly, hands spreading in the universal sign for *Drop it*. "We can send a thank you note later."

"Marks that grow are rarely souvenirs," Crow observed.

"Great," Abel said. "I'll exchange it for store credit."

I shot him a look. He met it, defensiveness rising like heat. "I'm not the emergency," he said, chin tipping toward the bed. "She is."

He was right. I turned back to Opal.

"Blossom," I breathed, and the room pressed in to listen. "Hear this wherever you are: I will spend the rest of the unending future making this bearable. You can be furious. You can set me on fire. I'll stand still."

The new heart ticked under her ribs, slow, stubborn, learning. The sound was nothing like a human rhythm and everything like the only one I'd ever trust again.

Behind me, Crow's voice softened in a way I'd only heard him use for the dying and the moments after. "She'll need a tutor," he said, "in rules you've never obeyed."

"I'll find one," I said.

"You'll be one," he said back sternly. "She'll need to know how to fight too."

I laced my fingers with hers and let the room breathe around us. Abel pulled a chair close and slouched into it like he planned to be difficult by being present. His eyes kept sliding to the window, to the pit's direction, then back to the mark beneath his shirt like he could hold it still by will alone.

"I'm not leaving," I told her. "Not ever again."

Outside, the Deadlands turned to morning without changing color. Inside, a crow pretended not to look worried, a demon-turned-brother tried not to touch a mark that wasn't going to be ignored, and a god of endings counted heartbeats he had no right to hear.

CHAPTER 33

Opal

I came back the way a maelstrom does: lungs first. Air punched into me like I'd been held underwater too long. My chest hitched, then learned the rhythm, slow and strange, a new metronome stitched into bone. I didn't open my eyes right away. The world arrived in pieces: the weight of a hand wrapped around mine; linen under my cheek; the smell of smoke, and mint—him. A thousand small hurts reported in.

When I finally dragged my eyes open, the room swam into focus. Dark stone, lamplight low, shadows clinging to the corners like they'd decided I belonged to them. Cain sat beside the bed, my fingers trapped between both of his. Crow stood at the footboard, composed, eyes a little too bright. Abel sprawled in a chair, trying not to look worried and failing.

They were all staring at me like I was a miracle they didn't quite trust.

"Hey," Cain said, voice wrecked-soft. "Blossom."

My throat made a sound that wasn't a word. Everything felt dry, like I'd been dusted in ash. I swallowed. It didn't help.

"Don't move too fast," Crow warned, gentle and clinical at once. "Your body is . . . adapting."

My tongue worked. "What—" It came out a rasp. I coughed, and it hurt, not in the way it used to. New pain, clean and cold. "What happened?"

Cain's jaw flexed. He didn't let go of my hand. "Lucian killed you . . ." He squeezed my hand and let go. "And there was only one way to bring you back. I did something unforgivable," he said quietly. "And I'd do it again." He lifted his shirt to reveal a hole punched in his chest, shielded by shadows like a bandage.

Abel scrubbed a hand over his face. "He means he saved you," he muttered. Crow shot him a look that said *Not now*.

Cain leaned closer, forehead nearly touching mine. "Lucian—" He stopped, and I knew what that meant. "I was too late." He swallowed hard. "I couldn't put your name in a book I'm supposed to keep. So I . . . split my heart." His mouth twitched, almost a laugh, almost a sob. "Gave you half. Took half of yours. It keeps you here."

My free hand went to my chest on instinct. The fabric there was stiff with dried blood. Under it, something cold and soft pressed back. Shadows. I pushed them aside and found the wound by touch: skin puckered into a jagged ring, edges tender, the center . . . covered. I couldn't see it. The darkness stitched over it like a second skin, warm as breath, hiding what I had become until I could bear to look.

I didn't realize my hands were shaking until Cain stilled them. "Don't," he said, sounding like he hated his own voice for saying it. "They're . . . helping. While you heal."

I stared at him. "Heal into what?"

He held my gaze, as if he wanted to take the sentence out of my mouth and carry it for me. "Death," he said. "Like me." The room went small and huge at the same time.

Crow's voice came quiet, a professor offering the page no one wanted to read. "Your appetite will change. You won't take food or drink ever again. Your touch"—he glanced at my hand wrapped in Cain's—"is dangerous to the living now. Except him. You can touch him." A pause. "And he can touch you."

"I'll teach you how to carry it," Cain said quickly, as if he could shield me with verbs. "How to satisfy the curse without breaking you. You won't be alone in it." His mouth hardened. "I won't let you be alone in it."

"So, I can't eat," I said flatly. "Or taste. Or touch anyone. Ever again." I glanced at Abel, then Crow, then back to him. "Except you."

Cain nodded once, like it hurt. "Except me."

"And I'm stuck." I let out something like a laugh and heard it echo wrong. "Permanently."

His face broke, just for a second. "I hate that I did this to you," he said, every word grated raw. "I hate that I'm relieved you're here."

Something lit inside me, anger, love, grief, too many wires sparking at once. I couldn't tell if I wanted to kiss him or hit him or crawl inside his ribs and sleep. "You should," I said. "Hate it."

"I do," he said. "And I don't."

We hung there in that terrible, honest place. Crow looked down, granting us privacy.

"And Lucian?" I asked finally, my voice knives wrapped in cotton.

"Handled," Cain said. There was no theater in it. No gloating. Just a door closed that would never open again.

"Should I ask?"

"No." He looked away and that was all I needed to see. Lucian was dead.

I stared at our hands. His thumb had settled over my knuckle, absent, steady. The warmth of him threaded through the cold that had taken root in me, and my new senses woke one by one: the hush at the edges of the room that wasn't silence but waiting; faint murmurs like pages turning where the ledger kept small accounts; the shape of Crow's life flickering at the edge of my vision, precise, bright; the wild, burning echo of Abel's, gold heat layered over something dark and new.

I looked up and caught Abel watching me with a slanted grin he was failing to sell. Concern tugged at the corner of it. For a beat, one, two, I could almost see the outline of something stamped on him, coal-dark, a shadow crown hiding in the space behind him.

"What happened to you?" I asked.

He dropped his gaze, shrugging like a stray committing to charm. "Tripped," he said. "Fell into an old god with my face."

"Later," Crow said, and the word was a scalpel again. "Opal first."

Right. Me first. I tried to sit up. Cain's hand tightened, then helped me, slow, careful, like I was made of glass. The shadows obeyed, peeling and settling like a blanket. The wound didn't throb the way it should have, but I felt it nonetheless.

"I don't know if I love you or hate you," I told him honestly. I didn't have the energy to be anything else.

His mouth twitched. "I'll take either," he said. "So long as you're here to throw it at me."

I should have said something brave. Something decisive. Instead, I got stuck on a small, practical truth. "I can't taste coffee anymore."

His eyes went wet at the edges. "I'll make you tea just to be petty."

"You're insufferable," I whispered.

"I know." He squeezed my hand. "But I'm yours . . . Forever."

The heat that ricocheted through me was new and old at once: fury, tenderness, terror, a grief so big it would take chapters to map. I let it wash over me. It didn't knock me down. I was, inconveniently, still here.

"Okay," I said at last, and the word felt like accepting a crown I hadn't asked for. "Teach me."

Steel flashed. Shadows braided the air, blades ringing, boots skidding on stone, my hair sticking to my cheek in sweat-slick strands while Cain's grin did that infuriating, pretty thing like he wasn't even trying.

"Your footwork is sloppy," he taunted. "Were you raised by influencers?"

"My footwork is flawless," I snapped, cutting left. "Your face is the problem."

"Ouch," he said and slid inside my guard with a move so lazy it felt like flirting.

I swung; he wasn't there. His arm hooked mine, momentum doing the rest, and suddenly my blade clattered wide, and I was in a headlock with a blade to my neck, pinned against a chest I could survive. The flat of his knife kissed my throat.

"Where'd you go wrong?" he murmured against my temple, heartbeat steady as a metronome I could hate and love.

"Trusted a smug reaper with good hair," I gasped, trying not to laugh.

"No," he drawled, all mock-patient. "You were too occupied by the kill and left yourself open. Anyone with a pulse could see that." A beat. "Present company included."

I elbowed him; he laughed and released me. Our blades scraped as we stooped to collect them. The shadows along the training hall uncoiled like cats who approved.

"Again?" he asked.

"In a minute," I said, rolling my shoulder. It would bruise. I liked that. We leaned on our blades like canes. The quiet came in, companionable.

Abel flashed through my head then. The last I'd seen of him was at the rift, tossing that cocky grin over his shoulder. *Explore my newfound humanity and get some space*, he'd said, refusing every question about the pit and the mark like he could out-smirk a curse. Cain had watched him go with that knotted look he tried to pass off as indifference, then sent Crow after him—because love is a verb and paranoia is proof.

"If he starts any trouble," Cain had called, deadpan as law, "I will personally come and find him."

He meant it. Of course he did.

It took three days for the ache to come for me. Not grief but the *other* ache, the hunger of the job. Three days of pretending I could breathe through it. By sunset of the third, I was on my knees in the chamber, teeth gritted, vision edged in white. Cain didn't touch. He didn't flinch. He just opened the ledger and walked me through names like a lullaby.

My first kill was smaller than my fear. So was the second. By the fourth, the rhythm had lodged itself under my tongue like a psalm I didn't want to admit I knew. It never got pretty. It got precise. Satisfying, sometimes, in the way truth can be.

The curse would never end, but Cain made it bearable, because he was there every step of the way, making tea I couldn't taste or drink just to be petty, checking my stance, letting me be furious without apologizing for saving me.

Somewhere between the second month's bruises and the thousandth quiet night where he fell asleep beside me with a book on his chest and his hand on my thigh like a promise, I forgave him. Not all at once. In handfuls. In the ways a life insists on being lived.

"It wasn't all bad," I said now, surprising us both.

Cain blinked. "What wasn't?"

"Dying," I said. "You. This." I twirled the blade. The shadows purred. "You made it . . . worth the trouble."

He tried for smug. Failed. The relief in his eyes could have flooded a small country. "I'll keep earning it," he said. "Every day."

"Good," I said, and flicked his wrist with my blade just to hear him swear.

He grinned, reset. "Again?"

"Again."

We moved, steel and shadow, callout and correction, the give-and-take that felt more like partnership than penance. The Deadlands kept their weather. Somewhere in the mortal world, a golden-eyed menace with a coal-black mark and a stolen shirt was learning how to be Abel again without burning cities for the fun of it.

"Shoulder," Cain warned, and this time I smiled, feinted wrong on purpose, and took his knife clean. I let him think he had me, pressed, cornered, posture perfect. Then I shifted my weight, feinted high, and hooked my ankle behind his heel.

Sweep.

Cain's eyes went wide a split second before gravity remembered his name. He hit the floor on his butt with a very undignified *oof*, blade skittering, shadows snickering along the walls like they'd been waiting for this.

I planted my boot lightly on his chest and offered the world's smuggest bow.

"Good girl," he breathed, surprised and pleased.

"Lady Death," I corrected and let the blade ring.

His fingers hooked behind my ankle, quick as a thief. A soft tug. I tipped, and he caught my wrist, pulled me down into him like it was always meant to end here. Mouth to mouth. Heat and smoke and the taste of copper-sweet adrenaline. He smiled against my lips. I bit his lower one because he deserved it. He groaned, hands firm at my waist, and the shadows crowded close like nosy witnesses.

I pulled back first, breathless, blade resting across his throat in a lazy warning. "Cheater."

"So punish me," he said, voice gravel and sin.

I kissed him once more, slow, then let the steel kiss air.

I stayed on him a moment longer than I needed, chest rising and falling against his. Shadows curled around us like curious cats, reluctant witnesses to our private riot.

"You're insufferable," I murmured, brushing my nose along his jaw.

"And you love it," he countered, voice thick with laughter and something softer, something warmer, that had nothing to do with teasing.

"I tolerate it," I corrected, sliding my hand down to rest over the hollow of his ribs. He tensed, and I smiled, careful, slow. "Just . . . for now."

He huffed a laugh, low and amused, and rolled us onto our sides so that the shadows pooled around us in a protective embrace. "You know," Cain said, voice rough, breath tickling my ear, "if we keep this up, I'm going to start charging for private lessons."

I turned my head, lips brushing his temple. "I'd pay in nightmares."

He groaned, playful and feral, and his hands found my waist. "Bad students deserve punishment," he murmured, dragging his thumbs lightly across my hipbones.

I smirked, watching a strand of hair fall across his forehead. "Is that a threat or a promise?"

"Both," he whispered.

I laughed, soft and unsteady. We stayed like that a long while, entwined, each moment a slow burn of reclamation. Shadows curled around his fingers where they held mine, wrapping us in a private covenant, silent and sacred.

"You're . . . different," he said eventually, voice low, almost hesitant. "The darkness . . . You carry it, and yet—you're still you. Alive. Infuriatingly stubborn. Terrifying."

I lifted my chin, challenging him with green eyes that had seen too much to shy away. "I died and didn't stay quiet about it, and I still know how to get under your skin."

He laughed, head falling back, shadows dancing across his features like a flame. "I don't know if I hate you or love you more for that," he admitted, voice raw. "Maybe both."

"Both's good," I said, tracing a line across his collarbone with a fingertip. "That's exactly how it should be."

He caught my wrist and pressed a kiss to the back of my hand. "Forever," he said. "You and me. All of this, together. No exceptions."

"Forever, huh?" I teased, rolling my eyes, letting my lips brush his jaw. "That's a long time to be stuck with me."

His grin was lazy, confident, and infuriatingly smug. "I'd endure a thousand lifetimes if it meant you could be mine," he said, brushing a thumb along my cheek. "Besides, I've already split my heart with you. You're stuck too."

I laughed softly, tipping my forehead to his. "I guess I can live with that."

Then, without warning, he pulled me closer, lips brushing mine in a soft, deliberate kiss. Slow, teasing, the kind that made your knees weak before it even reached your heart.

"You are my favorite disaster."

I bit back a laugh, leaning into him, lips brushing the corner of his mouth. "Disaster, huh? Sounds about right."

"And," he said, voice low, velvet-dark, "you're exactly the kind of chaos I've been trying to catch my entire life. Impossible to hold, impossible not to love."

I smiled, teasing, brushing my nose along his jaw again. "Good. I'd hate for you to be bored."

He groaned, a sound that was half-laughter, half-promise, and tugged me closer, wrapping an arm around my shoulders. "Never," he said, voice gravel and warmth. "Never bored with you."

We stayed like that as the night stretched on, shadows draping around us like a velvet curtain. Fingers twined together, touches featherlight, laughter and whispers carrying us through the darkness until we both fell silent, hearts syncing in a rhythm that wasn't human, or even truly alive, but it was entirely ours.

Cain wasn't the only one with work to do. By dawn, the name in the ledger burned soft and gold against the page. Mine. My first solo call.

He watched from the archway, all shadows and quiet pride.

"Don't hover," I told him, snapping the clasp on my cloak.

Yes, it was pink. A long sweep of rose-tinted silk stitched with tiny skulls at the hem. I'd made it. Crow said it was "morbidly charming." Abel called it a "war crime." Cain hadn't said a word, just looked at me like he'd never seen something so alive.

I stepped through the rift into the mortal world. The air was damp, smelling of rain and hospital sanitizer. A woman lay on a gurney, monitors stuttering. The nurse didn't see me—they never did when I hid in the shadows—but the woman's eyes flicked open. She smiled, soft and tired.

"Are you here for me?" she whispered.

"Yeah," I said, voice gentler than I expected. "But I promise, it won't hurt."

The scythe, or what passed for one, shimmered into my hand: polished silver, handle wrapped in pink ribbon, tiny charms dangling from the haft like trinkets from a magpie's dream. Ridiculous. Beautiful. *Mine.* I technically didn't need it, not like the reapers did, but I wasn't as practiced as Cain yet, and the scythe made the souls less . . . sticky. It made the process painless.

When the blade touched air, it sang, not grim or cold but bright, like chimes. I guided her soul free, easy as untangling thread. She exhaled, relief blooming across her face like spring.

"Pretty," she murmured.

"Thanks," I said and meant it.

The shadows gathered, curious, and I winked at them. "Don't look so surprised. Death can wear pink."

CHAPTER 34
ABEL

Before the old god died

I pulled the hood up to hide the gold in my eyes and the arrogance in my smile. Cain's hoodie under his leather jacket, his scythe in my palm, his shadows stitched to my wrist like a borrowed sin. In bad light, we're the same problem with different hair. Tonight, that was the point. They were calling for Cain, and I answered.

The Deadlands looked sick. Sky a low bruise of gold and pink. Wards muttering like old men who knew they were about to be ignored. Then, the ground fractured, and something crowned in bone hauled itself up, hell-bent on finding my brother.

"Looking for me?" I said, cocky on purpose.

He turned. Not a he—not really. A cathedral of absence with a crown built from kings who didn't need their bones anymore. He tasted the air, tasted the hoodie and the shadows and the history sewn into both, and the world tilted like it had just been corrected. "Cain," the darkness said without moving. Good. Let him be stupid.

I walked like a storm that had learned manners. The scythe loved my hands even if it wasn't mine. Shadow followed like a trained dog pretending to heel. I didn't give him a speech. I gave him steel.

He moved like gravity that had learned how to stand. I moved like what I was: a weapon first, man second, brother last. I was forged to fight angels and taught to win ugly. Muscle memory sang. I cut him. He laughed like a sinkhole. I grinned wider. I have always been at my worst when I'm winning. It goes straight to my head every time.

He tried to talk. Old gods love it. Puzzles and monologues. But I wasn't here to chat. The faster I moved, the less of a chance he realized I wasn't my brother. He wanted a pretty bargain and a bow. I wanted a body. So, I obliged. I stepped in close and let him smell the wrong brother on purpose.

"Cain," he said again, pleased with himself, and reached. The darkness moved faster than light. Inky hands unrolled from his ribs and slid around my waist the way hunger hugs. I twisted for the clean kill, blade kissing bone, and the pit yanked me backward like a stagehand with a hook. Down we went. Curtain call.

I hit stone hard enough to see white. Air punched out of me. Gravel in my teeth. The pit smelled like old rot and wet mud.

"You still owe me," it said. The voice came from everywhere. "The price you agreed to. The burden. My power is yours to carry now."

I froze.

Power? That word was catnip to a man like me. I didn't pretend otherwise.

I stayed down on one knee, because theatrics matter. Head tilted. Hood shadowing my face. Cain's scythe braced across my thigh like I owned it. I let him keep talking. People tell on themselves if you let silence do the heavy lifting.

"I am tired," the old god said. "To end, I must pass on my darkness, my power. The Mark carried me this far. It will carry you farther. You are worthy, Cain."

There it was. The mistake. I didn't correct him. Why would I? I'd crawled out of worse graves for far less.

He wanted Cain. He got me wearing my brother's shadow like a borrowed sin. Good enough. Besides, I had a few items on my to-do list. Revenge for the fall. Humiliation served cold. I used to be damn near royalty. Now I was a cautionary tale. Now I had my memories back, a face that still made mirrors nervous, and a choice I hadn't fully made about the day Cain killed me. Should I burn him for that someday, or keep the only useful ally I've ever had and aim higher? That was a problem for later. I could multitask.

"Go on," I said, light. "Tell me how worthy I am."

He lowered, a ruin pretending to be a king. Crown clicking. Jawless smile. The pit shivered like a held breath.

"If Cain can carry one curse, he can carry two," he said. "Bear it. End me."

"Glad to help," I said, and smiled where he couldn't see it. My favorite kind.

He moved faster than stone should move. A spear of night slid out of his ribs and punched into my chest. I didn't get a hero's pose. No warning. Just impact. Skin splitting like paper. Heat burning clean through the breastbone. It felt like someone had poured a furnace into me and locked the door.

I saw white again. Then gold. Then nothing. My hands convulsed around the scythe. The blade shrieked against the floor. The hood fell back, and the pit poured its light into my eyes until tears burned tracks down my cheeks I refused to wipe.

"Good," he whispered. "Take it."

The power crawled in, slow and sure. Every vein in my body lit up. My heart became a fist. A mark over my sternum flared black. I stayed standing for a second. Pride is stupid like that.

It hit again. The world blurred. My knees went soft, and the floor came up and kissed my cheek like an ex-lover. I heard myself laugh. It sounded wrong. Hungry. I didn't hate it.

The old god sagged. You could hear him coming apart. A cathedral becoming scaffolding. The crown slipped. Vertebrae clattered around my knees like dice.

"Worthy," he said, fading. "Worthy."

"Obviously," I muttered.

He collapsed into himself the way stars do when they're done existing. The dark went small. It tried to take the whole pit with it and failed. When it settled, what was left of him looked like an apology.

I rolled onto my back and stared up at nothing. The power kept coming. A tide that didn't care if I drowned.

I thought about the courts that cheered when I fell. About the hands that pushed. About the smile I wore while I took it like a gentleman. I thought about the day my brother put me down like a dog and how my bones still remembered the angle of his mercy. I thought about the Deadlands shaking when the pit called his name and how easy it was to steal it all for a while.

Cain was useful. He had a girl who made him stupid and soft and brave. He had a plan for the world written in new handwriting. He loved me in a way that kept my teeth in my mouth. For now, that won. For now, I would keep this secret and let him think I was just the same old disaster with better jokes.

For now, I aimed my hate at bigger targets. The pain flared, and I went out with the darkness like a light.

www.ingramcontent.com/pod-product-compliance
Lightning Source LLC
Chambersburg PA
CBHW021845130726
47988CB00009B/3421